W9-BVR-060

Praise for Heather Gudenkauf

"[A] scintillating psychological thriller.... The stunning plot builds to a chillingly realistic ending. Gudenkauf is at the top of her game."
—*Publishers Weekly*, **starred review**

"Eerily page-turning and wonderfully twisty."
—**Kimberly McCreight,** *New York Times* **bestselling author of** *Reconstructing Amelia* **and** *Where They Found Her*

"[*Not a Sound*] kept me reading till the birds started chirping—think Mary Higgins Clark or Lisa Scottoline." —*Washington Post*

"A truly original, immersive experience."
—*O, The Oprah Magazine*

"Heather Gudenkauf is one of my favorite new authors."
—**Lisa Scottoline,** *New York Times* **bestselling author**

"Heather Gudenkauf has written a spell-binding thriller which reminds us just how strong the human spirit can be, and yet how fragile life is." —*Suspense Magazine*

"[Heather Gudenakuf is] rendering some of the most compelling and likable female characters in print today... Recommended for all fans of Jennifer McMahon and Jodi Picoult." —*Booklist*

Also by Heather Gudenkauf

THIS
IS
HOW
I LIED

HEATHER GUDENKAUF

PARK
ROW
BOOKS

If you purchased this book without a cover you should be aware
that this book is stolen property. It was reported as "unsold and
destroyed" to the publisher, and neither the author nor the
publisher has received any payment for this "stripped book."

PARK
ROW
BOOKS™

Recycling programs
for this product may
not exist in your area.

ISBN-13: 978-0-7783-0970-3
ISBN-13: 978-0-7783-8811-1 (Library Exclusive Edition)

This Is How I Lied

Copyright © 2020 by Heather Gudenkauf

All rights reserved. No part of this book may be used or reproduced in any manner whatsoever
without written permission except in the case of brief quotations embodied in critical articles and
reviews.

This is a work of fiction. Names, characters, places and incidents are either the product of the
author's imagination or are used fictitiously. Any resemblance to actual persons, living or dead,
businesses, companies, events or locales is entirely coincidental.

This edition published by arrangement with Harlequin Books S.A.

Park Row Books
22 Adelaide St. West, 40th Floor
Toronto, Ontario M5H 4E3, Canada
ParkRowBooks.com
BookClubbish.com

Printed in U.S.A.

For my sisters—Jane Augspurger and Molly Lugar.

THIS IS
IS
HOW
I LIED

PROLOGUE
EVE KNOX

Friday, December 22, 1995

Eve wasn't even supposed to be in these caves. They had a dizzying number of stony corridors and with one wrong turn she could become lost. At fifteen she knew these paths better than most people twice her age, and she moved as quickly as she could, being careful not to slip on the icy cave floor. Eve had come here to clear her head, to think about things and now she may never make it out alive.

Fear made Eve's skin buzz, numbing the pain in her head and her wrist. She considered her options. She could try to talk her way out or she could try to run from the cave and to safety.

She didn't get a chance to decide. Before she could speak fingers were digging into her arm trying to push her more deeply into the cave. Eve managed to wriggle free but lost her balance and stumbled to the ground. Her fingers swept the floor in search of some kind of weapon and her hand landed on a jagged piece of limestone. She clutched onto the rock and with a cry of frustration she swung her arm hoping to strike but only cut through the damp air. She swung again, this time grazing flesh.

Eve tried to get up but was pulled back to the ground with

a teeth-rattling crash. She twisted around to see talon-like fingers clinging to her boot.

"No," Eve cried, kicking out at her captor. She tore away from the grasp and ran toward the cave's opening, hopscotching over jagged stone. *Almost there*, Eve thought as her right foot plunged into a narrow crevice and she tumbled forward.

The sickening snap of her ankle filled her ears and Eve howled in pain. Using her good hand, she tried to push herself up to her knees but her right foot was still snared. Only twenty yards more and she would be free. She gave her leg a desperate yank, the gasping, ragged breath closing in. Her skin tore and her Doc Marten was lost, but the foot came free.

She army-crawled across the rough stone toward the mouth of the cave, the ends of her scarf cascading down her back as she moved. *Almost there.* Suddenly, the scarf pulled tight at her throat. Eve froze but still the pressure. She scrabbled at the fabric, desperately trying to slide her fingers between the wool and her skin. Her legs felt weak and her lungs screamed for oxygen. Night had fallen and the only light came from the houses far up atop the bluffs, twinkling cold stars. Tiny beacons. *Only a little bit farther*, Eve thought. *I'm so close.*

With one frantic effort, she managed to flip onto her back but the scarf didn't loosen. It cut still deeper into her throat. Her screams became lodged in her chest. Her vision blurred and her arms fell uselessly to her side. Above her, Eve found eyes filled with rage. There was no fear, no regret, no sorrow. No air could pass through to her lungs. The cold crept through her skin, settling deep into Eve's bones until she became one with the slick limestone.

How did things go so wrong? Eve wondered. *Why?* Just beyond the cave, night had fully arrived. Snow came down in dizzying swirls. Dark places made it so much easier to be cruel, to exact revenge.

MAGGIE KENNEDY-O'KEEFE

Monday, June 15, 2020

As I slide out of my unmarked police car my swollen belly briefly gets wedged against the steering wheel. Sucking in my gut does little good but I manage to move the seat back and squeeze past the wheel. I swing my legs out the open door and glance furtively around the parking lot behind the Grotto Police Department to see if anyone is watching.

Almost eight months pregnant with a girl and not at my most graceful, I'm not crazy about the idea of one of my fellow officers seeing me try to pry myself out of this tin can. The coast appears to be clear so I begin the little ritual of rocking back and forth trying to build up enough momentum to launch myself out of the driver's seat.

Once upright, I pause to catch my breath. The morning dew is already sending up steam from the weeds growing out of the cracked concrete. Sweating, I slowly make my way to the rear entrance of the Old Gray Lady, the nickname for the building we're housed in. Built in the early 1900s, the first floor consists of the lobby, the fingerprinting and intake center, a community room, interview rooms and the jail. The second floor, which once held the old jail, is home to the squad room and offices. The dank, dark basement holds a temperamental boiler and the department archives.

The Grotto Police Department has sixteen sworn officers; that includes the chief, two lieutenants, a K-9 patrol officer, nine patrol officers, a school resource officer and two detectives. I'm detective number two.

I grew up in Grotto, a small river town of about ten thousand that sits among a circuitous cave system known as Grotto Caves State Park, the most extensive in Iowa. Besides being a favorite destination spot for families, hikers and spelunkers, Grotto is known for its high number of family-owned farms—a dying breed. My husband, Shaun, and I are part of that breed—we own an apple orchard and tree farm.

"Pretty soon we're going to have to roll you in," an irritatingly familiar voice calls out from behind me.

I don't bother turning around. "Francis, that wasn't funny the first fifty times you said it and it still isn't." I scan my key card to let us in.

Pete Francis, an overconfident rookie officer, grabs the door handle and in a rare show of chivalry opens it so I can step through. "You know I'm just joking," Francis says, giving me the grin that young ladies in Grotto seem to find irresistible but just gives me another reason to roll my eyes.

"With the wrong person, those kinds of jokes will land you in sensitivity training," I remind him.

"Yeah, but you're not the wrong person, right?" he says seriously. "You're cool?"

I wave to Peg behind the reception desk and stop at the elevator and punch the number two. The police department may only have two levels but I'm in no mood to climb even one flight of stairs today. "Do I look like I'm okay with it?" I ask him.

Francis scans me up and down. He takes in my brown hair pulled back in a low bun, wayward curls springing out from all directions, my eyes red from lack of sleep, my untucked shirt, the fabric stretched tight against my round stomach, my sturdy shoes that I think are tied, but I can't know for sure because I can't see over my boulder-sized belly.

"Sorry," he says, appropriately contrite, and wisely decides to take the stairs rather than ride the elevator with me.

"You're forgiven," I call after him. As I step on the elevator to head up to my desk, I check my watch. My appointment with the chief is at eight and though he didn't tell me what the exact reason is for this meeting I think I can make a pretty good guess.

Protocol can't dictate when I have to go on light duty, but seven months into my pregnancy, it's probably time. I'm guessing that Chief Digby wants to talk with me about when I want to begin desk duty or take my maternity leave. I get it.

It's time I start to take it easy. I've either been the daughter of a cop or a cop my entire life but I'm more than ready to set it aside for a while and give my attention, twenty-four/seven, to the little being inhabiting my uterus.

Shaun and I have been trying for a baby for a long, long time. Thousands of dollars and dozens of procedures later, when we finally found out we were pregnant, Shaun started calling her Peanut because the only thing I could eat for the first nine weeks without throwing up was peanut butter sandwiches. The name stuck.

This baby is what we want more than anything in the world but I'd be lying if I didn't admit that I'm a little bit scared. I'm used to toting around a sidearm, not an infant.

The elevator door opens to a dark-paneled hallway lined with ten-by-sixteen framed photos of all the men who served as police chief of Grotto over the years. I pass by eleven photos before I reach the portrait of my father. *Henry William Kennedy, 1995-2019*, the plaque reads.

While the other chiefs stare out from behind the glass with

serious expressions, my dad smiles, showing his straight, white teeth. He was so proud when he was named chief of police. We were all proud, except maybe my older brother, Colin. God knows what Colin thought of it. As a teenager he was pretty self-absorbed, but I guess I was too, especially after my best friend died. I went off the rails for a while but here I am now: Grotto PD detective, following in my dad's footsteps. I think he's proud of me too. At least when he remembers.

Last time I brought my dad back here to visit, we walked down this long corridor and paused at his photo. For a minute I thought he might make a joke, say something like, *Hey, who's that good-looking guy?* But he didn't say anything. Finding the right words is hard for him now. Occasionally, his frustration bubbles over and he yells and sometimes even throws things, which is hard to watch. My father has always been a very gentle man.

The next portrait in line is our current police chief, Les Digby. No smile on his tough-guy mug. He was hired a month ago, taking over for Dexter Stroope who acted as the interim chief after my dad retired. Les is about ten years older than I am, recently widowed with two teenage sons. He previously worked for the Ransom Sheriff's Office and I'm trying to decide if I like him. Jury's still out.

I use my key card to gain access to a small vestibule lined with shoebox-sized lockers and then push through a door that leads to a large room with exposed brick walls inset with a row of six-foot-tall windows. In one corner of the room is the chief's office and on the opposite side are two old jail cells with the swinging iron bar doors removed and converted into office space. I call the jail cell on the left home.

Francis and two other patrol officers are getting ready to head out for the day and pause to tell me good-morning. Francis avoids making eye contact with me. Good. He knows he already overstepped a line with me this morning and will stay out of my way the rest of the day. I cross the worn industrial gray carpeting, past the coffee machine which beckons me. I'd kill for a cup of coffee but the caffeine isn't good for the baby. I drop my purse atop my old metal desk and grab a legal pad and pen.

The door to Chief Digby's office is slightly ajar. I take a deep breath. I probably should have had this conversation with the chief much earlier, but the thought of sitting behind a desk for eight hours a day makes me want to scream. Besides, I've been doing just fine; it wasn't until a few weeks ago that my stomach began to inflate at an alarming rate and started slowing me down.

My husband, after watching me struggle to fasten my gun belt to my waist, finally spoke up. *Maggie,* he asked, *are you really comfortable having a gun so close to the baby?*

I was. But I saw Shaun's point. I kept telling him that I'd talk to the chief but hadn't. This morning, I got the text from Digby telling me he wanted to see me in his office first thing. I guess this is as good a time as any to have the conversation.

I tap lightly on the door and I hear muffled voices coming from inside.

"Good morning, Maggie," Chief Digby says as he opens the door. Digby is built like an NFL linebacker and his large frame blocks my view of the interior of his office so I can't see who else is in the room. "How are you doing?" he asks, trying not to stare at my stomach.

"Just fine, Chief. What's up?" I ask. Digby steps aside and sitting in a chair next to the chief's desk is my fellow detective, Dexter Stroope.

"Take a seat," he says gravely, closing the door behind us. I lower myself into the remaining empty chair and look to Dex. He shrugs. He doesn't know why we were summoned either.

"I'll get right to it," the chief says. "A piece of new evidence in the Eve Knox case may have just been discovered."

His words are a punch to my gut. I haven't heard my best friend's name said out loud in a long time. I try to keep my face neutral and wait for Digby to continue.

"A woman brought her teenage son into the station late last night," he says. "The kid and his friend were screwing around in Ransom Caves the other day and found this." He pulls a large plastic evidence bag from a cardboard box. Inside is a boot. Filthy and caked with dry mud, but still I recognize it immediately. Maroon and covered with graffiti-style flowers, the leather Doc Martens were among Eve's prized possessions.

"Jesus," I whisper.

"Yeah, Jesus," Chief Digby says. "Kid dropped his cell phone between some rocks and came out with this. Matches the one in the crime scene photos." Digby holds out a photograph and I recoil as I see a close-up of my best friend's feet, one bloodied and shoeless and the other clad in a Doc Marten that matches the one in the evidence bag. I feel the banana muffin I had for breakfast roil up in my stomach but force it back.

"Why'd the kid bring an old shoe home?" Dex asks. I can't tear my eyes away from the picture.

"The mom went to school with Eve Knox, told her son horror stories about the caves trying to keep him from messing around in there. That obviously didn't work. He brought the boot home and was showing it off to some friends and the mom overheard. When she found out where it came from, she marched the kid right over here and wasn't going to leave until she talked to me."

"It's Eve's boot," I say numbly, remembering the day she bought them while we were on a shopping trip to Des Moines. It was the only thing Eve ever paid full price for. She loved those boots. "I'm positive. She wore those things all the time. Who was the woman who brought them in?"

The chief looks down at his notes. "A Karen Specht and

that's what she said too." He gently places the boot back into the cardboard box.

I nod. "Karen was in our class." A cold sweat breaks out on my forehead. I'm glad I'm sitting down.

"I worked in the sheriff's office early during the joint investigation with Grotto PD," Chief Digby says. "The case should have been solved twenty-five years ago but maybe we can do it now."

"What's that supposed to mean?" Dex says quietly, but from his tone I know he's pissed. "We all worked that case hard, especially Chief Kennedy." Dex glances my way. Dex Stroope is in his midsixties, big-bellied with a face that always looks like it could use a good nap. Dex would be well over six feet tall if not for his slumped shoulders. *The weight of all the crap I've seen over the years*, he jokes.

He and my dad have always been tight and I feel a surge of gratitude toward him for sticking up for my dad. The investigation into Eve's murder and the inability to find her killer nearly broke my dad.

"I'm not pointing fingers," Chief Digby says, looking directly at me. "I just think we now have the technology and resources to solve it. Twenty-five years ago, I looked Eve's mother and sister in the eyes and promised them that I would do all that I could to help find Eve's killer."

"You're not going to find much forensics on that shoe," Dex says, nodding toward the evidence box. "Two decades of sitting in rain and mud will have washed anything of use away. Plus, the kid and his friends had their paws all over it."

"We're going to send it all in," the chief says, spreading his arms open wide. "Have the state lab retest all the old evidence. A lot has changed in forensics in the past twenty-five years."

"Have you talked to the family about this?" I ask, successfully tamping down my emotions for the time being. Nola Knox, Eve's little sister, has always been her own person, to

17

put it diplomatically. To put it less diplomatically, Nola is crazy. Weird shit happens when she is around. People get hurt, small animals go missing. In one of my earliest memories of Nola she is ripping the wings off fireflies and pressing the abdomens to her earlobes for a pair of glowing earrings. Then there was the baby squirrel Nola found when she was nine.

It was going to die anyway, Nola had said as a group of us kids stood around her staring horrified at the bloody knife in her hand. No one has ever forgotten that and never let Nola forget it either.

Chief Digby shakes his head. "Not since Nola was a kid, but I'm sure they'd be glad to know that we are reinvestigating. Now that I'm chief, I'm in a position to bring a fresh look at the case. Let's get it retested and if there is any usable DNA maybe we'll find a match.

"Genealogy sites like Ancestry aren't charging law enforcement agencies for their services, so that won't cost the city."

While Digby talks, snippets of memories shuffle through my head. The day Eve and her mom and sister moved across the street and we became instant friends. The sleepovers and bike rides, the hikes down the bluff behind our homes to the caves where we laughed and shared secrets and tried to hide from Nola and my brother.

I've tried for over two decades to stuff the memories deep down. It's too painful to conjure up images of Eve's shy smile, her red hair and the sprinkle of freckles across her nose. I can't walk past a secondhand shop without thinking of all the vintage clothing she'd buy and wear with pride.

And then there are the flashbacks of Eve's dead body splayed out as my flashlight swept across the cave floor. Her head matted with congealed blood, her eyes open wide and staring blankly up at Nola and me, her mouth contorted into an ugly grimace. The two of us running to the nearest neighbor's house for help. I rub my eyes, trying to scrub away the images.

"You've been pretty quiet, Maggie," Chief Digby says. "What are you thinking?"

I look to Chief Digby. "Can I have it?" I ask. "The case? Eve was my best friend and I'm the one who found her," I say, suddenly knowing that no matter how sad, how traumatic it will be to relive Eve's final days, I'm the one who must do this. "It's time I go on desk duty until the baby comes anyway." As if on cue, the baby does a quick somersault, a trick she does whenever I sit still for too long. I wince at her antics and lay my palm against my midsection.

Digby quietly considers this for a moment and then asks, "Are you sure this is something you want to take on right now?"

"It won't be a problem," I assure him. "It makes the most sense."

This seems to quell any doubts Digby might have. "Great, it's yours," he says. "Just make sure Dex is up to date on your other cases. Anything new on those arsons?" he asks.

There has been a series of old buildings being set on fire, mostly abandoned farm buildings out in the county, but the most recent was within Grotto city limits. I shake my head. "Nothing new. I'm working with the sheriff's department and the state fire marshal. They agree they are all connected. Fires are all set at night with the same kind of setup and chemicals. Other than that, we are at a standstill."

"Okay, keep me posted on the fires. In the meantime," Chief Digby says, rising from his desk, "inform the Knox family and you better review the case files for reference. Once word gets out I'm sure we'll get a slew of tipsters. And let's get a press release ready. There will be lots of inquiries. Then gather all the evidence in the Knox case together and send it to the state lab. Let them know it's coming."

I slowly get to my feet, my mind whirling. I think of the last time I saw Eve and the angry words we spewed at each other. "You got this, Maggie?" Dex asks as we leave Digby's office and step back into the squad room.

"Yeah," I say with forced confidence. "I'm going to go talk to Charlotte and Nola Knox right away. I don't want them finding out about this from someone else. I should talk to my dad too."

"That's probably a good idea," Dex agrees. "Nola Knox is hell on wheels when she gets her back up. Tread lightly," he warns. "Remember what she did to Nick Brady?"

"I remember," I say, but it's the flashes of Eve's bloodied face that have been seared into my memory. "See you later, Dex," I say, heading for my desk, my feet heavy with dread. It's time to get to work.

NOLA KNOX

Monday, June 15, 2020

The fawn-colored mare lay in the dry dirt, rolling from side to side, hooves kicking. Dust swirled around her like ground fog. Nola reached for the horse's lead and urged the animal to her feet. She ran a calloused hand along the mare's belly. It was distended and rock hard.

"How long has she been like this?" Nola asked, facing the horse, one hand on the mare's scapula and the other over the hip joint, a stance that was meant to calm. Bijou, an American quarter horse, huffed and reared. She was suffering, her eyes wild with pain. Nola reached into her bag and prepared a syringe. Something to take the edge off. Experience told her that this horse was beyond help.

"She started acting weird yesterday," the rancher said as he kicked dust off his expensive cowboy boots.

"Weird how?" Nola asked, biting back an impatient sigh. She needed details. Specifics.

"She kept pawing at the ground with her hoof like she was trying to dig something up," the owner's teenage daughter, a mousy wisp of a thing, said. "What's wrong with her?"

"Was she looking down at her abdomen, biting at it and sweating a lot?" Nola asked, though she was already certain of the answer.

They both nodded. "We thought she got overheated because of the high temps," he said. "We gave her plenty of water," he said defensively. "She just wouldn't drink it." Father and daughter both winced as Nola inserted the needle into the thick muscle of Bijou's sweaty flank.

"Hopefully this will relax her, ease some of her pain. Let's get her to the stable," Nola directed. "I can examine her better there." Bijou fought as they made their way to the barn, a brand-new structure that had more windows and square footage than most homes. Inside, an acrid ammonia smell prickled Nola's nose. "No one changed her bedding," she said, glancing down at the foul-smelling straw. She couldn't keep the irritation from her voice.

Uneaten grain remained in Bijou's bin—a perfect petri dish for mold. Right now, the state of Bijou's living quarters was the least of her worries. *Some people shouldn't have the right to be horse owners*, Nola thought as she got Bijou situated into the stall's doorway.

The close quarters settled the mare a bit. Though Bijou was no longer rearing back on her haunches she stretched her neck out, her mouth opening and closing in a series of yawns.

"She's sleepy," the girl said. "That's good right? The medicine is making her feel better?"

"She's not sleepy," Nola murmured and reached for her stethoscope. "It's one way a horse tries to calm itself. She is stressed and in pain." Nola inserted the ear tips and pressed the chest piece to Bijou's flank, moving the silver disc every few seconds while the two looked on anxiously. "You should have called me right away." Nola ripped the stethoscope from her ears and tossed it aside. "Looks like a twisted bowel."

"Is that bad?" the daughter asked.

"Very bad when it's not caught early enough." Again Nola reached into her bag and this time pulled out a package of surgical gloves and a large tube of topical anesthetic. She applied the cream while Bijou pawed at the ground and snuffled, her nostrils flaring.

"I've been out of town for work," the rancher stammered. "We had no idea she was this bad off."

Despite the size of the barn, the air was stifling. The rancher's shirt was stained with sweat and beads of perspiration dotted the girl's nose, magnifying her freckles. Nola used her forearm to wipe her own face, her eyes burning from the salt. "Did you do zero research when you decided to buy this animal?" Nola asked angrily.

The man wasn't used to being talked to in such a manner, not accustomed to being challenged in the boardroom let alone his own backyard. "Now listen," he began but trailed off when Nola slid her gloved hand into Bijou's rectum.

"Her large colon is twisted. You have two choices here," Nola explained. "We transport Bijou to the clinic for emergency surgery or we euthanize her."

"Wait, what?" the daughter squeaked, eyes wide with fear. "She's dying?"

"As we speak." Nola pulled off the gloves with a snap. "What do you want to do?"

"How much will surgery cost?" The father rubbed a smooth hand across his face.

"Daddy!" the girl cried. "We want the operation."

"Six to eight thousand and that's just for the surgery. Follow-up care will be more," Nola said and gently ran her fingers across Bijou's back. "What do you want to do?" There was no response. She reached into her bag for another syringe and another vial. She pulled back the plunger and inserted the needle into the rubber top, filling the syringe with a clear liquid.

"What is that?" the rancher asked staring at the long needle. "What are you doing?"

"It's sodium pentobarbital." She tapped the syringe to remove any air bubbles. "What do you want to do?" Nola repeated. "Every second you wait lessens her chance of survival, increases her suffering."

"I don't know," he said uncertainly. "I don't know." He looked back and forth between Bijou and his daughter.

"Make a decision," Nola snapped. "The pain medication I've given Bijou isn't keeping up with the strangling of her bowel."

"Daddy," the girl cried, grabbing onto her father's arm. "She has to have the surgery."

"The surgery," he said in a rush. "We want the surgery."

"Okay," Nola said, returning the syringe to her bag. "Let's get her loaded into your trailer and to the clinic."

The man ran to his truck while the girl hesitated, eyes red with tears. "You can save her, can't you?" she asked.

"I can't promise anything. She's very sick. You should have called me a lot sooner," Nola said gruffly. "We have to hurry." The girl ran, crying, toward her father's truck. Some people were just so stupid, Nola thought. Once the man and the girl were out of sight, Nola retrieved the syringe from her bag and in one swift move plunged it into Bijou's jugular.

"There, there," Nola whispered into Bijou's ear. "It won't be long now." Black flies gathered at Bijou's open eyes, nostrils and ears. *They find the dying so quickly,* Nola thought as the rancher pulled his truck up to the barn. Nola guided Bijou into the trailer and secured the rear doors.

Nola trotted to the open truck window. "I'll call ahead to the clinic so they'll be ready for you," she said glancing over at the girl, who was chewing frantically at her thumbnail.

"You're not going to do the surgery?" the rancher asked in confusion.

Nola shook her head. "No, every second counts. The surgeon will be waiting for you to arrive. He'll take good care of her. You need to hurry." Nola slapped the hood of the truck as if to prod it forward.

The horse would make it to the clinic but wouldn't survive the surgery. Nola had an excellent perioperative success rate so she was glad to pass the surgery off to someone else. Let Dr. Rasmussen deal with it. Nola didn't like him anyway. Maybe the rancher would ask for a necropsy; those she enjoyed. Nola hadn't performed a postmortem on a horse in a long time.

She checked her cell phone in case the hospital in Willow Creek had called. Her mother had fallen down the basement steps a week ago, breaking a hip, her right ulna and three ribs. The surgery on her hip went as well as could be expected for a woman with diabetes, smoker's lung and osteoporosis.

There were no calls from the hospital but there were three missed calls from the clinic she worked for—Ransom County Animal Health Center. RCAHC, owned by two vets, was a mixed practice, meaning it served all your veterinary needs from your guinea pig's mange to artificially inseminating your cattle.

Nola's specialty was with large animals. Pets, or rather pet owners, were not her strong suit according to the partners.

Nola rang the clinic and spoke before Becky, the receptionist, could say hello.

"I've got someone coming in with his horse. He'll be there in ten. Twisted bowel. Dr. Rasmussen should be ready to scrub in."

"Got it," Becky said. "Don't hang up. I need to talk to you. There was a police officer here looking for you," she said, her voice just above a whisper and laced with a *what have you done now* tone. "I'll be right back." Muzak filled Nola's ear.

Nola knew what this was about. She'd heard two women talking at the convenience store this morning while in line to pay for her coffee. They were scraping away at their scratch-off lottery tickets while they talked, unaware that she was standing right behind them. "I heard they found that Knox girl's shoe," said June, a woman Nola knew from the vet clinic. She lived on a farm outside of town and raised goats. "In the cave where she was murdered."

Nola didn't recognize the other woman, but she nodded knowingly. "Really? You know, I always thought the sister killed her. She's one strange bird."

June paused in her scratching. "My bet is on the boyfriend," she said and brushed away the silver dust from her ticket with a flick of her fingers. "It's always the boyfriend."

"Naw, it's the sister. My son went to school with her. Said she had a nasty temper, stabbed a kid once."

"Really?" June asked and then caught sight of Nola standing behind them. Nola gave them a tight smile but didn't say anything. They scooted away with their scratch-offs held tightly in their fists.

So it was no surprise to Nola that the police were looking for her. Nola waited for Becky to come back on the line and passed the time by scraping horse shit from the bottom of her boots across the scorched grass. "Like I said, the police were here," Becky said when she returned. "I said you were at the Niering place. What's going on?"

"Are they coming here?" Nola asked. "Seriously? I have to get over to Goose Lake to see about a bull." She opened the truck door, tossed her bag on the seat and climbed inside. "Couldn't you have just taken a message?" Nola asked, starting the truck and pulling onto the road.

"It's the police," Becky said defensively. "What would you have done?"

"I would have taken a message." Nola sighed and hung up on her. The last thing Nola needed was for a police officer to pull her over in front of a client's home. It wasn't good for business. Besides, she promised Richard Madden that she would be there before noon. She glanced at the clock on the dashboard. The police could wait. She had a feeling they would be taking up a lot of her time in the weeks to come.

Nola turned onto a county road, heat rising from the pavement in ripples when a car came into view, flashed its lights, slowed down and then did a quick U-turn. Nola knew the car. A black sedan belonging to her former neighbor, Maggie Kennedy. So this was the cop looking for her, Nola thought with newfound interest.

Nola pressed down on the accelerator, drove a mile and then took a sharp right. A shortcut to the Madden farm. Nola knew these back roads inside and out; she'd been crisscrossing them since she was sixteen. But Maggie knew them too. Nola floored the gas pedal, kicking up gravel as she sped down the deserted road past rows of spindly corn struggling to stay upright in the crumbly, dry earth. *I've got work to do*, she thought. Maggie could wait. It wasn't like Eve was going anywhere.

THE WILLOW CREEK GAZETTE
December 24, 1995

The identity of a deceased female found on December 22, 1995, in an isolated area just north of Grotto, Iowa, has been released. Grotto Police officials say that Eve Knox, 15, of Grotto was found in an area known as Ransom Caves Friday by an unnamed family member and family friend. The death has been ruled a homicide by the Ransom County Coroner's Office though the manner of death has not been made available to the public at this time.

The high school sophomore was last seen at the Knox residence around 3:15 p.m. on Friday afternoon. According to police sources, a family member went in search of Knox late Friday evening and came across her body. A call to 911 was made at 9:48 p.m. and emergency personnel were dispatched to the scene where Knox was pronounced dead.

In the days since her death, the Ransom County Sheriff's Office and the Grotto Police Department, in a joint investigation, have conducted several searches of the area, mainly focusing on the bluffs between her family's home and the caves.

Ransom County Sheriff Abe Pellitier says that they are considering all scenarios, including that Knox may have come into contact with a drifter passing through the area who caused her harm, but emphasized that all leads are being vigorously investigated. Sheriff Pellitier declined to comment on reports that the mutilated carcass of a dog was discovered near the spot where Knox was found and may be related to the crime.

In the days leading up to her daughter's death, Charlotte Knox said everything appeared normal. "Eve was her regular, happy self. I can't believe she's gone," Knox said. "I can't imagine life without her. We're heartbroken."

Over four hundred mourners attended a candlelight vigil at the high school in Grotto, Iowa, in Knox's honor. Funeral services are scheduled for 11:00 a.m. on Tuesday, December 26, at St. Theodosius Church in Grotto.

If you have any information pertaining to the death of Eve Knox, please contact the Ransom County Sheriff's Office or the Grotto Police Department.

EVE KNOX

Nick unlocked the door and Eve followed him inside. The Brady entryway, warm and inviting with its dark oak floors and soft lighting, was bigger than Eve's entire bedroom. Sometimes she couldn't believe she was inside a house like this, with someone like Nick Brady. He was cute, smart and rich. What he saw in Eve, she didn't know. But then Eve was beginning to wonder what she ever saw in Nick.

They'd spent the evening in Zeke Berger's basement eating pizza and playing video games. Well, at least that's what Nick did. Eve sat in the corner watching the boys shoot and chop up zombies. Later, Zeke came over and sat next to Eve and they talked about tomorrow's English final and how they both should have been studying instead. Zeke was nice, easy to be around, but Eve could tell by the way that Nick glared at them out of the corner of his eye that he was getting pissed. Then when they were leaving Zeke's house and walking to the car, Nick suddenly pushed her from behind. Eve tripped, her shoulder catching the side view mirror before falling to her knees.

"Fuck, watch where you're going," Nick snapped. "Damn it," he said examining the damage. "My dad is going to be pissed."

"I'm sorry," Eve whispered, getting to her feet and rubbing her shoulder.

They drove back to Nick's house in silence. Eve was tired. Exhausted really. She never knew what might set Nick off, only that something would. It could be that Eve was talking too much or not enough. It could be the clothes she was wearing or that she wasn't giving Nick enough attention or she was being too clingy. She couldn't win.

Nick had only hit her outright once. A quick smack to the face that left a quarter-sized bruise on her cheek. It had shocked them both and when Eve started crying Nick had tried to play it off as no big deal. Eve tried to cover the purple bruise with heavy makeup but people noticed. Eve mumbled something about getting elbowed during PE.

Now Nick was much more careful. A jab to the ribs, a pinch, a shove, a yank on her hair didn't lead to unwanted questions. No one noticed the halo of bruises around her forearm or the way she favored an elbow, except Nola. Eve brushed her questions aside, but from the smirk on Nola's face, Eve knew she didn't believe her.

Nick drove up the steep private drive lined with towering pines that led to the Brady home. Unlike Eve, Nick had no neighbors. On a bluff only a few miles away as the crow flies was Eve's house but they couldn't be more different. Nick's massive house had tall white columns and triangular pediments and a park-like front yard with a circular driveway. Eve's house had a cracked foundation and a crumbling garage so filled with junk that there was no room for their mother's run-down hatchback.

Once inside, Eve pulled off her boots and set them neatly on the rug. Nick's parents weren't home. They never were. His dad worked in Willow Creek as the boss of a lumber company. His mom owned a little shop downtown called Grotto Gifts & Things that sold everything from candles and cookbooks to artwork by local artists. Eve's mother couldn't even afford to shop there.

Though Nick and Eve had been dating for eight months, she'd only met his dad a few times. He was nice enough, just seemed like he was always in a hurry though Nick's mother tried to make Eve feel welcome. Eve appreciated the effort but it was hard to feel at ease when the floor she was standing on cost more than her entire house.

Nick grabbed two cans of pop from the fridge and handed Eve one. "You hungry?" he asked.

"No," Eve said, though she hadn't eaten anything since that morning. Her shoulder ached and all she wanted to do was go home.

"Let's go upstairs," Nick said, tugging on Eve's hand.

"I've got to get home soon," Eve said, pulling her hand away. She already regretted coming all the way over to Nick's house and wondered how she was going to get home. She had decided on the ride over that she was finished with Nick and his possessiveness and hot temper. She just needed to get the nerve up to tell him. "Let's just stay down here. My mom has to work late and she doesn't like it when Nola stays home alone."

"I don't think you need to worry about Nola," Nick said popping the metal tab and taking a long drink. "She's fine on her own. Unless of course she's out drowning puppies or something."

"Ha, ha," Eve deadpanned. "That's really funny, Nick. That's just a stupid rumor. Nola never did anything like that." Normally she wouldn't dare call him out on his meanness but Eve wasn't going to do this anymore. "Don't talk about my sister."

Nick set his can on the marble countertop and stared at her in disbelief. "What did you say?"

Eve didn't respond, her eyes fixated on Nick's clenched fist.

"You're feisty tonight," he laughed meanly.

He reached for Eve and she flinched as he wrapped his arms around her waist. Being hugged by Nick, Eve thought, was like being swallowed whole. At first you feel loved and warm and safe then suddenly you can't breathe. Eve jabbed him gently with her elbows and laughed. "Too tight," she said.

Nick eased his grip but still pushed Eve toward the stairs. Again Eve wished she had never come inside the house. She should have told him in the car.

"Nick, I really have to go," Eve said as she wriggled away. "Let's just talk for a minute."

"Talk about what?" He arched one eyebrow suggestively and slid his fingers through Eve's belt loops, pulling her close. His breath was hot and smelled sweetly of bubblegum and pizza. He was hard against her stomach.

"Just talk," Eve said, trying to squirm away.

"Like the way you and Zeke were talking earlier?" Nick asked. So here it was, Eve thought. She knew he was going to bring it up. Nick had given her the cold shoulder in the car. She should have just asked him to take her home.

"That was nothing." She gave a little laugh.

"Nothing?" Nick aped back at her.

"Come on, Nick." Eve tried to laugh again. "Zeke? Really?"

"Are you laughing at me?" Nick asked and he roughly snagged her arm.

"Ow!" Eve cried. "No! I'm not interested in Zeke. It was nothing."

"Prove it," he breathed into her ear, his hands on her zipper. She tried to bat his fingers away but that just made him smile, and not in a nice way.

"No," Eve said, afraid to meet his eyes.

"Come on," he said. His voice was low, urgent. Eve considered running out the door, but knew she wouldn't get far. He was bigger, faster than she was.

"Someone might walk in," Eve said as she took small, slow steps backward.

"They won't," Nick murmured as he crept closer to her. "My dad's out of town and my mom is doing inventory at the shop late tonight. We're alone."

Eve felt trapped. She knew if she argued, protested, things would go downhill fast but she had to get out of here. She shivered under Nick's stare.

He stepped toward her and kissed her. Gently at first and then more fervently as they sank to the Italian marble floor. Nick slid his hand beneath her shirt while a silent scream clanged around in her head. *Get off, get off, get off*, she wanted to scream. His weight pressed the air from her lungs and Eve struggled to catch her breath. Nick nuzzled his face against her neck and whispered, "I love you, Eve," as he tried to unzip her jeans.

"I have to go," Eve said abruptly and squeezed out from beneath him.

"Hey," Nick said, his forehead wrinkled with worry. "What's the matter?"

Eve swiped at her wet eyes. "I can't see you anymore," she said, her voice cracking.

Confusion filled his face. He was so handsome, Eve thought. People would say she was crazy for breaking up with him. "What? Why?" he asked.

"It's my mom," Eve said. "She said we can't go out anymore. She said we're getting too serious." This was a lie. Her mother loved that Eve was dating Nick Brady, thought that she was the luckiest girl in the world.

Her mother didn't have much luck with her own love life. Pregnant at sixteen, married and pregnant again at eighteen, divorced at nineteen. Now bitter and alone, she didn't have much positive to say about the opposite sex, except when it came to Nick. *He's a keeper, Eve, hold on to him, and don't let go.*

"Well, don't listen to her," Nick said angrily. "Let me talk to her. I can change her mind."

"No." Eve shook her head. "You won't change her mind. I can't see you anymore. I'm sorry."

She moved toward the door. "She can't do that," Nick said, yanking her back by the arm.

Eve bit back a gasp of pain and the tears broke through and streamed hotly down her face.

"Eve," Nick said pulling her to his chest and pressing his fingers deep into the small of her back. "Don't worry. She can't keep us away from each other. She can't. I love you, Eve," he said.

He sounded so sincere, so honest. For a brief moment, Eve kicked herself for telling him they couldn't be together anymore. What were the chances that someone would love her as much as Nick? Slim to none, Eve thought. *No,* Eve scolded herself. *Don't back down now.* A small mutter of frustration escaped from her lips.

"Don't worry, we'll change her mind," Nick said, mistaking the sound as anger toward her mother. "I can be pretty persuasive. Let me drive you home." Nick entwined his fingers through Eve's. "I can talk to her. It will be okay."

"No thanks," Eve said, eager to leave the house. "She's pretty mad. Maybe we can give it a few days until she calms down." She just needed to get out the door. Nick kissed her one more time. Hard, desperate. Eve waited for Nick to break away first before pulling on her boots. She opened the door and stepped outside. The cold air felt good against her skin. The complicated part was over, Eve thought. She didn't dare look back.

She couldn't wait to get home even though her mother would be mad at her for being so late and would shake her head when Eve told her that things were over with Nick. Nick was too much. Everything about Nick was too much.

Eve moved through the streets of Grotto on autopilot, barely feeling the bite of cold on her cheeks. The bare tree branches swayed in the brittle wind and the shiny slick sidewalk gleamed like glass beneath the streetlights.

Eve knew blaming her mother for the breakup was the easy way out. Nick still thought she loved him and with that believed there was the chance Eve would disobey her mother so they could be together. She should have just told Nick the truth. That *she* was the one who wanted things to end, that when they were together she felt anxious and weak, like some smaller version of herself. But she could never say these words out loud. Look at tonight for instance. Why did she let Nick talk to her the way he did? Let him push her around? Why was she so weak?

Eve could just imagine how Nick would react to this. He would blink back at her with his gray-blue eyes, trying to work out what she was trying to say. *But I love you*, he would tell her as if that was all that mattered. Nick believed the world spun around him like he was the sun and everyone else were lesser planets. And, Eve guessed, for the most part that was the truth. But not anymore. She was done spinning.

Eve spent the first four blocks looking over her shoulder checking to see if Nick was creeping up behind her in his car but finally her limbs relaxed, her legs felt light, her arms swung easily. She began to sing softly to herself, a catchy one-hit wonder about common ground and that old movie with Audrey Hepburn or maybe it was Katharine, that she and Maggie made fun of, but right then, in that moment, it was perfect.

For the first time in a long time, Eve felt free. Hopeful.

The grumble of a car engine revving drowned out her song. *Just keep walking*, she told herself. *Don't turn around*. The song fell silent on her lips. Nick always played this stupid game. Creep up behind her, rev the engine, make her jump, veer the car toward the sidewalk like he was going to run her over. All the while, laughing.

When Eve finally turned, Nick's silhouette was outlined through the windshield and a familiar anxiety wrapped itself around her midsection, weighing her down. He lowered the passenger-side window. "Get in," he beckoned, looking at Eve in that way that still made her stomach flip.

Why couldn't this be easier? Eve wondered as she reached for the door handle. Why did goodbyes have to be so hard?

MAGGIE KENNEDY-O'KEEFE

Monday, June 15, 2020

It isn't a surprise that Nola doesn't stop when I try to pull her over. As she speeds past me my head fills with memories of the day that Eve died. Her mother was frantic when she came home and found that Eve wasn't there. I had just gotten home from babysitting for the Harpers when Charlotte Knox came scurrying across the street wanting to know if I'd seen Eve. I told her I hadn't, that I'd been babysitting all afternoon and evening. She tearfully asked me where I thought Eve could be and I ticked off all the usual haunts: Nick's house, the library, some classmates' homes.

Can you help Nola look for her? Charlotte asked. I looked to my dad who nodded and told us to stay together. Nola looked put out but ran inside her house and came out with two flashlights.

They still live next to my dad though I haven't talked to Nola in years. I know what Nola's like, but even so I want to get to her before I talk to her mother. Charlotte Knox has always been fragile and I want someone there with her when I tell her about the kids finding Eve's boot, even if that someone has to be Nola.

As I drive through the streets of Grotto, images of Eve's

battered face pop into my head. For many years the only way to keep the memories at bay was alcohol. This worked only for so long. Today, I try to keep the happy ones front and center. Eve and me at thirteen exploring the maze of caves below our neighborhood at the bottom of the bluffs, talking and laughing and just being kids. It was all so innocent then. Nola lagging a few steps behind saying that she was going to tell on us the entire way.

Eve and me babysitting at the Harper house, their two young kids, Riley and Rebecca, running circles around us as we painted each other's fingernails with Nola sitting all alone on the Knoxes' front step. Mr. Harper, an attorney, and Mrs. Harper, a stay-at-home mom, didn't like Nola hanging around their kids. No one did. *I don't want her in my house*, Joyce Harper would say. When Nola was ten, Mrs. Harper found her outside holding Riley's hand and heading toward the edge of the bluff behind the house.

She's dangerous, I remember Mrs. Harper angrily telling my dad. *If I hadn't looked out the window and gotten to him, Riley would have gone right over. I swear to God she was going to walk him right off the ledge.*

My dad calmed her down, said he would go talk to Nola and Mrs. Knox, but Mrs. Harper never forgot.

Since Nola ditched me, I decide to touch base with the next person on my list. Nick Brady.

Nick was Eve's first and only boyfriend. I've never been a big fan of Nick. He was Adonis handsome but beneath his seemingly good nature, I thought he was an asshole. Everyone else thought that Eve was the luckiest girl in school. Nick's parents were rich and he liked to flaunt it. Dressed in the most expensive clothes and shoes, he sped around in his BMW like he owned the town. That's not why I didn't like Nick though.

What I hated about Nick was the way Eve changed when-

39

ever she was around him. The way she became meek and mild and seemed to forget every single opinion she ever had.

I know I'm not one to talk. At the same time that Eve and Nick were dating I'd been in love in that irrational, soul-sucking kind of way that leaves you heavy-limbed and thick-tongued. But Eve knew better. Was better. Plus, I had a sense that Nick hurt her. Emotionally, for sure, but I thought he could be abusing her physically too. I saw the marks. The fingerprint-sized bruises on the small of Eve's back. I saw the way she winced when she pulled her hair back in a ponytail or slung a backpack over her shoulder. She always had an ex-cuse: *I tripped; Nola and I were messing around; I'm such a klutz.*

But why do you like him? I remember asking Eve and she could never give me a real answer. *What's not to like?* was the best she could come up with.

Adult Nick, against everyone's expectations, did not fol-low in his father's footsteps into the lumber business. Instead, he took over his mother's gift shop which he ran with his pretty, docile wife, at least until their famously contentious divorce. There were rumors of domestic abuse and affairs. The ex-wife got the house, the kids and a whole bunch of money. Nick got the boutique and a crappy apartment next to the bowling alley.

Of course Nick was the top suspect in Eve's death at first, but he was cleared pretty early on in the investigation. One of his friends vouched for his whereabouts and there wasn't any physical evidence to link him to the crime. The only reason I want to talk to Nick is because Charlotte and Nola Knox were convinced that Nick was Eve's killer and made his life a living hell for a long time. Not that he didn't deserve it. He did. Just not for Eve's death.

I drive to Juniper Street. Grotto Gifts & Things is still the upscale, expensive tourist trap it's always been except that it could use a fresh coat of paint and a good scrubbing. Ever since Nick's wife made an exit, the shop has taken on a ne-glected, forlorn air. Much like Nick himself.

I see a few of my brother's smaller art pieces for sale in the display window. Metal sculptures twisted and welded into whimsical shapes. Colin is a very talented artist, I have to give him that. Beyond the sculptures, I see that the shop is empty except for Nick who is sitting behind the counter and star-ing down at his phone. A bell jingles as I come through the door. The air smells like a cinnamon-scented candle and fast-food French fries. Nick doesn't bother to look up. So much for service with a smile.

"Hey, Nick," I say. "How's it going?" Nick takes his time responding to me. He slides one finger across his phone a few more times before looking up.

"Living the dream," he says, finally setting his phone aside. Panting, he heaves himself up from his stool. His once hand-some face is now fleshy and formless and his girth spills over his belt. He breathes heavily at the exertion of getting to his feet. "How about you, Maggie? You look like you're about to pop."

"Not just yet," I say. "Listen, I'm not sure if you heard, but…"

"Yeah, I know. Everyone knows. You're looking into Eve's murder again," he says in a bored tone that infuriates me. He was supposed to love Eve and now he can't even be both-ered. He's pissing me off. "This means Nola Knox is going to go on a frickin' rant about me again." Nick shakes his head. "That bitch," he says. "She better not come anywhere near me. I swear to God I'll claim *Stand Your Ground* if I have to."

"Geez, don't say stuff like that, Nick," I say. "Don't forget who you're talking to. Besides, that's not a law here."

Nick comes out from behind the counter and peers out the window as if expecting to see Nola standing outside with a baseball bat. "Can you blame me?" he asks, looking back at me.

I can't, but I don't say anything. In the corner of the store is a wall of merchandise expressly for babies. I walk over and run my fingers over a toppled pile of onesies with *Gotta Grotto* across the front. *What does that even mean?* I want to ask but instead I begin to refold them into a neat stack.

"No offense, but what makes you think you can solve it now?" Nick asks. "It's been twenty-five years. What's an old boot going to prove?"

I give him a stiff smile but don't answer. "I'm reviewing all the files, reinterviewing witnesses. Do you mind if I ask you a few questions?" With hotheads like Nick Brady, it's always good to make them think they've got a choice.

"You?" Nick laughed. "You're investigating? Isn't that a little weird? You were best friends."

"It is upsetting," I say. "I loved Eve like a sister. I feel like I owe it to her, don't you?" I'm laying it on a little thick. It's much more effective to get a guy like Nick to think he is doing you a favor. That you hate to inconvenience him, but his thoughts and insights are imperative, crucial to the investigation.

Nick puffs out his already massive chest. "Yeah, I guess so. What do you want to know?"

"Just the basics." I pull out my notepad and a pen. "Can you think of anyone who might have wanted to hurt Eve?"

Nick shrugs. "No. I mean, everyone liked Eve. Hell, I loved her. I always thought we would get married." These were the words I found in the file, almost verbatim to what Nick said twenty-five years ago.

"That's funny," I say, tapping my pen against my front teeth.

"What?" Nick asks.

"That's not the vibe I got from Eve."

"What do you mean?" he asks. A flush begins to creep up his wide neck.

42

"You guys only dated for a short time," I remind him. "A few months, right? Eve never said anything about you guys talking about marriage. She always said she was moving away after graduation and going to college."

"We dated for eight months and would still be together if she hadn't died," he says. I wonder what Nick's kids and ex-wife would think of this speculation.

The only thing Eve told me was that she broke up with Nick, told me he didn't handle it well.

"I know there were rumors that Eve broke up with me," Nick says heading off my next question. "But they weren't true. We loved each other. I bought her a promise ring. I was going to give it to her for Christmas that year. Her mom told me that Eve bought me a present too. She found it in Eve's room. A video game. She gave it to me at the funeral."

I stare him straight in the eye. "Eve told me she broke up with you. It wasn't a rumor." I had said some mean things to Eve the morning she told me about the breakup. I felt bad the second the words came out of my mouth. I never told her I was sorry. I could have though. If only I would have apologized maybe the day wouldn't have ended the way it did.

"That was her mom, not Eve," Nick contests. "She loved me." By the look on his face I can tell Nick really believes this to be true.

"Uh-huh," I say noncommittally. "And you were where on the afternoon of December twenty-second?"

"I was with Jamie Hutchcraft and then I was here at the shop with my mom until about ten. I was at home the rest of the night."

"Where is Jamie these days?" I ask.

Nick squirmed. "I don't know, we lost touch. Why?" I let the question hang there, let him think that I'm searching for Jamie to once again confirm the alibi.

Nick rubs his elbow and he catches me watching. "Still

aches sometimes," he says, rolling up his shirtsleeve to show me the scars. "Twenty-five stitches because of Nola, that crazy bitch."

"Just stay away from trophy cases and large windows and you'll be fine," I joke. Nick doesn't think I'm funny.

"I'm serious," Nick says, pulling down his sleeve with a snap. "It took an hour for them to get all the glass out. You're going to make sure she stays far away from me, aren't you?"

Nick has a point. A week after Eve's funeral, Nola, who stopped at the high school to pick up Eve's things, shoved Nick into a glass trophy case. She overheard him describing in minute detail to a group of friends how sad it was that Eve was dead because she gave the best blow jobs.

"Nola isn't going to bother you. But if she does," I hand him one of my business cards, "just call me."

He looks at my belly. "You're going to stop her?" he asks. What a sexist pig.

"Maybe," I say.

"Wait, did your dad ever look into that guy Eve used to babysit for?" Nick asks. I freeze, pen in midair.

"What guy?" I ask.

Nick looks up at the ceiling trying to retrieve the name. "Harper, I think. I don't know for sure."

"Cam Harper?" I ask. "The man who lived next door?" I was not expecting this name to pop up. Not now. Not ever.

"Yeah," Nick says. "Eve mentioned once that he kind of creeped her out and on the day she died I saw them together. He was holding her hand."

I give my head a little shake as dread spreads through my body. "Why would Cam Harper be holding hands with Eve?" I ask.

"I figure she would have told you," he says. "I thought the two of you talked about everything." I respond with a non-committal grunt. "I called him out on it. Told him to stay

44

away from my girlfriend. He just blathered on that I had gotten it wrong."

"Maybe you did," I offer, still thrown by this revelation. Cam Harper and Eve holding hands? "When did this happen?" I ask.

"In the morning, on the way to school. It was weird." Nick drums his fingers on the counter. He's getting restless.

"And you told the police this?"

"Yeah." Nick shrugs. "At least I'm pretty sure. Your dad must have made note of it somewhere."

"I thought Dex Stroope interviewed you," I said, "but you talked to my dad?"

"Yep, just once. I did talk to the new chief when he was working for the sheriff's department. Three or four times. I've got to say, it made me really nervous. He was awful to me. Treated me like a criminal."

That didn't really sound like Chief Digby. From what I could tell, he was the epitome of decorum and respect when it came to suspects. That didn't mean he was soft—he would never have made chief. He just played good cop really well.

I remember my dad saying that Nick was cleared and that he hoped people would stop dragging his name through the mud. "Well, he was just doing his job," I say. "What else can you tell me about Cam Harper?"

"Nothing really. Just that Eve was ready to quit babysitting for them. Said that Harper made her real uncomfortable but it was the only way she had to make money so she kept doing it."

"And you told my dad this?" I ask again. Nick nods. "But not Stroope or Digby?"

"No, by that time I was the main suspect," Nick says. "Besides, I had a lawyer and she wasn't letting me say much."

"Will you let me know if you think of anything else?" I ask him. "Even the smallest detail?"

"Sure," Nick says, walking me past displays of rustic pottery and hand-poured candles to the door. "I miss her too," he calls as I push through the door. I almost believe him.

I turn back to him. "How'd you find out?" I ask. "About Eve?"

"My mom woke me up and told me the next morning," Nick says, his forehead furrowing at the memory. "It was awful. I really don't need this, Maggie. I was cleared twenty-five years ago and now you're telling me that I might have to go through all of this again. Eve's mom told everyone who would listen that I killed her and Nola is just freakin' nuts. Things finally died down and now they are going to be all over me again. It's going to be a shit show."

"I have no intention of letting this become a shit show, Nick," I assure him, "but I have to do my job."

"Then check out Cam Harper," Nick insists.

"I will," I say. "But do me a favor, Nick. Don't say anything about Cam Harper to anyone. I don't want him to get wind that I'll be talking to him. Sometimes it's better when they don't see you coming, you know what I mean?"

"Yeah, sure. Just keep Nola Knox out of my face, okay?"

I try not to roll my eyes. "You've got my card."

Either Nick is lying about Cam Harper to deflect any suspicion or my dad didn't think it was important enough to note. The third option is more disconcerting. Was my dad's memory failing way back then? I do this a lot—scan my brain for any evidence, any precursors that might have warned us of what was to come.

As I leave Nick's shop and step back into the heat of the day, I think of the night that Nola and I found Eve and banged on Vivian Benson's door for help. My dad came to take us to the police station to be questioned. I sat in a chair in a conference room, shivering despite the blanket that Mrs. Benson had wrapped around me. *I want to go home,* I told him. *I don't feel good,* I cried. *I can't stop seeing her face.*

You can't leave just yet, honey, he said. *We've got to find out what happened to Eve and we need your help.* He kissed my cheek. *I love you,* he whispered. *It's going to be okay.*

But it wasn't okay. My stomach twisted and cramped and a wave of nausea rolled over me. I rushed to the bathroom, and when I emerged, my dad laid a cool hand against my forehead.

She's feverish, he told the sheriff. *She needs to go home and go to bed. You can ask her more questions tomorrow.*

They finally let us go home and as I leapt from the car I was aware of Cam Harper's eyes following me on my way to the house. I passed my pale, wide-eyed brother and ran up the steps to the bathroom where I slammed and locked the door as a new round of sobs coursed through my body. I stripped off my clothes and stepped into the shower, letting the hot spray of water pound over me. I scrubbed at my face with a washcloth, trying to scour away Eve's cracked skull and blood-matted hair from behind my eyes.

As I drive away from Nick's shop I think about what he said about Cam Harper. Could it be true? Could Cam have gone after Eve? For a long time, I thought I was the only one. Stupid, naïve, I know. I was just too caught up in my own melodrama to pay attention to what was going on around me.

As much as I don't want to, I'm going to have to visit the Harpers and I'm going to have to talk to Cam Harper. The last thing I want is for anyone to find out about my relationship with my neighbor. *Not relationship,* I chide myself. *It wasn't my fault. I was fifteen. I was a child.* And though I thought I was in love with him, it wasn't a relationship. It was manipulative, sick and against the law. As much as I tell myself this, I still haven't come forward and told my story. I've never even told Shaun.

From afar, I've kept my eye on Cam Harper. I know men

like this don't stop. I've watched his comings and goings to see if he has targeted another young girl. So far, I've come up with nothing but that doesn't mean it isn't happening. Predators like Cam work hard not to get caught.

EVE KNOX

Friday, December 22, 1995
12:30 a.m.

Eve quietly slid her house key into the lock and slowly opened the door. More than anything she was mad at herself. Why did she get into the car with Nick? She thought the hardest part was behind her, breaking things off, but then she went and climbed right back into the car with him.

They ended up parking below the bluffs at the bottom of a dead-end street that led to the caves. Not the caves that all the tourists went to in the summer, the ones with guides and a gift shop, but the forgotten ones just below their neighborhood. This time Nick had been gentle, the earlier anger and fervor melting into soft touches and kisses. In those minutes she loved him again. Why? How did he do this to her? Why did she keep going back for more?

The living room was dark except for the glow of her mother's cigarette. Eve unwound her scarf from her neck, pulled off her coat and hung them both on the hook next to the door.

"Aren't you going to say anything?" her mother asked. Her voice was thick. She'd been crying.

"I'm sorry," Eve said softly. She was aware of Nick's odor emanating from her skin and hoped the scent of cigarettes would keep her mother from noticing. "We lost track of time."

"I bet you did," her mother said, a slyness in her tone that Eve hated. Eve didn't respond. "I almost called the police. I work sixty hours a week to make sure you have food and clothes and heat." Her mother shifted in her seat, the burning ember from the cigarette moving jerkily through the air. "The least you can do is respect my rules. I'm tired. I shouldn't have to wait up for you."

Eve knew she was right. She knew how much her mother tried. She was a single mother who worked hard and was even harder on herself. Nothing was easy for Charlotte Knox. Because of this Eve did her best to make things painless for her mom. She helped out at home keeping things neat and tidy. She tried to keep her grades up which was challenging because she was no Nola. Eve stayed out of trouble and, most important, she tried to keep Nola out of trouble. Not easy because not only was Nola scary smart, she was also always getting into trouble for fighting or lying or stealing.

"I'm sorry, Mom," Eve said again, meaning it. Eve wanted to tell her that she had broken up with Nick or at least tried to. Maybe then her mother would understand. Eve thought that maybe saying the words out loud would make them true. Final. But Eve couldn't quite do it. Her mother would probably be angrier with her for breaking up with Nick than for being late.

"You're grounded," her mother said flatly. "For a week. School and home, that's it."

"But it's winter break," Eve protested. "What am I supposed to do all week?"

"Not my problem. You're grounded," Charlotte said, a rare finality in her voice.

"But that's not fair," Eve said, her voice rising. "I'm never late. It was just this one time."

"Too bad," her mother said, extinguishing the cigarette and flipping on a table lamp. She was curled up into a corner of the sofa still wearing her work uniform. The ashtray on the side table was overflowing. "You should have thought of that before. You need to start thinking of other people once in a while."

Eve emitted an involuntary huff of air. *What a joke*, she thought. Her mother did work hard but in all other aspects Eve played the role of the adult. Eve was supposed to be the child, the moody teenager. Instead she got a mother who worked all the time tethering Eve with an evil genius little sister who creeped everyone out.

"You think it's funny?" her mother asked, getting to her feet. "Know what? Make it two weeks. You think it's so easy doing what I do? You can be in charge for a while. Home and school. That's it."

"What else is new," Eve muttered. She shouldn't have to worry about these kinds of things. She had her own problems.

"I give you a hard time because I don't want you to make the same mistakes I did." Her mother's voice rose.

Anger sizzled in Eve's chest. Her mother always made everything about herself. "Don't worry, Mom," Eve said indignantly. "I will never, ever, make the same mistakes you did. I will not get pregnant and married at sixteen. I won't have another baby and a divorce before I turn nineteen. I won't make one kid be the grown-up in the family and I won't let the other one, no matter how smart she is, turn into a freak and a bitch, which in case you didn't know, is the worst kind of combination there is. Yeah, don't worry, Mom, it's not going to happen."

"I've given up everything for you," her mother whispered, holding her hand tight against her chest as if she couldn't trust it not to strike out at Eve.

"Well, you shouldn't have," Eve mumbled, trying to brush past her mother and up the stairs. The slap came like a slingshot. Fast and hard against her cheek. The cheap green stone in her mother's ring nicked Eve's skin.

"How dare you," her mother cried. "Ungrateful brat! Make it three weeks!"

Pressing her fingers against her cheek, Eve stormed up the stairs and into her bedroom. She slammed the door, the thunderous vibration echoing through the house. Tears pricked at her eyes. Eve looked in the mirror on the back of her door. A bright red handprint covered her cheek and a small trickle of blood trailed from the cut.

Eve pulled off her sweater and threw it on the floor and began rifling through her dresser in search of her pajamas. She knew she should have stayed quiet but she couldn't stop the words from spewing forth. Her mother had no idea what her life was like.

She was pulling out an oversize tee when she heard a noise behind her. She turned to find Nola standing in the doorway, staring at her. Eve pressed the T-shirt to her chest.

"So she smacked you, huh?" Nola said. She was dressed in a pair of shabby sweatpants and a thermal shirt. Her yellow curls were pulled up into a messy topknot.

"Yeah, well, she didn't mean it," Eve said turning back to the bureau and retrieving a pair of flannel pajama bottoms.

"She's been crying all night. I wasn't able to get any reading done," Nola said. "All I could hear was her annoying sniffing and then she kept coming into my room to *talk*."

"Wow," Eve deadpanned. "Such a big heart you have, Nola."

Nola shrugged. "I had stuff to do."

Eve shook her head. "I'm going to bed," she said turning away from Nola to pull the T-shirt over her head.

"Where'd you get the bruises?" Nola asked, her head tilted to the side as if daring Eve to lie. Eve didn't answer. "The ones on your neck, those are obvious. Gross but obvious. But what about the ones there and there?" Nola stepped into the room and reached out for Eve's arm.

Eve shook her off. "They're nothing. Go to bed."

"That's what they all say." Nola lowered her voice to a whisper. "Do you like it? When he hits you?"

Eve's breath caught in her throat. She felt sick. "He doesn't hit me. I wouldn't let that happen. Get out of my room," Eve ordered.

"Uh-huh," Nola said, nodding knowingly. "I wonder what Charlotte would say if she knew?"

Eve tried to keep her face blank, untroubled. But what if her mother found out about the bruises? What would she do? Would she call Nick's parents? The police? Knowing her mother, she would probably say a mean boyfriend was better than no boyfriend at all. Part of Eve wanted Nola to tell. Then maybe it would be out of her hands for good. It would end things with Nick. But what would her friends say? Would they believe her? Most wouldn't but Maggie would believe her. She didn't like Nick.

No. Nola wouldn't tell. Maybe it would be different if her sister actually seemed to care about the way Nick treated her, but she didn't. Everything was a game to Nola to see who was smarter, who could get the upper hand.

"You tell Mom, I'll tell her about your box. Go to bed, Nola," Eve said quietly, not letting the panic reach her voice.

Eve held Nola's gaze. This was an old game for them— who would blink first? Usually Nola won, hands down, but this time Eve would not flinch.

Her eyes began to water but still she didn't look away.

"If a guy did that to me, I'd kill him," Nola finally said. "But that's just me."

She turned and left Eve's room, gently closing the door behind her.

THERAPY TRANSCRIPT

Client Name: Nola Knox, 13 years
Therapist Name: Linda Gonzalez, LMHC, NCC
Date of Service: Tuesday, Jan. 30, 1996

LG: Good morning, Nola. I'm Linda Gonzalez. Please make yourself at home. Take a seat.

NK: I'd rather stand.

LG: If that will make you more comfortable.

NK: It does.

LG: Have you ever seen a counselor before?

LG: Why don't you tell me about why you think you are here today.

LG: I know this is hard, Nola. I know you are going through a difficult time. Your sister was murdered. You found…

Loud crash

Notes:
Nola was mandated by the juvenile court to at-

tend no less than 12 counseling sessions after pushing a sixteen-year-old boy into a glass trophy case causing significant injuries to the boy and to herself.

Nola refused to answer any of my questions and did not make eye contact in this initial session. When asked about her sister who had been murdered just before Christmas, Nola knocked a lamp off my desk and left my office. I followed her but she left the premises before I could talk more with her.

MAGGIE KENNEDY-O'KEEFE

Monday, June 15, 2020

I'm still processing what Nick Brady told me about Eve and Cam Harper holding hands the day she died. I know that Nick is not the most reliable of sources but if it's true, this could change the course of the investigation. For a long time, I thought I was the only one. That Cam loved me. But as time passed I realized that this most likely wasn't the case. If Cam Harper preyed on me, chances are there were others. The thought that Eve could have been one of them makes me want to punch a wall.

I slow the car as I come up on Bates Avenue, named after a decorated Civil War soldier from Iowa named Norman Bates. I kid you not. We learned all about him in middle school—awarded the Medal of Honor by President Johnson in 1865. Great soldier. Unfortunate name.

Bates is a narrow street that winds sinuously upward with homes appearing to lean at painful angles like crooked teeth. The street evens out at the top and comes to an abrupt dead end. There are five homes atop the bluff. Two on each side, and the Harper house at the end of the cul-de-sac. Each seemingly built in a different era.

I park in front of my childhood home and look across the

street at the Knox house. Even though I visit my dad several times a week, I do my best not to stare too long at the Knoxes' shabby two-story. It was a second home to me before Eve died and I haven't been inside in twenty-five years.

Not that I didn't try. Charlotte didn't let anyone come inside except for my dad so he could give her updates about the case. It must have been too painful for Charlotte to have Eve's friends come around. I wanted desperately to be able to go inside, up the stairs to sit in Eve's room even for just a minute.

Decades later the siding of the house is pocked, the front lawn is overgrown and the walkway that leads to the front door is split. The cheeriest bits about the whole scene are the dandelions that sway with the weight of their furry yellow heads.

I also avoid looking at the Harpers' house. In the years after Eve died, I would look out my bedroom and see the sprawling rambler and my face would flush with shame and hurt and regret. That faded over time, but the anger stayed. Over the years, I lost my mom, my innocence and my best friend. This street has been a graveyard to me.

I inhale deeply and step from my car. My dad is sitting in his usual spot on his front porch, his affable home health aide, Leanne, sitting next to him. "I'll stop over in a few minutes," I call out to him. "I have official business," I say, pointing at the Knox house. My father looks at me blankly and continues swinging. The minute I walk away he'll forget I was even here.

I walk up the cracked pathway and try to look through the front windows but the drapes are pulled tight. Though we are in the throes of summer, a Christmas wreath with a limp silver bow hangs on the front door. I knock. The receptionist didn't give me many details when I called back after missing Nola out on her vet call. I'm hoping that I can catch her here.

I shift from foot to foot. The baby is pressing on my bladder and I already have to go the bathroom again. I knock over and over until the door finally opens a crack revealing one green eye.

"Nola," I say.

"Maggie Kennedy," she responds, not opening the door any farther.

"It's O'Keefe now," I say flatly. Could Nola really be that out of touch? I've been married for ten years. I'm guessing she knows my new name but is choosing not to use it. I'm not sure why it bugs me, but it does. "Do you have a few minutes to talk?" I ask.

"About what?" Nola asks. She's not budging. I look around the neighborhood. Mrs. Harper has come out to her mailbox and is staring at us curiously. My brother has appeared on the front porch, a welder's helmet tipped back atop his head and he and my dad are leaning against the front porch rail watching us. Colin must be taking a break from his art, I think. "Come on, Mags," Nola says, using Eve's nickname for me, "just tell me."

"Can I come in?" I ask.

"I'll come outside," Nola says. As she squeezes through the small opening in the door I catch a glimpse of the living room, a slew of plastic bins and a couch piled with clothes.

"Are you moving?" I ask in surprise.

"No," Nola says and quickly closes the door behind her. In front of me stands Eve's little sister, slim but strong looking, nearly six feet tall, now a grown woman. Though her oversize eyeglasses have been replaced with a more fashionable pair, her green eyes are still as intense as I remember. Curls spring from her head in a pale yellow halo. Her lips are thin, her nose long, but over time Nola has grown into her features. Not beautiful like Eve was, but certainly attractive. Too bad her insides don't match the outside.

"It's been a long time," I say. I can't remember the last time

I was standing this close to Nola. Maybe Eve's funeral. While everyone else was crying over Eve's casket, Nola stood by, dry-eyed. Through the years I've seen her from a distance but remarkably we never ran into each other at the bank or the grocery store. Not even at the vet clinic where Shaun and I take our cats, Skunky and Ponie.

"Has it?" Nola asks as if she hasn't given it a thought over the years.

"Time marches on," I say dumbly. The afternoon sun is beating down on my scalp and I'm feeling a bit light-headed.

"Why are you here?" Nola asks. She was never one for mincing words.

"Is your mom home?" I ask. "I'm here to talk to both of you."

"She's in the hospital," Nola says. "Fell and broke her hip. I would have thought your dad would have told you about all the commotion over here last week."

"I'm sorry to hear that," I say. It doesn't shock me that my dad didn't tell me about Charlotte's fall, his short-term memory being what it is. Out of sight, out of mind. "I'll get right to it then," I say, hating that I already sound defensive. "A new piece of evidence has been found relating to Eve's murder." I watch Nola's face for a reaction and get nothing.

"How gallant of you to deliver the news," Nola says with a barely perceptible smile. "But you're a bit late. I already heard about it."

"I'm sorry," I say. "I wanted to tell you first. I started looking for you the minute I found out about it myself."

"A shoe, right?" Nola asks. Normally, we wouldn't release this information but since the Specht kid has already shown the shoe to a third of Grotto's teen population, I don't see the harm in confirming.

"It was one of the boots Eve was wearing that night. Some

59

kids were messing around in Ransom Caves and found it wedged in a crevice between two rocks," I explain.

"I'm surprised you even bothered to come over here," Nola says dismissively. "I thought the police gave up on finding Eve's killer years ago."

"No one ever gave up, Nola," I say gently. "My dad never did."

"Could have fooled me," Nola shoots back. "Your dad had decades to solve it and he got nowhere. What makes you think it will be any different this time?"

"Technology. The chief thinks there's a chance we can get some usable DNA."

Nola gives a derisive snort. "Really?" she asks.

"Really," I assure her. "The evidence will be sent off to the lab this week."

"Interesting," Nola says, eyebrows arched. "My mother tried to get you people to look for new DNA years ago and got nowhere."

"My dad never gave up on trying to find out who killed Eve," I say, my voice rising. "He read through the files all the time." I thought back to the many hours my dad would sit in our wood-paneled den with boxes and file folders strewn on the floor and across his desk. If I would come into the room while he was reviewing the files, he'd quickly close the folder or cover up a photograph, but I knew it was Eve. *I'm working here*, he'd snap and I'd quickly retreat. Later, he'd apologize for his sharp tone.

"A lot of good that did," Nola sniffs.

"I thought you'd be happy about this," I say in exasperation. "I thought you'd be glad that we're focusing on the case again."

"And you're leading the investigation?" Nola asks, looking down at me skeptically.

"I am," I confirm.

"Like father, like daughter," Nola says. "Though I must say, you are the last person I would have expected to go into law enforcement."

"Oh, why is that?" I ask, my hackles raised.

Nola shrugs. "Just that you weren't known as much of an upstanding citizen back in the day."

"You can talk," I snap. "You grew up to be a vet. With your history, no one would have ever predicted that. A taxidermist maybe, but a vet?"

"You're going to have a baby," Nola says suddenly, seemingly noticing my condition for the first time. She reaches out and lays both hands on my belly. Her fingers are cold even through my shirt. Her fingernails are chewed ragged, the skin around her cuticles raw and red. I take an involuntary step backward from her touch and her hands remain outstretched, hanging in midair as if giving the baby a blessing.

"Yes, I'm due in August." I cross my arms over my stomach.

"Your first?" Nola asks and I nod. "You planning on giving it a sister?" she asks.

"Let me have this baby and then I'll let you know." I give a forced laugh. If Nola only knew the journey that Shaun and I had to take to get here, she wouldn't make such an offhand comment. Except, this is Nola, so of course she would.

"Everyone should have a sister," Nola says and moves to go back inside the house, then stops suddenly. "Do you ever think of the night we found her?" Nola asks.

The switch in conversation is so abrupt that it takes me a second to catch up. "Of course I do. I still have nightmares about it."

"You were the one who wanted to look there. At the caves," Nola says accusingly.

"What's your point?" I ask. Sister of the victim or not, I am losing patience with Nola. "We looked everywhere else. It made sense."

"I guess I should be thankful for that," Nola said, sounding anything but grateful. "If you hadn't suggested it, we might still be looking for Eve. But your dad wasn't able to find who killed Eve so I don't have a lot of faith in your investigative abilities either."

"Yeah, well, who do *you* think did it then?" I ask before I can stop myself. It does no good to engage with Nola.

She shrugs. "Based on the beating that Eve took, I'm guessing it was someone pretty angry with her. Who do you think did it?"

"I can't make any judgments until I see the whole picture."

"Judgments." Nola laughs.

"I have to go where the evidence leads me," I say diplomatically.

"Me too," Nola says before going back inside the house and shutting the door in my face, the limp Christmas wreath swinging precariously from its nail.

Now what the hell did that mean? I wonder. Did Nola know more about what happened to Eve than she let on? Or was she trying to mete out some kind of homespun justice? She's done that before, just ask Nick Brady.

I move across the street to my dad's house. He's still sitting on the porch but alone now. Leanne must have left for the day. Eve's was the only case I recall my father bringing home with him. It was also the only case I remember my dad obsessing over. My dad would come home from the station and then go directly to his den and shut the door.

He spent decades poring over the few known details of Eve's murder over and over again. Like an archaeologist he'd carefully hold the gruesome artifacts in his hands in search of a new detail, a new angle. He'd come home from the station or materialize from his den, pinched-faced and pale. I can't help but wonder if his memory issues are his body's way of saying, *Enough. This is too hard. It's too much. I don't want to remember these sad, violent things anymore.*

It didn't help that he was trying to parent Colin and me on his own. My mom died of an aneurysm when I was nine and Colin was twelve. One day she was making breakfast for us and taking us to school and the next she dropped dead at the grocery store.

Eve's case hasn't killed my father like many people predicted, not yet anyway, but I do think it played a hand in his deterioration. He didn't know how to help me through the grief of losing my best friend and he didn't know how to help his artistic son find his path in the world.

After Eve died, I couldn't get out of bed. All I wanted to do was sleep, to forget. My dad was patient for a while, tried to give me some space. The turning point came when the school called and said that I had missed so much school I was in danger of not being promoted to the eleventh grade. My dad stormed into my room, threw open the shades and told me to get out of bed.

Enough, Maggie! he shouted. *Eve can't live the life she was meant to, but you can. You owe it to her, to your mother and to me to get it together.* I stared up at him in shock as he continued his tirade. *Get up, take a shower and get to school. You let me worry about what happened to Eve and live your life.* It wasn't easy, but I did get up and with many fits and starts I was able to get back on track.

My dad didn't realize that he was doing the best he could with us and that he wasn't to blame for not finding the person who killed Eve. He didn't believe people's reassurances though. He blamed himself for not bringing the closure that the Knox family deserved.

I think that's partly why I became a cop—to make my mom proud of me and to be closer to my dad. Be more like my dad. He worked his ass off his whole life to make Grotto a safer, better place. I couldn't fully appreciate that when I was young. Now I do.

I don't want to tell my dad that we are reopening Eve's case but at some point I'll have to. I know it will upset him. He'll get anxious and sad and frustrated. Then he will forget that I told him. Just like that. I wish it could be that easy. To forget, to shed painful memories like a dried-up snakeskin. I've had so much loss. Eve, my mother, the babies. All the babies that could have been.

Eve would have been so happy for me. For a moment I allow thoughts of what might have been: picking out baby clothes and paint colors for the baby's room, me calling Eve to run baby names by her. Maybe we would have even been pregnant together—sharing morning sickness and stretch mark stories.

My dad's face brightens when he sees me coming toward him. "Hi, Dad," I say.

"Maggie," he says as if he hadn't seen me just a few minutes earlier. "What are you doing in this neck of the woods?"

Normally, I come over and he moves over on the porch swing to make room for me. He loves talking shop, reminiscing about his glory days on the force. He peppers me with questions about whatever case I'm working on and I tell him with no fear that he'll relay the details to Colin or his home health aide. He can remember a collar he made forty years ago but forgets what I tell him after a few minutes. But I don't want to bring up Eve's case, not today.

"I heard that Charlotte Knox was in the hospital. I just wanted to make sure that she was doing okay," I tell him.

"Oh, that's too bad. What happened?" he asks. I was right. He had forgotten.

"Apparently she fell down the basement steps. Nola says that she broke her hip. She'll be in the hospital for a bit longer," I explain and then change the subject. "What's Colin up to? Is he around?"

"He's around here somewhere, I think," my dad says looking around. "You're pregnant?" he says looking at my stomach. "When is the baby due?"

My dad asks me this nearly every time I see him and the joy on his face is just as genuine as it was the first time Shaun and I told him the good news. "August tenth," I tell him. "We're having a little girl. We can't wait."

"A girl," he says with wonder. "That's great! I'll have to go out and buy a gift. I wish your mother was here for this."

"I do too," I say. My mother would have loved this. I miss her more than ever now. I have so many questions about giving birth, about being a good mom. Even though I've read as many books on the subjects as I can get my hands on, it's not the same. I still need her even though I'm older than she was when she died.

Cam Harper pulls into his driveway and I watch as his garage door rises and he maneuvers his car inside. Bile creeps into my throat but I swallow it back.

"You okay?" my dad asks.

"Just heartburn." I wave away his concern. "Dad, what do you know about Cam Harper? Did he run into any trouble when he was younger?"

"Trouble?" my dad repeats. "No, I don't think so. He's always been a nice guy. I remember you babysat for them all the time. I think you were over at the Harper house more than you were here."

"Great baseball player, too," Colin says coming out the front door carrying a glass of water and a handful of pills for my dad.

"Cam Harper?" I feign surprise. "I didn't know that." In fact, Cam told me all about his baseball glory days. It was one of his favorite topics.

"Oh, yeah, all-American in college. Could have gone pro but hurt his shoulder." Colin hands Dad the glass. "Ended up coaching his kids' Little League teams back in the day. Now he helps coach the softball team," Colin says as he presses one pill at a time into our dad's palm.

"Softball?" I ask as dread spreads through my body.

"Yeah, the freshman team at the high school in Willow Creek," Colin says.

How did I miss this? I'd been watching Cam Harper for years, making sure that he didn't get too close to any girls. I ran checks on him through the police computer. There were no complaints, no indication that he was abusing another girl. Could I have been the only one? I didn't think so. Men like Cam Harper never were satisfied with just one.

NOLA KNOX

Monday, June 15, 2020

Nola pressed her back to the closed front door. She honestly didn't think it would have taken them this long to start looking for Eve's killer again. Her mother pushed it for years, but the response was always the same: no new leads.

Nola tried to remember when her mother gave up fighting for Eve. Was it after Charlotte had written the letter to the editor a few years ago going after the sheriff's department and Grotto PD, specifically Chief Kennedy? That's when some people really turned on them—started publicly going after Nola, accusing her of hurting Eve. That had hurt her mother badly. *Ignore it*, Nola had told her. *People will always talk.*

Now Maggie was talking about looking for new DNA. As a doctor and a scientist, Nola knew all about the advancements in forensics, though she wondered if the Ransom County Sheriff's Department could say as much.

It was a long shot, getting any meaningful DNA. It all depended on how well preserved the evidence was. After twenty-five years there could be cross contamination and degradation.

She should probably go to the hospital and tell her mother that Eve's case was reopened but the thought of it made her head ache. Her mother would cry and ask questions that Nola didn't know the answers to. She would make a scene.

Nola shoved aside a pile of newspapers from the sofa and they fluttered to the floor. She'd tie the papers together with twine later, add them to the others. The look on Maggie's face when she got a peek into her mother's living room was priceless. It's probably what the entire town was expecting though. Nutty Charlotte Knox and her daughter buried alive in a house filled with junk.

Nola hadn't wanted to come home to Grotto fifteen years ago. After graduating vet school with zero debt because of scholarships Nola moved to Louisiana but ran into a little bit of trouble at the lab she worked at in Baton Rouge. There were some research results and necropsy reports that were called into question and rumors of an inappropriate relationship with a supervisor. Nola had to admit they had her on the falsified data. The affair with her married boss, not so much. But the suggestion of a lawsuit got her out of there with a sterling letter of recommendation and a decent severance.

Now she was back home and Nola had to admit she was comfortable here among the clutter. Maybe *clutter* was too kind a word. To be fair, Nola thought, most of the garbage belonged to her mother but over the years Nola added her own collections.

Dusty rolls of carpets sat against the walls, plastic garbage bags stuffed with random items filled corners, their black mouths gaping open as if vomiting mildewed clothing, board games and VCR tapes. The living room was covered with newspapers and magazines stacked neck high forming a rat's maze. It had gotten a bit out of hand, but her mother would freak out if Nola tried to purge the house. Nola liked having her things nearby; how could she begrudge her mother the same? Besides, it was good cover.

Nola reached for the television remote, wanting to see if the local news station had a story about Eve and the new investigation. She flipped through the channels and found nothing.

She stood and followed the labyrinth of rubbish through the living room, passing a bucket filled with acorns, a dressmaking mannequin and tangles of extension cords up the steps to the second floor. Nola paused at her sister's bedroom door and turned the knob.

The room was dim, the plastic shade drawn, light seeping through only at the corners and edges. Eve's bed, a narrow twin, was made up with a pieced quilt stitched together with scraps of fabric in shades of pink, orange, green, yellow and blue. One of Eve's thrift shop finds. Nola remembered their mother being irritated when Eve brought it home. *Why did you bring that dirty thing home, Eve? God knows who's slept under that thing.* Funny, considering the state of the house now.

If Eve could see their house now she would be mortified. She was the one who always kept it clean. After she died their mother gave up on day-to-day activities like cooking and cleaning and taking the garbage out. Nola had other things on her mind. She didn't have time for housework.

Over the years, Eve's bedroom stayed the same. No newspapers or garbage bags filled with junk encroached the sacred space. Nola and her mother never spoke about it. Eve's same grunge-band posters still hung on the walls along with a mosaic of photos of Eve with her friends pinned to a large bulletin board. Since her mother had difficulty getting up and down the steps, a thick layer of dust covered every surface. Nola didn't like coming in here, but she had run out of space in her own room and had resorted to storing some of her collection in Eve's room.

After Eve died, the sheriff's department came through and searched for any clues or evidence as to who might have killed her. They were respectful. Dressed in booties and white gloves, they went through every drawer and pocket and looked at each scrap of paper. When finished, they tried to put everything back where it came from.

Nola plucked a snapshot of Eve and Nick from where it was tucked into the corner of Eve's mirror. Eve was sitting on Nick's lap, his arms around her waist. They were both smiling into the camera. Smiling at Nola. Nola remembered how Eve had handed her the black-and-yellow disposable camera and Nola grudgingly took the picture. Through the lens, they looked so happy, but Nola knew better. She knew what he did to her. At the time Nola wasn't sure whom she hated more. Nick for hurting Eve, or Eve for putting up with it.

Less than a month after the picture was taken Eve was dead. Not long after that Nola pushed Nick Brady into a glass trophy case at the high school. They both ended up with scars. Nick needed stitches on his arm and Nola had to have a shard of glass extracted from her lung. It had been worth it, worth the scars, worth expulsion and counseling, Nola thought, just to see his blood pool onto the tiled floor. Of course, they charged Nola with the assault. No one would have believed her if she had told them what really happened.

Nola had always thought they would end up arresting Nick for Eve's murder. It never happened. Maybe it was time that changed. Nola finally told her mother about the bruises that she suspected Nick gave Eve. At first Charlotte protested, couldn't believe that someone like Nick would be abusive but over time she came around.

Her mother once tried to throw the picture of Eve and Nick away, but Nola stopped her. *It needs to stay,* Nola insisted. Charlotte argued with her, said she couldn't stand looking at the picture of the person who killed Eve but Nola was insistent. *It stays,* she said with such ferocity that Charlotte jumped. The photo stayed. It fueled Nola's anger.

Nola wandered to Eve's bookshelf and ran her fingers along the spines and retrieved one of the books. The pages were stained and dog-eared. Nola replaced the book and chose another, *The Thorn Birds.* Most of Eve's books were swollen and warped from a number of reading sessions in the bathtub. Eve would light scented candles, fill the tub with hot water and bubble bath, lock the door and disappear. This book had been cared for. No dog-eared pages, no food stains. Nola had been waiting for just the right time to pull this book out and use what was inside. It looked like the time was now.

Nola peeked inside Eve's closet. The hatbox was right where she'd left it. She didn't think that the police would need to search the house after all these years. If they did, they'd get an eyeful, Nola thought, that was for sure.

Kurt Cobain and Pearl Jam and REM looked down on Nola from the walls and she suddenly felt closed in, claustrophobic in the cleanest room in the house. Nola hurried from the bedroom and into the hall, book in hand, and opened the door to her own room.

Nola's room hadn't changed much over the years either. The dresser with the sticky drawers, the lamp and rickety bookshelf filled with vet textbooks and journals occupied the exact same spots. More books overflowed to the floor and were stacked flush against the walls.

Where Eve had her band posters, Nola had her drawings. Sketched directly onto the plaster walls were brightly colored diagrams of a cat, a dog, a finch, a horse and dozens more that she'd added as recently as last winter. All anatomically correct with realistic depictions of hearts, lungs, livers. Nola wondered what Maggie would think when she saw the cross section of Winnie, the Harpers' corgi mix.

But it wasn't the sketches that Nola was worried about. Pressing her back to the wall, she sidestepped along the perimeter to the closet door. She turned and pulled on the knob, opening the door just enough so that she could squeeze inside.

Nola reached into a corner of the shelf, shifting books aside until she found what she was looking for. An old tackle box that Charlotte said once belonged to her father. The tackle box, painted a deep hunter green, was chipped and corroded in spots with a clasp that didn't work any longer. Nola carefully removed it from the shelf, eased it through the small opening in the door and set it on her bed.

Nola opened the tackle box and inside were over a dozen small clear museum-quality display cases stacked neatly on top of each other. Nola chose one that she acquired years ago and opened it. Sitting inside were three tiny bones, each not much bigger than a grain of rice. The ossicles: malleus, incus and stapes. Hammer, anvil, stirrup. *The better to hear you with, my dear,* Nola thought.

Nola doubted that Maggie Kennedy, or anyone else for that matter, would know what they were looking at if they came across her tackle box, but still, questions would arise. Nola closed the box, replaced it with the others and shut the tackle box lid. The Knox home appeared to be in total chaos, but she knew where everything was. Everything.

Besides, it wasn't the tackle box Nola worried about. She inched her way to the other side of the room where buried beneath a pile of vet journals and unfolded laundry was an old oak cedar chest. Nola cleared the surface, tossing the journals and socks and underwear onto the bed. She lifted the lid with a rusty squeak and the bite of peroxide filled her nose.

What was inside the cedar chest would be much more difficult to hide.

MAGGIE
KENNEDY-O'KEEFE

Monday, June 15, 2020

I'm at my desk with the approved press release in front of me.
I know I need to get it out to media, but I also know once the
information is released to the public we'll be overwhelmed
with phone calls from armchair detectives and well-meaning
townspeople trying to help. Eve's case will distract from our
other work. The ongoing arson case, for instance. With calls
coming in about Eve, tips about the arsons could get lost in
the shuffle.

I'm still puzzled by Nola's response to finding out we're
looking into Eve's death again. I thought she would show
some kind of emotion besides scorn. I know that Nola drove
Eve crazy but Eve loved her little sister, was incredibly protective of her. Too bad Nola didn't seem to reciprocate, even
after Eve's death.

I decide to go to the archive room and review Eve's files.
I open the binder that holds Eve's background information.
Name, address, birthday, family contacts. It also holds the
transcript of the call to 911, crime scene photos, initial interviews and the coroner's report. I take the elevator to the
basement. It may be windowless and stuffy but there's room
to spread out and chances are I won't be interrupted.

I open the binder, flip past the photograph of Eve's sophomore year school portrait and find a brief synopsis of the case. Too brief. It's typed on Ransom County Sheriff's Office letterhead and is just a few sentences long.

After reviewing the facts in the murder of Eve Marie Knox, it is my opinion that the perpetrator is a white male, between the ages of twenty-one and fifty. The perpetrator may or may not be known to the victim. Because of the positioning of the victim's clothing, an attempted sexual assault may be a motive. While several men have been named persons of interest, there isn't sufficient evidence for an arrest.

In the mess of paperwork, I find that law enforcement focused on three specific males. Nick Brady, of course, but also Daryl Olhauser, the creepy adult son of our next-door neighbor, and a drifter known as Pedals. No one knew Pedals's real name or where he lived, but he traveled around on an old Schwinn, even in the snow, and passed through town every few weeks or so. There were no clear ties between Eve's death and these men.

I turn to the 911 transcript. As I read, flashes of that night come back to me.

We've looked everywhere but the caves, I said. *Let's go check them out.* Nola gave me an odd look but agreed. It had started to snow and I remember the cold and wet seeping through my tennis shoes. Nola had handed me a flashlight when we got to the last streetlight at the end of the dead-end street that lead to the caves.

I remember the whistle of the wind and the way we had to step over a litter of fallen leaves and dead branches until we were swallowed up by the pine trees. I tripped on a snaggle of exposed roots and grabbed at a low-hanging branch to steady myself.

About a half an inch of snow had fallen since Nola and I began our search and the stepping stones across the creek were dusted with a slippery layer.

Once over the creek the caves weren't far off. Nola led us directly to Rattlesnake, a cave whose main tunnel stretched out like a long sinuous snake. I knew that bats hibernated during the winter but I still covered my head as we entered the mouth of the cave. Our breaths seeped from our mouths in ghostly puffs, illuminated by a flashlight that only let us see a few feet in front of us. Though the air in the cave was warmer than outside, my teeth chattered. I kept one hand on the damp, rough wall of the cave to help guide my way though I knew that if we kept following the curves and didn't veer off into one of the side caves we would eventually come to the opening that would lead us out the other side.

We walked for about fifteen minutes, the only sounds the soles of our shoes scraping across the rocky ground and the soft plop, plop, plop of water and our occasional calls of Eve's name. Was it possible for there to be running water in a cave in the dead of winter? I had visions of bat shit dripping from above. But as scared as I was to stay put I was even more frightened of moving forward.

I focused the beam above us, half expecting to see a colony of bats curled up in furry balls on the craggy ceiling. There was nothing there. I lowered the flashlight spotlighting first the icicle-shaped stalactites and then the pocked gray walls. Still I heard the bubble of water running—an underground stream somewhere off in the distance.

The trail slanted upward and the temperature gradually rose. The all-encompassing black pitch we were traveling through shifted to an inky charcoal and I knew we were finally close to the cave's exit.

She's not here, I breathed with relief. *Let's go*, I said, picking up my pace, my thigh muscles burning as we climbed the steep path.

Wait, what's that? Nola asked, grabbing the flashlight from me. The beam bounced off a kaleidoscope of colors fanned

75

out across the stone floor. It was Eve. Her bright red hair incongruous against the drab limestone, her face stained dark with blood, her wide, staring eyes.

I screamed and skirted past the body out the mouth of the cave into the gently swirling snow, not knowing if Nola was behind me or not. I stumbled and fell and got up again only to slip again and again. I paused and vomited into the nearly frozen creek.

By that time Nola had caught up with me and together we hurried to the closest house, Mrs. Benson's.

The 911 transcript is pretty straightforward but transcripts can be deceiving. They chronicle what the caller says but not the raw emotion. I flip through the binder and sure enough in the back is a three-hole plastic page protector containing an audio tape labeled *Eve Knox 911 Call*.

I have to do some hunting in order to find a cassette recorder. I find one, coated with dust in a box in the IT office. I dig out a pair of earbuds from my purse and realize, of course, they aren't compatible. I press Play, adjust the volume by spinning the wheel on the side of the player and listen. The tape is slightly warped with age. Sluggish, so that each word is lazily drawn out. Even so, I can hear the alarm in the caller's voice.

Vivian Benson, the woman who initiated the call, sounds breathless and panicked, stumbling over her words as she tries to provide the dispatcher with the requested information. I don't remember much about pounding on Mrs. Benson's door that night after Nola and I found Eve but I do remember shaking with cold and terror.

When Nola comes on the phone line, I'm immediately struck by her composure. She sounds cold. Mechanical. A stark contrast to the woman who handed her the phone and to my jagged crying in the background.

We had just found Eve dead. Could Nola's reaction have

been shock, like the dispatcher suggested? I scan the notes that the first officer on the scene jotted down as he talked to Nola for the first time. *Thirteen-year-old juvenile doesn't seem v. upset. Matter-of-factly led us to the body of her sister. No emotion. Follow up.*

My dad must have thought so too because on one of the hundreds of sticky notes that freckle the pages of files, he wrote in his familiar, messy scrawl: *Nola Knox—psychological eval.* My heart squeezes. My dad doesn't write anything anymore. Now he can't harness his thoughts long enough to put them into written form.

Next come the crime scene photos. They are hard to look at, even for a law enforcement officer. The baby kicks at my stomach and I wonder if looking at such disturbing pictures is unhealthy, that I'll be inflicting some psychological damage on my child. "I need to do this," I murmur to my belly. "Someday maybe you'll understand."

I take a deep breath and look at the first photo. It's a shot of Eve's body lying just inside the mouth of the cave and looks like it was taken from at least two hundred feet away. This was smart thinking by the officer. He knew how a flurry of activity could soon destroy any possible evidence at the scene. The photo shows the area in front of the cave, unmarred except for a jumble of footprints in the snow. Eve's body was how I remembered it—bloodied and broken. I stand, nauseated.

I force myself to sit back down. *I can do this,* I tell myself. I'm good at compartmentalizing. I always have been. This is what made me a good cop and makes me an even better detective. There are several other photos of the crime scene and I examine them carefully, looking for anything that might jump out at me.

I feel like I'm missing something. Something obvious. I shake my head in frustration. Nothing.

I flip through the binder in search of a list of evidence

found at the crime scene but can't find one. This is a problem. I can't send the evidence to the lab to be retested until I know exactly which items to send. I'm sure it's somewhere within the files, but where? I get up and grab a second binder and flip through it. This one holds the medical examiner's report and Eve's autopsy photos.

I take a deep breath and try to fully enter my cop state of mind. Unemotional, analytical, unfazed. I open the binder to the first page.

DECEDENT: *Eve Marie Knox*
Autopsy Authorized by: Dr. Felicia Waller
Saturday, December 23, 1995
Identified by: Henry Kennedy, Grotto Police Department

I never knew that my dad was the one to identify Eve's body. I never really thought about it, but it makes sense. I couldn't see Eve's mother being capable of doing it, Nola was much too young and as far as I knew there was no other family.

Rigor: present
Livor: red
Distribution: posterior
Age: 15
Race: White
Sex: Female
Length: 60 inches
Weight: 57 kilograms
Eyes: Green
Hair: Red

As I read through the reports it becomes clear that Eve died a long, painful death. According to the pathologist, Eve had a broken wrist, a skull fracture resulting in significant swelling of the brain and dozens of contusions. There was also indication of ligature strangulation.

The doctor determined that the time of Eve's death was between 4:00 and 9:00 p.m., give or take. The plunging temperatures that day made it difficult to pinpoint the exact time of death.

The last time Eve was seen was by Nola at around three thirty at their home just before Nola left to go visit her mother at work. Eve could have been lying there on the edge of death for hours.

Nola stayed with her mother at the motel, watching TV in the rooms her mother cleaned until six and arrived at the public library at six fifteen. The librarian backed up Nola's account, even providing documentation that Nola checked out several books that evening and stayed there until eight. Nola then walked home where her mother was waiting for her. Eve was nowhere to be found.

I flip through the files. They found tree sap on Eve's hands but not much else. Nola's clothing was taken and examined. Hair consistent with Eve's was found, but that isn't surprising; they were sisters, lived in the same home. There was no evidence of Eve's blood found on Nola's clothes.

I go back to the report and continue reading. It also chronicled the state of Eve's clothing. She was wearing a coat, jeans and a turtleneck sweater. Testing back in 1996 showed the blood found on Eve's clothing belonged to Eve. No other physical evidence—semen or hair—was found.

I move to the autopsy photographs but can't stand looking at them except for a cursory glance. Instead I return to the crime scene photos.

The next several pictures were taken from the same distance away but using a zoom lens focused on Eve's body. She's lying on her back, arms at her side as if in the midst of making a snow angel, except for the crimson pillow of congealed blood beneath her head.

When I've looked at them all I realize that my face is wet with tears. I've had enough for today.

I reach for my phone and besides missing a half a dozen calls from Shaun, I'm surprised to see that it's just about five o'clock.

I call Shaun back and say I'm sorry before he even says hello. "I didn't see your texts," I say.

"I was worried. You missed your doctor appointment. We were supposed to meet there at four," he says, his voice tight with irritation.

"Dammit," I say. "I completely forgot. I came back to work to follow up on a few things and time got away from me. I'm sorry."

Shaun doesn't respond. I really screwed up.

"I'll call the doctor first thing in the morning. I'm sure everything is fine. I feel fine."

"I just can't believe you'd take this chance, Maggie," Shaun says. "We've gotten this far, we can't have anything happen now."

"Nothing's going to happen," I snap. "It's just one appointment. I said I'll call tomorrow."

"Okay, fine," Shaun says. I know it's not fine.

"I'm on my way home," I tell him, softening my tone.

"Don't hurry because of me," Shaun says flatly. "I'm working late tonight." Then silence. He hung up on me.

I sigh and rub my forehead. Obviously from the sheer number of documents collected, my dad and the sheriff's department were very thorough in their investigation but their organization skills left something to be desired. That wasn't like my dad. Were his memory issues already surfacing? I couldn't put my finger on exactly when my dad began to fail but I'm almost positive it wasn't back then.

Our new chief, on the other hand, had no history of neurological decline. What was his excuse? I would have to tread lightly. Digby not only had decades more experience than I did in law enforcement, he was my boss. It would do no good to openly criticize their investigation.

I pull the lid off a cardboard box labeled *Eve Knox—Interviews* and am met with a stack of papers that nearly spill over the edge. "Jesus," I murmur.

What a mess.

I start with the page at the top and begin to arrange the interviews in alphabetical order. Once I have them organized and inserted into a new binder I begin to read.

I see names of classmates that I haven't thought about in years. Most don't have anything useful to add. No, they didn't see Eve after she left school on December twenty-second. No, they didn't have any idea as to who might want to hurt her. She was nice, she had no enemies, she loved her boyfriend and he loved her, her sister was weird.

I knew what that was like—loving someone but being afraid of them. I wish Eve and I could have talked about it. Who we loved and what we feared. Maybe we could have helped each other through it, together. Maybe things could have turned out differently.

The statement from Miss Cress, the Grotto High art teacher, is kind of cryptic. She mentioned that Eve had come to her the day she died a bit upset but didn't reveal much about why. Eve was supposed to meet with Miss Cress after school but never showed up. I wonder what they were going to talk about.

I come across the transcript of the interview I did with Dex Stroope back in 1995 and immediately set it aside. I'm not ready to read it yet. That was such an awful night. I remember crying nearly all the way through and running to the bathroom several times to vomit. I couldn't believe my friend was gone. Forever. My dad finally stepped in to end the interview. *Enough*, he said.

I slam the binder shut. Enough. This was enough for now. Tomorrow, I'll do a few quick follow-up interviews and then pack up the evidence and get it sent off to the lab. It will take some time to get the results; there is always a big backlog at the state lab when it comes to testing evidence.

I rise from my seat. I need to go home to the orchard, to the apple trees and my cats and my husband. I want to lie on the couch with my hands resting on my abdomen feeling the baby move beneath my fingers. I want to be lulled to sleep by my little girl floating within the ocean of my womb.

My hand is on the light switch when I pause and turn back to the shelf. I reach for the thick binder of interviews and tuck it beneath my arm and shut and lock the door with a gentle click.

911 TRANSCRIPT

Item #1—911 Call

Grotto Police Department
Transcript of 911 Call for Service
12/22/95—9:48 p.m.

DISPATCHER: 911, What is your emergency?

VB: Someone's been killed. I've got two girls here who say they found a dead girl. Please hurry!

DISPATCHER: What's your address?

VB: 29 Ransom Lane. Please hurry. She said her sister was killed. What if he's still out there?

DISPATCHER: Killed? As in murdered?

VB: Yes!

DISPATCHER: Are your doors locked?

VB: I don't know. The back door, I need to lock the back door!

DISPATCHER: Go lock it and come right back.

VB: Okay, they're locked.

DISPATCHER: Good. Now tell me what happened.

VB: Two girls came knocking on my door and one said her sister is dead. Oh my God.

DISPATCHER: I'm sending someone to your home right now. What's your name?

VB: Shhhh, honey, I can't hear what they're saying. It's going to be okay. What? What did you ask me?

DISPATCHER: What's your name?

VB: Vivian Benson.

DISPATCHER: Okay, Vivian, did the girls say where the sister is right now?

VB: They say she's down at Ransom Caves. They came over here when they found her. Where are the police? What's taking so long?

DISPATCHER: Help is coming. I promise. How old are the girls?

VB: How old are you?

Muffled speech

VB: Thirteen and fifteen.

DISPATCHER: Okay. Can one of them speak to me?

Muffled speech.

VB: Yes, she can talk to you. Here she is.

NK: Hello?

DISPATCHER: Are you in a safe place? Are you okay?

NK: Yeah, I'm okay.

DISPATCHER: Good, good. Can you tell me your name?

NK: Nola Knox. We found my sister.

DISPATCHER: Where did you find her? We'll send help.

NK: I don't think you can help her.

DISPATCHER: Do you know what happened? What are her injuries?

NK: She's dead. Someone killed her.

DISPATCHER: Are you sure? Could she just be hurt very badly?

NK: No, she wasn't breathing. I checked her pulse. Be quiet, Maggie! I can't hear!

DISPATCHER: You checked her pulse?

NK: Yes. No pulse. Her skin was blue.

DISPATCHER: Okay. You're doing a great job. How do you know someone killed her?

NK: Her head. I could tell by her head.

DISPATCHER: Someone hurt her in the head?

NK: Yes. It was bashed in. She was pale. There were little dots on her skin. Around her eyes.

DISPATCHER: Did you see her being attacked? Do you know who hurt her?

NK: No. I don't know.

DISPATCHER: Okay, Nola. I want you stay where you are. A police officer is on his way over.

NK: Okay.

DISPATCHER: Can you put Vivian on the phone for me, Nola?

Muffled speech

VB: Yes? What now? What should we do? She's hysterical. She can't stop crying.

DISPATCHER: What's her name?

Muffled speech

VB: It's Maggie Kennedy. She said her dad is Chief Kennedy. It's going to be okay, Maggie, the doors are locked. No one can get in. Nola, go get Maggie a glass of water from the kitchen.

DISPATCHER: Just do your best to keep everyone calm. An officer will be there shortly. Can you get blankets for the girls? Keep them warm? They could be in shock.

VB: Yes, but the other one is fine. She's calm. Very calm. It's not right.

DISPATCHER: Okay. Stay on the line until the police arrive.

VB: I hear the siren. They're here.

EVE KNOX

Eve sat on the edge of the bathtub staring at the blue tiles, trying to think of a way to keep Nola from telling their mother about the bruises.

They called this room the Larimar Bathroom even though it was the only bathroom in the house. Many years ago, Nola christened it Larimar after seeing a picture of the pale blue mineral in a book she borrowed from the library. So now it became the Larimar, like it was some fancy hotel powder room with gilded mirrors instead of a pukey-yellow-and-blue bathroom with a leaky faucet, moldy tub and shower and cracked tiled floor. Maybe it would be better if it all came out. How Nick treated her, the name-calling, the pushing and roughness. He always claimed he was just joking, that she was overreacting. Was she? And anyway, who would even believe her? She was a nobody.

Now Nola rapped on the locked bathroom door. "Hurry up, I need to get in there!" she yelled.

"Just a minute," Eve called back. She was biding time, wanting to leave for school at the very last minute so she didn't have to talk to her mom. She rose and leaned heavily against the sink and looked in the mirror. Her mother's crimson handprint was long gone and the small cut, now covered with concealer, was barely noticeable.

Her mother had never hit her before. Never. She yelled and screamed and threw things once in a while but never once had she gotten physical with her daughters.

For a fleeting moment, Eve wondered what might happen if one of her teachers noticed the mark on her face. They would have to call family services and report an incident of possible abuse, right? Eve would be hauled into the counselor's office and asked a million questions. *What happened to your face? Does your mother hit you often? Are you afraid to go home?*

Then, she imagined, a social worker, a gray-haired woman with tired eyes but a reassuring smile, would show up at their house and inform their mother that the children were being removed from the home pending an investigation.

Eve quickly slammed the door on this scenario. She didn't want to leave home. Not now anyway. She just wanted her mother to leave her alone and for Nola to be normal. She'd be moving out of the house in a few years anyway, hopefully going off to college and it would be nice to know they'd be okay without her.

"Eve! We're going to miss the bus!" Nola pounded each word out on the door.

Eve took a breath. The key was not to engage. Not to get caught up in her mother's roller coaster of emotions and in Nola being Nola. She opened the door, her face a blank canvas. "I'm walking today, Nola."

"Walking?" Nola repeated. "We can't walk, it's cold outside. Come on, if we hurry, we'll make the bus."

"I want to walk today. It's not that cold out." Eve breezed into her bedroom, went to her closet and pulled out a long multicolored scarf that was as wonderful as it was hideous. Knitted together in an array of pink, red, purple, blue and green blocks with fat, furry yellow puff balls dangling from the ends, Eve knew she had to have it when Maggie spotted it last winter at a secondhand shop in Maquoketa.

When she arrived home with it wrapped around her neck, Nola had scoffed. *That is one butt-ugly scarf.*

Someone made this with their own two hands, Eve marveled. *She picked out the colors and the yarn...*

Someone color-blind, Nola interrupted.

Maybe she sat in a rocking chair in front of the fire or on the front porch and pieced it all together, Eve had mused. *I love it.*

And she had worn it every cold day since. Eve looped it around her neck, retrieved her backpack and started down the steps.

"Whatever," Nola called after her. "Go ahead and freeze to death. I don't care."

"Eve," came her mother's voice from the kitchen. "Eve, are you leaving? Aren't you even going to say goodbye?" she asked as Eve opened the front door and stepped outside into the cold, brisk morning. It was still dark outside and no streetlights lined their street but both the Harper and Kennedy houses had their front porch lights on.

She wanted to tell Maggie about breaking up with Nick, wanted to just talk. Eve had been so consumed with Nick the past few months that she was just realizing how quiet and withdrawn Maggie had been.

Now she wondered if Maggie had been sick or if something was going on at home. Colin was always in some kind of trouble and Eve had walked in on a number of shouting matches between Colin and Chief Kennedy. Well, Chief Kennedy yelled and Colin just kind of simmered.

Once Eve's second home, the Kennedy house had taken on an aura of anxiety and unease. When Eve did go over there, Maggie rushed them up to her bedroom and shut the door soundly against the tension below.

There was a time when Eve would simply announce her

presence with a loud hello and then let herself into the Kennedy home, but not anymore. She never knew what argument she might walk in on and instead knocked and waited for someone to answer. Colin opened the door. "She's upstairs," he said. "But I'd turn around and go home—she's in a mood." Colin was dressed in his usual uniform of black jeans and paint-splattered black tee. He held on to the door frame with fingers that were perpetually smudged with black ink and brightly colored paint from the shop and art classes he took at school.

"I'll take my chances," Eve said squeezing past him.

"I warned you," he called after her as she ran up the stairs. When she reached the top she glanced back down to find that Colin was gone. Colin was like that. One minute he was there, the next minute he disappeared. He always stayed off to the side, moved along the periphery watching, listening. He never had much to say, but Eve figured that when he did talk it was filled with ideas that were too big for a small town like Grotto.

Maggie's bedroom door was closed and like the front entrance, there was a time when she would burst right in, but it had been such a long while since they spent any time together, she felt shy, hesitant. She rapped lightly on the door and was immediately answered with a, "Go away, Colin!"

"It's me," Eve called through the door. There was a moment of silence then the sound of footsteps across the wood floor. The door opened and Maggie stood before her, eyes red-rimmed and swollen.

"Sorry," Maggie said. "My brother is such a jerk. Come on in."

Eve stepped over the threshold and into the bedroom that she had always thought of as a sanctuary from the rest of the world. It was painted in a soft sage green and all the furniture matched. Substantial real wood furniture—and not covered in the half-ass coats of paint Eve's mother gave everything. There was a tall dresser and two side tables on either side of a double bed. There was a bookshelf that went to the ceiling and a desk where Maggie could do her homework in the privacy of her own room.

Maggie, still in her pajamas, flopped down on her bed and patted the floral-sprigged comforter for Eve to join her. Eve climbed up and lay on her back staring up at the textured popcorn ceiling. "You're going to be late for school. Are you okay?" Eve asked, peeking over at her friend's tearstained face.

"Yeah," Maggie said. "My brother is an idiot."

"I can relate. Nola is insane."

Maggie flipped over onto her back. "She is insane. Certifiable."

"I broke up with Nick," Eve blurted out. "I can't believe it, but I did."

Maggie sat up suddenly and gave Eve a playful punch in the arm. "Why didn't you start with this information? This is huge! Was he okay about it? I mean, did he freak out?"

Eve shook her head. "I don't think he really believes I'm serious. When I left he acted like we were going to start right back up the same way."

"You always say you're going to break up with Nick. Don't you dare get back together with him," Maggie said firmly. "You deserve so much better, Eve." When Eve rolled her eyes, Maggie grabbed her hand. "No, I mean it. Nick is a jerk and I know he didn't treat you well." Eve felt her face flush.

She never told Maggie about the grabs, the pushes, the occasional slaps, but somehow her best friend seemed to know.

"Is there someone else?" Maggie asked.

Eve thought about mentioning Shaun O'Keefe but something stopped her. He was just a friend from class. "Nope, nope and nope." Eve shook her head from side to side. Seeing the skepticism on Maggie's face she protested. "I mean it, there isn't anyone. Boys are stupid."

"Most boys," Maggie agreed. "But not all. You just haven't met the right one yet."

"Oh, and you have?" Eve asked and a dark look passed over Maggie's eyes as she swung her feet over the side of the bed. "Wait? What? Oh, come on!" Eve scrambled to her knees. "Who is it?"

"There's no boy," Maggie said but Eve wondered if she was being completely truthful. Ten years of friendship made Eve an expert on Maggie's body language. It was subtle, but when Maggie lied she did this thing with her hands. She'd pinch the soft skin between her thumb and index finger. Eve had seen it a hundred times. The bigger the lie the harder the pinch. There were more obvious signs that Maggie wasn't herself. She had lost weight and the circles under her eyes stood out in dark contrast against her pale skin.

"Tell me," Eve begged. "I know something's wrong."

"I think I might have gotten in over my head with someone," Maggie said, tears filling her eyes. "Someone too old for me."

Eve reached for her friend's hand. "Who? What happened?"

"I can't talk about it." Maggie swiped tears from her face. "Not right now." Maggie glanced at her alarm clock. "Oh my God, I still have to shower. You want to ride to school with Colin and me?"

"No, I'm going to walk today," Eve said. "Are you sure you're going to be okay?"

"I'm fine. Really. It's nothing."

"Okay," Eve said doubtfully. "But call me later, we'll talk more." Eve scanned Maggie's bookshelf. "Hey, can I borrow a book? I have a feeling I'm going to be spending a lot of time at home over break."

"Sure, take whatever you want," Maggie said as she got

to her feet and began flicking through the clothes hanging in her closet.

Eve ran her fingers across a row of spines until they landed on a thick book. She pulled it from Maggie's shelf. *The Thorn Birds.* She read the back cover and decided that she could use a good long book to read over winter break. One that she could lock herself away with and not have to deal with her mom or Nola. One that would keep her mind off Nick.

"You know you'll probably just get back together with him," Maggie said offhandedly as she pulled a shirt from a hanger.

"No, I won't," Eve said. "Not this time."

"I've heard that before," Maggie mumbled beneath her breath. "You always go back to him."

"Not this time. I really mean it," Eve said with conviction.

Maggie gave a derisive snort.

Eve stared at her friend. Why was she being like this? "Why don't you worry about the guy who's too old for you and you let me worry about Nick," Eve snapped.

Maggie grabbed a towel off the floor. "Why don't you just shut up?" Maggie shot back. "I wish I'd never said anything to you about it."

"Thanks for your support, Maggie," Eve said, shaking her head. "You're a great friend."

"And you are?" Maggie's voice rose in anger. "You spend all your time with Nick and now all of a sudden you break up and you're the friend of the year? I don't think so. You're only there for me when it's convenient to you."

"That is not true," Eve said, her voice quivering.

"Just go," Maggie said in disgust. "I have to get ready for school."

Trying to hold back her tears, Eve rushed down the steps, meeting Chief Kennedy at the bottom.

"Hello, stranger," the chief said with a smile. "We haven't seen you around here lately."

"Yeah, I've been kind of busy," Eve said, not making eye contact. She couldn't wait to get out of there.

"I'm glad you stopped by," he said wistfully. "Maggie hasn't been herself lately. Maybe you can cheer her up."

Eve couldn't answer, afraid that she would burst into tears. She kept her head down and hurried out the front door.

Eve slipped the book into her backpack and scurried past the Olhauser house, sure that the creepy neighbor was staring at her from behind the curtains, and trotted down the hill. What in the world was going on with Maggie? She wiped at her nose as she reached the bottom of the hill. A gaggle of kids, ranging from six to sixteen were already gathered at the bus stop on the corner. Two little girls in matching pink parkas stood beneath the streetlight, experimentally blowing frosty breaths into the air and giggling, while three preteen boys tossed a football back and forth. A cluster of older kids stood in a circle, laughing raucously. Eve's stomach plummeted.

"What are you going to do?" asked Robby Scheckel, a gangly sophomore with cheeks laced with acne, his voice rising above the crowd. "Dissect me? I'm so scared." Again the group laughed.

"Get the fuck away from me," came Nola's voice. It was steely and composed.

"Leave her alone," Eve called out as she ran toward the band of teens.

"Hey, Eve," Robby called out. "How does it feel to live with a freak? Aren't you afraid to go to sleep at night?"

"Real mature, a bunch of high schoolers picking on an eighth-grader," Eve scoffed. "Your mothers must be so proud."

"Just looking out for small children and squirrels," said a boy named Jason, sending the crowd into another round of laughter.

"Just knock it off," Eve said in resignation.

"Or what?" Jason baited her. "What are you going to do?"

"I'm not going to do anything, but maybe Nick will," Eve snapped. She hadn't meant to invoke Nick's name but it was easier than continuing this stupid back-and-forth.

"We're just messing around." Jason tried to smooth things over. Eve knew that if she asked Nick to shut the boys up, he would, except they were supposed to be broken up. "Come on, lighten up." Jason scooped Nola up in a big hug.

"Get off." Nola lashed out, sending an elbow into his side. "You're disgusting!"

"Jesus," Jason said, releasing her and then rubbing his ribs. "I was just joking. Relax."

Nola wasn't going to relax. "Keep your hands off me," she spat, shoving Jason away so that he fell backward into the crowd of teens. Eve saw Nola reach into her pocket and a surge of alarm coursed through her. She knew what Nola kept in her pocket.

"Come on, Nola," Eve said sharply, reaching for her sister's arm. "Let's go."

"I don't need your help." Nola shook her off. "And I don't need your asshole boyfriend's help either."

"Seriously?" Eve said in disbelief. "You know I'm your only friend, right? I'm so sick of you treating me like crap."

"I treat you like crap?" Nola raised her eyebrows. "I think you should be more worried about the way your boyfriend treats you." Nola grabbed at Eve's coat and shirt, lifting them to reveal her bruised ribs.

The boys laughed again, this time uneasily.

"Stop it," Eve cried, slapping Nola's hands away. "Get away from me." She looked to the boys. "Forget what I said. Do whatever you want to her. I don't care. But do it at your own risk."

First Maggie and now Nola. Everyone was turning against

THIS IS HOW I LIED

her. Eve turned and hurriedly moved down the street but after a short distance she felt a tug on her scarf.

"I told you to get away." She whirled around expecting to find Nola. Instead it was Shaun O'Keefe.

"Whoa, sorry!" he said, raising his hand, stick-up style.

"Sorry," Eve said, instantly contrite. Shaun was a good guy, nothing like those other morons. He was two years older than Eve and they shared a study hall. Shaun would help Eve with her biology homework and Eve would proofread Shaun's term papers.

"You okay?" he asked with concern. Shaun lived outside of town and Eve found it odd that he was here.

"Delivering a Christmas tree," Shaun explained, seeing the questioning expression on Eve's face. Shaun was nice looking in a wholesome, unimposing way, not especially handsome but he had a quick smile.

"Yeah, I'm fine. I'm just having a bad morning," Eve explained. "Bunch of jerks at the bus stop."

"You want me to beat them up for you?" Shaun gave a crooked grin.

"Nah." She laughed. "They aren't worth going to prison for."

"Want a ride the rest of the way to school?" he asked, pointing to his truck.

Eve shook her head. "Thanks anyway."

"All right, see you later." Shaun turned and walked away.

The screech of brakes made Eve turn around. The bus had made its way back down the hill and paused at the stop sign to pick up the kids. One by one they filed onto the bus. Only Nola didn't get on.

Eve saw the arm worm out the window but it was the pop bottle in the kid's hand that caused Eve's stomach to drop. The dark-colored liquid flew from the window showering over Nola who stood there as if in shock. The bus began to inch forward and then the hand released the bottle, which struck Nola's head and went bouncing across the pavement.

"Freak!" came a shout. The bus erupted in laughter so loud that Eve heard it from a half a block away.

Nola stood there dripping and looked back at Eve, her face filled with a helplessness that Nola rarely, if ever, saw. "Nola," Eve called out to her sister, backtracking toward her. "Are you okay?"

Nola ignored her and turned toward home.

Eve made her way down another steep hill and once at the bottom turned left onto First Street. Two and a half more years. Two and a half more years and she could move out of the house. That seemed like an eternity.

While she walked, the sun rose milky white behind leaden clouds awakening a brisk north wind. Eve had twenty minutes to make it to school before the first bell rang.

The sun was rising about the treetops, splashing cold light across the windshield and the bus groaned and hissed as it crept past. Eve knew she should go after her sister to make sure that she was okay, but couldn't bring herself to do it. Maybe this would teach Nola that she couldn't treat people this way. Besides, Eve had bigger problems. Nick would be waiting for her at school and now, more than ever, she was resolved to end things with him. She would prove Maggie wrong. Eve hunched her shoulders against the cold and trudged toward school.

MAGGIE KENNEDY-O'KEEFE

Monday, June 15, 2020

With the binder in hand, I stare up at the elevator ceiling. Dark splatters stain the tiles. My feet are swollen and joints ache and I'm ready to go home to Shaun and the cats. My phone vibrates and I press it to my ear. It's Peg, the receptionist.

"You better get up here," she says tensely.

The doors open and I see a Channel Four reporter and a camera operator standing in front of Peg's desk. "Can I help you?" I ask and they turn.

"I'm Robert Shay. We're here for the press conference," the young reporter says. He is young and handsome with close-cropped hair and a disarming smile complete with dimples. I predict he'll move on from Channel Four to greener pastures and a bigger TV market within the year.

"Press conference?" I repeat.

"Regarding the Eve Knox murder case," Robert explains earnestly. "We got a call that there was going to be an update." The woman holding the camera lifts it to her shoulder.

"Whoa," I say. "Don't turn that thing on." I'm mindful of my wrinkled shirt and messy bun. "I'm not sure where you got your information but there isn't going to be a press conference."

"But you are reinvestigating the Knox case, correct?" Robert asks, pulling out a small notebook.

"No comment," I say.

The reporter isn't giving up so easily. "We have a source who tells us that new evidence was found. Is that true?" He nods toward the binder in my arms. I move my hands to cover up Eve's name.

I repeat the mantra. "No comment. Where'd you get your information?" I ask.

"Anonymous tip," the camerawoman says.

"We're running a story," Robert adds. "Don't you think it would be better if the police department had an official comment?"

I sigh. I really didn't think it would make the jump from gossip to news this fast, especially since we are such a small town and don't even have our own local paper or TV station. "Give me a second." I step away from them and tell Peg to get Chief Digby on the phone.

Peg rings Digby's office then hands me the phone. I fill him in. I'm hoping that he will come down and deal with the press himself but it seems he's perfectly comfortable with me making the statement.

I pull the press release from the binder and take a deep breath. "Okay, let's get this over with," I say and lead them to an empty conference room. "I'm just giving a statement, not answering any questions. Got it?" Both Robert and the camerawoman nod.

I tuck wayward strands of hair behind my ears and try to smooth the wrinkles from my clothes. I stand behind the podium and the camerawoman raises the camera to her shoulder and nods to let me know she's filming.

"Twenty-five years ago, fifteen-year-old Grotto resident

Eve Knox was murdered. Despite the tireless work of investigators, the case has not been solved. Yesterday, potential new evidence connected to the homicide was discovered. As a result, all the evidence is being resent to the state lab for testing. With the advancement of forensic technology, we are cautiously hopeful that we will be able to bring closure to this case and for Eve's family. Thank you."

"It's been said that the new evidence is a shoe that the victim was wearing the night she was killed," Robert says off camera. "Can you confirm this?"

"No comment," I say.

"Have you spoken to the family? What is their reaction?"

"No comment."

"Do you have any suspects or persons of interest at this time?"

"No comment. Thank you, that is all I have right now," I say and step out from behind the podium and move toward the conference room door.

"Weren't you one of the people who found Eve Knox's body?" The reporter steps into my path and sticks his microphone in my face.

I try to keep my face impassive though I want to smack the mic out of his hand and tell him to get out of my way. Part of me also wants to tell him that the night Nola and I found Eve's body was the worst day of my life. But more than anything I just want to get the hell out of that room. "No comment," I manage to say with authority. When the reporter realizes that I'm not going to give him anything more, he shakes his head and the camerawoman lowers her camera.

"Will you give me a call if there's something new to share?" Robert asks as he holds out a business card. "Anything at all?"

"Sure," I say, plucking the card from his hand. "Thanks for stopping by," I tell them. "You'll be the first I contact if something comes up." Once out of the room I rip the card in half and drop the pieces into the nearest garbage can.

As I head out of the police station to go home, I can see the headline now: *FROM FINDING THE BODY TO FINDING THE KILLER: Twenty-five years later, detective hunts for clues in the slaying of best friend.* I don't want this kind of attention.

NOLA KNOX

Monday, June 15, 2020

After Maggie left, Nola opened each closet carefully, fearful that an avalanche of musty dish towels or cardboard boxes filled with old shoes would crash down on her. Nearly every nook and cranny of the house was crammed with their things. Nola hesitated. She wasn't sure if she should dismantle her bone collections and stow each piece into its own hiding spot or keep each memento together.

She was overthinking this. There was no reason to think that the police would want to come back in and search the house after twenty-five years but it was prudent to be prepared. The discovery of her collections would be shocking and difficult to explain even among the miscellany that filled the house.

She finally settled on the basement. Dank and dark with its cobwebbed corners, concrete floors and exposed joints, it too was overflowing with items her mother had no room for on the other two floors and garage but wasn't able to part with. There were garden tools, empty mason jars, sets of dishware found in thrift stores and boxes of baby clothes that Charlotte enthusiastically bought when there was still a chance that Nola might give her grandchildren. There were golf clubs and lawn chairs and garbage bags filled with empty cans of Diet Coke at the bottom of the steps creating a black barrier.

First, Nola taped old sheets over the small drafty windows with rotting panes that provided a ground level view of the yard. It wouldn't do to have peering eyes.

Beneath a dimly lit, exposed lightbulb, Nola placed each group of specimens into bigger plastic bins, secured the lids, and then covered them with boxes filled with holiday decorations of red-and-green glass ornaments, sparkly gold-and-silver garland, and Christmas stockings cuffed with red velvet and embellished with felt snowmen and reindeer and elves.

Up and down the steps, Nola went, picking her way through boxes and bins and garbage bags, positioning her boxes beneath the stairs where they had less of a chance of being crushed by toppling junk. Over these boxes she set thick loops of fake Christmas garland.

Behind an old kitchen table stacked with empty cardboard boxes was a pocket door that led to a smaller storage room. Nola nudged the table aside, unlocked the padlock and slid the door open. Nola flipped the light to reveal a nearly empty room. In the center of the room sat a stainless steel table on wheels and against one wall was a large utility sink. That was all. The storage room was incongruous with the rest of the house; the walls were bare, the floor spotless. It looked completely out of place.

Nola dragged a few boxes into the space and set an old paint can and dirty brushes in the sink. Grabbing a broom with half its bristles missing she swept dust from the main storage area into the room. That was better, Nola thought.

She closed the door then pushed the table back into place. This time Nola didn't lock the door. She looked around. It would have to do.

Back upstairs in the kitchen, Nola navigated around more newspapers and boxes of old mail. Cans of peas and beets and corn and every kind of bean imaginable filled every inch of counter space. The only clear space was the small kitchen table where they used to sit as a family. Nola rarely ate at home, preferring to grab her food while on the road.

She chose a can of green beans from the tower, popped the top and dumped the contents into a glass bowl. She wrestled to open a drawer crowded with knives and forks and spoons but gave up and took the bowl outside and sat down on the front step and began eating the green beans with her fingers.

She had been so absorbed in her work that hours had passed unnoticed. The humid night air felt good on her skin after the chill of the basement, the dark a welcomed camouflage from the eyes of her neighbors.

The Kennedy house was unlit and quiet. Nola knew that Colin Kennedy, Maggie's brother, had recently come back to town to help care for their father. *Alzheimer's,* Nola's mother said and laughed bitterly. *It's not fair,* she had said cradling one of the china dolls she collected. *I'm the one who needs to forget. What bliss that would be.*

The door to the Harper house opened and out stepped Joyce Harper with her dog. Curious, Nola watched from the shadows as the corgi mix sniffed the grass and circled the yard. Joyce Harper hadn't changed much over the years. Austere and sharp-angled—just like her house. She had never been a fan of Nola's. Not since that unfortunate incident with Riley. Or was it Rebecca? No, it was the boy. Nola wasn't really going to push the kid off the edge of the bluff, she was just curious to see how far they could go. And anyway, what kind of mother doesn't notice that her three-year-old isn't in the house? So really, it was her own fault.

What a scene she had caused. Joyce Harper running barefoot through her perfectly maintained backyard, her long skirt gathered up in her fists so she wouldn't trip over the fabric, sleek hair barely moving, a look of terror on her face. Joyce had struggled to open the back gate that led to the bluffs, her manicured fingers scrabbling at the latch. When she finally reached Nola and the child, Joyce had yanked the boy away from Nola so hard that the little boy's head snapped back violently, snatching the air from his lungs. When he finally opened his mouth to take a breath, blood dribbled down his chin where he had bitten his tongue.

Joyce picked up the boy and clutched him to her chest and scurried to the Kennedy house, screaming bloody murder. When Nola caught up to her, Joyce was crying and ordering the chief to arrest her. Nola talked her way out of it. She always did. *I saw him wandering around outside by himself*, Nola said innocently. *I was just trying to help.*

Joyce Harper was having none of it. *Stay away from my children!* she had squawked. *Stay out of my yard.*

Nola laughed softly at the memory and the dog lifted her head as if catching a scent and cocked her head in Nola's direction.

"Come on, Winnie," Joyce urged. The dog ignored her and trotted away and began exploring the Knoxes' burnt, brown lawn.

Nola set aside her bowl and clicked her tongue. The dog paused and looked at Nola.

"Winnie, come!" Joyce called. "Come here!"

"Here, Winnie," Nola whispered in the tone she used with all the animals she worked with. They liked the sound of her voice. Calm, reassuring, mesmerizing. Winnie approached her cautiously and sniffed the back of her hand.

"Winnie, get back here, now!" Joyce yelled but Nola scooped her up and began stroking her fur.

"Good girl," Nola soothed and ran her fingers across the soft hollow of Winnie's throat.

"Winnie," Joyce called again, her voice edged with panic.

Nola stood and started walking over to the Harper house, an austere Frank Lloyd Wright constructed of concrete and ribboned with lead glass windows. Commissioned by a wealthy newcomer to Grotto in the 1920s, the house was an anomaly around here. Modern and sleek, so different than the simple traditional Dutch colonial and ranch homes that most townspeople lived in. The original owners left and the house went through many owners until the Harpers purchased it in the early nineties.

"Hello, Joyce," Nola said, emerging from the shadows and causing Joyce to jump.

"Nola," Joyce answered, her eyes darting around the neighborhood as if in search of a friendly face. No one was around. "How's your mother doing? We heard about her accident." Joyce held out her arms for Winnie but Nola took a step backward, just out of reach.

"Holding her own," Nola said though she hadn't been to the hospital to visit or even called for several days.

"Tell her we're thinking of her." Again, Joyce reached for Winnie but Nola held tight, her fingers massaging the dog's ears. The front door opened and out stepped Cam Harper. Above him moths banged their wings against the porch light.

"Nola," he said. "Did Winnie sneak off again?" he asked, sliding an arm around his wife's waist. Cam Harper was tall, handsome with a quick smile and eyes that snapped with mischief. Nola had always thought he was a pompous ass.

Nola forced a smile. "She just came over to say hello." Nola craned her neck to peer inside the house. She'd only been inside a few times and the final time was when she was ten. She had never been invited back. Joyce tried to take a nonchalant step to the right to block her view but Nola loomed over her and could see that except for some new furniture, the interior was just as she remembered it: expansive maple floors, wood-encased radiators, the fireplace big enough to hide a body in.

"Why don't you come on in for a minute," Cam offered

in a smooth voice. "Joyce and I were just sitting down for a glass of wine. Please join us."

Joyce shot her husband a venomous glare. "Yes, please, come in," she echoed tightly. Joyce would make Cam pay for this later.

Nola stepped inside. The air was so cold that even the honey-colored walls and the inviting glow of the wall sconces gave only the illusion of warmth. Again, Joyce reached out for Winnie. Nola finally handed her over.

"I'll just go put her to bed for the night," Joyce said, whisking Winnie from the room.

"How have you been?" Cam asked. "Don't see you around much." Cam Harper had to be about sixty years old now, Nola thought. Still trim and fit looking, Nola would see him jogging through the neighborhood in the early morning hours on her way to the clinic.

"I work a lot," Nola said as she wandered around the living room following the progression of photos that chronicled the growth of their twins. First as newborns, wrapped burrito-style and tucked into each crook of their father's elbows, as towheaded toddlers with matching outfits and as devilish gap-toothed seven-year-olds wearing T-ball uniforms. There were photos of the twins as high school seniors gazing importantly into the camera and a few years later with their spouses. Riley looked just like his father, Rebecca like her mother, Nola thought. If the photos were part of an art installation it would be entitled *De-evolution*.

"Cabernet okay?" Cam asked, coming up behind Nola, his breath in her ear.

"Sure," Nola said, turning so that her back was against the wall, Cam just inches away.

"I heard on the news that some evidence in your sister's case was found." Cam handed her a delicate glass filled with red wine. "Is that true?"

So this was why Cam had invited her inside the house. He wanted the latest scoop on Eve's murder. "Apparently," Nola said, taking a sip from her glass.

"Eve was a nice girl," Cam said reaching around Nola, brushing his hand against her shoulder to pull a photo of the twins from the wall. "Did you know we're grandparents now? They have their own kids now. Rebecca has a five-year-old boy and Riley has girls, seven and nine. Eve was good with our kids. They still talk about her."

"Eve was good at a lot of things," Nola said, taking a step closer to Cam so that they were nearly nose to nose.

"She was," Cam agreed. "So the reporter said something about a shoe. Is that the new evidence?"

"Her boot," Nola answered.

"After all these years? That's remarkable," Cam marveled. "It's a shame they never caught anyone. I'm glad to hear that they are looking into Eve's case again."

Nola leaned in until her lips were nearly touching Cam's ear. "Are you?" she whispered.

Cam's eyes narrowed in confusion. "Of course I am."

"What kind of recovery is your mom looking at?" Joyce asked, stepping back into the room, unaware of the tension between Nola and her husband.

"You know, hip injuries can be so unpredictable." Nola eased away from Cam and waved her hand around as if to indicate the nebulous nature of broken bones. "Cam was just asking me about Eve's case," Nola said. "They're hoping that they'll be able to find some new forensics. Who knows? Stranger things have happened."

"Oh? That's good," Joyce said. "I imagine it dredges up a lot of sad memories for your mother." She paused. "And for you too, of course. It was such a frightening time. Not knowing what crazy person was out there killing people."

Nola nodded in agreement. "I'm sure Maggie O'Keefe will be around to talk to you."

"Why would Maggie talk to us?" Joyce asked. "We don't know anything."

"Just routine, I'm sure." Nola smiled. "In fact, Maggie stopped over to talk to me today. I figure she'll be making the rounds."

Joyce steered the conversation to the weather and Nola quickly drained the last of her wine. "Well, I should probably get going." Joyce looked relieved when Nola handed over her empty glass.

"I'll walk you out," Cam said. Cam closed the door behind them and walked Nola to the end of the driveway.

"Does your wife know?" Nola asked.

"Know what?" Cam asked. "What are you talking about?"

"About how you have a thing for young girls?" Nola asked.

"What?" Cam exclaimed, a shocked expression on his face. It almost looked sincere, Nola thought. "What? That's a lie," he blustered.

Nola didn't respond, just met his gaze.

"You can't go flinging around rumors like this, Nola." Cam grabbed her forearm and the searing look she gave him made him instantly let go. "I'm a lawyer, remember that, Nola," he said, regaining some composure. "You start spreading these lies, I'll sue you and you'll lose everything you have, got it?" He nodded toward the house. "Even if it's only that piece of crap house you live in."

"You could," Nola said. "But I bet your wife wouldn't appreciate the entire town knowing what you've been up to."

"Watch yourself." Cam pointed a finger in her face. "You utter a word of these baseless rumors and I will destroy you." With that, Cam turned and strode back up the driveway into the house, the door slamming behind him.

Joyce looked out the window, arms folded, rubbing them as

if cold. She was probably running through the list of people she needed to call and tell that the police had reopened Eve's case. Not that it was ever closed. It wasn't. It just lay dormant for the last twenty-five years like a cicada long buried and ready to dig its way out.

Nola knew that publicly, there were no official suspects in Eve's murder, just many persons of interest. The police looked closely at Eve's boyfriend, Nick, and at the sex-offender son of their neighbor, Mrs. Olhauser. And there was Pedals, the homeless man who rode his bike around town.

Suspicion had fallen on Nola, though she didn't realize it until she walked into the bathroom at school and caught a group of girls whispering about how they heard she was the one who beat and strangled Eve. Charlotte told the police that Nola had stopped by the hotel to see her at the time of the murder, that there was no way she could have had anything to do with it. But it didn't make much of a difference.

Word of mouth in a small town was a powerful thing. A kids' game of operator on steroids. Even now, Nola could tell by the way Maggie O'Keefe and Joyce Harper looked at her, they still didn't quite know what to think of her, those old assumptions were so deeply ingrained. Second chances meant shit in small towns.

MAGGIE KENNEDY-O'KEEFE

Monday, June 15, 2020

I hurry out to my car in case the reporter suddenly comes up with another question and as I open my door something on the windshield catches my eye. I stretch across the hood of the car, the metal hot against my midsection, and pull it from where it's pinned beneath a wiper. It's a red piece of paper folded into the shape of a cardinal.

My heart thumps in my chest. I look around the parking lot to see if any other cars have one slid beneath their windshield wipers but find none. Maybe a child dropped the bird, a school art project, on the way home and someone found it on the ground, picked it up and placed it on my car. But deep down I know that's not the case. Cam made one of these for me once. Decades ago. It was our little secret.

I get inside the car and turn on the engine, cold air flooding the space. He wouldn't have left this for me now. I'm well beyond his preferred demographic. I quickly unfold the bird and search for any written message. It's blank. I toss the bird onto the seat next to me. It has to be some weird coincidence.

It's a twenty-minute drive to the tree farm that Shaun and I call home. Outside Grotto, hills and bluffs flatten into acres of farmland reserved for soybeans and corn and alfalfa. I prefer the predictability of open country. I like being able to see what's coming, something that isn't possible in a town built atop cliffs and in deep valleys.

Before long O'Keefe Orchards & Landscaping comes into view. Shaun took over the family business when his folks decided to move down to Florida year-round. Around that same time, we ran into each other at the grocery store and struck up a conversation. Two years after that, we got married and I moved to what is now my favorite spot in the world.

The orchard fills both sides of a lush valley and I love walking the rows of apple, fir, spruce and pine trees. Each row has its unique scent—sharp, sweet, woody. I've always imagined our children playing beneath the trees trying to catch the falling delicate pink-and-white apple blossoms that cling to their hair like confetti.

But the children never came. Only hope, anticipation, disappointment, despair. We mortgaged the orchard in order to pay for the fertility treatments. Now we are in major debt, but that doesn't matter. I would sell my soul if it meant that this baby comes to us in good health. And now that I'm at thirty-two weeks I can almost believe it will happen. Shaun and I are going to be parents.

Our home, an old farmhouse, white with green shutters, is my oasis from the grimness of police work. Yes, we live in a small community but we still have our fair share of domestic abuse, breaking and entering, drug offenses, and even a murder now and then, so coming home to the orchard is heaven.

The orchard is just off Highway 22, and I always feel a sense of relief when I see our big red barn with *O'Keefe Orchards & Landscaping* scripted across the side in crisp white paint. I turn into the small parking lot next to the barn where the shop is located and then veer left down a long gravel drive that leads to our home. In the summers, the shop is open until six and Shaun is often out on landscaping jobs even later depending on the weather. Tonight, especially after our phone call, I won't count on seeing him until the sun sets.

I park in the garage, get out of the car, reach back inside to retrieve the case files I brought home with me and let myself inside the house. My feet feel like they are going to burst out of my shoes and I've got a raging headache.

Instead of being greeted with the cool blast of the air conditioner I'm met with hot, stagnant air. The central air has conked out again. "Oh, Jesus," I say, dumping the binder on the kitchen counter.

I go from room to room, the cats following me, opening windows hoping for even a hint of a slight breeze. By the time I reach the top of the stairs my shirt is wet with sweat and I'm nauseated. I wrestle with the window in our bedroom, finally forcing it open but the sheer white curtains remain still.

I turn on the ceiling fan and strip down to my bra and underwear and lie down on top of the covers. I try to stay completely still while the warm, recycled air sweeps over me. I want to close my eyes but every time I do, I think of Eve. I think of the case files waiting for me on the kitchen counter. It's taken a long time, but I've been able to push thoughts of my best friend so far back that I only allow myself to really think about Eve a few times a year. September fourteenth, the day she was born, and December twenty-second, the day she died.

Eve and I met the August before we started first grade. Her family had just moved to town. They didn't show up to their new house with a moving truck or even a U-Haul. I remember sitting on my front porch in my brand-new school shoes. Bright white tennis shoes with a pink stripe. My mom told me not to get them dirty so I just sat on the porch and admired them while I waved away mosquitoes.

I heard the Knoxes arrive well before I saw them. The rattle and screech as their canary-yellow car with a queen-size mattress strapped to the top pulled up in front of the old Miller house. I'd never met the Millers, they were long gone before I was born and replaced with a parade of renters, none lasting longer than a year. Every time a U-Haul or a moving van appeared I'd excitedly be on the lookout for someone my age. There never was.

The doors to the car opened and I leaned forward in anticipation. First, a pretty girl emerged from the driver's side door. She wore cutoff shorts and a bright blue tank top half-hidden by her waist-length blond hair. She looked way younger than my mom. No other adult appeared to be in the car. Maybe the mom and dad were on their way and were going to show up with the moving van.

The driver fiddled with the front seat, pushing it forward and out launched a girl of about four with dandelion fluff hair. She was wearing a scowl and denim overall shorts with cowboy boots. Without a backward glance she marched up the walkway and to the front door and tried the knob. It didn't budge.

I let out a huff of disappointment. It didn't look like I was going to get the neighbor girl I wished for. But then there was movement from inside the car and I stood to get a better look. Another figure stepped out from the rear of the car and my heart soared. She had long red hair and was about my size. She had to be about my age, give or take a year. That would be okay, I told myself. We could still be best friends.

At age six, I'd never seen someone with hair that color before. Not in real life anyway. And it was hard to name. *Red* was too common a word and that hair wasn't the color of fire engines or the tomatoes that my mother grew in the garden in our backyard. But it was pretty and I wished away my own ordinary brown hair.

Hurry up! the child at the door yelled. She sounded just like she looked, screechy and bad-tempered. *Eve!* She stomped her foot.

Mom, make her stop! the redhead implored. *Mom?* I thought in amazement. The girl I thought was the sister was the mother? And Eve. What a pretty name to match such a pretty girl. I itched to cross the street and introduce myself but I couldn't do it. I was too shy.

The little sister scanned the street and her eyes found mine. They were sharp and angry. I didn't like her and from the way she stared at me, the feeling was mutual.

"Maggie." Shaun's voice startles me back to the present and I open my eyes to find the room in shadows and my husband standing in the doorway looking down at me. I'm self-conscious at my near nakedness but I'm too tired, too hot, to try to cover up.

"Hey," I say sleepily. "What time is it?"

"Eight thirty," he says. "Is everything okay?"

"I'm fine," I say blearily. "Just tired. I'm so sorry about today."

"I can't believe you missed the appointment," Shaun says. "I waited at the doctor's office and you didn't show up. I was worried."

"I know, I can't believe it either." My hands travel to my stomach. "I completely forgot about it."

"Yeah, I got that," Shaun says, miffed.

"I'm so sorry," I say, using my elbows to prop myself up in bed. "I'll call first thing in the morning and reschedule. I had a crazy day at work today. I can't believe it slipped my mind." It's then when I notice a white binder in his hands.

"I'm on light duty," I explain. "Digby assigned me to look into a cold case."

Shaun flips on the overhead light. I squint at the harsh brightness that showcases the network of purple veins that lie just below the surface of the skin of my swollen breasts and taut belly. I swing my legs over the side of the bed and reach for my clothes. It's not that I'm ashamed of my pregnant body. I'm not, but it's foreign to me, nearly unrecognizable.

"This is about Eve Knox," Shaun says. He's still dressed in his dirt-stained work clothes, but his hands are spotless, fingernails scrubbed clean. He smells like fresh-mown grass.

"And?" I say, playing dumb.

"And, do you think it's a good idea for you to be looking into your best friend's murder?"

I knew that Shaun would have these concerns. Shaun never knew Eve. He was older than us, ran with a different crowd but he knew she was my best friend.

"It can't be good for the baby," Shaun says again, knowing this is his best argument. I slip my shirt on but leave my pants next to me. It will take too much effort to thread my legs through them.

"Have you seen these pictures?" he asks.

"You shouldn't have opened it," I tell him and hold out my hand so he can help hoist me to my feet. With a groan I stand and reach for the binder and he places it across my palms.

"I didn't know what it was at first," he says. "Jesus, Maggie, if I could go back and unsee them, I would. It's bad."

"I'm sorry, I shouldn't have brought them home," I tell him. I've seen dead bodies before and Shaun hasn't, should never have to. "You go ahead and shower first."

"But you knew her." Shaun begins to shed his clothes. "How can you look at the dead body of someone you knew?" He turns on the shower and the bathroom begins to fill with steam. I don't know how he can stand it on such a hot day.

"It's my job," I say simply.

"I don't think you should do it," Shaun says again as he steps into the shower, submerging his head beneath the stream of water. His insistence surprises me. Shaun isn't new to this rodeo. He knows what I do for a living. I was a cop when we met and started dating. The fact that I'm pregnant shouldn't make a difference.

"Turn that handle to the left a few notches and I'll join you in there," I say as I once again remove my shirt and the rest of my clothes. Shaun turns the knob and as the water cools I step in next to him. Close quarters for two people and the beach ball between us.

"I just don't want you to be stressed out," he says, tucking a wet strand of hair behind my ear but what he really is saying is, *We have to keep the baby safe. We can't let anything bad happen to this one.*

"The fastest way to stress me out is to tell me not to be stressed," I say as anxiety rises in my chest. "Everything is going to be fine." I, more than anyone, know this isn't necessarily true.

Shaun nuzzles my neck. "If it gets to be too much just promise me you'll stop. You'll just walk away."

"I promise," I say to appease him, but I know I won't be able to walk away.

An hour and a half later, Shaun is sleeping and I'm wide-awake sitting on the family room couch with Eve's files in front of me and the TV playing softly in the background. I start reading again.

There are interviews with the librarian at the public library and the shop owners on Grinnell Avenue who saw Eve the afternoon of the twenty-second. They all reported that Eve was looking for her sister and that she seemed distracted but not upset. Nola was always running off, getting into some kind of trouble.

A familiar image pops up on the television screen. There I am in all my pregnant glory talking to the camera. The chyron at the bottom of the screen reads, *New Evidence Discovered in Twenty-Five-Year-Old Murder Case of Grotto Teen.*

"Oh, Jesus," I say out loud. "Here we go."

The house phone begins to ring and I rush to get to it before the sound wakes Shaun. "Hello," I answer breathlessly. No response on the other end. I hang up and before I sit down, it rings again. I lift the receiver. "Hello?" I say and again nothing. Irritated, I lower the receiver and go back to the sofa. My abdomen contracts, a brief squeeze and release, the baby's way of telling me it's time for bed. *Not just yet*, I tell her. Before I can sit down the phone rings again. "Yeah," I say when I answer, in no mood for this nonsense. This time a voice on the other end responds.

"Home wrecker," comes a harsh whisper. "You should be ashamed of yourself, sinner."

"You must have the wrong number," I say. "Don't call again." I move to hang up the phone when the voice speaks again.

"This is the right number," the voice hisses. "You'll pay for what you did." It's impossible to tell if the person on the other end is male or female but they're clearly angry.

"You're threatening a cop," I say. "Don't call back." I hang up again and this time I leave the phone off the hook. I don't have time for stupid, random prank calls. I flip off the television and return to the files.

My fingers land on a transcript of an interview with Sarah Reiss, the office secretary at Grotto High. If there was something to know about a student, Ms. Reiss was the one to ask. She knew every student's name and schedule, who was dating whom and all the day-to-day dramas associated with high school life.

According to Ms. Reiss, Eve was called to the school office at around 10:30 a.m. on the twenty-second to take a phone call from her mother. Before Eve got to the office, Ms. Reiss said she saw Eve in the hallway talking to Nick Brady, stating that the two looked pretty cozy. After Eve talked to her mother, Ms. Reiss said that Eve abruptly left the building saying that she needed to go find her sister.

But it's the last line of the report that takes my breath away. When asked if anyone else was seen with Eve as she left the building, Ms. Reiss gave one name. Shaun O'Keefe.

THERAPY TRANSCRIPT

Client Name: Nola Knox, 13 years
Therapist Name: Linda Gonzalez, LMHC, NCC
Date of Service: Feb. 6, 1996

L. Gonzalez: Good morning, Nola. How are you doing today? I'm glad that you decided to come back.

N. Knox: I didn't have a choice. It was this or being sent to the detention center.

L. Gonzalez: Everyone who comes here expects something different. What do you want out of our time together?

N. Knox: Nothing. I just want to get it over with.

L. Gonzalez: Well, let's look at why the court ordered you to attend these sessions. Maybe that will be a springboard for us. Okay?

N. Knox: Fine.

L. Gonzalez: You had an altercation with a young man. You pushed him into a glass trophy case.

N. Knox laughs

L. Gonzalez: You disagree?

N. Knox: No. That's what happened.

L. Gonzalez: But you find something humorous in the situation?

N. Knox: Not funny. Inane.

L. Gonzalez: How so?

N. Knox: I find it inane that a thirteen-year-old girl can get in trouble for standing up to a big, sixteen-year-old asshole.

L. Gonzalez: You were standing up to the boy?

N. Knox: Yes. He's a bully. He was being gross. He was talking about my sister. I didn't like it.

L. Gonzalez: What did he say?

L. Gonzalez: You don't want to talk about what he said?

N. Knox: No.

L. Gonzalez: Okay. You stood up to him for being a bully. He was bullying you?

N. Knox: No one bullies me.

L. Gonzalez: But he said something crude about your

sister and you lashed out. That must have made you very angry.

L. Gonzalez: Something must have made you very angry to push that boy into the glass.

N. Knox: He deserved it. People get what they deserve.

EVE KNOX

Friday, December 22, 1995
7:45 a.m.

Eve knew she should have gone after Nola, but she just couldn't deal with her right now. Besides, Nola obviously didn't want her help.

Eve backtracked a few blocks and then took a right on Third Street. She was going to be late for school going this way but surprisingly didn't really care. Winter vacation started at twelve thirty and then they'd be off for two full weeks. Eve had been looking forward to the break: sleeping in, no homework, lounging around and watching TV and reading. But after the fight with her mother she dreaded it. The thought that she would be stranded in the house with her mother and Nola for two weeks was excruciating.

The soft beep of a car horn startled her and Eve turned to see a black BMW creeping down the street next to her. The driver's side window rolled down and their neighbor Mr. Harper smiled up at her. "Hi, Eve," he said. "I'd been hoping to catch you."

Everyone, including her mother, said that Cam Harper was handsome in a soap opera star kind of way. *That Cam Harper,* she said, *he's one nice-looking man.* But in the last few months he'd made Eve uneasy, making offhand comments about how pretty she was and how all the boys in her school must want to date her.

Over time Eve saw that Cam had these intense eyes that one minute were warm and laughing and then the next turned hard and cold like a snake's. Because of this, Eve had been babysitting less and less for the Harpers. She was happy to let Maggie take the jobs even though it meant less money in her pocket.

Eve had always felt a little bit sorry for his wife. She tried so hard. Joyce was always careful to look her best. Perfect hair, perfect makeup, perfectly kept house. When Eve first began babysitting for the Harpers she thought that this must be what a marriage was supposed to look like, what a home was supposed to be. Her own father was a ghost of a memory and her mother, to be honest, was kind of a hot mess.

When Eve looked carefully at the Harpers she could see that nothing was quite as it seemed. The toll that maintaining this perfection took on Mrs. Harper was always just below the surface and her once open, sweet face became closed and guarded. Resigned.

"You're still babysitting for us tomorrow night?" He smiled hopefully, a deep dimple appearing.

"Yep, I'll be there. Six o'clock, right?" Eve wasn't thrilled about accepting the job but knew that Maggie wasn't able to watch the kids and that the Harpers were desperate.

"It's cold out there," Cam said, giving an exaggerated shake to prove his point. "Hop in, I'll take you to school."

Eve's cheeks were numb and her fingers stiff from the cold and she was definitely going to be late for school but she would rather be late and frozen than get into the car alone with Mr. Harper.

"No thanks," Eve told him, rewinding her scarf around her neck so that it covered her ears. Mr. Harper reached through the window and grabbed her hand.

HEATHER GUDENKAUF

"You're freezing," he said, enveloping her cold fingers in his warm ones. "Come on, let me give you a ride." His skin against hers was moist and sent a spasm of revulsion through her.

"No thanks," Eve said again, trying to pull her hand free but Mr. Harper held tight. "Ow," Eve said with a nervous laugh and he finally let go. Eve shoved her hands into her pockets, eager to get away.

"Alright," Mr. Harper said with an easy smile. "Better run off to school. Don't want to be late. See you tomorrow."

Eve turned and started walking, well aware that Mr. Harper was still sitting there in his car, watching her. The weight of his gaze scraped across the back of her neck and she picked up her speed.

The awkwardness with Mr. Harper didn't happen all of a sudden. It was so gradual and natural and innocent that it took Eve forever to figure out. The way his knuckles grazed against her hand when he paid her, the way his shoulder brushed against Eve's when he insisted on walking her across the street when she finished babysitting late at night. Cam Harper was a creeper. Maggie suddenly came to mind: in over her head with someone too old for her. Could Cam Harper be that someone? The thought made her sick. Maybe this was why Maggie was acting so weird this morning, why she was so quick to start an argument. Eve would find Maggie when she got to school and try to work things out.

"Hey," came a shout. "Eve!"

Eve spun around and found Nick inching along in his car close behind. "Jeez, you scared me." Eve pressed a hand to her chest.

"Who was that?" Nick asked through the open car window, his hands gripping the steering wheel tightly. "Who were you talking to?"

Eve looked back to where Mr. Harper was still parked. "I

126

babysit his kids," Eve explained. "He was asking if I could watch them tomorrow."

"He was holding your hand," Nick said accusingly.

"No," Eve said, laughing nervously, knowing that it probably looked pretty bad from Nick's point of view. "No, he wasn't. He was just checking for frostbite."

"Get in the car, Eve." Nick glowered.

"That's okay," she said taking a step backward.

"Get in the fucking car," Nick hissed, putting the car into Park and throwing open his car door.

"Nick," Eve said looking around. Mr. Harper was still sitting in his car looking curiously at the two of them through his windshield. "Why are you being this way? It was nothing." Nick jetted from the car and yanked on Eve's elbow, pulling her toward the passenger side. "Ow," Eve cried, this time in real pain.

"Hey," Mr. Harper called as he stepped from his car. "Eve, is everything okay?"

"I'm fine," Eve answered, her voice shaking. "Everything's fine."

"Get in the car," Nick demanded, still holding on to her coat.

"Hey, man, let go of her," Mr. Harper said, trotting toward them.

"Hey, man, mind your own business," Nick mimicked.

"I know who you are," Mr. Harper said in a low voice. "You think this is the right way to treat a girl? I know your parents and I don't think they'd be happy to hear you're acting like an asshole."

The two stared at each other until Eve was sure it was going to come to blows. Nick was the one who balked first, dropping Eve's arm and looking away.

"You okay?" Mr. Harper asked Eve and she nodded. "You want me to call your mom?"

"No, I'm okay," Eve whispered.

"At least let me give you a ride to school," Mr. Harper urged.

"Real original," Nick muttered as he climbed back into his car. "Screwing the babysitter."

"What did you say?" Mr. Harper said, striding toward Nick's car. Nick ignored him and sped off with a squeal of the tires.

"He gets mad sometimes," Eve said apologetically. "He doesn't mean it."

"Guys like that always mean it, Eve," Mr. Harper said, gently brushing a wayward strand of hair out of Eve's face. "You deserve better than this."

"I better get going," Eve said, biting back tears. "I'm sorry that happened." She turned and moved down the street toward the school.

Eve couldn't make sense of it. Nick said he loved her but could be so mean. Mr. Harper could make her feel so uncomfortable one minute and safe the next. She was so confused.

She felt eyes on her and looked around, fearful that Nick was following her. He wasn't. But standing beneath the naked branches of a black maple was Nola, watching, taking in the entire scene.

THE WILLOW CREEK GAZETTE
December 20, 2015

Letter to the Editor
Online Edition

From Charlotte Knox, 1325 Bates Street, Grotto

My daughter, Eve Knox, was murdered twenty years ago this month. She was only fifteen years old. On the night she died, police chief Henry Kennedy gave me his word that he would find the monster who killed my daughter. He promised me justice.

Chief Kennedy broke his promise.

Enough is enough. There is a murderer in our town and someone knows something. It could be your neighbor or son or husband and because of Chief Kennedy's incompetence we may never know.

I hope no one else has to go through what my family has but if you do, don't count on Chief Kennedy, the Grotto PD or the Ransom County Sheriff's Department. Twenty years is too long to not know the truth.

Tags Letters-to-the-editor Crime Nola-Knox Cold-case

57 COMMENTS

Bethany Lincoln
I remember this like it was yesterday and I can't believe they haven't made an arrest yet. I'm so sorry for your loss.

Jessalyn Fagan
It's always the boyfriend!

Orrin Wenman

It's easy for someone to blame the police when it's too hard to look at one's own actions. Why didn't the parents know where she was? I've always thought there was a lot more to this story than meets the eye.

Dawn Iverson

I agree. Someone knows something and the police dropped the ball here. I've tried to give eyewitness evidence to the police and have been ignored at every turn. It's a shame, especially since all they have to do is literally look in their own neighborhood. This poor family hasn't gotten the closure they deserve.

Rick Meadows

Own neighborhood? How about own kitchen. Everyone is pointing fingers at the boyfriend or some homeless dude. What about the family? Aren't most murders committed by relatives?

MAGGIE
KENNEDY-O'KEEFE

Tuesday, June 16, 2020

Last night, after finding Shaun's name in the interview transcripts, I couldn't sleep. That and Shaun's less-than-enthusiastic reaction to me taking on Eve's case had me tossing and turning all night. Could he have seen or heard something that might lead to Eve's killer?

And I had forgotten about my ultrasound appointment. How could I have forgotten something so important? I had been counting down the hours until I could see the comma curve of her spine, count her fingers and toes, hear the pulsing thrum of her heart. Already this case has me addled, forgetting the most important things.

When I woke this morning, Shaun was already gone. I had hoped to ask him about seeing his name in Eve's file before he left for the day. It probably meant nothing but still I was curious. It kept me wondering if Shaun might have seen something he didn't even realize was important.

I dump cat food into the bowls and Skunky and Ponie come running, winding their sleek bodies around my legs in appreciation. I check the calendar on the wall while I toss back my prenatal vitamin and take a swig of water. I grab a banana and a muffin from the kitchen counter and head out the door. The morning sky is bright blue and cloudless and already hot. Someone is burning brush off in the distance. Stupid because of the dry weather. We need rain and it's careless to burn leaves and weeds in these dry conditions.

I drive up our lane past the big barn and the orchards and the old saltbox barn near the main road. A flicker of light in a window of the small barn catches my eye. This makes no sense. The old barn isn't wired for electricity. We use it as a catch-all space for orchard supplies and a four-wheeler and a snowmobile that we use to get around the property.

I pull the car to the side of the lane and put it into Park. Most likely what I saw was a reflection from the morning sun glinting off the pane of glass but I still want to check it out. I walk toward the window but I'm too short to peer over the ledge so I move to the barn doors. That's when I see the thick iron padlock lying in the tall grass. With difficulty, I bend down to pick it up. It's been snapped with a bolt cutter.

Dammit, I think, *we've been robbed.* There are thousands of dollars' worth of equipment in there. We are going to have to get a better security system. I fling open the barn door and a whoosh of heat and black smoke sends me reeling backward.

I clutch the door frame to catch my balance and peer through the haze. The fire is concentrated in the far left corner of the barn and isn't out of control just yet. There's still time to put it out. I scan the space in search of something to smother the knee-high blaze. I spy an old tarp draped over the riding lawn mower and yank it free.

Within seconds the flames unfold themselves from a crouch and scale the wooden walls until they are licking the rafters. It's too late. I should have never opened the barn door. My eyes burn and I wipe away the tears. The oxygen only fuels the fire and a thick fog rolls over me and my nose fills with a biting, chemical odor. My lungs suck in the dense smoke and I struggle for breath. There's nothing I can do to save the barn and its contents. The air around me cracks and pops and I know I need to get the hell out of here. Hot sparks rain down on me and I can hear the sizzle of fabric burning and feel the sharp bite of fire against my skin. I turn and bumble blindly toward where I pray the barn door is.

Once outside I lurch toward the road. All I can think about are the bags of fertilizer stacked against the barn walls and the grease and gasoline pooled in gas tanks. I'm barely aware of hands grabbing at me, pulling me away from the flames.

"I was driving by and saw the smoke," the man says, guiding me to the top of the lane. "I called 911. What happened?" Out of breath, I lean against my car, coughing.

"I don't know," I gasp. I think of the broken padlock lying in the grass. "At first I thought someone had tried to break in, but when I opened the door there was a fire." I spit out a wad of black phlegm. This can't be good for the baby.

"You're hurt," he says, reaching for my arm. I look down and see a constellation of blisters across my arm. I'm suddenly aware of pinpricks of pain across my shoulders. I crane my neck and see tiny singe marks dotting my shirt. I was lucky I wasn't burned alive.

"It happened so fast," I rasp. "I have to call my husband," I say, opening my car door and reaching inside for my phone. His phone rings and rings. Finally, he picks up.

"The saltbox is on fire," I tell him over the roar of the fire. "Come home," I say hoarsely, my throat stinging from the smoke.

"Are you safe?" he asks. The house is well away from the barn but I know how quickly fire can spread, especially in a dry season.

"I'm okay. Someone stopped and called the fire department." We disconnect and the man and I watch helplessly and in a matter of fifteen minutes the barn burns and crumbles, collapsing in on itself in an ashy heap. It's a total loss.

"Where are they?" I ask, my teeth chattering despite the waves of heat rolling over us. "What's taking so long?" I can only hope that the fire department will get here soon and contain the blaze before it can move to the orchards.

Finally, in the distance comes the wail of sirens and a caravan of bright red fire engines comes into view. I wave my arms to let them know where to go as if the heavy smoke and burning rafters aren't enough clues.

"She needs to be looked at," the man tells a paramedic who leads me to the back of her vehicle.

"I'm fine," I say. "Just a few small burns."

"How much smoke did you breathe in?" the paramedic asks.

"Some," I respond and promptly begin coughing. My throat feels like I swallowed glass.

"How far along are you?" she asks.

"Seven months?" I murmur.

She quickly slides an oxygen mask over my face and begins taking my vitals.

"We'll take you in and have you and your baby checked out by the docs."

I know she's right, but I don't want to leave. I want Shaun. If it wasn't for the baby I'd stay put. "Okay," I acquiesce. "My husband is on his way here. Can someone let him know that I'm okay?" The paramedic waves over the man who stopped to help me and tells him we are heading to the hospital over in Willow Creek just as a precaution. The man promises me he'll let Shaun know I'm perfectly okay and that I promise to call him when I'm done getting checked over.

I lie down in the back of the ambulance and suck in the clean, fresh air from the oxygen tank. I try to close my eyes but all I can see are angry flames scaling the barn wall and engulfing the rafters. I lay a hand over my abdomen waiting for the baby to move. *Come on*, I urge. *There's no way you could have slept through all that. Unless you take after your dad. He can sleep through anything.*

I think of the cut padlock and the weird phone calls from last night. Then there's the origami figure left on my car. Are they all related or strange coincidences? I rack my brain trying to think who might have it out for me. It could be any number of dirtballs and criminals that I've come into contact with. The most obvious is my involvement in investigating the recent arsons in the area. If our barn fire and the arsons are connected, what are the chances my barn was chosen randomly? All I can do now is wait and see what the fire marshal determines as the cause. Whatever the reason, someone has crossed a line. They have stepped onto my property, come to my home, and that is not acceptable.

The baby shifts, swinging an elbow or a foot in the process. I laugh with relief. "Don't worry," I whisper to her, imagining that she is pressing her fingers flat against the walls of my uterus so that only a thin layer of skin separates our hands. "I'll protect you."

NOLA KNOX

Tuesday, June 16, 2020

Nola woke to the muffled alarm from her cell phone and rose stiffly from the sofa's lumpy cushions where she'd fallen asleep. The night before, Nola kept walking up and down the basement steps to check on the boxes hidden beneath the stairs, trying to determine whether or not they looked out of place among the other mildewed cardboard boxes and broken rattan furniture.

Around one in the morning she pushed the mountain of clothes from the sofa to the floor and tried to rest but with little luck. She kept thinking she could hear the scritch-scratch of rodents in the walls and wondered if there might be more in the basement.

The ringing continued and Nola found her phone buried beneath the pile of clothes and silenced it. There were dozens of missed calls from her mother's number. She couldn't put it off any longer; she needed to go to the hospital and talk to Charlotte about Eve's case.

Nola called the vet clinic to let them know that she wouldn't be coming into work today. That she would come into the clinic tomorrow but then wouldn't be in for the remainder of the week, that she needed to spend time with her mother. Nola hadn't missed a day of work in ten years. The last time being when she received a nasty bite to the arm. She had been in too much of a hurry, too careless and it cost her a trip to the emergency room to get cleaned up and be prescribed some antibiotics. Good thing the ER was busy and the physician didn't ask too many questions.

Nola moved to the kitchen and blearily poured herself a cup of coffee from the automatic coffee maker. Sipping the hot liquid, she opened the front door and stepped outside. The warm air was still and thick with moisture, the sky a hazy blue.

Nola felt someone's eyes on her and looked around to find Colin Kennedy standing on his front porch, cigarette and coffee cup in hand, watching. Colin, Maggie's older brother, had always been an enigma to Nola. She remembered him being so different than his pretty, popular sister and his big strong police chief dad. He was a common sight riding around town on his skateboard wearing his flannel shirt and cargo pants. He was brooding, quiet and dumb as a box of rocks. Or, Nola thought, that was what he wanted people to think.

A screen door slammed and Henry Kennedy stepped out onto the porch to join his son. Nola hadn't seen him in a long time. She left for work early in the morning and often didn't return until late evening.

Nola remembered Henry exuding confidence and authority, but now he was stooped and frail looking. Puzzled, Henry stared at Nola for a long time as if trying to place her. She had heard that he had memory issues. What would that be like, Nola wondered, to gradually forget all that you've ever known? She had the opposite problem. She never forgot a thing she read, heard or saw.

Henry leaned close to his son and spoke into his ear. Colin nodded and lifted his coffee cup toward Nola in a greeting. She didn't wave back. Henry shuffled back inside the house with Colin close behind. Nola wondered if they were talking about her.

Across the street, Joyce Harper dragged her garbage cans out to the end of the driveway, the plastic wheels clacking against the concrete, and nearly tripped when she spotted Nola.

Her eyes lingered on Nola's face, probably wondering why Nola was still at home at this hour. Or, Nola thought, Cam had told Joyce about their little conversation the night before, but Nola doubted it. The last thing Cam Harper would want is his wife to know about his proclivities. Joyce quickly placed the garbage can on the curb and rushed back into the house without saying a word. Nola had to smile. Joyce was clearly nervous around her, perhaps even afraid.

Or maybe Joyce's nervousness had nothing to do with Nola at all. After all, Joyce Knox lived with her own kind of monster.

Nola glanced down at her watch. Eight o'clock. Normally she would be on her way to do her herd health rounds, visiting dairy farms, performing pregnancy checks on cows and looking in on the new calves. Now the entire day stretched out in front of her like a black void. She was restless, jumpy.

Nola thought of Charlotte, sitting in the hospital in Willow Creek, probably waiting for her to call, to come visit. Nola sighed. She would go see her mother and combine the visit with her other errands. It was time.

Nola made the drive to Willow Creek and the hospital in twenty minutes. After Eve died and Nola was expelled from Grotto High for pushing Nick Brady into a glass trophy case, her mother enrolled her in Sacred Heart, the Catholic high school in Willow Creek, a pretty college town with acres of woods and hiking trails nearby. Sacred Heart was better than Grotto High, Nola thought, but not by much.

Nola moved through the halls of Sacred Heart in a fog, attending classes but not paying attention, not interacting with her new classmates. What she really wanted was to graduate early but her mother refused to even consider the idea. *You can't leave me too*, she cried. *Not yet.*

Nola drove by a handful of farms that she had visited many times. She passed the Ransom County Fairgrounds where 4-H kids showed their pigs and calves and rabbits each summer at the fair. As she sped down the highway she passed a hand-painted sign for O'Keefe Orchards & Landscaping and wondered if Maggie had slept as poorly as she had that night. Together they had found Eve sprawled out across the cave floor, eyes open wide, staring up at them. It was a terrifying sight. One that Nola relived often, mostly at night under the cover of darkness. She imagined that Maggie did the same.

Nola came into Willow Creek and drove directly into the hospital lot and let the engine idle. Having her mother out of the house the past few weeks was freeing. She felt like she could breathe again. She could pull out her display boxes and examine the contents and she could add to her collections without having to worry about Charlotte barging into her room or yelling down the basement stairs complaining about the odd smells. Turning off the ignition, Nola was confident as to what she needed to do next. It was for her mother's own good.

Leaving the cool air of the truck, she advanced through the half-filled parking lot, the hot sun beating down on her scalp, and pushed through the hospital entrance. Once inside she found the elevator that would take her to the skilled care floor.

Nola tapped on the door of 318 and a creaky voice told her to come in. Her mother was sitting up in her hospital bed, one arm in a cast; her long ash-gray hair hung in stringy hanks against her shoulders.

"Nola?" Charlotte wheezed. "Where the hell have you been? You haven't been back to see me since the surgery." Charlotte's face, pale and puffy, was strained with pain and fatigue. "I saw the news. Are they really looking into Eve's murder again?"

"Hi, Charlotte," Nola said.

"She's always called me Charlotte," her mother said. "Ever since she could talk. It was never mommy or mom or mama. Always Charlotte."

Nola looked around, unsure who her mother was talking to but then a young man dressed in yellow scrubs stepped from the bathroom. He pulled the latex gloves from his hands, tossed them into a nearby wastebasket and smiled.

"I'm Ray, your mom's nurse," he said. "It's nice to meet you."

Nola gave the man a nod and turned back to her mother.

"I tried to call you. Why didn't you call me back?" Charlotte shifted in her bed and winced.

"I'll let you two catch up. Holler if you need anything," Ray said and left the room.

"I didn't realize that it would be on the news and I wanted to tell you in person." Nola peered at the label on the nearly empty IV bag connected to Charlotte. "They're giving you morphine? Strong stuff."

"I am in pain," Charlotte said tremulously. "You have no idea how bad my hip hurts. Not that you care. What evidence did they find?" she asked. "And why is that Kennedy girl in charge?"

"Some kids found Eve's boot in the cave and I don't know why Maggie's the one in charge. I thought it was strange too," Nola tried to pull Charlotte's sheet back from her legs but Charlotte held tight. "I just want to see the incision," Nola explained, releasing the linens. "See if your surgeon is as good as I am."

"It's not right," Charlotte said, bringing a cup to her mouth and tipping it back. Water dribbled down the corners of her mouth. "I don't think that's a good thing at all. I gave Henry the benefit of the doubt for years and what do we have to show for it? No." She shook her head. "The Kennedy family had their chance."

"That's what I said." Nola plucked a tissue from the box on the windowsill and handed it to Charlotte. "Maggie Kennedy isn't the most impartial person to investigate. She's too close to the case."

"If they would have only listened to me, they would have solved it a long time ago." Charlotte dabbed at her face with the tissue. "I'm just worried that Maggie Kennedy will go down the same dead ends that her dad did."

"We all know who you think killed Eve," Nola said distractedly, looking out the window. "Too bad there was never enough evidence to prove it."

Charlotte sniffed. "Nick Brady killed Eve and I'll go to my grave saying so. When I get home, I want to talk to Maggie Kennedy. I want to tell her that they can't let him go this time. The doctor said I will probably be able to come home by the end of the week."

"Charlotte, that's not going to happen," Nola said as she glanced behind her to see if anyone could hear her.

"What?" Charlotte asked in confusion. "But the doctors said..."

"It's the house," Nola said eager to get this conversation over with. "They'll never let you come home to it the way it is now."

"But how will they know?" Charlotte's voice cracked. "You aren't going to say anything, are you?"

Nola didn't respond.

"Nola, you're not going to tell the doctors I shouldn't come home, are you?" Charlotte asked fearfully. "You can't do this to me."

"It's for your own good," Nola said, keeping her voice neutral, calm.

"You've never done anything unless it was for your own good," Charlotte shot back. "The only person you care about is yourself. I'll tell them you pushed me down the steps. I swear I will."

"You know that's not true, Charlotte. I was trying to help you and you tripped. Why in the world would I push you?"

"You've always hated me. You hated your sister and you hate me. You want me out of the way."

"That's not true." Nola went to the small closet in the corner of the room and pulled out a pillow and walked back toward Charlotte. "I loved Eve and why would I have stayed with you all these years if I didn't care about you? You look uncomfortable," Nola said as she slid the pillow behind Charlotte's head. "If you tell them that, there's no way they will ever let you come home." Nola spoke in a low, soothing voice. "You would be put in an old folks' home. Let me get things organized for you. Then you can come home," Nola said as she looked to the doorway. "I've got to go now, Charlotte. You get some rest now. I'll call you later."

"You're lying! You always lie. I can't stay here." Charlotte's eyes widened with fear. "Don't leave me here, Nola. Don't you dare leave me here. I'll tell them you weren't there with me until six on the day Eve died."

"You can't say that, Charlotte." Nola sighed. "That will just make it all the harder to prove that Nick was the one who killed Eve."

"I don't want you throwing away my things." Charlotte was shouting now. "They're important to me. They're all I have! Nola, don't leave me here!"

Nola stepped from the room, meeting Ray as she moved down the hallway, her mother's cries following her. "Is everything okay?" Ray asked. "Did something happen?"

"She'll be okay," Nola answered as she breezed past him. "She'll be just fine."

Nola hurried back to her truck but she took her time heading back to Grotto, taking back roads and country lanes, swiveling her head from side to side looking for any movement in the ditches that hugged the road. She was getting that urge again.

Her mother would forgive her. She always did. Nola just needed her mother out of the way for the time being and, well, if it turned into a permanent thing, that was okay too. Her mother would thank her in the end, especially if it meant the downfall of Nick Brady.

The rustle of tall grass and a sleek striped tail caught her eye and she pulled over to the side of the road. Poor thing was scrawny and flea-bitten. If Nola didn't step in, it would probably die a long and painful death. She reached into her bag and retrieved the can, a snare pole and a thick pair of work gloves. No need to get scratched up.

Nola stepped from the truck. Black gnats swirled around her head and she waved them away only to have them disperse and quickly return. She popped the lid on the tin of cat food and set it near where she saw the tabby, took five steps backward and with the snare pole in hand, crouched down and waited.

THERAPY TRANSCRIPT

Client Name: Nola Knox, 13 years
Therapist Name: Linda Gonzalez, LMHC, NCC
Date of Service: Feb. 13, 1996

L. Gonzalez: How was your first month at your new school?

N. Knox: It was okay. Pretty much everyone ignored me.

L. Gonzalez: What are your classes like? Do you have a favorite?

N. Knox: They're too easy. I can already tell. I just sit in the back and read my own book and keep my mouth shut.

L. Gonzalez: What would happen if you told your teachers that the work was too easy? What do you think they would say?

N. Knox: They already know it is. They know I'm smarter than they'll ever be. It's just easier if I work on my own things. They leave me alone and they don't look stupid.

L. Gonzalez: What are you working on?

N. Knox: Have you heard of Alec Jeffreys?

L. Gonzalez: I can't say that I have. Tell me about him.

N. Knox: He knew he wanted to be a scientist since before he was even eight years old. His dad bought him a chemistry set and he liked to do experiments. Blow things up. When he was around my age he found a dead cat. He brought it home and dissected it on his dining room table. He was curious, you know, about what was inside. But his parents got mad at him for bringing a dead cat into the house. It smelled bad. But it paid off. Eventually he discovered DNA fingerprinting.

L. Gonzalez: You like learning about scientists?

N. Knox: I want to be a scientist. A veterinarian—a really good one. I feel like there's all this information out there but because I'm only thirteen I can't get my hands on it. It's not fair. I could be this amazing scientist but I'm stuck here, in the middle of nowhere.

L. Gonzalez: You feel like you're missing out because you are in middle school?

N. Knox: Yeah. I'm smart enough to be in college but no one cares.

L. Gonzalez: Have they talked about grade level acceleration with you?

N. Knox: Yeah, but they always say that I'm not socially ready to be moved ahead. So I'm stuck.

L. Gonzalez: What would make you un-stuck?

N. Knox: If I could get out of Grotto, go to college.

L. Gonzalez: Wouldn't you miss your mother? Your friends?

N. Knox: My mom misses Eve. I don't even think she would know I was gone.

L. Gonzalez: Why do you think that?

N. Knox: Because all she does is cry and say how much she misses Eve. It's pretty obvious. Do you think it was okay, what Alex Jeffreys did?

L. Gonzalez: Dissecting the cat? What do you think?

N. Knox: I think that it's the only way to learn. Really learn. If you don't get in there, cut through the skin and muscle and tendons, hold the heart in your hand, how can you really understand? If you don't understand how things die how can you understand how they live?

EVE KNOX

Friday, December 22, 1995
8:10 a.m.

Mr. Orso barely looked at Eve when she slunk into class ten minutes late. He handed her a copy of the semester test and went back to sipping his coffee.

Eve stared down at the exam and dread filled her chest. The confrontation between Nick and Mr. Harper kept running through her head. She was mortified that Mr. Harper knew that Nick was abusing her and she couldn't believe that Nick accused her of having sex with Mr. Harper. How was she going to face either of them?

Nick never meant to hurt her, he just got so mad sometimes. And in the beginning, she had to admit, she liked the way he hovered over her, the way he wrapped an arm around her like he owned her. No one ever loved her in that way.

Tears blurred her vision. She swiped them away with her fingers and tried to focus on the exam.

1. A phrase that uses ambiguity in service of rhetorical humor is which of the following rhetorical devices?

A. Pun

B. Metonymy

C. Synecdoche

D. Zeugma

E. Alliteration

Eve should have known the answer to this. Last week she would have known the answer, but her head was muddled and confused and it didn't help that Nick was sitting a few rows behind her staring daggers into her back. Eve circled letter *B*. Metonymy. "Hey," Eve heard and turned her head. The girl behind her shoved a folded piece of notebook paper at her. Eve looked back at Nick who was staring intently at her. Mr. Orso, oblivious, was bent over a stack of essays. Eve quickly snatched the note and covertly slid it beneath her exam.

She just needed to push Nick, Mr. Harper and her mother and Nola and even Maggie out of her mind. English was her best subject and she didn't plan on blowing the chance for her one and only A because she had a bad few days.

A sharp poke to the back made Eve sit upright and again she spun around. The girl behind her gave her an exasperated look and held out another piece of paper. Eve wanted to ignore the offering but she knew Nick too well. He'd keep writing and passing notes until she was buried in them. She took the note and slid it beneath her test paper along with the first.

Eve looked at the clock. She had fifteen minutes before the bell rang and she was still on page one of the test. No matter how fast she wrote, she'd never finish in time. She shifted her paper and opened the first note. *I'm sorry*, it said and was signed with a sad face. Nick was always sorry, Eve thought as she unfolded the second note. *Why are you being such a bitch?* Eve abruptly stood, causing her desk to teeter precariously then right itself. The scratch of pens on paper stopped and all eyes were on her. Mr. Orso looked up with irritation. When he saw her face it was replaced with concern.

"Eve," he said, "are you okay?"

Eve shook her head. "I don't feel well," she said, her voice croaking as if she had a sore throat.

Mr. Orso scribbled out a nurse's pass for her and leaving the test and the notes from Nick behind, Eve grabbed the pass and hurried from the room. Nick would be pissed that she didn't take the notes with her though Eve figured he would finagle a way to get to them before Mr. Orso found them.

From the classroom, she heard the scrape of a chair and heavy footsteps. "Sit down, Nick," came Mr. Orso's booming voice. "You can see your girlfriend later."

In the empty corridor, she reviewed her options. She could go to the nurse's office and feign illness though she really didn't feel great. Her head pounded from lack of sleep and her heart hammered with worry. The nurse's office was the first place Nick would look for her. She could go hide out in the girls' bathroom for a while but Nick would look for her there too.

Eve approached the art room and paused in the doorway. The room was filled with several tables that sat six students each. The concrete block walls were covered in students' artwork. There were self-portraits done in the style of Picasso and brightly colored tessellations and Neo-pop realistic pen and ink drawings. On the cluttered shelves were ceramic Faberge eggs and papier-mâché sculptures.

The room looked empty and Eve decided she could hide out here until the bell rang and then head to her next class. Nick would probably come looking for her there too.

"Eve?" A soft voice came from behind. "Are you looking for me?"

Eve turned around to find Miss Cress looking at her expectantly. Eve had taken an art class as a freshman and was hopelessly inept at drawing a straight line or any line for that matter, but it didn't matter. Eve loved the class or rather loved Miss Cress.

"Come on in," Miss Cress said to Eve. "You can help me set up for class." This was another thing about Miss Cress. She seemed to know what you needed even if you didn't. Eve followed her into the classroom. Jazz was playing in the background and the smell of paint and clay and dried flowers filled her nose.

"How about passing these out for me?" Miss Cress handed Eve a stack of heavy paper and Eve began to place one at each seat. "What brings you to my neck of the woods?" Miss Cress asked as she followed behind Eve with a box filled with jars of ink and narrow wooden skewer sticks.

Eve shrugged. What was she supposed to say? That her boyfriend could be scary? That her mother slapped her and her sister was exhausting? That she thought her neighbor was hitting on her? That her best friend was mad at her and might be involved with an older man? No way.

Eve finished passing out the papers and Miss Cress pointed to a table where jars filled with water sat. Eve picked up two jars at a time and began placing them in the center of the other tables. "Have any fun holiday plans?" Miss Cress asked.

"Not really," Eve murmured as she arranged the wooden skewers and paintbrushes just to the left of each paper. She felt like she was setting a table for dinner. "Just Christmas with my mom and sister."

"Listen, Eve," Miss Cress said, "if something is going on, you know you can talk to me."

Eve hesitated. "I don't know what to think anymore," she said, trying to keep back the tears. "I don't know if I'm making too big of a deal out of something."

Miss Cress twisted her hair into a tight knot and using one of the paintbrushes as a hair clip, fastened it into place at the back of her head. "If you're worried about something then you're not making too big of a deal—sometimes saying the words out loud helps."

"It's a lot of things. It's just really complicated. I think I'm in over my head," Eve said, using Maggie's words. "I'm not sure if I should say anything. People could get hurt."

"Eve, but if someone is hurting you, physically or emotionally, I can help." Miss Cress gave her a sad smile. "You deserve the best, you know."

Eve felt her face grow hot. Miss Cress was the second person who told her this today but why did it sound so different coming from her mouth than Cam Harper's? "It's not like that, really. I'm fine. I'm worried about someone else. I just... I'm sorry I even mentioned it. It wasn't anything."

"Hey, Eve," came a voice from the hallway and Eve stiffened. "What are you doing in here? I thought you were sick." It was Nick. Why couldn't he just leave her alone?

Miss Cress put a protective arm around Eve's shoulder. "Aren't you supposed to be in class?" she asked.

"I just wanted to make sure she was okay. Are you okay, Eve?" Nick asked gently. He was so good at making sure that adults saw this side of him. Attentive, affable.

"I'm better now," Eve said, not quite able to meet Nick's gaze.

"Good. I'll walk you to class." Nick reached for her hand. "Come on. Let's go." Eve took a step forward but Miss Cress stepped between the two of them.

"I asked Eve to help me out for a minute," she said and the bell trilled, signaling that it was time to move on to the next class. "You better get going, Nick," Miss Cress said. "You'll be late for your next final." With a scowl, Nick stomped down the hallway. Nick wouldn't openly defy a teacher. He might slash her tires in the dark of night, but he wouldn't argue with Miss Cress in public.

"You better get to your next class too," she said to Eve. "You're going to miss your test."

"Can I stay here for a while?" Eve asked hopefully. "I'll talk to my teacher. She'll let me make up my test. I just can't concentrate right now."

Miss Cress hesitated but then nodded. "Do you want to

tidy up the supply closet for me? I've been meaning to do it for ages."

"Sure," Eve said. "Thank you."

Eve stepped into the dimly lit supply closet as the classroom flooded with students and their happy chatter. In a few hours it would be holiday break and they would all bolt from the school to their own homes, their own lives. Despite her trepidation about Nick and the fights with her mom and sister, an almost childlike excitement wrapped itself around her. Eve knew she wasn't going to get much for Christmas, but she would get a book or a pair of silly socks and they would make homemade pizza for dinner. Maybe it would be a happy Christmas this year. That's all Eve really hoped for.

Eve spent the next forty-five minutes organizing paint bottles, reams of paper and boxes filled with random art supplies. A student came to the closet. "Miss Cress was wondering if you can find another box of ink in here."

Eve scanned the shelves for the box filled with jars of ink and found it next to bottles of paint and glue. She wrestled the box down, turned to go back into the classroom. Miss Cress was standing at her desk, phone pressed against her ear, her face tight with concern. She murmured a few words into the receiver and then hung up and her eyes landed on Eve.

"Eve," she said, "you need to go to the office right away. It's about your sister, but let's plan on touching base right after school. Come back to my room after the final bell and we'll talk for a few minutes in private, okay? We need to talk about Nick."

Eve stepped from the supply closet and nodded but she wasn't scared or worried. Nola must have done something to get into trouble. Maybe she exacted revenge against the kids on the bus or got kicked out of class for mouthing off to a teacher. Eve didn't know, but whatever it was, it was usually Nola's fault.

She handed the box of ink to Miss Cress and slunk from the room. Miss Cress followed her out to the hallway. "Do you want me to walk with you to the office?" she asked. "In case Nick shows up?"

Eve shook her head. "No, I'm fine."

"Okay, if you're sure." Miss Cress looked at her face carefully for confirmation. Eve nodded. "Remember to stop back and see me later, okay?" she said with concern. "We'll talk some more."

Eve told her she would and moved down the hallway toward the office. Eve was in no hurry. She was always reminding herself that Nola's emergencies weren't her own. She knew the drill. The middle school office would try to call Eve's mother at work with no luck. Then they would call the high school and the office would summon Eve.

Eve's mother had no problem ignoring a call from school administration but for reasons unknown to Eve, her mother would return a call from her within five minutes. Eve figured she should have felt flattered.

Eve felt a forceful tug at her elbow and she realized her mistake. She shouldn't have dawdled. "Hey," Nick said, spinning Eve around to face him. "What the hell is up with you?" he asked. He was smiling but it was strained and his fingers dug into her skin. "Why are you avoiding me?"

"I've got to get to the office," Eve said, wriggling out of his grip and continuing quickly down the hallway. "Something happened with my sister."

"What? Was she like in an accident or something?" he asked. Eve was taken aback. Usually Nick couldn't care less about Nola.

"I don't know, I don't know," Eve said, her voice high and shrill.

"It's probably nothing, like usual. Are you coming over after school?" Nick said. He sounded put out. Did he not remember this morning and the way he grabbed her in the middle of the street in front of Mr. Harper? Did he really think everything was okay?

Eve stopped suddenly and looked up at him in disbelief. "Nick," she said. "Something happened to my sister. I'm not thinking about after-school plans. I'm not thinking about anything but Nola. Besides, you were a jerk this morning."

Nick stared down at her as if he couldn't believe what was coming out of her mouth. She never talked back to him. His slack-faced surprise quickly turned to anger. "You're the one screwing the old guy and I'm the jerk?" He looked her up and down. "You'll be back." Nick's shoulder grazed Eve's as he brushed past her, knocking her off balance, and she tripped into the lockers.

Eve knew she should stay quiet, just let him walk away but she couldn't help herself. Resentment bubbled caustically through her. Maggie's prediction that Eve would end up getting back together with him kept running through her mind. "And I told you," she spat at his back, "I can't see you anymore. I can't. I'm not coming over after school. I'm not coming over ever."

Nick stopped in his tracks, his back stiffening. He turned back toward Eve. A ruddy tint spread across his face and he looked around to see if anyone heard how Eve had spoken to him. The corridor was empty. His eyes narrowed and in two long steps he was in front of Eve, boxing her in against a locker. The smell of his cologne was overwhelming, nauseating. The hard metal of a locker handle dug into her back and her books tumbled to the ground. A red piece of paper fluttered from the book that Maggie had lent her and spun lazily to the ground. "What did you say?" he asked, his voice low, angry.

Eve didn't speak. It was better to keep quiet. No matter what Eve said it would just make him angrier. He hooked a finger onto her turtleneck and pulled down, exposing her neck and the spot where he left the hickey. He ran a finger along the bruise as if admiring his handiwork. In that moment, Eve hated him and promised herself that she would never let him touch her again.

"Meet me at my car after school. Don't make me come looking for you," he said as he nuzzled his face against her neck.

"Eve, come on now," a voice rang out. "Your mom is on the phone. She needs to talk to you about your sister." It was Ms. Reiss, the school secretary. "Hurry along." From her vantage point she couldn't see how Nick had Eve pinned against the locker, that he was holding her wrist so tight that it was growing numb from lack of circulation.

"Coming," Eve said, trying to keep her voice even, confident.

Nick held her there for a moment longer before grabbing her by the face, his fingers digging into her cheeks. She wanted to bite his face off. "Don't fuck with me, Eve," he hissed into her ear and then let her go.

Eve pushed past him and bent down to gather up her books and the red piece of paper that had fluttered to the ground. It was in the shape of a bird. Eve didn't pause to look too closely at it but slid it back into the book and rushed the rest of the way down the hallway and through the office doors where Ms. Reiss was waiting for her. "Your mom is on line one," she said, pointing to the phone on the counter.

Eve picked up the receiver and pressed the flashing button. "Mom?" she asked. "What do you want?"

"It's Nola," her mother said and from the panic in her voice, for a moment Eve began to think that something bad might have happened. But drama was a given with Nola. Their mother didn't help things with her overreactions.

"What happened?" Eve asked, checking the clock.

"She didn't show up to school. They have no idea where she is." Her mother was on the verge of tears.

Eve let out a sigh. "I'm sure she's fine," she said. Nola had run off before. "She's probably hiding out at the library. She'll come to school or home when she calms down."

"I've called the library. They haven't seen her. No one has." Charlotte's voice rose. "She's gone, Eve! No one knows where she is. What if something bad happened? What if she's hurt? I need you to go look for her."

"Mom," Eve began to protest but her mother interrupted.

"I can't miss any more work. I don't have any more personal time for the year or sick days," Charlotte said. "I'd leave if I could, but I can't. You have to go, Eve. I'm so worried. You know she hates missing school."

Her mother was right about that.

But still, Eve wasn't really concerned. Nola was just off pouting somewhere, licking her wounds. She would show up sooner than later. "I can't just leave," Eve whined, aware that Ms. Reiss was listening from her spot behind the counter. Eve turned away from her and lowered her voice. "Seriously, Mom, I've got a class." The office door opened and Shaun O'Keefe walked in, gave her a little wave and stopped to wait for Ms. Reiss at the counter.

"Eve," her mother begged, her voice loud enough for Shaun and Ms. Reiss to hear. "I need you to go look for her. I don't have a good feeling about this."

"Fine," Eve snapped and held out the phone to Ms. Reiss. "I have to go," Eve said. "I don't know if I'll be back today."

"Are you okay?" Ms. Reiss asked, taking the phone from her hand. Eve nodded and rushed from the office more from embarrassment than concern for Nola.

Though Eve didn't want to risk running into Nick, she had to stop at her locker and grab her coat. She scanned the hallway for any sign of him but the coast was clear.

"Hey, are you okay?" came a voice from behind her. Shaun again. Great. Everyone wanted a front row seat for the Knox family freak show.

"Yeah," Eve said. "My stupid sister took off. My mom wants me to go look for her." She paused in front of her locker. "They drive me crazy."

"I'll help you look," Shaun offered as Eve fumbled with her combination.

"That's okay," Eve said, opening her locker door and pulling out her coat. She was mortified.

"Seriously," Shaun said as they walked down the hallway toward the front doors. "I just finished my last final for the day. I can leave." He smiled at her. A soft smile so different than Nick's mean smirk. Shaun, while not nearly as handsome as Nick, had a kind, sweet face.

Eve was tempted but no, Nola had always been something that she had to deal with on her own. "Thanks, but I'm good," Eve said as they paused at the exit. "I'll see you after break. Have a good Christmas."

"You too," Shaun said. And that was all. He stepped aside to let her pass but when she looked behind her, down the hallway, there was Nick again. Always there. Always watching.

MAGGIE
KENNEDY-O'KEEFE

Tuesday, June 16, 2020

When I arrive at the hospital in Willow Creek I'm surprised to see that Shaun is already here to meet the ambulance.

"I called a friend in the fire department," Shaun says as they wheel me into an examination room. "He told me that you were on your way here."

Shaun holds my hand as the ER doctor squeezes a curlicue of gel on my belly and skates the transducer across it. I hold my breath as we wait for the sound waves to be collected and transmit on the screen. Finally, the pixels arrange themselves into a recognizable shape and the first thing I see is the open and closing fist of a beating heart, the thump filling my ears like a psalm. Tears slide from my eyes, rinsing the soot from my face and onto the pillow in ashy streaks.

"She looks perfect," the doctor says with a smile. My breath releases in a stream and Shaun lowers his head to my chest in relief. "Strong heartbeat," the doctor says, "amniotic fluid looks good and she's just the right size for thirty-two weeks."

"Thank you," I say to the doctor. "Thank you so much." My voice is thick with emotion.

"We'll get those burns of yours tended to and then you can

hit the road," the doctor says. "And stay away from burning buildings."

Thirty minutes later Shaun and I are walking hand in hand to his truck. As he helps me into the passenger side seat, I see Nola hurrying across the parking lot. A smile plays on her lips and her step is light. She looks happy. She must have gotten good news about her mother. We both got good news today.

"I don't like that you have to deal with her," Shaun says, staring at Nola as she climbs into her own car.

I can barely deal with the fact that the barn nearly collapsed on me during the fire; there's no way I'm going to bring up the files right now. Instead I close my eyes and by the time we hit the Willow Creek city limits I'm dozing. Twenty minutes later, I'm awakened as Shaun steers the truck down our bumpy lane. Deep ruts in the grass from the fire trucks crisscross the property. The air still smells like a barbecue and vapor rises from the blackened remains of the barn in smoky fingers. "At least it didn't reach the orchard," I say glumly.

"Yeah," Shaun agrees. "Are you okay with staying at the house tonight?" he asks.

"Because of the fire?" I ask. "I'm okay. Are you?"

"Could be arson," he says as he pulls up to the front door. "You said so yourself."

"I'm a cop, Shaun," I say tiredly. "And we don't know that it's arson. Not yet anyway." I don't tell him that I have the same inkling. Though I don't have the details regarding accelerants and burn patterns of our fire, I do know that the other arsons have involved old structures in rural, out-of-the-way spots. "I'll call the fire marshal tomorrow when I go to work," I say. "Hopefully he'll be able to give us some more info."

"You're going into work tomorrow?" Shaun asks in surprise. "Don't you think you should take it easy for a few days?"

"The doctor said I'm fine. The baby's fine," I say, shaking my head. Shaun steps from the truck and comes around and opens my door. I see the concern on his face. "How about we see how I feel in the morning," I tell him, leaning in for a kiss. "I promise that if I'm any bit tired I will stay home in bed."

"Fair enough," Shaun acquiesces and holds out his hand to help me down.

We go inside and the cats are there to greet us, as is an answering machine filled with messages. A few are friends checking in on us because of the fire but there are dozens accusing me of adultery and all sorts of awful things.

"What's going on?" Shaun asks after we listen to the final message. "You have something you need to tell me?" he says with a small laugh.

"I have no idea what's happening," I say, pressing the heels of my hands into my eyes, trying to stanch the tears that are beginning to form. "You know I would never cheat on you," I tell Shaun.

"I know that," he says gently. "But first the fire and now these phone calls. It can't be a coincidence. Do you think it has to do with Eve's case?"

"Maybe," I admit.

"Walk away," Shaun says as he hands me a glass of ice water for my sore throat. "You don't have to do this. Give the case to someone else. No one could blame you for taking a step back."

"I can't do that." I shake my head. "It's probably just some guy I pissed off when I busted him. It will blow over," I say but the tremble in my voice gives me away. The fire, the bird on my windshield, the phone calls. Bad things happen in threes.

"Really, Maggie?" Shaun yanks open the refrigerator and pulls out a bottle of beer. "You could have been killed in that fire. Our baby could have been killed. And you're blaming this on *some guy*." Shaun twists the cap from the bottle and tosses it to the kitchen counter and we stare at each other from behind our drinks.

I sigh, set my glass down and go to Shaun and he wraps his arms around me. "I couldn't stand the thought of something happening to you and the baby," he murmurs into my hair.

"When I saw those flames, when the barn ceiling started coming down, I was really scared," I admit.

"Then please step aside. At least for now," Shaun begs.

At this moment, I want so badly to do just this, but I can't. Being a cop isn't just a job, it's who I am. I take a deep breath and lean back so I can look Shaun in the eyes. "Let's see what the arson investigator finds out and go from there. As for the phone calls, they're just calls. They're harmless."

"I hope you're right," Shaun says, shaking his head and walking away.

"Me too," I whisper as I move through the house to double-check that the windows and doors are locked.

NOLA KNOX

Wednesday, June 17, 2020

Nola woke up and padded into the bathroom, bleary-eyed. She pulled the box from its plastic bag and squinted at the directions. She had chosen the shade that most closely matched Eve's hair color—Sedona Sunset. It only took thirty minutes or so for her to transform from a blonde to redhead. It was really quite remarkable, she thought after she dried and straightened her hair. Nola and Eve could never have been mistaken for twins by any means, but the essence was there, Nola thought as she stared into the mirror. Close enough for people to do a double take. That's all she wanted.

Nola dressed and ate breakfast then glanced down at the mewling cat in the kennel. She rummaged through the canned goods until she found a can of tuna. The cat hissed and clawed at her when she opened the carrier to slide in the can and fresh water. She was hoping to deal with the cat today but had to head to the vet clinic to perform the postmortem on the horse from the other day.

She drove to the clinic and was met with curious stares by the other staff members. Nola barely combed her hair, let alone colored it. "It suits you," said the receptionist. "I like it."

Nola smiled and thanked her though approval wasn't really what she was looking for and the clinic staff wasn't her intended audience. That would come later.

Nola scrubbed in and stepped into the large animal surgery suite to find Bijou there waiting for her. Even in death Bijou was a beautiful animal. But she hadn't been cared for the way she should have been.

The owner had requested the necropsy after Bijou had died. For insurance purposes, he said. Horse necropsies tended to be rare. They were expensive so Nola was happy to take on the task.

She already knew how Bijou had died. Technically, it was the injection of sodium pentobarbital she had given the suffering horse the other day. But in reality it was the idiot rancher and his daughter. Their inadequate care of Bijou was the real cause. Nola was just trying to ease the animal's suffering but she couldn't very well put that detail in the necropsy report. Instead, Nola sliced open Bijou to reveal what was obvious—the horse had a twisted bowel. She would have died eventually anyway.

Nola examined every part of Bijou's body. She scanned the abdomen and chest for any sign of abnormalities; she collected tissue and blood samples and examined them beneath a microscope and noted her findings. Since Nola had postgraduate residency training in pathology, she wouldn't need to send the samples off to another lab to be tested for pathogens or toxicants. No one needed to know about the sodium pentobarbital.

Next Nola prepared the carcass for disposal. Since she euthanized with the pentobarbital, Nola wouldn't be able to extract the tiny ear bones. Bijou was toxic. Too bad, she thought. She didn't have a horse in her collection.

While she worked, Nola thought of her mother. Charlotte wasn't all that different than Bijou after all. Ill and destined to die younger than she should. Charlotte was suffering, had a long recovery in front of her. Perhaps Nola would stop by the hospital after she was finished here. Twice in one week. Charlotte would be so excited to see her.

MAGGIE KENNEDY-O'KEEFE

Despite all my bravado I get little sleep. Every time I close my eyes I see orange flames behind my lids, I can feel the heat and hear the growl of the fire as it tears through the barn, can smell the acrid scent of burning wood. In my dream, I'm not pregnant anymore and I'm desperate to find my baby. I run from the barn, the blaze close at my heels and I find myself at Ransom Caves. When I step inside, the cavern is pitch-black but the air is blissfully cool. In the distance, the cry of an infant echoes off the rocky walls. My baby. I flounder through the dark trying to find the source of the crying that morphs into the high-pitched trill of a telephone.

At six, when the alarm goes off, it's a relief to slide out of bed. My muscles are sore and my throat still aches so I decide to compromise with Shaun and spend the morning taking it easy.

While Shaun is off cleaning up the mess from the fire, I sit in a rocking chair in the baby's bedroom. I stare at the crib that I assembled and buttery yellow walls that Shaun painted. I doze, my hands cradling my belly and I can't believe how soon I'll be able to hold her in my arms.

I also can't believe how close the baby and I came to being

seriously injured in the fire. Just the thought of it brings tears to my eyes. As a police officer I know that danger lurks around every corner. I know that there is no way that I will be able to protect my baby from all the bad in the world. But I have to try. That's what cops do. What moms do.

At eleven thirty, I heave myself out of the rocking chair, get into my car and make the drive to the police station. I'm on high alert, keeping an eye out for anything out of the ordinary but see nothing unusual. It doesn't make any sense, the origami bird, the phone calls, the fire. I'm not ready to say out loud that the three might be connected but I can't help feeling like I'm being targeted.

I have to tread lightly here. If I'm wrong, the chief might pull me from Eve's case. I don't want that. When I arrive at the station I decide to park in a spot where I know the security camera is pointed, just in case.

The squad room is buzzing. There is a constant ringing of phones. Tips in Eve's case. An officer is clicking away on his keyboard, a phone receiver beneath his chin, and another is speaking loudly into the phone trying to talk over the annoying groan of the ancient copy machine. Francis is staring intently at his computer screen. A few people stop and ask me about the fire and how I'm doing. I assure them that I'm just fine and make a beeline for my office.

My phone is also ringing and after talking to a woman who is positive her ex-husband was the one who killed Eve, I listen to a confession to Eve's murder from a boy who sounds like he's no more than sixteen. I also get a handful of calls from someone who calls me a bitch and a whore and I'm tempted to trace the calls and arrest the caller for harassment. No time to do that now though.

I think about taking my phone off the hook but instead I try to call the fire marshal and end up leaving a message. I hang up and drop the origami figure on my desk and pull out

Eve's case folders. I stare at them, trying to decide what I'm going to tackle first. I can't deal with the bird in my view, so I stick it in my bottom desk drawer.

I turn my attention to the interview Ms. Reiss did with the police after Eve died. According to her, on the day Eve died Shaun walked out of the school just after Eve did. Shaun was a senior when we were sophomores and while he knew me as the police chief's daughter, we never interacted. He didn't give me a second look until years later in the grocery store. After the fire, Shaun's name in the police file doesn't seem all that important anymore but I'm still pissed he didn't tell me about it.

I call his cell and he answers on the first ring.

"Maggie, is everything okay?" he asks.

"Everything's fine," I say. "I was just going through some files on Eve's case and your name was mentioned."

"My name?" he asks in surprise. "Why?" I read him the quote from Ms. Reiss saying that she had seen him leaving the school with Eve.

When he doesn't say anything I tell myself that this one piece of paper probably means nothing. Ms. Reiss misspoke or misinterpreted. I remind myself the man I'm talking to is my husband, not some suspect to interrogate.

"I didn't know you knew Eve," I say.

"I *knew of* her. Grotto High isn't that big of a school, you know."

"You never mentioned her. Not once. You never told me you had a class together," I say. I'm trying to keep my voice easy, neutral. It's hard.

"What are you trying to say here, Maggie?" Shaun asks. I hear the hurt in his voice.

"I want to know why you didn't tell me about this," I say. "I want to know why I have to read that you knew my best friend, who was murdered, in a police report."

167

"Maggie..." Shaun begins but I keep going.

"Of all the times that I cried to you about Eve and all the times I told you about how much I missed her. You never once told me that you knew her, let alone that you talked to her on the day she died."

"That's because it wasn't a big deal, Maggie," he says. "We were in the office at the same time on that day. We talked."

"Jesus, Shaun," I say in frustration.

"And I told the police about it," he says defensively. "You're more worried about it than they were." He's mad now. I can't blame him. This conversation isn't going the way I hoped.

"You need an alibi for me for that day?" His voice rises. "Well, it was just before Christmas, right? Then I was at the tree farm loading Christmas trees onto the tops of people's cars. I'm sure I can line up some witnesses if I need to. Is that what you want?"

"No, no, Shaun. I'm sorry," I say. "I'm not accusing you of anything. I was surprised to see your name and I'm following up. It's my job to find out what people might know about Eve's last day."

"There's nothing more to know, Maggie," Shaun says. "But it's always fun to be interrogated by my wife. I've got to get back to work." He hangs up.

I screwed that up, I think, but I still don't understand why he never mentioned it and I wonder what he and Eve talked about that day. His interview from back then must be somewhere in the mess of paperwork.

Twenty-five years later and I'm still sticking my foot in my mouth. The morning of my fight with Eve, I had looked for her at school hoping to apologize for how mean I'd been to her. I never got the chance.

As I pick up the phone to call Shaun back and apologize I sense someone watching me and look up.

"Hey, Maggie," Francis says from the doorway. I bite back a sigh. "Got a minute?" he asks.

"Yeah, what is it?" I ask, setting down my phone and shoving my desk drawer shut.

"There's something on the department's Facebook page that I think you need to see."

"Is it a tip in the Knox case?" I ask. "If it is, write it down and I'll add it to the hundreds of other ones that have been coming in."

"It's not that," Francis says. Something in his voice makes me take a closer look at his face. He's uncharacteristically serious. Nervous.

"What is it?" I ask. "Show me." Francis pulls up a chair and I turn my computer screen his way and push my keyboard toward him. He brings up the Grotto Police Department Facebook page and scrolls down to a post that features a picture of me. It's an old photo and I'm wearing my dress blues. "What am I looking at here, Francis?" I ask.

"It's the link and the comments beneath your picture," Francis says. "I thought you should know."

"Know what?" I ask, losing patience.

He points the cursor at the link and I feel his eyes on me as I read. *Police officer Maggie O'Keefe is supposed to be protecting the community but instead she is...*

"Click on it," I order. Francis does and a website fills the page. The banner reads *WreckedNest.com* and features an illustration of a bird's nest with cracked eggs. "Oh my God," I say as I read. *Police officer Maggie O'Keefe is supposed to be protecting the community but instead she is sleeping with married men. I came home early from work one afternoon and found Maggie O'Keefe and my husband in our bed. This is not okay! Let the Grotto Police Department know that one of their own is screwing around on the clock and ruining marriages while she's at it.*

"This isn't true." I look up at Francis. "This is a lie! Take it off. Delete it." The comments are just about as bad as the article. There are calls for me to be fired. I'm called every name in the book: bitch, slut, skank, home wrecker and worse.

"I can take it off our page," he says, clicking back to Facebook, "but it's been shared dozens of times and it will still be on this website."

There's more. I scan the rest of the page and am horrified to see my home phone number is listed for the entire world to see. I think of all the phone calls we've been getting. All the nasty things the callers are saying. It all makes sense now. "Take it off!" I say again frantically.

Francis taps the keyboard and the link disappears. My brain is reeling. It's not true. I would never cheat on Shaun. "Who would do this?" I ask Francis helplessly. "Why?"

"I don't know," Francis says. He's embarrassed for me. "Police officers make enemies out of a lot of people. I'm sure it's someone just thinking they're being funny."

"It's not funny!" I say. "Is there a way you can find out who posted it?"

"Yes," Francis says. "But chances are it's a fake account. I can ask IT to look into it."

"It's gone, right?" My voice is shaking.

"Like I said, it's off the Facebook page, but it's not gone. It's still on this website. Are you alright?" Francis asks as he stands. "Do you want me to say something to the chief?"

"No!" I exclaim. I refuse to cry in front of Francis. "I'll do it if this doesn't blow over. Like you said, we piss people off all the time. Some idiot thought he was being funny. If I make a big deal out of it, they win."

Francis hovers in the doorway.

"I'm fine, Francis," I say, clearing my throat. I busy myself with looking through Eve's files but still he lingers. "Seriously, Francis, you can go now."

Once he leaves, it's all I can do to hold it together. The fire, Eve's case, this. It's all too much.

I've decided that all I can do is throw myself into Eve's case knowing that I will have to talk to Shaun about everything sooner than later.

I've barely made a dent in organizing the files but at least I'm getting somewhere. I create two documents on my laptop. The first is an index to inventory all the different reports I come across. I enter the type of report—interviews, lab reports, photos and so on, and then note which binder, section and page number they're on.

This way I'll be able to quickly find a report that I need to refer to without having to dig through binders and boxes. I also create a media section. Peppered throughout the files are newspaper clippings that discuss the case so I make note of where I can find these if I need to.

I go back to my laptop and a wash of memories flows over me. Eve and I huddled together over a fashion magazine. Eve braiding my unruly hair into a French braid. Eve and I down at the caves on hot summer afternoons talking about boys, our parents, school and about nothing at all. And Nola is always there, on the edges, lurking.

Stuck among some random paperwork, I finally find the list of the evidence collected at the crime scene. This is what I've been looking for. I scan the items and nothing unusual jumps out at me. All of Eve's clothing is listed: the second-hand pair of brand-name jeans that she had bought at the thrift store, her boot, socks, underwear, bra, sweater, a light jacket.

Then it hits me. What I found odd about the crime scene photos. Eve wasn't wearing her scarf. She wore that thing all winter long. With a coat, without a coat, it was always hanging around her neck. She should have been wearing it.

I remember her wearing it the day she died. I flip back to the crime scene photos to take a look.

It's not there. It doesn't make sense. I push away from the table and stand up. I blink back tears. How Eve loved that scarf. I remember the day we found it at the secondhand store. I told her it was hideous but she said it was beautiful.

That was just like Eve. She saw something or someone who was different or damaged and took him or her under her wing with little or no forethought. She always fought for the underdog. Case in point—Nola. Even if it was true Nola could fend for herself. Eve just didn't want Nola to have to. I look back through all the crime scene photos just to be sure. It's not there.

Then I skim back through my dad's notes until I find a notation in his messy handwriting: *Charlotte Knox and others indicate that Eve often wore a multicolored knit scarf. The scarf wasn't found at the scene nor with her belongings at home. Did killer take it with him? Poss. trophy?*

My phone rings again. I'm tempted to ignore it but I know I can't.

"This is Maggie O'Keefe," I say cautiously into the receiver.

"Maggie," my brother says. "Dad took off."

"What do you mean, he took off?" I ask. "Where would he have gone?"

"I don't know." Colin sounds panicked. "Leanne is beside herself. She says she went inside to get Dad's medicine and when she came back out to the porch he was gone."

"He probably just went for a walk. Have you gone looking for him?" I try to keep the irritation out of my voice. I'm honestly not alarmed. Our dad has taken off before; he never goes far.

"Of course I went looking for him," Colin snaps. "I've been looking for him for the last thirty minutes. I wouldn't call you if it wasn't important."

I prop my elbow on my desk and lower my forehead into my hand.

Just outside my office door the phones are ringing in a constant cacophony. I should be answering phones, I should be in the evidence room preparing to send the samples from Eve's case off to the lab, I should be looking into the arson files to see if there is a connection to the fire at our place. But something in Colin's voice tells me that he truly believes my dad is in trouble.

"I'm sorry," I sigh. "I'll be right over." Colin hangs up without saying goodbye. He's pissed and I can't blame him. I've been so caught up in my own personal dramas that I haven't been paying attention to the people I need to. My family.

I grab my keys and head to the elevator. When I reach my car I'm relieved to find there's no note on my windshield to greet me.

When I pull up to my dad's house, Cam Harper is just pulling out of his driveway. I park and unlatch my seat belt. The restraint is rubbing against my blistered shoulder. And just like every time I see Cam, a bubble of rage rises in my chest. I remember the first time I noticed him looking at me as something different than his babysitter. I had put the twins to bed hours earlier and I was curled up on the couch watching a movie and trying to keep my eyes open. I didn't even hear them come inside. Mr. Harper jostled my shoulder and I awoke with a start to find him looking down at me. *Wake up, Maggie*, he said. *We're home.* He smelled like cigarettes and alcohol. He held out his hand to help me from the sofa. His fingers were warm and smooth and completely enveloped mine. His eyes never left mine and my skin burned beneath his gaze. It was electric and I went to bed that night with the memory of my hand in his.

It progressed quickly after that. I loved him. And Cam Harper did what any thirtysomething man who is sleeping with a fifteen-year-old does. He manipulated me.

173

I sit there for a moment trying to gather my thoughts. I haven't been inside the Harper house since the night Eve died. In fact, Cam Harper and I haven't spoken since. Though God knows I tried. He tossed me aside like a piece of garbage, which is exactly what I felt like. Now when our paths cross, he doesn't look me in the eye. He doesn't dare.

I throw open my car door and step out into the street. Leanne comes down the porch steps to greet me.

"I'm so sorry," she says tearfully. "I only left him alone for a minute."

"It's okay," I say, placing a hand on her arm. "Don't worry, we'll find him. Where's Colin?"

"He's driving around looking for him," she says. "I'm so sorry," she repeats.

"It's okay, really," I assure her again. "Did you go check with the neighbors?" I scan the street. All is quiet. The trees are still, American flags droop limply from their poles and doors and windows are shut tight to keep out the simmering afternoon heat.

Leanne nods. "I checked with everyone but there." She points to the Knox house. "I saw her drive off in her truck a while ago."

"Stay here and let me go look around," I tell her. I start to make my way over to Nola's house and despite my order for her to stay put, Leanne is right behind me.

The driveway is empty; it doesn't look like Nola is home. The shades are still pulled tight. I knock but there's no answer. I press my ear to the door and listen. I dig into my pocket for my cell phone and call the Knoxes' home phone. It rings and rings and I hear it echo from inside the Knox house. It eventually goes to voice mail and I hang up without leaving a message.

"It doesn't look like he came over here," I tell Leanne. "You go back to the house in case he comes back and I'll go around the back and see if he's wandering around someone's yard." Leanne nods and just as we are walking away, a crash comes from inside the house.

I pound on the door again. "Nola?" I call. "Are you in there? We're looking for my dad." No answer. I give an experimental twist of the door handle. It's not locked.

Because I'm a police officer and I heard a crash, I tell myself it's my duty to go inside and make sure everything is okay.

The muscles in my abdomen tighten and then release. Braxton-Hicks contractions—I've been getting a lot of them lately. They don't hurt, just intermittent reminders that the baby is getting ready to join us on the outside.

"Too soon, Peanut," I murmur to her. I push on the door and it swings open and I step inside.

My senses are assaulted with the scene in front of me. I cover my nose with my hand, my stomach protesting against the rotten, sour smell.

"Oh my God," Leanne breathes as she comes up behind me to get a closer look.

The state of the living room is straight out of *Hoarders* casting. Layers upon layers of junk fill the room. Boxes and baskets crammed with odds and ends are stacked neck high. Newspapers and magazines cover nearly every surface. Bottles of bleach and glass cleaner and laundry soap and rubber gloves are in a jumble in one corner. From somewhere inside the house there is an insistent mewing.

"I have to talk to her," comes a familiar voice.

"Dad?" I say in disbelief and then turn in a slow circle but he's nowhere to be found. It's Leanne who peeks behind the open front door and there is my dad, his back pressed against the wall.

"Dad, what are you doing here?" I ask, my voice sharper than I intend.

For a second, his eyes cloud with shame at being scolded by

his daughter but then it disappears. "I need to talk to Charlotte," he says more forcefully.

"Charlotte's not here. She's in the hospital, remember?" I say and then kick myself. Of course he doesn't remember. "Is Nola here?" I ask. "Did she let you in?"

"I always give Charlotte an update on Friday," my dad insists, running his fingers across his thinning hair. There's a stain on his shirt and he looks exhausted. "I'll just wait until she gets back."

I know that when my dad gets like this it does little good to argue with him. It's better to try to break the persistent loop that plays in his head and redirect the conversation. "That's why she's not here. It's only Wednesday," I say, showing him the calendar icon on my cell phone. "We'll come back on Friday. You can talk to her then."

My dad takes my phone from my hands and examines the display more closely. "Oh," he finally says in a small voice. "I got my days mixed up."

"That's okay," I say, blinking back tears. "I get my days mixed up too sometimes." It's so hard seeing him like this. Confused, unsure of himself.

To Leanne I say, "Can you take him home? I want to make sure everything is closed up tight here. I'll call Colin and say we found him. I'll come in a few minutes."

Leanne places an arm around my dad's waist and steers him through the door. I watch as she leads him across the street and back to the front porch. I do want to make sure that Nola's house is shut up tight but I also want to see the rest of the house. I'm shocked at its condition.

I squeeze through the narrow path that I know leads to the kitchen. The smell is worse in here. The meowing is louder. A small kennel sits by the back door and from inside a cat arches its back and hisses and screeches at me.

Every counter is covered with mounds of mail and dishes

and canned goods. The sink is brimming with forks and spoons and knives. One drawer is pulled open and piled with coffee cups. I open a cupboard—cans of tuna and bags of sugar. I open the oven—again more canned goods. Soup this time. It appears that Charlotte and Nola Knox have a system. I bend over and look in the cupboard beneath the sink and it's filled with the usual: dishwasher liquid, drain opener, rags, garbage bags and carpet cleaner.

I open the door that leads to the basement that is as black as Ransom Caves. I flip the light switch on, hold tightly to the railing and take a few steps downward. It's just as bad as the main floor. Garbage bags and boxes cover every inch. There is a rusty old bicycle sitting in a corner and a treadmill draped with winter coats. I look down. Dark spots dot the steps. Blood from Charlotte Knox's fall? I don't go any farther. The basement is a minefield and I know I need to turn around and head upstairs and back into the kitchen.

I open the refrigerator door and a putrid, rotten odor assaults my nose. It's stuffed with moldy cheese and packages of black lunch meat, shriveled apples and slimy carrots. There's a quart of congealed milk with the lid missing, containers of half-eaten takeout and liquefied heads of lettuce. I gag and slam the door shut and tear from the kitchen, knocking over a pyramid of mason jars that crash to the floor.

Back in the living room, I lean over, hands on my knees and inhale deeply trying to expel the rancid smell. Once the nausea passes I fight the urge to flee the house. How did Eve's mother and sister come to live this way? Though the Knox home was never fancy it was clean and cozy. I always liked spending time here, though we spent most of our time hidden away in Eve's room.

Stacks of books line the staircase and I have to step carefully, clutching onto the railing so I don't tumble backward. *What happened here?* I wonder as I reach the landing to find a mattress and folding chairs leaning against the walls. I barely fit through the narrow pathway to get to Eve's bedroom door.

I'm afraid to open the door, afraid of what I might find. Only the worry that Nola will come home prods me forward and I push the door open and step inside. "Oh," I breathe and spin around slowly. Eve's room hasn't changed a bit and I feel like I'm transported back twenty-five years in time. The small desk where Eve did her homework is still there, her nubby pink cardigan sweater draped over the back of the chair. There was the gray stuffed rabbit with the worn velvet ears that Eve rubbed between her fingers when she was nervous and brought with her to every overnight.

I bite the sides of my cheeks to stave off the tears. A ratty, slightly yellowed white robe hangs on the front of Eve's closet and I brush it aside to open the door. Eve's closet is filled with her secondhand store finds. I smile as I thumb through the jeans and the Grateful Dead and Jimi Hendrix T-shirts. Her shoes are lined up on the floor of the closet and her book bag hangs from a hook on the back of the door. There are half a dozen scarves but not the one she was wearing the day she died.

I glance down. A floral hatbox sits on the floor of the closet. I've been in Eve's room a million times as a kid and I know every inch of the space. Twenty-five years ago there was no hatbox. This wouldn't be remarkable except that everything else in this room has not changed a bit. I give the box a shake and its contents rattle.

"What the hell are you doing in here?" comes a voice and the hatbox tumbles to the ground. My heart lodges in my throat as I swing around to find a redheaded woman standing in the doorway. The box spills open and the ivory-colored items scatter across the hardwood floor. My hand flies to my sidearm, but I had taken it off when I got into my car. The girth of my belly was making it uncomfortable to wear.

The woman is Nola. Nola with red hair. "Nola, I..." I begin but before I can finish she is backing me against the closet door.

"What are you doing in here?" she repeats, her voice shaking with anger. She towers over me and is standing so close that I can see the shiny puckered skin below her collarbone. Scarred from her altercation with Nick Brady years ago.

"Calm down, Nola." I press my palms against her shoulders, trying to make some distance between us. "Back up, I can explain." Nola holds her ground. I'm losing control of the situation. I was caught off guard, in a home I legally have no right to be in, and I'm unarmed. "I mean it, Nola, take a step back, now." Somehow the words come out forcefully, with no tremor or hesitation.

Nola steps back and folds her arms across her chest and looks down at me waiting for an explanation.

"My brother called me. My dad was missing. We came over here and heard a crash. My dad was here. Inside. We got him out quickly, but..." Nola is unmoved by my explanation. "And I thought you might be up here. I didn't want you to be scared." This part is a lie but I couldn't bring myself to tell Nola that I was wandering around her home out of morbid curiosity.

I sidle past Nola and move to Eve's small bookshelf. "I remember when she got that shelf," I say. "She wanted to decoupage it with pictures from old magazines. We cut out pictures and words for hours..." Nola has a cold, unreadable expression on her face. I need to get out of here, now.

"I obviously should have just left and called you from outside," I say contritely.

"Maggie," Nola says in a singsong voice. "Are you in here?"

"What?" I ask in confusion but Nola keeps talking.

"I want to be alone," Nola cries. Her face remains smooth, dispassionate, but her voice cracks with emotion and her eyes are wild and filled with a crazy glint.

"Are you okay?" I ask but she doesn't respond. "I'll go," I say, inching toward the door, eager to get out of the house, but Nola blocks my way.

"Maggie," Nola says as if confused. "What are you doing here? Did you leave the kids all alone?" Her voice has taken on a different quality, one I haven't heard in decades. She sounds just like Eve.

"Let me pass, Nola," I say. She's lost her mind. I never should have come here.

"He'll probably never talk to me again," Nola says, her voice heavy with tears. "Why did you have to come over? You can't tell anyone. You have to promise me."

"Nola, you're not making any sense. Let's go outside. Get some fresh air, talk about this." Even if I get past Nola I have to maneuver my way through the maze of junk. I'm pregnant and slow, there's no way.

"Because it's wrong. I want to help you," Nola says in Eve's voice. "It's going to be okay, Maggie, we can work this out together."

Then her tone changes again, becomes venomous. "It's not okay and I don't want to work it out. Eve, I'm pregnant. I need to figure out how to tell him," she pretends to sob. "You ruined it. You ruined everything. I hate you for this, Eve. I hate you."

Realization begins to sweep over me. I've heard this conversation before. I was part of this conversation. The baby gives a sudden kick as if prodding me forward. I have to get out of this room, out of this house. I feign moving left in hopes that Nola will shift that way and I can run past her but she stays put. I can't catch my breath and tiny pricks of light dance in front of my eyes. I sway on my feet and sink down on the edge of Eve's bed.

Nola glowers down at me. "I saw you and Eve at the caves that day. I know what you did to her, Maggie. I saw everything and heard everything. I was there."

EVE KNOX

Friday, December 22, 1995
11:00 a.m.

Eve searched each one of Nola's usual haunts. First she checked the library, Nola's second home. She moved past a blue Schwinn bicycle propped against the side of the building. Odd, she thought. You didn't see very many bikes out in the middle of winter. Eve stepped into the library vestibule and peered through the glass doors hoping she'd spy Nola right off since she had a feeling that Nola wouldn't be so easily extracted from her spot among the shelves today.

Eve pushed through the doors in resignation. Walking into the Grotto Public Library was a bit strange, like walking uninvited into someone's home. The building, the former residence of a wealthy Grotto family, was donated to the city for the express purpose of housing books. Each room held a different section of the Dewey Decimal System. Books on philosophy and religion in the master bedroom. Applied and natural sciences in the dining room. Social sciences and languages in the family room and so on.

Eve breathed in the dry, dusty smell of old paper. Nola wasn't the only one who liked to read. Eve read, just not the thick, boring reference books that Nola was obsessed with. Eve preferred romances and sweeping historical sagas.

The space that was once a parlor now held the circulation

desk where patrons checked out their books. Standing behind the desk was Rita, the librarian. She glanced up from the pile of books in front of her. "I haven't seen Nola today," she said, smiling apologetically at Eve. Rita was used to Eve coming in and hunting for her sister. "I may have missed her though. It's been kind of busy today."

"I'll go take a quick look," Eve said.

The library's former dining room alone was larger than the entire first floor of the Knox home and still it was crammed with books. Dimly lit with rows of floor-to-ceiling bookshelves, it was difficult to see if anyone else was in the room with her. A perfect hiding place for Nola.

Eve walked down the length of the room, her footfalls muffled by the worn, frayed carpet. She glanced down the narrow stacks. Usually Nola could be found sitting cross-legged, her back pressed up against the shelves that held books about anatomy and physiology, with a heavy science text on her lap. *Nola*, Eve would say in exasperation and Nola would take her time reading to the end of the page before looking up. *Mom says it's time to come home now*, Eve would grouch.

Nola would get to her feet and carefully, lovingly, replace the book in its rightful spot on the shelf. Eve's irritation never lasted very long. It was hard to get too mad at Nola when she lost track of time at the library. It meant that she wasn't antagonizing anyone else for the time being. But today there was no sign of Nola.

Eve turned to leave when at the far end of the room something caught her eye before it quickly disappeared behind a shelf. Was Nola playing a childish game of hide-and-seek? This was exactly what she would pull. Eve was having none of it.

She retraced her steps in hopes of cornering Nola before she could escape but as she hurried down the rows she saw that they were empty. Eve had been certain that someone was in the room with her. She should have parked herself in front of the exit and waited for Nola to appear. She couldn't stay hidden forever.

Instead, Eve found herself in a far corner of the stacks opposite the exit, out of breath and sweating beneath her coat and scarf. "This is so stupid," Eve muttered, deciding she'd had enough. There was no reasoning with Nola when she got like this, so it was useless to try to track her down.

Once again, Eve headed down one of the rows toward the exit when the damp, acrid scent of unwashed clothing pricked at her nose. Eve stopped short. Someone else was in the room with her, but not Nola. A barb of fear swept through Eve and she swung her head around, sure that someone was directly behind her. There was no one.

The foul odor grew stronger and Eve slowly turned toward the shelf of books to her right and staring back at her between the spines was one rheumy blue eye and a gray stubbled cheek. The man reached his tobacco-stained fingers across the shelf and stroked Eve's hand. A yelp of fear leapt from Eve's throat. She forced her legs to move and in a matter of seconds she was across the room and out of the room. Heart hammering, she made a beeline to the circulation desk.

"No luck?" Rita asked.

"No," Eve said as the man from the stacks emerged carrying an armful of books. Her stomach churned at the thought of his grimy, rough fingers on her skin. The man, tall, bone thin and wearing a grubby red sweatshirt that smelled like damp, rotting wood. "I'm going to go check the bathroom," Eve said and breathed a sigh of relief as the man passed by her without a second look. She had overreacted like always. The man was scruffy looking and had poor hygiene but that didn't make him a serial killer.

Eve made her way to the women's restroom and closed the door firmly behind her. "Nola, are you in here?" she called out. "Mom says you need to get back to school. Now." No answer. "Nola, seriously." Silence. Eve turned to leave, thought better of it and went back inside to check each individual stall. All vacant. Eve opened the bathroom door to find the man in the red sweatshirt was right there staring back at her. Eve slammed the door shut and pressed her back against the door, heart pounding. Surely someone would come along and the man would go away. She would stay in here all day if she had to.

Minutes passed and through the heavy door Eve heard a light tap, tap, tap of someone knocking and felt the door push open. Eve planted her feet and pushed back. The door opened an inch, then two, before the person on the other side gave up and the door closed. Was it the man or someone waiting to use the bathroom? Eve screwed her eyes shut and waited, still pushing against the door. She waited five more minutes and when she cautiously opened the door again, the man was gone.

With relief, Eve walked slowly back down the steps to the circulation desk. "I'll be sure to tell Nola you're looking for her," Rita assured her.

"Thanks," Eve sighed. "But she might not listen to you if she knows I'm the one looking for her. Maybe just tell her my mom wants her to call her right away. Technically, that's true. Can I use the phone?"

Rita nodded and Eve reached for the phone and dialed the house number. It rang seven times before the answering machine picked up and her mother's voice came across the line. "Nola," Eve said in a low voice. "If you are home, you better pick up. I mean it. Grow up!"

Eve banged the receiver down harder than she intended and it trilled back at her in protest. Eve looked around, embarrassed, to see if anyone had seen her mini tantrum but she was alone. Her eyes drifted toward Rita's desk and there was the man's pile of books.

Eve ran her finger over the green cover. Why would the man dump his books on the counter? Maybe he had forgotten his library card or maybe he just decided he didn't want to check out these particular books.

Eve had seen this man before. Supposedly homeless and always riding around on his bicycle. Maybe he just wanted to get out of the cold for a little bit. Did Grotto even have any homeless people? Eve considered calling Rita and asking her about the man, if she knew who he was, but then thought better of it. She would sound paranoid. Silly.

Eve tried to push the thought of the strange man out of her head as she stepped back out onto the street but she couldn't help scanning the street in search of his red sweatshirt. A few flurries danced around her head but then the snow abruptly would stop, as if the sky was frozen in indecision. Eve couldn't decide what to do either. Where to look next.

Finally, the cold pushed her into action. She hurried down the street, poking her head in the doorways of businesses and asking if anyone had seen her sister. Everyone knew Nola but no one had seen her that morning. At the pharmacy Eve chose a candy bar from the dusty display and dug into her pocket for a dollar bill to pay the clerk.

He hadn't seen Nola either.

The caves? Eve wondered as she peeled the wrapper from the bar and took a small bite, hoping to make it last as long as possible. Would Nola really run off to sulk in Ransom Caves in the middle of winter? Eve didn't think so. But the caves were secluded and would offer a spot for Nola to be alone and out of the elements. It was worth a look anyway, but after this she was going home.

Eve hunched her shoulders against the rising wind and

headed in the direction of the caves, all the while alert for any sign of Nola or Nick or the man from the library.

Eve heard the rumble of a car behind her but forced herself to ignore it and not let every little sound scare her. She expected the car to speed past her but it continued its slow trek behind her and it was all she could do not to take off running. Instead, she whipped around ready to tell Nick to get lost but the words died on her lips. It was Shaun O'Keefe in his junky pickup truck. He pulled up next to her and leaned over to roll down the passenger side window.

"Any luck?" Shaun asked.

"No," Eve said. "I'm checking one more spot then I'm going home."

"Hop in, I'll drive you," Shaun said.

Eve was tempted. From here, the walk to the caves would take forever. "You don't have to," Eve said. "I'm sure you probably have better things to do."

"Not really. If I go home now I'll have to help load Christmas trees onto people's cars. I'd much rather look with you." Shaun gave Eve a lopsided smile. "Come on, I bet you're freezing."

"I am," Eve admitted and against her better judgment opened the door and stepped up into the truck and slid in next to Shaun.

"Where do you want to go next?" he asked.

What Eve wanted was for Shaun to put his truck into gear and drive her far away from Grotto. Somewhere warm and sunny and miles away from her mother and Nola and Nick. But she knew that wasn't going to happen so instead she said, "I think we should go to the caves. The ones on Ransom Road."

Shaun looked at Eve quizzically. "Really? Why would she go there?"

Eve shrugged. "Nola goes there sometimes."

"Okay." Shaun revved the engine. "Let's go."

The cab of the truck was warm and smelled like pine needles. Eve's muscles, tight from the cold, began to relax. Her eyes grew heavy and she had to fight to stay awake. She told herself that she'd only close them for a moment and leaned her head against the window.

As she dozed, Eve was vaguely aware that they had been driving for too long. They should be at Ransom Road by now. She opened her eyes with a start and scanned her surroundings. Eve had no idea where they were. A surge of panic ran through her.

"Shaun," Eve said, grabbing onto the dashboard. They were out in the country on some rural road she didn't recognize. They sped past bare, lonely-looking farm fields and Eve searched for some familiar landmarks but found none. "Where are we? Where are we going?" Eve demanded.

"I thought you said Ransom Caves." Shaun looked over at her, his forehead wrinkling in confusion. "That's what you said, right?"

"This isn't the way," Eve said. How could she have been so dumb? Why would she get into a car with a guy she barely knew? Nola was right, Eve thought. She was stupid. "Go back. Go back!" she insisted.

"Whoa," Shaun said taking one hand off the steering wheel and reaching out for Eve. She scooted out of his reach and pressed herself against the door. "We're almost there," he said. "I'm taking a back road. It takes longer to get to but we won't have to walk as far. Look."

Eve followed Shaun's gaze as he slowed the truck and took a left on a gravel road lined with towering pine trees. "I still don't know where we are," Eve said. "I told you Ransom Caves, right below my house."

"I know, I know." Shaun laughed. "Calm down. That's where we are. This is an old service road. It will take us pretty close to the caves and we won't have to cross the creek or climb over any rocks."

They bumped down the winding gravel road that ended in a wall of trees. Shaun stopped the truck and put it into Park. "The caves are just through there. You still want to go look?" He asked.

Eve didn't know what to do. No one knew where she was. No one knew who she was with.

"We can leave if you want," Shaun said. "Just tell me and I can take you home."

Eve reminded herself that not every guy was Nick or the jerks from the bus stop or Cam Harper. This was Shaun, a person she'd spent an hour with nearly every single day that school year. In study hall he was a good guy, Eve thought. She was being an idiot.

"No, I'm okay," Eve finally said. "I just never knew there was another way in."

"Yeah, not too many people do," Shaun said, throwing open the truck door and stepping out onto the gravel.

Eve hesitated, not wanting to leave the warmth and safety of the truck. Shaun started walking toward the caves and then stopped when he realized she wasn't following him. Eve knew she was being ridiculous. Shaun had never given any hint that he was interested in her. He could be doing a million different things this afternoon, but he was just being nice, a friend.

Eve opened her door and walked to Shaun's side. Before them was a grove of tall, spindly pine trees. Their footsteps were soundless beneath the soft rug of fallen pine needles as they began to move forward. It smelled like Christmas.

They were walking for only a minute when Eve saw the back of Nola's coat. A dingy purple hand-me-down. A double hand-me-down, Nola called it. Eve had picked it from a secondhand store a few years ago and when she was done with it, Nola claimed it as her own. Nola never cared what she looked like. Clothes kept her warm, kept her covered. That was enough. Eve and Shaun ducked behind a copse of trees.

Nola was on her knees and bent over, as if praying. But that didn't make sense. Nola didn't believe in God. She once tried to explain to Eve why the existence of a higher being was irrational. Eve refused to listen. Though the Knoxes weren't churchgoers, Eve didn't feel right entertaining the idea there was no God. It made her feel small and lonely and like she didn't matter, that she wasn't important.

Eve was just about to call out to Nola. To shout at her for being so bullheaded and selfish and inconsiderate when Nola suddenly sat back on her heels. Lying in front of her on the dead grass was an animal. Eve wasn't sure what kind but from its paws, her first thought was a dog. It was still, not moving, just lying there.

"Jesus," Shaun breathed. "What's she doing?" Eve pulled her eyes away from the animal and turned her attention to Nola. In her hand something shimmered in the sun. "Is that a knife?" Shaun whispered in disbelief. Eve squinted to see better. It was a knife. The Swiss Army knife that Nola had started carrying in her pocket. Why was Nola out here in the middle of nowhere with a knife? Eve stepped forward but Shaun reached out and snatched her back.

Nola shifted her weight again revealing the animal, and yes, Eve clearly saw that it was a dog. Brown and white with bushy, wiry fur, of indeterminate breed. "Nola," Eve cried, her voice swept away by the sharp wind that whistled through the trees.

Nola held the knife like a surgeon, index finger atop the blade, and slid the sharp edge down the dog's soft belly. A surge of bile rose in Eve's throat and she felt the ground tilt beneath her. "Nola," she shouted, stepping out from behind the trees and into the open. "Stop it!" Eve sobbed. "Stop it!"

Nola's head snapped up and she quickly hid the substitute

scalpel behind her back like a toddler caught hiding a stolen cookie. The dog was laid open, a grotesque tableau. Tendrils of steam rose from the open wound.

Eve turned and ran back to the truck, stumbling over frosty ridges in the ground and into the cover of the trees, her head swimming with the horror of what she just saw. She wrenched open the truck door and scrambled inside. Nola was crazy, Eve thought. That's all there was to it. Her sister was crazy.

Where was Shaun? She had left him behind. Had Nola turned the knife on him? No, Eve shook her head at the thought. Nola would never hurt someone, at least without being provoked first. But that dog. That poor dog.

Finally, through the windshield, Shaun came into view. He jogged lightly toward the truck and climbed in next to Eve. He inserted the key into the ignition and the engine turned over with a roar. "You okay?" he asked.

"Let's go," Eve said biting back tears.

"That was crazy." Shaun shook his head from side to side.

"Please just drive," Eve whispered.

"She took off," Shaun said. "Toward Ransom Road."

"Just drive," Eve snapped.

Shaun put the truck into gear.

Eve was immediately contrite. It *was* crazy. The entire situation was insane. Her sister was insane. Shaun was in shock, just like she was and trying to make sense of what he had seen.

Shaun drove them up the service road and onto the highway that would lead them back to town. Eve wanted to apologize but the words wouldn't form so instead she looked out the window and tried to erase the memory of the dog and its innards and Nola holding the knife. Her stomach churned and flipped with each bounce on the uneven road. Throwing up in Shaun O'Keefe's truck would only make this day even more unbearable.

"Do you want me to drop you off at your house?" Shaun asked cautiously as they entered the town limits.

"Can you just drop me back off at school?" she asked. It was as good a place as any.

"You sure? School's pretty much done for the day," Shaun said. "I can take you home if you want."

Eve didn't know where she wanted to go but she was sure she wasn't ready to go home just yet. "Yeah," she said and turned back toward the window. "I have to grab something from my locker." They drove in silence the rest of the way and when Shaun turned into the school parking lot, Eve said flatly, "You can drop me off here."

Shaun pulled into an empty parking space and Eve reached for the door handle as if ready to make a quick getaway but then stopped. "Please don't tell anyone," Eve murmured, looking down at her hands. "I know it looks bad. I know there's something wrong with her, but please don't tell anyone. Please. I'll take care of it."

A tear slid down Eve's face and plopped into her hand. Using one finger, Shaun wiped the moisture from her palm. Eve wanted to grab his hand, hold it tight. She wanted to bury her face in his neck and sob but it would do no good and she'd just end up being embarrassed.

"Please," she said again.

"I won't say anything, I promise," Shaun said, his hand still on hers. "She didn't even see me. Are you going to be okay?"

"I'm fine," Eve said extracting her hand and swiping at her tears. "Have a good Christmas."

Shaun looked as if he wanted to say more but settled on, "You too," as Eve pushed open the truck door and stepped out. Head down, she started to walk toward the school but veered away once he pulled out of sight.

Eve didn't really need to get anything from her locker, she just needed to get out of the confines of Shaun's truck. She needed to try to clear from her head the image of Nola looming over that dog with a knife. Besides, if she ran into Ms. Reiss she would ask if Eve found Nola and she'd have to lie and say no. It was better to just wander around and pretend to be searching for her sister.

As Eve stepped off the curb to cross Sherman Street she caught sight of Nick and two friends leaning against his BMW. Their horselike laughs slammed into her. What if they saw her get out of Shaun's truck?

A crackle of dread went through her. Nick hated to be embarrassed, one-upped. He would find a way not only to get back at Eve but Shaun too. She'd have to warn him.

She hurried down the block, deciding her best bet was to stay on busier streets, the ones with more foot traffic.

There goes another friendship, Eve thought, looking over her shoulder to see if Nick was trailing her. After today, there was no way Shaun would want anything to do with her.

First, he encountered her crazy sister and if Nick saw them together, Shaun was sure to face the wrath of Nick. Eve was sure they both would.

THE WILLOW CREEK GAZETTE
January 7, 1996

In the third week since her sister and a friend discovered the beaten and strangled body of fifteen-year-old Grotto resident Eve Marie Knox, law enforcement have made no arrests in the brutal homicide. According to the Ransom County Sheriff's Department spokesperson, Les Digby, hundreds of tips have been called in and dozens of interviews have been conducted. Despite all leads, no official suspects have been named.

Digby did say investigators are interested in speaking with a man seen at the Grotto Public Library at the same time as Knox. The man is described as being in his late fifties, wearing a red sweatshirt and blue jeans and riding a blue Schwinn bicycle with a basket on the front. He is thought to be a drifter passing through town. Digby reiterated that the man is not a suspect but a possible witness and asked that anyone with any information as to his whereabouts please contact law enforcement.

NOLA KNOX

Wednesday, June 17, 2020

Nola stared down at Maggie sitting on the edge of Eve's bed. Maggie looked as if she might pass out. "I was there, Maggie." Nola, certain that Maggie wasn't going to make a run for it, moved toward the bookshelf. "I was down at the caves the night you killed my sister."

Maggie shook her head from side to side, arms wrapped protectively around her belly. "No, you're crazy. Why would I kill Eve? She was my best friend, I loved her."

"Shhh." Nola pressed a finger to her lips. "It's my turn to talk. I know you loved Eve, but you loved someone more. Cam Harper. He liked young girls, didn't he? And you fell for it."

Again Maggie shook her head but didn't speak.

Nola reached for a book on Eve's shelf. Nola opened its pages to reveal a bird folded from red paper. "The cosmos has a way of vomiting up pieces of the past, Maggie," Nola said.

"That's not mine," Maggie whispered. "I don't know where it came from."

"Come on," Nola scoffed. "The book has your name in it, the note is addressed to you. Do you want me to read it out loud to you?"

Maggie closed her eyes tightly as if willing Nola, the book, the bird to disappear. "No, I remember what it says. I was just a child. I was fifteen. The man was a predator."

"But you killed your best friend to protect him," Nola said. "Not so innocent were you?"

"Stop it, Nola." Maggie got to her feet. "No one is going to believe you."

"You're going to want to hear me out," Nola said, pushing Maggie back onto the bed.

"Don't you touch me," Maggie snapped but Nola could smell the fear rolling off her. A bitter, desperate scent. Not altogether unpleasant, Nola thought. She'd smelled it before.

Nola slowly unfolded the origami bird. "He called you Bird, didn't he? Because you were like a little bird flitting around all over the place, always moving, always chattering. It was his pet name for you."

"You left that bird on my windshield, didn't you? Did you start the fire? Put that crap online about me?"

Nola's eyes narrowed and then she shrugged. "Sure, why not?"

"I'm going to leave now," Maggie said, her voice trembling.

"Just a little bit longer, Maggie," Nola said. "You can spare five minutes for your best friend's sister, can't you? I saw Eve running off toward the caves that day and you chasing after her. She found out about you and Cam Harper. She was going to tell. She was going to tell your dad and Cam Harper was going to be arrested and taken away from you and you couldn't stand the thought of that."

Nola's eyes sparkled. She was enjoying this.

"You followed her to the caves and you attacked her to shut her up. You killed her and for what? A middle-aged pedophile who probably had done the same thing to dozens of other girls. You thought you were so special," Nola said with disdain.

"You are crazy," Maggie spat.

"I still have three minutes," Nola said holding up her fingers. Her voice changed again and Eve's earnest words fell from her lips, "Please, Maggie, we can work this out together." Then another shift in tone. "I don't want to work it out! I'm pregnant. If you tell, it will scare him away. I need time to figure out how to tell him. You ruined it. You ruined everything. I hate you, Eve, I hate you!" Nola ended her soliloquy with a childish stamp of the foot.

"You need help," Maggie whispered.

"Actually, I think it's you who needs the help," Nola said, matching Maggie's soft tone. "You of all people should know what happens to pregnant women in prison. You'd have to give birth in leg irons. And how long do they let the baby stay with a convicted murderer? Your baby would be taken away. And what do you think your husband will do once he finds out that the mother of his child is a monster? Do you really think he'd want the baby? Off to foster care she'd go."

"Enough," Maggie said, once again getting to her feet. "I'm leaving now. I suggest you get some professional help."

Nola slid the paper cardinal back between the pages of the book and stepped aside to let Maggie pass. Maggie didn't move. "I think I'll ask Chief Digby to put another detective on Eve's case." Nola tapped her chin thoughtfully. "He wouldn't approve of you showing up in my house without a warrant. He might think you were trying to manipulate the investigation or something. Another detective will make sure that the evidence in Eve's case gets sent off safe and sound. And we'll just see what they find. Oh, and maybe Chief Digby would be interested in seeing the bird. Who knows, maybe it has some kind of evidentiary value.

"And what do you think they are going to find once they send the evidence to the lab for retesting?" Nola asked. "Maybe nothing. But maybe they'll find that tiny speck of DNA from when you knocked Eve to the ground. Maybe not.

Maybe a small drop of your blood didn't get on Eve's clothing when she was fighting back." Nola shrugged. "Who knows? Maybe the new advancements in forensic testing won't detect the touch of DNA you left behind. But I guess that's a chance you are willing to take. Good luck, Maggie." Nola reached out to touch Maggie's belly and Maggie swatted her hand away. Nola just laughed. "Good luck to you and your baby. Maybe you'll actually be able to hold this baby in your arms."

"You're bluffing," Maggie said but her voice was unsure, shaky.

"You can go now, Maggie," Nola said haughtily. "If you don't want to talk about this like adults, I think I have a few phone calls to make."

Maggie brushed past Nola and out of the room. Nola smoothed the quilt on Eve's bed from where Maggie had rumpled it. She heard Maggie's feet slapping against the steps as she rushed down the stairs. A rapid-fire staccato. Nola was surprised at how fast Maggie could move given her condition. Then there was silence. No slamming of the door, no roar of an engine being turned. Just the whir of the overhead fan. Nola sat on the edge of Eve's bed and waited. Maggie would be back.

EVE KNOX

Eve didn't want to have to march past Nick and his friends so she decided to just keep walking in the opposite direction. The wind was picking up and moved her along with an icy push.

Eve passed by the police station where Maggie's dad worked and up Juniper Street past Grotto Gifts. Nick's mother spotted Eve through the window and waved happily but Eve turned her head and kept on going. She passed by the pharmacy and the Maid-Rite. So familiar, but Eve felt oddly out of place. A funny thought to Eve. Of the three of them in the family, Eve was the one who seemed to have found her place in their hometown.

Eve never really understood how her mother ended up in Grotto. Her mother's job, she guessed. But why she chose a place with few single men and no social scene to speak of never made sense to Eve. Her mother used to be pretty. Beautiful actually, and at least in a larger town her mom would have had the chance to meet a nice guy—any guy for that matter—and could have had a life beyond her daughters. But the longer they lived here, the more worn down, faded her mother became.

Eve thought Nola would have benefited from living in a

larger, more diverse town. A city where there were more kids like her, more opportunities to learn and explore. But as she got older, Eve realized that there weren't a whole lot of people like Nola. No matter where she lived, Nola would be scary.

Out of the corner of her eye, Eve saw a flash of the pale moon yellow of Nola's hair but just as quickly it disappeared. She knew it was Nola, across the street but lagging a bit behind Eve, ducking into doorways whenever Eve glanced her way. Nola had taken the quick route from the caves.

"I see you!" Eve hollered but kept walking. Something bounced against her coat and fell to the ground. "Go home!" Eve shouted, sensing that Nola had crossed the street and was walking directly behind her. "Real mature!" Eve called out and picked up her pace. "Go home!" Her job was done. Their mother told her to find Nola and that's what she did.

Eve heard the pounding of feet against the sidewalk. "You probably thought it was hilarious," Nola said coming up behind her. "Those assholes making fun of me."

Eve swung around and was flabbergasted at the hurt expression on Nola's face. Eve could always tell when Nola's feelings were hurt. She bit down so hard on the inside of her cheek that a rarely seen dimple formed. Her voice shook and lost the haughtiness that everyone was used to.

"I tried to help you," Eve cried. "I was trying to get them to leave you alone and you went after me. What the hell is wrong with you, Nola?"

"The only thing wrong is that I'm stuck in this town and forced to go to school with idiots," Nola shot back.

"Yeah, well, if you weren't so crazy maybe people would leave you alone," Eve snapped.

"Well, maybe if you didn't spend so much time with Nick you wouldn't be such an asshole," Nola barked back.

"Nick and I broke up," Eve said, pausing to look both ways before crossing the street.

This announcement seemed to take Nola by surprise. She was quiet for a moment. The only sound was their breathing. The sky was heavy with snow and for a second Eve's heart gave a little childlike leap. Eve may be over fifteen but she wasn't too old to be enchanted by a Christmas snowfall. Normally they had piles of snow by this time of the year.

"Good," Nola finally said. "Maybe you won't be such a bitch anymore."

Eve stopped short while Nola kept walking. Eve was aware of other people on the street carrying on with their normal, everyday activities. A man digging into his pocket for coins to feed the parking meter. A woman carrying bags of groceries. A group of middle school boys huddled together laughing and talking excitedly about winter break.

"I may be a bitch," Eve said, "but at least I have friends." Her voice was low and singsong sweet. "Unlike some people I know. Maybe if you weren't such a freak show you'd have some friends."

Nola went stock-still and though Eve hated to admit it, she felt exhilaration in finally saying those words. Eve couldn't stop herself.

"Maybe if you didn't read books about string theory and dissecting small animals—if you didn't dissect animals—you wouldn't be alone all the time."

Nola slowly turned around. Her face was stripped of emotion as if Eve's cruel words meant nothing, but the stony glint in her eyes told Eve that her words had hit the mark.

"And I saw you. I saw what you did," Eve hissed. "Did you really kill that dog, Nola?"

Seeing the rage on her sister's face, all the confidence and righteous anger that Eve felt disappeared and was replaced with a fist of dread and all she could think about was getting home. Eve turned to leave.

She only made it a few steps when she felt the blow. It was

sudden and knocked the breath from her chest. Eve stumbled to the ground, her jeans snagging against the coarse sidewalk, taking a layer of skin from her knee with it. Eve looked up and Nola was standing above her, arms on her hips, her mouth pinched in anger, her hand in her pocket. Fingering her knife, Eve was certain.

The nearby group of boys stopped their playful shoving and laughter to watch and the woman with the grocery bags changed course and crossed the street. Nick's mom stepped outside the shop and was joined by two others to look on.

"You ruined my jeans," Eve said, shifting to a seated position. She felt the cold concrete through the seat of her pants. "I only have one other pair. You're going to buy me new ones," Eve said, examining the bloodstained rip. When she looked back up to demand an apology she could tell by the look on Nola's face that she wasn't going to get one.

A thousand responses ran through Eve's head but she remained silent and hastily got to her feet. "Nola, what is wrong with you?" she whispered, well aware of all the eyes on them.

Nola didn't answer, only walked away as if nothing had happened. The boys went back to jostling each other and Nick's mom walked toward Eve, a worried look on her face.

"Eve," she called. "Are you all right?"

"Just messing around. I'm fine," Eve said, waving her off. Mrs. Brady said something more but what, Eve couldn't hear. She limped quickly away, turning down a side street and out of sight.

Nola and Eve had arguments before, loud, wall-shaking ones. They even had ones that involved hair pulling and pinches. Nola held a mean grudge but they didn't seem to last for too long. At least not toward Eve.

Usually all she would need to do is give Nola some time to cool off and then things would go back to normal. But what did that even mean? There was nothing normal about Nola. Eve knew she would have to talk to Nola about the dog. It was going to be an awful conversation but something had to be done. Nola was out of control. Eve was scared of her sister.

MAGGIE
KENNEDY-O'KEEFE

Wednesday, June 17, 2020

I pause at Nola's front door, one hand on the brass doorknob. Every fiber of my body is screaming at me to turn around and run, to get the hell out of this house and never return. Nola Knox is crazy but she's not wrong.

That night, when I left Eve behind in the caves, I was sure she was still alive. Even when Nola and I found Eve's body, I didn't believe that I was the one who killed her. But I did. I murdered my best friend.

My heart is thumping and I'm crying so hard that I'm afraid it might hurt the baby. I can't catch my breath and the room is spinning. If I'm not careful I'm going to pass out and then God knows what Nola would do to me. I take long, deep breaths, the way that Shaun and I learned in Lamaze class.

A wash of different emotions floods through me. Disgust at what I could do to another human being and that I was able to keep it a secret for so long. For years I was able to almost make myself believe that it wasn't me who killed Eve. Most days I was able to convince myself that after our fight, Eve slipped and fell and that's what ultimately killed her.

But in the dark, quiet minutes before I drifted off to sleep, I've always known the truth, known what I was: a killer. For one brief moment, I feel something new. Relief. My secret is finally not mine alone.

Finally, my heart rate steadies and I release the doorknob and turn back to the stairway. Every word that Nola said was true. She repeated, verbatim, the fight that Eve and I had the afternoon she died. Nola had to be there, at the caves. Watching. Listening.

I should just leave, ignore Nola. I put my foot on the first step. Nola was there when Eve confronted me about Cam Harper.

But no one would believe her over me. I'm a respected police officer. Another step. Nola was there when I begged Eve not to tell anyone. She was there when I told Eve that I loved Cam and I was pregnant with his child.

My medical records are private. There is no way anyone could know I was pregnant. And even if they did, there was no way for anyone to know that Cam was the father.

I take another step upward. Nola was there when I knocked Eve to the ground, the two of us in a twisted heap. She was there when Eve kicked out at me, striking me over and over again with her foot until something inside me broke free. In that moment I knew my relationship with Cam was over and a caustic rage coursed through my veins and I wanted Eve dead. My best friend. Nola was there when I hit her and pulled tight on her scarf until she stopped fighting back.

I honestly didn't believe I had killed Eve. When I fled the cave, I swear she was still breathing. Hurt, yes, but still alive. At least I thought she was. I lurched back to the Harpers' and found the twins right where I left them, in front of the television watching Nickelodeon. They didn't even know I was gone. I stripped off my bloody clothes and showered. I pulled a shirt and a pair of pants from the back of Joyce Harper's closet and threw my clothes in the washing machine. I prayed the Harpers wouldn't come home early.

I tried to pretend everything was normal and must have done a pretty good job because Joyce gave me a five-dollar tip. When Nola's mother asked us to go look for Eve I thought we would find her at Nick's or maybe even at the caves. Angry and pissed off, but not dead.

Why had Nola kept the secret for all these years? Why hadn't she gone to the police, reported what she had witnessed? How could anyone stand by and watch their sister getting murdered and do nothing? The thing is, Nola isn't just anyone.

I reach the landing and place a protective hand across my midsection. Nola is crazy and devious and smart but I have one thing going for me that she does not. I'm a mother. I will do absolutely anything to protect the baby I'm carrying now. I will go back inside that bedroom and listen to what she has to say, get more information, but I will not let Nola get to me. I brush away the last of my tears and step back into Eve's room. For a long time, I tried to get inside Eve's room to search for the note from Cam but Charlotte didn't like having Eve's friends visit. It upset her. It took years, but I finally relaxed. If the origami note hadn't been found by then I figured it never would. And even if it was discovered no one could connect it to me. I shouldn't have let my guard down.

Nola is sitting on the edge of Eve's bed waiting for me. Of course she knew I'd come back. "Smart girl," Nola says.

"Nola, you have to believe that I didn't mean to hurt Eve. We argued, yes, but I didn't think I truly hurt her. I expected her to come out of the cave right behind me," I try to explain. Nola stares at me curiously. I think she's enjoying this. "Even when she didn't come out," I go on, desperate to make Nola understand, "I wasn't worried. For a long time after we found Eve's body, I didn't believe that I had killed her. I thought she must have fallen, hit her head, something. Please, Nola, you have to believe me."

"Don't look so worried, Maggie." Nola pats the spot next to her inviting me to sit down. I stay in the doorway. "I can help you. I want to help you."

I stay silent, willing my hands to stop shaking. How in the world could Nola help me? Why would she want to?

"Nick Brady," Nola says almost triumphantly. Seeing the confusion on my face she continues. "It makes the most sense. It's always the boyfriend." She leans in conspiratorially. "All you need to do is slip a little bit of his DNA into the evidence, reseal it, send it in and we wait for the results."

I shake my head vigorously. "I don't understand. Why would you want to blame Nick for something you say I did?"

"It's got to be Nick," Nola insists. "Otherwise, I go to the police chief and tell him everything."

"Look, I know that Nick was a jerk," I say, trying to reason with her. "He was awful to Eve. But if he is innocent why would you want him to go to prison for it?"

"Nick Brady is not innocent," Nola snarls with a ferocity I wasn't expecting. She rubs at the ropy scar on her chest and she catches me staring. "You think I was the one who went after Nick at the high school. That I was the one who pushed him into the glass case, caused this scar and the one on his arm."

"That's what I heard," I say carefully, not knowing if this is the answer Nola wants to hear.

"It's partly true," Nola says picking up a penny-filled jar from the bedside table and tipping it back and forth so that its contents jangle. As Nola holds the jar up to the window, the copper glinting in the afternoon light, her face changes, just slightly. There's a crack in her usually composed countenance, a vulnerability I've never seen before. Then it's gone. Like the flash from a firefly. "You want to know what happened that day?"

She doesn't wait for me to nod but plunges forward. "My mom made me go to the high school to pick up Eve's things.

207

I told her that Eve didn't need that stuff anymore, that she should just let the school deal with it all. Wrong answer." Nola gives a bitter laugh. "So I went to the school and gathered her things. My last stop was down in the girls' locker room."

"Yeah," I interrupt. "And Nick and a friend of his were down there and Nick made some stupid comment about Eve. You pushed him into the glass case." I wipe mucous from my nose with my sleeve. I need to get some semblance of control back or Nola will own me. "I'm not saying that Nick didn't deserve to get his ass kicked, but he didn't hurt Eve. At least not that day."

"But he hurt me." Nola's eyes flash angrily. "He made that sick comment about Eve and oral sex and then he and his friend followed me into the locker room and grabbed me. Nick pulled his pants down and tried to make me..." Nola trails off and shakes her head. "But I fought back. I managed to get out of the locker room and they chased me and we fell into the glass case."

"Why didn't you tell anyone?" I ask, thinking of thirteen-year-old Nola being accosted by Nick and his friend and no Eve to protect her. Nola has lied about a lot of things over the years, but in this case I actually believe her.

Nola gives a wry smile. "Like you said, no one would believe me. It was my word against Nick Brady and his friend. They concocted the story about me pushing Nick through the glass. They were pretty smart—just enough of the truth to make it believable." Nola rubs the scar on her chest again. "It was kind of a win-win. I got the satisfaction of watching the glass slice through Nick's arm and I got kicked out of the Grotto school system."

"Nola, I can't blame something on an innocent man," I say, tears filling my eyes again.

"Then I'll tell them you did it," Nola says sharply. When she speaks again, her voice is soft, cajoling. "But I know you didn't mean to hurt Eve. I know what guys like Nick Brady and Cam Harper do to girls. What they steal from them. If it wasn't for Nick or Cam, you would have never killed Eve. I truly believe that. You were desperate to keep Cam and you lashed out in the heat of the moment. Who could blame you? Eve should have kept your secret but she had her own secrets to keep." Nola says, taking a step toward me. "Nick hit her and demeaned her. And he sexually assaulted me." She brushes a strand of hair out of my face. I try not to flinch. "Together we can take down Nick Brady."

I begin to protest but she interrupts. "Remember, Maggie, I was there, I heard everything, saw everything. And I can make life miserable for you." She drops her eyes to my belly. "And for your baby." My heart skips a beat and I know that she's telling the truth.

"But Nick has an alibi," I say. "Jamie Hutchcraft was with him that afternoon and then he was with his mother."

Nola gives a derisive snort. "Not a solid alibi. I bet if you pressed Jamie, you'll find it's not so airtight. And what mother wouldn't lie for her child? And besides, DNA trumps alibi any day. DNA doesn't lie."

"But I don't understand," I manage to eke out. "Why would you want to lie for me?"

Nola examines me as if looking at a specimen through a microscope. "I told you, if it wasn't for Nick or Cam, it would never have happened. And I thought about it. If I went to the police, I'd have to explain why I was at the caves in the first place, why I didn't step in and help Eve. It would just complicate things.

"I'm giving you a gift, Maggie," Nola soothes. "All you have to do is grab it. You don't even have to do all that much. I'll get the DNA, and all you'll have to do is add it to an existing piece of evidence and send it in. When it's retested Nick will go down for being the disgusting creep we both know he is. Easy-peasy. It's another win-win." Nola smiles brightly as if she's just asked me to tear up a traffic ticket or something.

"It's not easy," I exclaim. "It's nearly impossible to tamper with evidence once it's been sealed and entered into the log. There's no way we'll get away with it."

"Okay, not easy, but not impossible either. Come on, Maggie, we're talking about the Grotto PD, not the FBI," Nola laughs. "No one is going to notice a tiny pinprick from a needle. All we need is one drop of blood. Now go on home to that husband of yours. I'll stop by tomorrow with what you need."

"Why didn't you…" I start, my voice deadened, flat. "Why didn't you try to help Eve?"

Nola looks me square in the eye. "Because I didn't really care." I hold her gaze. She's lying. For all her bravado, Nola is lying. She did care about Eve. She does care, or she wouldn't be doing this.

I turn and numbly move from the room, down the stairs and out the front door. I want to run into my old house, up the stairs and to my old bedroom. I want to be little again and have this all disappear. Instead, I ignore Joyce Harper who is standing on her front lawn and wave away my brother who is waiting for me on the front porch.

"I'll phone you later," I manage to call out to Colin as I climb into my car.

I always knew that one day my actions in the caves would come back to haunt me in a real, concrete way. I already have the bad dreams, the flashbacks, the crippling guilt. But now I have to face what I've done and make a decision that is, in my mind, equally as evil. If I do what Nola is asking me to do, I'm for all intents and purposes killing Nick Brady. I'll be branding him as a murderer. I'll be taking away his freedom, his life as he knows it.

As I pull away from the curb, another thought comes to mind. Maybe there's another way.

THERAPY TRANSCRIPT

Client Name: Nola Knox, 13 years
Therapist Name: Linda Gonzalez, LMHC, NCC
Date of Service: March 19, 1996

L. Gonzalez: Good morning, Nola. It's so good to see you smiling. You had a good week since I saw you last?

N. Knox: It was okay.

L. Gonzalez: What made it okay?

N. Knox: I don't know. I went to the doctor and he said my lung is all better.

L. Gonzalez: That must be a relief. It looks like the wound is healing nicely.

N. Knox: Yeah. After I got the stitches out, I practiced doing stitches too. I think I finally got the hang of it.

L. Gonzalez: Oh? How do you practice something like that?

N. Knox: I asked the doctor what they used in med

school and he said that pig's skin is the closest to what it would be like to work on a person. He also said oranges and bananas work too. I sliced through the peel of an orange and sewed it up with needle and thread. It took a few tries to figure it out, but my stitches actually looked pretty good.

L. Gonzalez: You mentioned during our last visit that you wanted to be a vet. It sounds like you've thought more about this?

N. Knox: Yeah. I've always wanted to be a vet. Animals are much more trusting than people; don't you think? Easier to deal with.

L. Gonzalez: In what ways?

N. Knox: Well, they don't talk back, that's pretty obvious. And all you have to do is talk gently to them, maybe offer them a treat, they calm down and you can get them to do anything you want them to. People don't work that way.

L. Gonzalez: Nola, your teachers say that your interactions with your classmates tend to be contentious...

N. Knox: I don't care about them.

L. Gonzalez: Who do you care about?

L. Gonzalez: There must be someone you care about. A friend, your mother?

N. Knox: My mother only cares about herself and Eve. Why should I care about her?

L. Gonzalez: Your mother is grieving Eve's death. It's very difficult to lose a child and sometimes people are so consumed by sadness they can barely take care of themselves let alone someone else. Are you being taken care of, Nola? Are you eating? Sleeping?

N. Knox: I'm not stupid. If I say that my mom isn't feeding me or say that she's neglecting me I know that I go into foster care. Not going to happen. I'm fine. We're fine.

L. Gonzalez: Fair enough. Let's go back to what you said about how dealing with animals is easier than people. What if you tried that with your mother and your teachers and classmates? All you have to do is talk gently and offer them a treat—obviously not a dog biscuit, but maybe a kind word or two—and perhaps things might get better. What do you say? Will you give it a try this week? See what happens?

N. Knox: I suppose.

L. Gonzalez: And you might want to think about using this same strategy with the boy you hurt. It could go a long way with the juvenile courts if you offer him a sincere apology for pushing him and causing his injuries.

N. Knox: I will never, ever, apologize to Nick

Brady. I don't care if I go to jail or have to come here every week for the rest of my life. I'm not saying sorry. He's lucky I didn't kill him.

MAGGIE KENNEDY-O'KEEFE

Wednesday, June 17, 2020

I don't know where to go. I can't go back to work and I can't go home. There's no way I can explain why I'm so upset. I just start driving, winding through the streets of Grotto on autopilot. Maybe I can just run away. Take off and start a new life somewhere. Raise my baby away from Grotto and Nola Knox. That's what I should have done in the first place, left Grotto for good. But no, I wanted to be near my dad and if I'm being honest, wanted to keep an eye on Eve's case, to be close if there were any new developments. Be careful what you wish for. Something new has definitely developed.

I nearly miss a stop sign and slam on the brakes, the seat belt snapping tight against my chest as I come to a screeching stop, narrowly missing an elderly man walking his dog. My heart hammers in my chest as he walks in front of my car, shooting daggers at me. I have to get myself under control.

Shakily, I move through the intersection, keeping my speed well below the limit and find myself heading toward Ransom Road. Only two houses sit on the quiet street and I pull in front of the house where Nola and I ran to call 911 the night Eve died. As far as I know, Vivian Benson still lives there. She would be about seventy-five years old by now. Over the years, we've only greeted each other with brief, hurried hellos, never acknowledging the night that Nola and I showed up on her doorstep. I park beneath a locust tree in front of Vivian's house, its feathery leaves blocking the sun from beating down on my car.

I remember how after she called 911, Vivian wrapped me in a blanket and settled me on her sofa until the police came. I remember how comforting it was to feel her weight there next to me as the full understanding of what I had done settled over me. Until the moment I saw Eve's dead body I didn't believe that I had hurt her that badly.

Confident I'm alone I allow myself something that I haven't done in twenty-five years. I weep for Eve. Shame and grief spew from me in great racking sobs. I meant to hurt Eve, but I hadn't meant to kill her. But she discovered the truth about Cam Harper and she was going to tell. I was pregnant and though I hadn't told Cam yet I was sure we'd have our happy-ever-after. I thought I was in love and Eve told me a truth that my fifteen-year-old self wasn't prepared to hear.

I lashed out. Eve fought back. I walked away from the caves and Eve didn't.

I search through the glove box for some tissues and blow my nose. There has to be a way out of this. No one would believe Nola Knox, would they? She has always been the town weirdo, angry, sometimes violent. Maybe her accusations would be written off as another one of her crazy rants. For years Nola and her mother bad-mouthed Nick Brady, saying he was responsible, so if she pointed the finger at me, would people take her seriously? A horrific thought flashes into my mind. I could get rid of the problem. Nola. Maybe I could frame Nola instead of Nick.

No. I don't think I can get away with it. I probably won't get away with Eve's murder either. With the reexamination of the evidence and twenty-five years of advancement in forensics, there is a good chance that my DNA will be found. My DNA wasn't in the system but I know that my brother had sent a swab into one of those genetic testing companies to find out what percentage of Irish and Eastern European he was. There is a good chance that his DNA could eventually lead to me.

I know there is a way out of this; I just need more time to think. Nola isn't giving me this luxury. She wants to act now, wants to implicate Nick Brady. I reach for my gun belt. Maybe there is a way out. I grasp the butt of my gun and release the thumb snap. I imagine lifting the gun to my temple and pulling the trigger. Instant relief.

The thought sends a surge of vomit up my gullet and I manage to get out of the car before I throw up all over Vivian Benson's lawn. I'm gasping for breath, hands on my knees, when I hear the squeak of a screen door. I look up and see a tiny woman with close-cropped, pearl-colored hair, coming down the Bensons' concrete front steps. "Maggie O'Keefe?" she asks, squinting at me.

I nod, wiping my mouth with my sleeve. Though I haven't seen Vivian Benson this close up in years, I recognize her immediately. "I'm so sorry, Mrs. Benson," I say. "I can't believe I did that."

"Don't you worry about it," she says, laying a hand on my shoulder. I wince from the pressure on my blistered back. I try to will my stomach to settle. "I remember when I was pregnant," Mrs. Benson continues. "I had morning sickness morning, noon and night. Come in and rest for a minute." She places a hand on my elbow and leads me up the front steps and into a room with faded floral curtains and a wall filled with black-and-white family photos.

I know I've been here before but when Nola and I came knocking on her door I wasn't paying any attention to the décor. "Take a seat," Mrs. Benson invites and then suddenly she is gone.

I sit down and sink into the lumpy cushions and close my eyes. Suddenly, I'm fifteen years old again and I've just discovered the dead body of my best friend. The best friend that I murdered. Another wave of nausea rushes over me.

"Here, honey," Mrs. Benson says, offering me a washcloth and a glass of water. I press the damp cloth to my face. I take a small sip of water. Mrs. Benson sits across from me in a straight-back chair, her feet barely reaching the worn carpet. "I heard on the news that there was new evidence. That was an awful night," she says. "When I opened the door to find you girls on my front step..." She shakes her head at the memory. "Seems like yesterday." Mrs. Benson looks down at her hands. She tries to smooth the wrinkles from her knuckles with a fingertip. "It was close to ten o'clock. I remember because I was watching *Picket Fences*. I loved that show."

She looks up at me as if expecting a response. I murmur something about how my dad watched it too.

"Anyway, I'm sitting right where you are when the doorbell rings, and I think to myself, *Who in the world would be here at this time of night?* At first I thought it might be that awful Iverson girl, Dawna, coming over to tell me that she saw a strange car coming down the street. Such a paranoid thing, always finding the bogeyman where there were only shadows."

Mrs. Benson sighs. "I wish it would have been Dawna, but instead I found Nola standing there looking up at me with those big glasses and green eyes like some kind of click beetle."

She leans forward in her chair, "It was ten o'clock and I just couldn't imagine who would be ringing my doorbell at that time of night. Right away I was concerned, but by the casual look on Nola Knox's face, you would have thought she was selling Girl Scout cookies or popcorn for her basketball team or something. But instead of asking me if I want a box of Thin Mints or Do-Si-Dos, she says, *My sister is dead*. She was so matter-of-fact I thought I heard her wrong. Then I saw you standing behind her, pale as a ghost.

"But she said it again, *My sister is dead. She was murdered.* I didn't know if her sister was on the street outside or what so I pulled you both into the house," Vivian says, making a motion as if tugging on a rope, "and then I shut and locked the door thinking that some crazy person must be out there. That's when I called 911."

"I remember," I tell her and take another drink of water.

Mrs. Benson nods knowingly. "Then you remember how strange Nola sounded."

I didn't remember, I was too busy thinking about how I ended up killing the girl who was like a sister to me. How we would never speak again. I was thinking about how I was going to go to prison for murder, how this would kill my dad.

What I wasn't thinking about was Nola. It hits me now. When Nola and I went searching for Eve, Nola *knew* I was the one who killed her sister, but she never spoke up. Never said a word.

"She wasn't right," Vivian says, getting to her feet and then joining me on the sofa. She smells like talcum powder. "And Nola was not in shock like the 911 operator thought. She said *My sister is dead* just like someone would say, *It's Tuesday* or *I had a bologna sandwich for lunch.* Do you have a sister?" she asks.

"A brother," I say dumbly.

"Then you know," she says with finality. "You would be devastated if something happened to your brother, right?"

"I should go," I mumble. "Thank you, for the water. I'm sorry about your lawn."

"Oh, don't worry about that," she says. She walks me to the door and wishes me good luck with the birth of my baby and I thank her.

Before I step outside, Vivian lays a hand on mine. It is soft, cool. "I should have spoken up twenty-five years ago but no one asked my opinion," she says. "So I'm going to say it now. I know it sounds crazy, but that girl killed her sister or knows who did it."

I almost laugh out loud. If she only knew. Then I go back to my car and start to cry again.

I need to compose myself before I head home for the day so I decide to drive around for a while. There's something calming about driving the back roads. The gentle twists and turns edged by ditches filled with waving black-eyed Susan and Queen Anne's lace.

I can't believe I considered, even for the briefest of moments, running away or killing myself. I could never do that to my baby, to Shaun. But I also never believed that I could murder my best friend. For years I was afraid to fall asleep, scared that Eve would come to me in my dreams. I was afraid to close my eyes and find her staring back at me with those dead, unseeing eyes.

The nightmares came, but not in the way I thought they would. Eve would come to me as her seven-year-old self, all red hair and knobby knees while I continued to age. She'd smile at me, her front tooth missing, her freckles forging a path across her nose, her scarf wound around her neck. In my dreams Eve would hold her hand out to me and though every fiber of my being told me not to take it, I always did. Together we'd run toward the caves and once there we'd stop and peer into the black hole at the mouth of the cave. *Come on*, Eve would urge. I would shake my head and beg her not to go inside. She pleaded but I refused until she released my hand and went forward without me.

Don't go, I cried and in desperation I grabbed at her scarf and pulled and pulled. Eve's eyes bulged and her lips turned blue, her fingers scrabbled at her neck, but still I pulled until

Eve dropped to the ground, her red hair spread out against the ground like a cardinal's wings. Then I would wake up, crying.

I'm not a bad person, at least that's what I tell myself. If it was just me, if I didn't have Shaun and the baby, I think I could turn myself in. But I do have them and why blow up the lives of two innocent people? Four, really, if you include my dad and brother. Nola has offered me a way out. All I have to do is frame a not-so-innocent man for murder.

I find myself driving past Sacred Heart High School. I think of what Colin told me about Cam Harper being a softball coach for the girls' high school team. I pull into the parking area that sits between the soccer field and the softball fields. On one side a horde of teen boys is running footwork drills warming up for a soccer match and on the other the softball team is running laps around the bases.

And there he is, grasping the chain fence that surrounds the field. Cam Harper is wearing a Sacred Heart Stallions T-shirt, khaki shorts and holding a clipboard. He spits off to the side and shouts something at the girls that I can't hear. I look at the girls, ponytails swinging. They look so young. Just babies really—fourteen, fifteen years old. Just like I was.

I watch as Cam comes around the fence and toward a girl with long dark hair who is standing off on her own, away from the team practicing her swing. Cam talks to the girl who looks like she is trying to adjust her feet based on what he's saying. Finally, he comes around behind her and begins to move her hands, repositioning her fingers along the shaft of the bat. He places his hands on her hips and thighs, adjusting her stance. His fingers linger too long, slide along her bare legs. The girl seems to lean into his touch. She looks up at him with adoration. Cam Harper definitely has a type. I turn away in disgust. He was back at it. He probably never stopped, just cycled through girls until they reached a certain age and then started all over again.

I know I wasn't a likely target for someone like Cam. I was the daughter of the police chief for God's sake. But Cam saw something in me. Something sad and broken and lonely. Somehow he knew I could keep a secret. If only there was someone who could have told me to watch out, to beware. Would I have listened? Probably not.

When I get home Shaun is sprawled out on the living room floor, a large cardboard box, tools and pieces of what could be a baby swing strewn around him. I stand in the doorway and watch him for a minute as he sorts screws into neat little piles. There's so much I've kept from him. So much that is unforgivable. Shaun could never find out about Cam Harper or Eve. He'd never look at me the same way again. "What's all this?" I ask, stepping into the room.

"Baby swing," Shaun says, looking up from the direction pamphlet. "This thing can actually detect when a baby starts crying and then adjust its settings to try to get her to stop."

"Wow," I say. I lean against the doorjamb. I'm drained of energy.

Shaun looks at me with concern. "You okay?" he asks.

"If something happened to me you'd still take care of the baby wouldn't you?" I ask thinking of Nola's warning to me: *And what do you think your husband will do once he finds out that the mother of his child is a monster? Do you really think he'd want the baby? Off to foster care she'd go.*

Shaun sets down his screwdriver and gets to his feet. "Are you feeling okay, Maggie? What's going on?"

"I'm fine," I say. "But if something happened to me and I couldn't be here to take care of the baby, you'd look out for her, right?"

Shaun stares at me like I've grown a second head. "Of course I would. She's my baby. Our baby." He pulls me into an embrace. "What's going on? Was it the fire? Did you find out who set it? Have you gotten more phone calls?"

"No," I murmur into his shoulder though it's so much more than the fire and the calls. It's the new evidence, it's Nola's threats, it's the knowledge that everything I love could be taken away from me. I could be going to prison. "Just promise me, okay?" I squeeze him tight, tears flooding my eyes. "Just promise me that you'll always be there for her, no matter what."

Shaun promises and this makes me feel better, that maybe this will all turn out okay.

I know one thing for sure. Nola isn't going away but an idea has already begun to form. Just a seed but it's been planted. Maybe there's a way I can keep Nick Brady out of this after all. And more important, maybe I can protect my family and even keep myself out of this entire tragic mess.

NOLA KNOX

Thursday, June 18, 2020

Nola parked her truck on Juniper, waiting for just the right time to make her move. It was still dark, that shadowy space between night and morning. Except for the bakery, the stores along the street were not due to open for a few hours. Nola wasn't worried about being seen. In fact, it was important that she was. She needed a reason to be on this street at this time of morning.

She stopped in the bakery and examined the case filled with frosted and filled donuts and pastries. She wanted the chocolate one with sprinkles but that could be too messy for the job she needed to do so she settled on the plain cake donut. She pulled it from the paper bag and took a bite.

Nola was a bit surprised by Maggie's reaction to her bombshell about what she'd witnessed at the caves. Nola thought it would take more convincing to get Maggie on board with the plan to bring Nick Brady down. Sure, Nola could go to the police and tell them what she had seen and heard that afternoon at the caves, but Maggie was right, it would be a hard sell.

Maggie was a well-respected cop and the daughter of the beloved former police chief. She was married to a hometown boy who sold Christmas trees for God's sake. And there was the meager little detail that Nola hadn't said anything about what she saw and heard at the caves for twenty-five years.

But Maggie, it seemed, after a brief hesitation, was all in with framing Nick for Eve's death. Maybe the two of them were more alike than she thought. Maggie could see what a scumbag Nick was then and probably still was. People don't change. That's one thing Nola had learned over the years. Once a predator, always a predator. Why should Nick have gotten away with treating girls the way he did? Though Eve never admitted it to her, Nola knew that Nick hurt her. She saw the bruises.

Then there was the day in the girls' locker room. She would never forget the feel of Nick's hands on her head as he forced her downward, never forget the hyena-like laughter of his friend. They had touched her in places and tried to make her do things that still made her face hot with shame. But why should she be embarrassed? She hadn't done anything but try to gather her dead sister's things.

Nola remembered the power she felt when she shoved Nick into the trophy case, the crack of the glass as it shattered into a million pieces. She didn't even care that Nick had dragged her down with him. She welcomed the bite of pain as the jagged shards penetrated her chest. But even as she was being stitched up in the hospital she knew that no one would believe her side of the story, so she took the punishment. She endured the psychological evaluations and the expulsion and the counseling sessions. She told them what they wanted to hear eventually, murmured an apology and waited. Waited for the right time to strike back. And now was the time.

Half-hidden in the early morning shadows, Nick Brady approached the door to Grotto Gifts & Things and pulled out a set of keys. He fumbled and dropped them to the sidewalk, bending over to retrieve them. With effort, Nick picked up the keys unaware that someone was watching. Nola pulled the long, narrow plastic case from the glove box then reached for her phone and punched in three numbers. She could use a little chaos in order to get what she needed. What better way than to get the Grotto PD on the scene?

"Yes," she cried, her voice shrill and panicked. "Someone is breaking into Grotto Gifts on Juniper. I think he's armed. Please hurry." Nola disconnected and watched while Nick finished unlocking the door and went inside. She waited for the cavalry to arrive.

She took the gold-plated lancing pen out of its plastic case, inserted the disposable needle into the pen cartridge, twisted the protective cap and rotated the pen until the lancer was screwed in. *There*, Nola thought. Who knew that blood collection tools came in pen form—for discreet blood testing, the description said. It was just what she needed. It was amazing what you could purchase at the local pharmacy. She held the pen tightly in her fist. Nola had two goals: to collect a sample of Nick's blood without being detected and to not get arrested while doing so.

It didn't take long. Two minutes at the most when a Grotto PD police car appeared and came to a slanted stop in front of the shop. Two officers hurried from the car. Nola was a little disappointed to see that their weapons remained holstered.

Curious, Nick returned to the entrance to see what was going on. After a short conversation with the officers, Nola stepped from her truck and started walking their way. Nick looked toward the street and his eyes narrowed in understanding. He gestured toward Nola and the two officers turned.

"I'm the one who made the call," Nola said apologetically. "I thought I saw a man trying to force the door open."

"He's the owner of the shop, ma'am," the officer explained. "There's no break-in."

"You knew damn well it was me," Nick said. Circles of sweat darkened the armpits of his shirt and he mopped his forehead with the back of one hand. Beneath the streetlight the raised, puckered scars on his arm glared white against his ruddy skin.

"I didn't," Nola said, contrite. She turned to the officers. "My apologies. I didn't mean to waste your time. I had no idea it was Nick."

"Bullshit," Nick said. "She's crazy. She thinks..." Nick finally noticed the small crowd of curious onlookers that had gathered outside the bakery across the street and paused to watch.

"I think what?" Nola asked. "That you killed my sister," she finished for him. "That you beat her up and strangled her because she broke up with you?"

"Jesus, Nola. Can't you get it through your head? I'm sorry about what happened to Eve. But. I. Didn't. Kill. Her," Nick said with disgust. "I loved her."

This was it. This was the time. Nola leaned into the arc of his waving finger and it grazed her cheek. "Hey," she exclaimed. "Don't you fucking touch me." She swatted away his hand with one hand and with the other, keeping the pen concealed beneath her sleeve, shoved the tip of the pen into his forearm.

"Ouch, dammit, you scratched me, you bitch," Nick said, instinctively grabbing onto Nola's arm. The momentum caused them both to lose their balance and Nola fell forward, striking Nick's face with the crown of her head.

Blood exploded from his nose. "Jesus Christ," he cried, pressing his fingers to his face.

"He touched me first," Nola insisted, dropping the pen into the deep pocket of her cardigan before anyone noticed it. "You saw it," she said to the police officers who were trying to step between the two. Blood coursed down Nick's face and dripped to the sidewalk. "He grabbed my arm and I fell into him."

"Whoa now, everyone settle down," the younger of the two officers said.

"Mr. Brady, let's get you inside and cleaned up and we can talk about it."

"I don't want her anywhere near my shop," Nick snapped. He turned to Nola, blood still streaming down his face. He pinched the bridge of his nose, trying to stanch the bleeding. "Go ahead and press charges and I'll go after you for calling in a fake emergency."

Nola turned on Nick. "She didn't love you back, Nick. She finally figured out what an ass you were." Nola kept her voice low, measured. "And you couldn't stand it."

"She's crazy. Make her stay away from me," Nick said and retreated into the store, letting the door shut with a glass-quivering slam.

"Ms. Knox," the officer began, "do you really want to press charges against him? You instigated the matter. I'm really hoping that your call was a case of mistaken identity because if not you could be in serious trouble."

"I'm sorry about that," Nola said trying to look apologetic. "I had no idea it was Nick and it looked like someone was breaking in, it really did. I was trying to help. And no, I don't want to press charges."

The two officers looked relieved. "Stay away from him," the older officer ordered and they climbed back into their car and drove away.

Nola walked back to her truck and carefully climbed into the cab. Once inside she slowly and methodically removed her right shoe and placed it on the seat next to her. Bright red beads of blood freckled the top of the leather. This worked out even better than she hoped. Nola glanced out the window. The sun had risen and the last of the bystanders had moved on.

Nola raised her phone to her ear and began the short drive

to the house where she would prepare the blood sample for Maggie.

"Jesus, Nola," Maggie hissed when she answered. "You shouldn't be calling me."

"Relax." Nola laughed. "I bet you get family members calling about cases all the time. No one is going to think twice."

"It's not a good idea." Maggie's voice was hushed and strained.

"I kept my end of the bargain," Nola said. "I have what you need."

"We need to talk about this." Maggie's voice dropped again so that Nola had to strain to hear her. "I don't think I can do it."

Nola turned onto her street and saw a U-Haul truck parked in front of the Kennedy place. She saw Maggie's brother, Colin, and three other men carrying two large sculptures. As she crept closer she saw that the metal sculptures were in the shape of horses.

"Nola, are you still there?" Maggie asked. "I mean it, we need to talk about this. Nola!" Maggie insisted. "I can't do it."

"You don't want to fuck with me, Maggie," Nola snapped into the phone. "Come over tonight and I'll give you what you need. We're doing this."

Nola disconnected and examined Colin's artwork. The faces of the horses were cut and carved into regal expressions and the manes, flanks and legs were bent and folded in ways that conveyed movement. The sculptures were stunning.

Colin Kennedy was full of surprises, Nola thought, remembering the awkward teen who was overshadowed by his younger sister. She stepped from her truck and watched as the men loaded the sculptures into the U-Haul. Maybe it was time to stop by and get reacquainted.

But first she had work to do. Nola reached inside the truck, grabbed her bloody shoe and went inside.

EVE KNOX

Eve trudged up the hill toward home. She was starting to feel guilty about the way she'd yelled at Nola but then made herself stop. Why did she do that? Eve was always the one to feel bad when it was Nola who was in the wrong.

A stitch gnawed at Eve's side and by the time she reached the top of the street she was sweating and out of breath. She loosened her scarf and leaned against the grimy telephone pole and bent over to examine the hole in her jeans. Her knee had stopped bleeding but bloodstains dotted the fabric. *Damn it, Nola,* she thought. Why did she have to be so childish? So mean? It was bad enough that Eve was constantly keeping their mother, who was so easily overwhelmed, on track with the bills and household chores, but she also had to serve as Nola's protector and moral compass. It was too much sometimes.

As she approached her neighbor's house, Eve crossed the street. Though the Olhauser home, a pretty periwinkle blue, with its sharp peaks and fanciful latticework appeared to be straight out of a fairy tale, the place made Eve uneasy. The son, Daryl, gave her the creeps. In his early twenties, Daryl would show up periodically at his mother's home for weeks, sometimes months at a time and from Eve's vantage point did little to contribute to the household.

To be fair, Nell Olhauser was a great neighbor. Petite and stooped, Nell would bring them freshly made *lefse* sprinkled with cinnamon and sugar and warm apple cake as thanks for shoveling her walk or mowing her lawn.

It seemed like Daryl would emerge from the house every time Eve would get home from school or Nick's. Like clockwork, he'd come out onto the front steps blinking rapidly into the bright sun as if he'd just woken up from a nap or had been waiting for her in a darkened room. He'd light a cigarette and watch her pass by. Through the haze of cigarette smoke, Eve could feel the heaviness of his eyes on her as she rushed into the safety of their home. Daryl never actually said anything. Eve couldn't remember a time when they ever exchanged a greeting but she knew she didn't like him.

She tried to tell her mother about how he made her feel like one of the bugs that Nola collected and pinned to index cards. Like she was a specimen, something to be examined, probed. Her mother just laughed and said that she should be flattered. She was a pretty girl; of course men were going to look at her.

Nola, on the other hand, had no problem calling Daryl out. *What are you looking at?* Nola would yell when she caught him staring at Eve. Or *Take a picture, it'll last longer.* Daryl would just smile lazily and blow a ring of smoke their way. Eve would hiss at Nola to shut up, to not encourage him.

Maggie said she had the same experiences with Daryl and the two finally went to Chief Kennedy to complain. *He's gross, Dad*, Maggie said. *He just stands there and stares at us.* Eve nodded her head in agreement. *It freaks us out.*

Chief Kennedy finally walked over to Nell's house, knocked on the door and went inside. Maggie and Eve watched anxiously from the window until he materialized thirty minutes later with a foam plate filled with star-shaped butter cook-

ies. He shouldn't bother you anymore, the chief said, holding the plate out to the girls. *But if he does, just let me know.*

Daryl still stared, though he tried to be less obvious about it. Now he watched out of the corner of his eye and Eve thought she could see shadows from behind windows. Whenever she was home alone, she made sure the curtains were closed tight.

Eve closed the front door and locked the dead bolt. Then she ran around the house, checking to make sure that each window and the back door were also locked tight. If only they had a dog, Eve thought and then caught herself. A sharp yelp of laughter erupted from her chest and she clapped a hand over her mouth.

Eve had begged for a dog for years, but her mother always said no. They were too busy; the house was too small; the girls were too irresponsible to take care of it. Now Eve wondered if there was more to their mother's decision. Had she known, on some level, that a dog, a pet of any kind would be in danger in this house? It was an awful thought.

Eve took the stairs two at a time and went directly to her bedroom. She lay back on the bed and stared up at the ceiling with its opaque stars that glowed in the dark when she switched off her bedside lamp. How had everything gotten so out of control, she wondered. Eve tried to push the thoughts aside and in the quiet stillness of the empty house her eyes grew heavy.

When Eve opened her eyes again the clock next to her bed read 2:45. With a sigh she slid from the bed and blearily made her way to the bathroom. She locked herself inside, wriggling the doorknob a few times to make sure it was secure. She hoped that Nola wouldn't come home anytime soon. Her mother worked until at least seven.

If she was lucky, she'd have the house to herself until her mother came home that evening. Eve pulled off her shirt, catching a glimpse of the bruises that Nick had left behind.

233

They were so ugly, made her feel so ashamed. At least it was the middle of winter and she could wear long sleeves and pants to keep the bruises covered until they faded.

Eve slid her jeans down, pulling them gingerly over her scraped knees. Why was it that every single person who claimed to love her found a way to hurt her?

Eve stared at herself in the mirror looking for an answer. Was there something in her eyes or in the way she held her head that said, *Pick me, I'm weak. I won't stand up to you.* But she did stand up for herself. She broke up with Nick and she stood up to her mother the night before. When Nola pushed her, she pushed back.

Eve turned the shower handle to the hottest setting, running her fingers beneath the spray until steam began to fill the room. She stepped over the lip of the tub and let the water stream over her body. Someone had used the last of the shampoo so Eve grabbed the chunky yellow slab of soap from the edge of the bathtub and rubbed it into her hair. Its sharp medicinal smell burned her eyes and nose but still she scrubbed and scrubbed her body until it ached.

She rinsed the suds from her body and then lathered up again trying to get the lingering smell of Nick's cologne and the stench of the dead dog from her skin. Eve knew she had to be imagining the odors that she was sure were clinging to her skin. Nick barely touched her today; the dog was too far away for her even to catch a whiff, but still the scents were there and when she finally stepped from the shower her body was rubbed raw and pink.

A sudden rap on the bathroom door caused Eve to startle and she pressed a towel to her mouth to stifle a scream. "Eve," came Nola's raspy voice. "I'm home."

Eve remained still, the water sliding down her body and into a puddle at her feet.

"Eve." Nola knocked again. "Open up."

Eve ignored her.

"Are you hungry? I can make you a grilled cheese," Nola offered.

Eve wrapped a towel around herself and ran a comb through her wet hair.

"Come on, I know you're in there," Nola said, frustration creeping into her voice. "Just come out. I want to talk to you."

Eve was used to Nola's attempts at apologies. They were always the same. First, Nola would pretend that nothing had happened. That there was no argument or harsh words. Then she would offer to do something nice for Eve. Wash the dishes for her or vacuum the living room or make her a grilled cheese sandwich.

Eve remained quiet knowing what was yet to come.

"Seriously, Eve." Nola's voice rose. "I didn't hurt that dog. I promise. It was already dead." Nola paused for a response. She wasn't going to get one. "Fine, don't talk to me. I don't care. You're supposed to be the mature one but you're not. You're just like everyone else. Mean and stupid and judgmental!"

Eve wanted to laugh. How could Nola not understand how twisted and awful her actions were?

"You're a horrible sister and I hate you!" Nola screeched, kicking at the door.

For a second, Eve thought the door was going to splinter but it held. Nola gave a few more kicks and then stopped. Eve could hear her breathing on the other side of the door.

Eve knew she couldn't stay in the bathroom forever. She put her ear to the door to see if she could hear Nola. It was quiet. Slowly she opened the door, looked to the left and to the right down the hallway. Nola was nowhere in sight. She stepped lightly so as not to let the floorboards creak beneath her feet and hurried to her bedroom.

She opened the door to find Nola sitting cross-legged on her bed. "Jesus, Nola," Eve said, pressing her hand against

235

her heart. "Get out of my room." Nola stayed put, her fingers digging into the bedding as if to prove she wasn't going anywhere without a fight. "I mean it. Get out of my room." Eve crossed her arms in front of her chest. "I can't even look at you. And you better call Mom and tell her you're home. You don't want me talking to her right now."

"It's not what you think," Nola said, and there was a desperation in her voice that Eve wasn't used to hearing. "I didn't hurt the dog. It was already dead," Nola explained again. "The school here is terrible. I don't get the chance to study real animals. Not really…"

Eve looked at Nola with disgust. "It doesn't matter why you did it, Nola. It's weird and creepy. You better hope that this doesn't get out or it will be another thing you'll never live down."

"You're not going to tell anyone." Nola said this, so sure of herself. So certain that she would get what she wanted.

"Maybe I will, maybe I won't," Eve said. "Now leave. I need to get dressed."

Nola hesitated as if wanting to argue some more but Eve didn't give her the chance. "Get out! Or I'm going to call Mom right now."

Nola slid off the bed and sidled past Eve, a knowing smile on her face. Eve slammed the door behind her.

Even if Nola was telling the truth about finding the dog already dead it was still wrong. Normal people did not behave this way.

Nola had always been fascinated with anatomy, had talked about studying to be a vet since she was little, but to dissect a dog? Surely the dog belonged to someone, had a name. This was someone's pet. How had it died then, if Nola wasn't the cause? Of old age or from being struck by a car? Maybe when she wasn't so mad at Nola, she'd ask.

Eve dressed in her only other pair of jeans and a clean

sweater. She trotted down the stairs to see Nola putting on her purple coat. "Where are you going?" Eve asked.

"None of your business," Nola snapped, pulling on a pair of gloves.

Eve went to the window and looked outside. "I think Daryl is back at it. Be careful. Have you seen anybody hanging around here? Nick or another strange man? An old guy wearing a red sweatshirt?"

"Paranoid much?" Nola asked. "I haven't seen Daryl and no, I haven't seen Nick or Hobo Santa Claus either." She opened the front door and stepped outside into the cold.

"Ha, ha," Eve deadpanned. Behind her the phone began to ring. She lifted the receiver and placed it to her ear.

"Listen, bitch," Nick hissed into the phone. "No one walks away from me."

NOLA KNOX

Thursday, June 18, 2020

Once inside the house, Nola went down to the basement and moved the junk from in front of the door to her workroom. When she stepped inside, she breathed a sigh of contentment. Using Nick's blood that dripped on her shoe, Nola prepared a small tube. She would get it to Maggie later today. She retrieved the pen with the dot of Nick's DNA from her pocket and put it in the refrigerator that hummed in the corner of the room. Nola had plans to use that sample for something else. Reluctantly, she stepped back into the main basement area and looked around at all of her mother's garbage. She had lived like this for way too long. Maybe it was time to reclaim some of the space for her own things.

She walked over to where she had hidden most of her collection. She moved the box filled with Christmas decorations and lifted the lid of the large plastic container that held dozens of small boxes. She dug around until she found the particular box she was looking for. It was smaller than you would think. When you peeled away the skin, muscle and tendons, when you lifted the organs from the cavities where they were nestled, what was left behind seemed so inconsequential. Bones and teeth. Smooth and bleached. Not white like the skeletons that are displayed in science classrooms. More like the color of an old lace tablecloth.

★ ★ ★

Back upstairs Nola quickly changed out of her clothes, stained from Nick's bloody nose, and then went back outside. Colin was loading the final sculptures into the U-Haul and his dad was standing on the front porch watching their progress.

"Thanks, guys," she heard Colin Kennedy say to his friends. "I got it from here. The buyer will help me unload them when I get to Willow Creek." He waved goodbye and spied Nola standing on her front step and came toward her.

"Oh, wow," Colin said, giving Nola a wide grin. "You changed your hair. I like it." Nola fingered a strand of her hair, the curls flattened into submission. "Our paths finally cross," he said. "I've been back for six months and I think this is only the second time I've seen you. What are you, a vampire?"

"Ha," Nola laughed. "I just work all the time. I took a few days off to deal with some personal matters."

"How's your mom doing?" Colin asked soberly. "I heard about the fall."

"She's holding her own," Nola said, her face falling. "She just needs time to heal. Hey, are these yours?" she asked nodding toward the U-Haul. "Pretty impressive."

"Thanks," Colin said. He was actually blushing, Nola thought. "I just sold them. I'm heading off to deliver them now."

"Congratulations." Nola smiled. The gesture felt foreign on her face. The chitchat that fell from her lips sounded unnatural even to her own ears. "How are you going to celebrate?"

"I hadn't even thought about that. With Dad, I have to stay pretty close to home. We'll probably grill out or something. Have a few beers."

"Alzheimer's?" Nola asked. "I remember my mom saying something about it. I'm sorry."

"Dementia, actually," Colin explained. "So far, he can tell

you about anything that happened decades ago but he has no idea what he ate for breakfast. Hey, I've got an idea." Colin's voice brightened. "Come over for supper one of these nights."

"Oh, I don't want to be a bother," Nola said half-heartedly. This was going to be easier than she thought.

"Yeah, but you've got to eat," Colin said. "And you are over at that house all alone."

"It has been a little lonely over there without my mom around," Nola admitted.

"Come on, I just sold my sculptures. This is big and this is how I want to celebrate." Colin lowered his voice to a conspiratorial whisper. "And honestly, I love my dad but it would be nice to have a fresh face around the house. We can share adult children living with their parent horror stories. How about tomorrow night at six?"

"Okay then," Nola finally agreed. "Tomorrow night."

"Hey, Mr. Kennedy!" Nola shouted. Henry turned his head toward her voice. Nola stepped past Colin. "It's Nola Knox," she said. "You remember me, don't you? I grew up next door." She stopped at the bottom of the porch steps.

Henry narrowed his eyes and looked her up and down. "You're the one who chopped the heads off all our peony bushes," he said leaning dangerously over the porch railing to get a good look at the top-heavy pink-and-white blooms that line the side of the house.

"Guilty." Nola held up her hands in defeat. "In my defense I was only nine at the time."

"Why'd you do it?" Henry asked gruffly.

Nola shrugged. "I guess someone must have pissed me off."

Henry laughed. Nola peeked over at Colin. He looked pleased.

"Dad, you ready to go?" Colin asked. "We're delivering the sculptures to Willow Creek today."

"I don't want to go," Henry said, gripping the handrail tightly. "Where's Leanne?"

"This is her afternoon off. Come on, Dad," Colin urged. "It's a horse farm. It will be fun to see the horses, won't it?"

"I don't want to go," Henry repeated stubbornly.

"I can't be late with this delivery. They're expecting me. This is a big deal." Frustration crept into Colin's voice.

"Or," Nola said, chiming in, "I can sit with you here on the porch, Henry. And you can remind me of all the mean things I did as a kid."

"Or," Colin said, "we can stop at Culver's when we're done. We can get something to eat. Dad, you like their ice cream."

"I'll stay with her," Henry said nodding at Nola.

"I don't think so," Colin said. "You have to keep a pretty close eye on him. He may end up in a stranger's kitchen."

Nola crossed her arms in mock offense. "I'm a doctor, Colin. I'm perfectly capable of keeping an eye on a fellow human being." Colin still looked hesitant.

"Here." Nola held her cell phone out to Colin. "Put your number in. I can call you if there are any problems." Colin still looked unsure. "I'll call if there are any issues. I promise," Nola assured him.

Colin didn't look convinced. He was going to be a hard sell. Just like his sister. "Seriously," Nola said, hand on hip. "Nothing bad is going to happen. I'll be here the entire time and if I need you, I've got your number."

Colin finally took the phone from Nola, punched in his number and handed it back to her. "I owe you," he said. To his dad he said, "See you in a little while. I won't be long, I promise."

Henry and Nola watched Colin climb into the U-Haul. He waved out the window as he drove away. Once he was out of sight, Henry sat down on the porch swing and began to rock back and forth.

"You look like her," Henry said, peering at Nola. "Except for the glasses. She didn't wear glasses."

"She got the good eyesight and I got the brains," Nola said and sat down next to him, their shoulders touching. Henry laughed and then abruptly stopped.

"It's not nice to speak ill of the dead," he said.

"You already know I'm not the nice one," Nola said and he chuckled again.

They swung in silence. Their feet pushing off the porch floor and lifting in unison. The warm air sweeping across their skin.

"So, Henry," Nola finally said. "They found new evidence in my sister's murder. Her boot. Wedged in between some rocks down in the caves."

"I didn't know that," Henry said, swinging a bit faster.

"It's been a long time since anyone has tried to find Eve's killer." Nola looked over at Henry. "I was beginning to think no one cared."

"I cared," Henry said softly.

"Then who do you think killed my sister?"

"Don't you think I would have arrested the guy if I could have?" Henry asked with irritation. Nola shrugged and Henry shook his head and planted both feet on the ground, bringing the swing to an abrupt stop. "I'm tired," he said getting unsteadily to his feet.

"I didn't ask you why you didn't arrest anyone," Nola followed Henry as he shuffled through the front door. "I just asked you who you thought might have killed Eve."

Henry continued on to the kitchen. He opened the refrigerator and scanned the contents.

"Come on, Henry. I'm curious," Nola pressed. "Just give me the name of your top suspect. Then I'll tell you what I think."

"I don't want to talk about this!" Henry said, slamming

the refrigerator door so hard that the contents rattled and the door popped open again.

"Okay." Nola crossed her arms. "You don't want to play. I'll go first." She took a step toward Henry. "How about this scenario? It was your perfect little daughter, Maggie." Henry looked at Nola in disbelief.

"I want you to leave now. You need to leave," Henry said, trying to step past her.

"I can't leave," Nola said blocking his path. "I promised Colin I'd stay until he got back. Did you hear me, Henry? Maggie killed Eve. She bashed her head in and strangled her." Her voice was calm, kind and didn't match the awful things she was saying.

"No," Henry said, bumping past Nola, accidentally knocking a glass of lemonade off the kitchen counter that shattered as it hit the floor. He turned and with surprising speed made his way down the hallway and into his den. Nola stayed close behind him.

"And you know what they were fighting over?" Nola asked. "A guy. Cam Harper to be specific. Your perfect little girl was banging the neighbor."

"Shut up!" Henry screamed. "You're lying! Get out of my house!"

"Eve found out and was going to tell and Maggie killed her." Nola laid a hand on his arm and he shook it away. "I'm telling you this for your own good, Henry. Your daughter did a bad thing. She smashed Eve's head against the ground over and over and over and then squeezed the life out of her."

"No!" Henry shouted and grabbed a picture frame from atop his desk and flung it toward Nola. His aim wide, it smashed against the wall behind her. She didn't even flinch.

"Come on, Henry," Nola taunted. "We both know that Maggie is no angel. You saw the way she acted the night Eve died. You can't tell me that it didn't cross your mind that Maggie knew more than she was letting on." Something flickered in Henry's eyes. Something sheepish and guilty looking. Nola stepped over the broken glass to get a better look.

"You knew," Nola whispered in disbelief. "You knew Maggie was the one who killed Eve and you didn't do anything about it. You protected her."

Henry shook his head. "No, no," he said over and over again. "That's not true."

But Nola knew the truth. None of the physical evidence pointed toward Maggie. Not one bit of DNA implicated Maggie because her father, the chief of police, was there to sweep it all away.

MAGGIE KENNEDY-O'KEEFE

Thursday, June 18, 2020

I make the drive to the station in under twenty minutes. After I hung up on Nola I told Shaun that I had to get in to work, that I needed to follow up on some of the tips that had been coming in about Eve's case. Not entirely true, but I was going to review the files.

As exhausted as I was last night, I couldn't stop thinking that Nola was going to report me to the police. Though I believe that the chief and Dex would initially support me one hundred percent, they would be obligated to listen to Nola. And she's persuasive. She would tell them about me and Cam Harper. My relationship with him would come to light, maybe my pregnancy. A few days after I killed Eve, I developed a high fever and chills. My dad took me to the doctor in Willow Creek and I broke down and told the doctor that I was pregnant and thought I lost the baby. He told me that I had.

The doctor was kind and promised me that he wasn't going to tell my father I was pregnant, that he couldn't tell him. But the information was in my medical records and if an investigation into me was launched, there was a slim chance those records could be accessed and used against me. Would Shaun ever be able to look at me the same way again? I would lose everything.

By the time I walk into the records room, I'm shaking with anger and fear. All of this goes back to Cam Harper and how he had gotten away with abusing me all those years ago. How he groomed me, impregnated me and somehow managed to keep me silent for so long. I still don't want people to know about it and for that I'm ashamed. I want to be brave; I want to stand up and tell the world that Cam Harper was—is—a predator.

I don't think I can do that, but maybe I can do the next best thing. I pull a box off the shelf and fan the files out in front of me. Before, I had no reason to look closely at the notes and interviews that I was half-heartedly organizing except to see if there was anything within the folders that could implicate me. Now I have something else to look for. Something that I had seen earlier. Notes referencing an interview that Joyce Harper had done with the police back in 1995.

I'm flicking through the pages when Francis pokes his head into the room. "Did you hear about this morning?" he asks.

"No, what happened?" I ask distractedly. I know the interview transcript is somewhere in here.

"It was a bloodbath," Francis says with a laugh. "Nola Knox drilled Nick Brady right in the nose with her head. Blood everywhere. I couldn't believe it." I look up from the papers, my attention piqued.

"She thought Brady was breaking into his own shop. Called us and when we went over there he nearly lost his mind."

I spin my hand in a circular motion to hurry him along.

"Nola started accusing Brady of killing her sister and he got right in her face saying she was wrong. Nola tripped and cracked him right in the face. Man, I thought the guy was going to kill her."

"Then what happened?" I asked, my mind racing.

"Then nothing." Francis shrugs. "Nola apologized and Brady went inside his shop bleeding like a son of a bitch. And then we left."

"No one pressed charges?" I ask, closing my eyes.

"Nope, but Brady looked like he was going to have a coronary." Francis gives a shake of his head. "Nola Knox better not go within fifty feet of him anytime soon. I swear to God he wanted to kill her. What's her deal anyway?" he asks.

"I have no idea." I play dumb. "Listen, Francis, I got a ton of work to do before this baby is born."

"Yeah, sorry," Francis says, but hesitates, and I know he wants to bring something up but doesn't quite know how to do it.

"I'm still getting calls," I admit before he asks. "We're going to have to change our home number. I disabled my Facebook account."

"Want me to keep looking to see if I can find out where the posts originated?" Francis asks and I hate the sympathy I see in his eyes.

"No thanks," I say. "I think I know who started this all and I'm going to ignore it." Francis looks like he wants to ask me who but he doesn't dare.

"Just let me know if you change your mind," he says then leaves.

I'm pretty sure it's Nola who accused me of having an affair with a married man on Wrecked Nest. It's the only thing that makes sense. It's another way to keep me off balance, keep me in line. I'm not going to give her the satisfaction of letting her know it's gotten to me. The fire is another story. Did I really think that Nola was capable of arson? Yeah, I did. Did she start the fire at my house? That I'm not sure about.

I settle back into reviewing the files, but this time my fingers fly faster through the pages. Nola really plans on going through with this and I will do just about anything to keep my secret.

A name catches my eye and I know I've found what I'm looking for. I read the interview and then flip through the pages until I find my dad's interview with Cam. "Bingo," I murmur.

In Joyce's interview she explained to Dex that she had been out Christmas shopping all afternoon and didn't return home until around eight o'clock that evening, when she paid me and I went home. She went on to say that her husband had meetings that afternoon and was in his office in Willow Creek until about six and then had a work-related dinner with colleagues. He arrived home, according to Joyce, at 9:00 p.m.

Cam Harper gave my dad just about the same story but added that he took a break to go for a run around 3:00 p.m. and returned to the office for a shower and more meetings. Except I know different. I don't know where he was between 7:00 a.m. and 3:00 p.m. that day, but I know Cam wasn't running between three and three forty-five because he was with me. That day Cam parked at the bottom of Ransom Road before coming up to the house. He was always very careful about not being seen at the house when I was there but was ready with the excuse that he was picking up his running gear.

The medical examiner thought that Eve died between four and nine. And Cam Harper did not have an airtight alibi. Even if he went directly back to work after he was with me, it would take about thirty minutes to get to his office. Cam was supposed to have been in Willow Creek all day. In that small window, he had the opportunity to kill Eve. With one pull of the thread, his entire alibi would unravel.

I shake the thought away.

"Hey, how's the investigation going?" I look up to find Dex Stroope standing in the doorway.

"Slow but steady," I say vaguely. "Verified a few things—have a few avenues I want to look more closely at."

"Good. Let me know if you need anything," he says then notices the files spread out in front of me. "That the autopsy report?" I nod. "You really want to read that?" he asks. "Pretty grim stuff. I can give you the CliffsNotes version."

My spine stiffens. "Would you ask a male detective that?" I ask. As much as I like and respect Dex, he was pretty old-school.

Dex raises his bushy white eyebrows at my tone. "I would ask that question to any cop whose best friend was the murder victim."

"I can handle it," I assert.

"I have no doubt," he says dryly. "What's your gut telling you?"

"Who do I think killed Eve?" I ask. "I'm trying to reserve judgment. How about you?"

"I have my suspicions," Dex says. "Finish your investigation and we'll compare notes."

Though I'm dying to know who Dex suspects, I let it go. "Fair enough," I say. "Hey, Dex," I call before he goes on his way, "I'm not judging, but the files in Eve's case are pretty jumbled. That wasn't like my dad."

"They didn't always look like that. There was a time they were organized nice and neat, like everything else. Your dad spent a lot of time on Eve and a few years ago, he went back into the files and pulled everything apart. He said he wanted to look at it with fresh eyes. I think he was onto something but," Dex's eyes shift away from me uncomfortably, "he started having his health concerns."

"But he didn't tell you what he found?" I ask.

"No, but I got the sense he thought the killer was definitely someone who knew Eve."

"As is the case with most homicides," I say. "That would

be three-fourths the population of Grotto. Eve knew a lot of people."

"True," Dex agrees. "Listen, I've gotta run..."

"Hey, can I show you something really quick? It will just take a second." I flip through the files until I find his interview with Nick Brady. "How solid was Nick's alibi?"

Dex reaches for the paper and brings it close to his face. He's left his reading glasses back in his office. He peruses it for a few seconds. "Looked pretty airtight to me. With his friend Jamie Hutchcraft from after school until five. Jamie verified it. And then went to help his mother out at their shop until ten. She backed that up too. Why? You think Brady killed her? We checked him out pretty carefully."

"No," I say, taking the paper from him. "I'm not saying that at all. Just trying to be thorough."

"Hopefully the DNA testing will clear things up and we can put this one to bed," Dex says. "Let me know if you want to talk more. I'm always around."

Dex leaves and fear blooms in my chest. Eve's boot and all of the other items from her case are still locked away in the evidence room. I could pack up all the evidence now and send it off to the state lab. The chief expected it to be done already, but still it sits. *You had one job*, I say to myself. There's only one person that the forensics can be tied back to. Me. I should just go to the chief and turn myself in. In the long run it would be easier.

Nola's words keep nagging at me. *I can help you. I want to help you. All you need to do is slip a little bit of his DNA into the evidence, reseal it, send it in and we wait for the results.*

And Nola had really done it. She had gotten a DNA sample from Nick and she expects me to do the rest.

I swing by the café and pick up three club sandwiches and some macaroni salad and drive to my dad's house. I try to stop by there for lunch a few times a week. My first instinct is to avoid my dad and Colin. I feel like all they have to do is take one look at me and they'll see right through me. See that something's wrong. But I have to do my best to keep up appearances, to keep things as normal as possible.

No one is sitting on the front porch so I push open the door. "Hello?" I call out. "Dad? Colin?" No one answers. "I've got sandwiches!" Bag of food in hand, I move to the kitchen. The refrigerator door is open wide. The floor is wet and sticky and covered with shards of glass. My hand flies instinctively to my sidearm.

A loud crash comes from somewhere within the house. I throw the bag on the counter. "Dad? Colin?" I call again then hurry back down the hallway toward my dad's den. I push open the door to see my dad's ancient desktop computer lying on a carpet of wayward papers along with the contents of the desk drawers. My dad is standing in the corner, clutching a lamp, his face red with rage. Kneeling on the floor in front of him is Nola.

"What the hell?" I ask.

"Jesus," Nola says from the floor. "He freaked out and started throwing things."

"What are you doing here, Nola?" I ask, my eyes sweeping the room, fingers still hovering over my holster. "What did you do to my dad? Where's Colin?"

"He had to run to Willow Creek to deliver some sculptures. He asked me to stay with your dad until he got back." Nola looks genuinely rattled. "I was trying to get him something to eat and he just went off on me."

I go to my dad's side and gently pry the lamp from his fingers. "Dad, what's the matter?" I ask. "What happened?" He is breathing hard and sweating. I'm afraid he's going to have a heart attack. "Why would Colin ask *you* to stay with my dad?" I ask Nola incredulously. "He wouldn't do that."

Nola gets to her feet. A broken picture frame is in one hand and the index finger on the other hand is oozing blood. "One minute he was fine and the next minute he started throwing things at my head." It's the most out of sorts that I've ever seen Nola.

I take my dad by the hand and get him seated in his desk chair. "It's okay, Dad, I'm here," I soothe. "What happened?" He just shakes his head, his eyes filled with confusion and shame.

"You wanted me to stay with you, Mr. Kennedy, don't you remember?" Nola asks, taking a step toward him. I give her a look that stops her cold. "He did," Nola says to me. "He didn't want to go with Colin. I said I'd stay. Call Colin and ask him."

"Don't worry, I'm going to," I say icily. "What did you say to him? You weren't talking to him about Eve's case, were you?" I cross my arms in front of me.

"No," Nola says. "We talked about peonies."

"Peonies?" I repeat. I glance at my dad but he's looking dumbfounded at the mess on the floor.

"Yeah, peonies," Nola says, meeting my eyes, daring me to challenge her.

"You need to leave now," I say. It's all I can do to not grab Nola by the arm and drag her from the house.

"Bye, Henry," Nola says as she turns to leave, dropping the picture frame she's holding. It crashes to the floor.

I track her footfalls as she moves through the hallway. I wait for the sound of the front door opening and closing. Certain that she's gone, I turn my attention back to my dad. He looks exhausted. "What did Nola say to you?" I ask, my heart hammering in my chest, afraid of what he's going to say.

"She ruined the peonies," my dad says. "Ripped the heads right off." He wades through the paper littered across the floor and out of the room. "But I found it. Don't worry, Maggie,

I took care of it." I stare after him, confused. I have no idea what he's talking about.

Once again Nola has swept in and somehow left a mess. Literally and figuratively. Nola leaves a toxic cosmic residue behind wherever she goes.

I look down at the shattered picture frame. A small smear of blood streaks the broken glass. In the photo my mother is sitting on the porch steps. She is gazing at the camera, a soft smile on her face. She looks content. Happy. This was the way my mom looked at my dad in the quiet moments of the day, when the chaos of running a busy household and chasing two young kids had slowed. I think about how I miss her.

I follow my dad out of the room and watch as he climbs the stairs up to his bedroom, his shoulders hunched, head bent as if he's climbing a mountain. What did Nola say to him that would cause him to start throwing things? Certainly it wasn't about his peonies. It could be that my dad was just confused, worried because Colin wasn't here. I return to the kitchen and survey the mess. This was definitely not about flowers.

I go upstairs to check on my dad and to bring him a glass of water. He sometimes forgets to drink and gets dehydrated. He's lying on his side, covers pulled up around his chin. He's already fallen asleep and is snoring softly. He's fine. For the first time I'm grateful that my dad forgets.

I call the police station and let them know that I won't be back in today, that my dad needs me. While I wait for Colin to come home I keep busy by cleaning up the mess in the kitchen. I put the sandwiches I brought for lunch into the refrigerator and sweep up the glass and scrub the floor. In my dad's office I return the computer to the desk and gather all the papers and the broken picture frame from the floor.

I'm transferring a pile of wet towels into the dryer when I hear my dad on the steps and I go out to meet him. "Hey,

Dad," I say. His hair is sticking up and his shirt is untucked. "How was your nap?"

"Where's Colin?" he asks sleepily. "What time is it?"

"Two o'clock. He went to deliver some sculptures to Willow Creek," I tell him.

"Oh, yeah," he says. My heart squeezes. He doesn't remember.

"Nola Knox was here," I say.

"I'm sorry I missed her. What time is it again?" my dad asks as he moves toward the front door.

"Two o'clock," I say. "Nola left when I came over. Have you eaten anything? I brought you a sandwich."

"Peanut butter sounds good," he says as he pushes through the screen door, steps out onto the porch and to his spot on the swing.

I don't know if it's safe to leave him alone on the porch, but he's got to eat something. As I go inside toward the kitchen, a renewed sense of frustration toward Colin rushes through me. He should know better than to leave our dad with Nola. In the pantry I find a box of crackers and a jar of peanut butter. It doesn't look like Colin has been to the grocery store anytime lately and I find myself getting angry again.

I slather the peanut butter on half a dozen crackers, arrange them on a plate and bring them out to the porch with a glass of iced tea and one of the sandwiches I brought to the house. "Here, Dad," I say, handing him the plate of crackers. I sit in a chair adjacent to the swing as he nibbles tentatively.

"Dad, Nola was here earlier and something made you very upset. Do you remember what she did? What she said?"

"Nola was here?" he asks through a bite of cracker.

"Yeah," I say with relief. He has already forgotten. "She was here."

"Bad business about her sister," my dad says, shaking his head.

"You didn't talk about it much," I say, picking at my sandwich. I need to eat but I've lost my appetite.

He takes a sip of iced tea. "It was a hard thing to talk about. How do you talk to your kids about the murder of a fifteen-year-old girl? Eve was your best friend and she was brutally beaten and then strangled." He points at the Knox house. He's getting worked up, agitated.

"Dad, I'm sorry, I shouldn't have brought it up…" I begin but he's not done yet.

"I tried to protect you from the ugliness of it. It was an awful thing that happened. So no, we didn't talk about it at the dinner table."

"Dad," I say reaching for his hand but he shakes it off and disappears into the house.

I hear the rumble of a vehicle and look up to find Colin pulling into the driveway. He gives me a big grin. I'm nauseous with guilt and anger at my brother for letting Nola Knox into my dad's home.

"Hi," Colin says trotting up the porch steps. "Did Nola leave?"

"What were you thinking?" I ask, rounding on him. "I came over and found Dad standing in a corner ready to throw a lamp at Nola's head. How could you have left him with her?"

"What happened?" Colin asks in alarm. "Is Dad okay?" He moves to go inside and I grab his arm.

"I just don't think it's a good idea to leave him with strangers," I chastise. "Especially crazy ones like Nola. Next time you have to go somewhere, take him with you."

Colin's face reddens. "Don't you think I tried that? Dad refused to come with me. He wanted to stay home. He wanted to stay with Nola. If I knew it would have upset him so much I would never have left."

I sigh. Who am I to judge Colin? He's the one who's here

all the time, the one who upended his entire life so Dad can stay in his home, and he's done so without complaint. But Nola Knox? "Next time just call me, I'll come over," I tell him gently.

Colin sits down on the swing and reaches for one of the remaining peanut butter crackers. He takes a small bite and tosses it back onto the plate.

"So you delivered the sculptures?" I ask, trying to smooth things over. "That's got to feel pretty good."

"It feels great," Colin says through the crumbs. "Man, there's nothing like it."

"We should celebrate," I say. "Go out for dinner or something."

"I already got it covered," Colin says, downing the rest of Dad's iced tea. "Dinner, tomorrow night. Right here. I want you to come and Shaun and the baby of course." He pats my belly. "And I've invited Nola too."

"Nola?" I ask in alarm. "Why?" This day keeps getting worse and worse.

"I don't know?" Colin shrugs. "Her mom's in the hospital and Nola's all alone over there and it was a nice thing to do."

"That's too bad, Colin, but it still isn't a good idea to have Nola over for dinner," I say. "I'm working on Eve's case. It doesn't look right for me to socialize with her."

"It's just a barbecue." Colin laughs. "Relax."

"It's not a good idea, Colin," I repeat, getting to my feet. "Nola Knox is not someone you want to get involved with. Don't you remember what she was like as a kid?"

"Maggie," Colin says, "it's just dinner."

"I've got to get going," I tell him, my irritation back in full bloom.

I go inside and say goodbye to my dad. He's sitting in front of the television with his feet propped up on the coffee table. "Bye, Dad," I say, leaning down for a hug. "You doing okay?"

"I'm fine," he replies, barely glancing away from the TV.

"So?" Colin asks, stepping into the house. "Will you come?"

"Yeah, we'll be here," I say grudgingly. It's better if I'm here, keeping an eye on Nola. God knows what she's up to. "What do you want me to bring?"

"Just your beautiful selves," Colin says.

I move outside and take a quick glance at the Knox house and a long hard look at the Harper house, a beautiful home with a lot of ugliness inside. I spent countless hours inside that house babysitting the twins and so much more. Over the years I've tried to keep tabs on the goings-on there but recently I've been so busy at work and with the baby coming I haven't been so diligent. I think of the way Cam was touching the young girl at the softball field and in my gut I knew he was doing it again. Most likely had never stopped. Men like him never change.

I walk up to the cherrywood front door and press the bell. The sound of Pachelbel's "Canon in D" echoes through the house and my stomach clenches. How many times over the years have I rung this bell? A hundred? Maybe more. I hear a dog bark from somewhere inside. No one comes to the door. I stand on tiptoe trying to see through the leaded glass window with the hand-painted pineapple medallion in the center and see Winnie.

I cross around to the back of the house where I know there's a large brick patio surrounded by a tall privacy fence. "Hello," I call out. "Anyone home?" Again, no answer. I thread my hand through a slat in the fence and lift the latch and let myself into the backyard. If someone comes upon me I have no good excuse for being here. I look around for security cameras but see none. I'm guessing Cam Harper doesn't want any trace of the comings and goings in and around his house.

I peek through the slats in the fence, and looking into the Harpers' backyard is like stepping into a different world. Spires of hollyhocks and star-shaped columbine and purple-and-yellow Johnny-jump-ups fill the flowerbeds and masses of clematis climb and tumble over the wooden fence in snow-white curls. The emerald green lawn a stark contrast to my dad's sad, anemic yard. The firepit with five Adirondack chairs situated around it is still there. I remember how Cam Harper would sit in one of those chairs with his tanned legs crossed, one hand holding a cigarette and the other a crystal tumbler filled with an amber-colored liquid. I thought he was beautiful. He told me I was beautiful. He was thirty-five. I was fifteen.

I shouldn't be here. My unborn child shouldn't have to breathe the same air that Cam Harper does. I lean against the fence and try to steady my shaky legs and slow my breath. On the ground, out of place among the deep-blue ladybells are a scattering of old cigarette butts. It looks like Cam still had that nasty habit. I rub a hand across my face.

The statute of limitations has long run out for any legal recourse for what Cam did to me, but I still have to find a way to make sure Cam Harper pays for what he has done. For what he's doing. He ruined my life. Why shouldn't I ruin his?

NOLA KNOX

Friday, June 19, 2020

Henry Kennedy was waiting at the front door as Nola walked up the porch steps carrying a pie in one hand and a small gray plastic bag in the other. If he remembered anything about what happened the day before he didn't give any indication.

"Dad," Colin said, coming up behind him. "I invited Nola to the barbecue." To Nola he said, "Come on in. What can I get you to drink?"

"I'll have whatever you're having," Nola said.

They traveled through the living room and into the kitchen to find Maggie and Shaun already there sitting at the table.

"Thanks," Nola said as Colin handed her a bottle of beer from the refrigerator. Nola stared defiantly at Maggie and took a long drink.

Sensing tension, Colin jumped in. "I just put the burgers on," he said. "They should be ready in about fifteen minutes. Hope you are all hungry."

"I'm starved," Shaun said, rubbing his hands together. "Hey, I wanted to ask you about making a sculpture for the shop at the orchard. You interested?" The two disappeared out the door and into the garage leaving Nola and Maggie alone in the kitchen.

"Here," Nola said thrusting the bag at Maggie.

"What's this?" Maggie asked. She peeked inside and the

color leached from her face. "What the hell, Nola?" She pressed the bag back into Nola's hands, noticing a Band-Aid wrapped around Nola's finger. "Why did you bring this here? Are you crazy?"

"Take it," Nola ordered. "I want this done. The sooner you get the evidence to the lab the sooner this will all be over with."

Maggie shook her head. "I don't think I can do this, Nola. I think I'll just take my chances."

"We've been through this, Maggie." Nola tipped the beer to her lips. "You're almost there. Remember what Nick did to me? What he did to Eve? Do you really think someone like that should be running around free?" When Maggie didn't answer she went on, "Think about your baby, Maggie. It's the most important part of all this, right? You have to do this for your baby."

"I should probably go sit with my dad," Maggie said, grabbing the bag and rushing from the room. Nola went to the refrigerator, retrieved another bottle of beer and went to the front door. From behind the screen she could see Maggie leaning into the truck.

Nola went outside carrying two bottles of beer and waggled one at Henry. "Here you go, Henry," she said. "I thought you might be thirsty."

"Thanks," Henry said, reaching for the bottle.

"Dad," Maggie said coming up the front steps. "You know that's not a good idea. When you drink your sleep gets messed up."

Henry took a deep swig and smiled mischievously. "One beer isn't going to make a difference," he said. "Tastes good."

Nola squeezed into the spot next to him on the swing and lifted her bottle and clinked it against his. "Salud," Nola said, and smiled.

"Time to eat," Colin called through the screen door. Nola lagged behind as they moved through the house and to the kitchen. "Help yourself," Colin said. "We can eat out back." They each grabbed paper plates and plastic silverware and dished up baked beans and potato salad and moved to the back patio. The air was still hot and humid with the temperature hovering in the eighties even though it was after six. A citronella candle sat in the middle of the table emitting its lemony scent.

"I'd like to propose a toast," Maggie said, tapping on her glass of lemonade with a plastic fork. "Colin, we are so proud of you. I remember when we were kids you always said you were going to be an artist. I know it's been a long road but all your hard work is paying off. Congratulations on your first big sale—and here's to many more." Maggie lifted her glass into the air. "Cheers."

"Cheers," everyone said heartily, raising their own drinks. Even Nola.

"Hello?" a voice from inside the house called out. "Anyone here?"

Nola looked to Colin. "Is someone else coming to dinner?" she asked.

"Yeah, Dad and I were on the porch talking about it and the Harpers came outside," Colin said. "He invited them to come too."

"Oh my God," Maggie murmured, rising from her chair.

"What's the matter?" Shaun asked with concern. "Are you okay?"

"I'm fine," Maggie said as the Harpers stepped into the backyard. Joyce carried a covered dish and Cam a small cooler. "Everyone's here."

Nola leaned over and whispered to Maggie. "All we need is Nick Brady."

Joyce glanced uneasily at Nola. "We are so sorry to hear about your mother, Nola."

"Thank you," Nola said. "She's getting stronger every day. I'll tell her you asked after her."

Nola watched as the Harpers fixed their plates and settled into their seats. She noticed how Cam Harper and Maggie didn't make eye contact.

"Maggie, you used to babysit for the Harpers when you were young, right?" Nola asked.

"Yeah, I did," Maggie shifted in her chair. "How old are the twins now?" she asked, directing her question to Joyce.

"Thirty-two. Can you believe it?" Joyce marveled spearing up a forkful of pasta salad. "They have their own kids now. Cam is just champing at the bit when Sophie gets to the high school so he can coach her in softball."

"Oh, you coach softball?" Nola asked, turning to Cam. "How old are the girls you coach? Fourteen, fifteen?"

"Somewhere around there," Cam said, focused on his plate. "I love the game."

"What's your next project, Colin?" Maggie asked, steering the conversation to a different topic.

"Actually, I have a few in the hopper," Colin said. "A sculpture of a family for the entrance area of the hospital in Willow Creek and one for the orchard." He gave Shaun a big grin.

"Nice," Nola said, leaning forward on her elbows. "I've always thought a sculpture of a bird would be pretty. Don't you think? Maybe one in red, like a cardinal." Nola looked first at Maggie and then at Cam as she spoke. "Some people say that when you see a cardinal, it's a dead loved one coming to visit you."

"What a nice thought," Joyce said, oblivious to the tension at the table. "I've never heard that before."

"How about it, Colin?" Nola asked. "Do you think you could do that for me?"

"Sure," Colin agreed affably. "I'll stop by next week and you can tell me more about what you're thinking."

"Excuse me for a moment," Cam said, pulling a pack of cigarettes from his shirt pocket. "I'll be right back." He went around the side of the house and toward the front yard.

"Such a bad habit," Joyce said once Cam was out of earshot. "He's tried quitting a million times but can't kick it. I swear it will be the death of him."

"So," Nola said, turning toward Maggie. "What's going on with my sister's case? What juicy tidbits can you tell us? When will the DNA come back? Any new suspects?"

"Why do you want to talk to Maggie?" Henry asked in annoyance. "That's my case, Nola. If you have any questions, you should ask me."

"Okay, then," Nola said, leaning in close to Henry. "Who do you think killed my sister?"

Maggie abruptly stood. "Sorry, I can't talk about the case."

"Are you okay?" Colin asked. "Do you need water?"

Shaun stood and gently put a hand on Maggie's back. "I think she just needs to go home and get some rest. It's been quite the week with the fire and all. You go on to the truck, Maggie, I'll grab our stuff."

"Ahh, the fire," Nola said, "I almost forgot about that. Any leads on how that started?"

Maggie ignored her question and Shaun's gesture and went into the house.

"I'll go after her," Colin offered.

"No, let me," Nola said. "You stay." Nola let herself into the house and watched as Maggie pushed through the front door and stopped short when she saw Cam Harper smoking a cigarette on the front lawn.

Nola watched as Maggie stared at Cam for a long moment, straightened her spine and walked directly toward him. Though she couldn't hear what was being said, Nola could tell by the stunned expression on Cam's face that Maggie was giving him an earful. Cam reeled backward and held up his hands as if they could shield him from the onslaught of words, then he regained his composure and stepped forward. Maggie held her ground, hand on hips, mouth moving rapidly. Cam looked as if he might explode but instead brushed roughly past her and toward the Kennedy backyard.

"Go, Maggie," Nola whispered, surprised at Maggie's vehemence. Nola could only imagine what Maggie had to say to Cam, but whatever it was, it hit its mark. This was getting more interesting by the minute.

Maggie awkwardly lowered herself to the curb. For a moment Nola wondered if something might be wrong with the baby, but Maggie was simply struggling to tie her shoe.

"I wonder what that was all about," Shaun said, looking over Nola's shoulder.

"I have no idea," Nola murmured. Obviously Shaun had no inkling of Maggie's past involvement with Cam Harper. Shaun stepped past her and down the steps. Nola watched with interest as he held out his hands to help Maggie to her feet. *So many secrets just waiting to be spilled*, she thought. Nola couldn't wait to see how it all played out.

MAGGIE KENNEDY-O'KEEFE

Friday, June 19, 2020

As we drive home from Colin's I vacillate between wanting to tell Shaun everything and keeping my mouth shut.

Shaun can see that something is wrong. He keeps glancing over at me as he drives. "Maggie, what's going on?" he asks. "Is it the baby?"

"We're fine," I snap. "Quit asking me that."

"Sorry," Shaun says, not sounding sorry at all. "Sorry for being concerned about my wife and our baby. I'll shut up now."

"Let me out," I say as we pull into our lane.

"What?" Shaun asks.

"Stop the truck, right here," I order. "I need to get out."

"Maggie," Shaun sighs. "What's going..."

"I said stop the truck!" I shout.

Shaun yanks the truck over to the side of the road and throws it into Park. I fumble with the door handle, throw open the door and step out into the humid evening air. I grab my purse from the truck's floor. It's where I put the bag that Nola gave me. I don't want to take the chance of Shaun finding it.

"I just need some air," I tell Shaun. His face is stony as he pulls away leaving me behind in a cloud of dust.

A new wave of shame comes over me. I'm not the woman my husband thought he married.

I take a deep breath and am met with the smell of fallen apples, decaying in the evening heat. I slowly walk beneath the canopy of leaves and reach up to pluck a red-and-green Cortland from a low-hanging limb. I roll it around in my hands until I come to one of the wrought-iron benches that we have placed intermittently throughout the orchard for visitors to take a rest.

I sit and take a bite of the apple, its sweetness exploding in my mouth. You'd think that living on an orchard, surrounded by thousands of apples would make me sick of them. But I'm not. If anything I crave them even more now that I'm pregnant. Shaun jokes that the baby will crave applesauce the minute she's born. He's probably right.

I confronted Cam. I can't believe it, but I did. All the rage and anger that's been bottled up inside of me for the last twenty-five years spewed forth when I saw him standing on my dad's front lawn smoking that cigarette.

Of course he said I was crazy. That nothing happened between the two of us, that it was all in my head and I had no proof. He said if I said another word about it, he would sue me for defamation and then he walked away.

I sat on the curb, tightened my shoelace and saw Cam's smoldering cigarette butt on the ground and I knew what I had to do. After Shaun helped me to my feet I asked him if he would go and get a few pieces of the pie to bring home with us. While he was gone I reached into the truck's glove compartment and fished out an old newspaper that Shaun had stuffed inside.

Making sure to leave no fingerprints I used the newspaper

to carefully scoop up the cigarette that Cam discarded and slid them both into the glove box.

I gnaw on the apple, surrounded by the buzz of cicadas. This should be one of the happiest times of our lives. We're just about to have the baby we've wanted for years, I've recently been made detective and the orchard is doing great but I know better than anyone that everything you love can be taken away in a second.

"That'll be seventy-five cents." I look up to find Shaun standing over me.

"It's worth it," I say, tossing the apple core to the ground. Shaun settles on to the bench next to me, reaches for my hand. It's warm and calloused and fits perfectly with mine.

"How's Johnny Appleseed doing in there?" he asks, laying his other hand across my belly. The baby swoons with his touch and we both look at each other in delight.

"Johnny's a girl," I remind him.

Shaun shrugs. "Who says a girl can't be named Johnny? We'll just drop an *ie* at the end of her name. All the cool kids are doing that."

I laugh. It feels good. We sit quietly for a moment, holding hands and gazing up at the red orbs swaying lightly with the breeze.

"I'm sorry," I say. "I was way out of line. It's just that I've been buried in Eve's case. And having to be in the same space as Nola and the Harpers, it was like being transported back in time twenty-five years. It's making me crazy."

Shaun is quiet for a moment. "You weren't out of line, Maggie. She was your best friend. You want to find out what happened to her."

I nod. "I'm driving the evidence to the state lab on Monday. Then I'm going to tell Digby that I'm not working the case anymore."

Shaun doesn't look as happy about this as I thought he would. "What?" I ask. "What's wrong?"

"I did see Eve that day," he says, kicking the dirt with his boot. "We were friends. Sort of."

"Friends?" I ask in confusion. "You and Eve?"

"Eve was looking for her sister that afternoon, so we drove around looking for her. I told the police all about it. They checked my alibi. You believe me, don't you?"

"Of course I do, but why didn't you tell me?" I ask, floored by this revelation.

He shrugs. "I thought you probably already knew and didn't want to discuss it. I could see how much it hurt you to talk about Eve. I didn't want to make it worse for you."

I reach for his hands; despite the hot weather, they are cold and clammy.

"We drove to the caves," Shaun says, rubbing my knuckles. "And we found her sister." Shaun goes on to tell me about seeing Nola with the knife, the dog, the blood.

"That's awful," I murmur. "Did you tell the police this?"

"I wanted to, but Eve made me promise I wouldn't. I dropped her off and drove away. Next thing I know she's dead. I thought for sure Nola did it, but then nothing happened. Her mother vouched for her and no one was arrested. The longer I didn't say anything, the easier it was to keep it a secret." I know exactly how he feels.

"It was easier to pretend that it was just some crazy person who killed her, that nothing I could do or say would help the police." Shaun looks at me helplessly. "I'm so sorry."

"I know." I lean into him. "It's okay."

Shaun lets out a breath of relief. "What about Nola and the dog? She didn't see me but she saw Eve. That's why I thought Nola might have killed her. It was awful, seeing her kneeling over that dog, its stomach all torn apart. Could she have done it? Killed her sister?"

"No, it wasn't Nola," I say. "Don't say anything to anyone about this," I tell him. "It isn't relevant anymore."

"She's crazy though, isn't she?" he asks.

"Yeah," I say. "She is."

We begin to feel the sting of mosquitoes and know it's time to go inside for the night. We walk to the truck and Shaun drives us back to the house. We spend the rest of the evening in front of the television watching sitcoms and eating the pie we never got to eat at Dad's.

Shaun keeps one hand atop my belly hoping to catch the baby moving. He's in luck. Little Johnnie is in rare form tonight. Rolling and kicking and punching her little fists into my ribs.

Just for tonight, I'm not going to think about Eve or Nola or Cam Harper. Just for tonight I'm only going to think of Shaun and the baby. Nothing else.

EVE KNOX

Friday, December 22, 1995
3:15 p.m.

Eve slammed down the phone. "Who was that?" Nola asked.

There was no way Eve was going to tell Nola that it was Nick and what he said to her. She wondered what it would be like to not be afraid all the time. Afraid of what others thought of her, afraid of what Nick might do, what Nola might do.

Eve breathed a sigh of relief once Nola walked out the door. She had a few hours of uninterrupted peace. No Nola, no mother, no Nick. These moments were rare. She went to the kitchen, pulled a pop from the fridge and went upstairs to her room. Eve shivered. Her windows rattled from a brisk wind, sweeping in heavy snow clouds along with the cold. She coiled her scarf around her neck, climbed beneath her quilt and reached for the book that she borrowed from Maggie this morning.

She flipped over on her stomach when something fell from the pages and to the floor.

Eve reached down and picked it up. It was a bookmark made from red paper. It was cute, in the shape of a bird. Curious, she pulled at one of the corners and began to carefully dismantle the bird. As she pulled back each fold a word was revealed.

Eve smoothed the pleated page with her hand and began to read.

For Maggie, my sweet bird ~
One day we will fly away from here and be together forever. Be
patient. We only have to keep it a secret a little longer. I can't
wait to touch you again. To kiss you, to be inside you.
I love you and only you.
C.

MAGGIE KENNEDY-O'KEEFE

Saturday, June 20, 2020

Somehow, amid all the fetal gymnastics, I must have dozed off because the house phone startles me awake. A blanket is covering me and Shaun is nowhere to be found. I struggle into a seated position on the couch and look around. The house is dark and the TV is off. The phone continues to trill and I get up to answer it. Since we changed our number we haven't gotten any hang-up calls but that doesn't mean they haven't started again. I reach for my cell phone sitting on the coffee table and see that I've had six missed calls from my brother. *Shit.*

By the time I get to the phone in the kitchen it's stopped ringing and I can hear Shaun coming down the steps. I look at the clock on the microwave. It's just after midnight. I use my cell to call Colin back and he immediately answers.

"Jesus, Maggie," he says. "I've been trying to call you for a half an hour. Dad took off."

"What do you mean he took off?" I ask, my heart thumping.

"What's going on?" Shaun whispers and I hold up my hand to silence him.

"I mean he's gone. I can't find him anywhere." Colin is breathing heavily as if he's been running.

"I thought you had an alarm on the door. Didn't it go off? Are you sure he left the house?" I shove my feet into my shoes and start searching the kitchen for my car keys.

"I forgot to set it. I'm sorry. I fell asleep."

"Jesus," I mutter.

"You want to deal with this?" Colin snaps. "Be my guest. It isn't easy."

"I'm sorry," I say. I have no right to judge Colin. He's the one with Dad all day, every day. "Have you called the police?" I ask.

"You are the police, Maggie." Colin's voice breaks.

He's right. We've already lost too much time and I need to take control of the situation. "I'll call patrol and have them meet us at the house. Where are you right now?"

"I'm walking around trying to find him," he says. "Do you think he might have gone down the bluff?"

"No," I say immediately. "He wouldn't have gone that way. He hasn't been down that way forever." For many years he walked up and down the rocky bluff in search of evidence, of anything that might lead to Eve's killer but once, a few years ago, he slipped and fell, scraping his knees and cracking his elbow. The fall scared him enough to stop his daily treks.

"He might have gotten confused," Colin insists. "He could be trying to get down to the caves."

"Go back to the house and wait there in case he comes back. I'm on my way," I order and hang up.

Shaun reemerges, dressed and with car keys in hand. "I'll drive," he says and together we rush out of the house and into his truck. While he speeds down the highway I call dispatch and request that a patrol officer meet us at my dad's house.

"I knew something like this was going to happen," I say

in frustration. "He's getting worse every day and Colin can't watch him twenty-four/seven."

"We'll worry about that later," Shaun says, reaching for my hand. "Let's concentrate on finding him first. He can't have gone too far."

I know he's probably right but I can't help thinking about all the bad things that could have happened. He could have gone through the woods behind the Harper house and fallen down the bluff, he could have stepped into traffic and been hit by a car, he could have pitched into the creek, or wandered into a cornfield and gotten turned around. All terrifying prospects.

When we pull onto my dad's street, it has started to spit rain and Colin and Pete Francis are standing in front of the house wearing rain jackets and holding flashlights. "Any sign of him?" I ask the second I get out of the truck but from the look on Colin's face I already know the answer.

"How many patrols do you have searching?" I ask Francis.

"It's just me," Francis says. "There was a bad car accident out west of town. The other units are over there and I was called in to cover everything else. Any idea where your dad may have gone to?"

I shake my head helplessly. "Your guess is as good as mine. But we can't wait around for him to just come back." I don't want to ask for help. I don't trust Nola or the Harpers but they are all I have by way of reinforcements and I'm desperate to find my dad. I would make a deal with the devil if it would help. I turn to Colin. "You go knock on the Harpers' door and see if they've seen him or if they would be willing to help search for him. Shaun and Francis, both of you drive around and look for him. I'll go get Nola to help look and I'll then ask Mrs. Olhauser to wait here at the house in case he comes back." I'm using my cop voice but inside my daughter's heart is racing in my belly. "Call me if you find anything."

Everyone scatters and I cross the street to Nola's house. It's dark and quiet. I pound on the front door. No one answers. "Nola," I shout through the door. "Wake up!" I knock louder. I turn and face the dark street. It's pouring now. Minutes are ticking by.

I peer through the window and see what looks like one of my dad's slippers. This is enough of a reason for me to enter Nola's home without her permission. I turn the knob and push the door open. I step inside and flip on another light. To my surprise, the living room looks somewhat less cluttered. The stacks of newspapers have shrunk and the path to the stairs has widened. I pick up the damp, muddy slipper. It's definitely my dad's. "Dad! Nola," I call up the steps. "It's Maggie, where are you?" Still no answer.

I get to the top of the landing and move toward Nola's bedroom. "Nola," I say, rapping on the closed door. "Wake up. My dad is missing." Nothing. I push open the door and light from the hallway splashes into Nola's bedroom. No one is here. I feel along the wall for a light switch and the room is filled with harsh light.

I bite back a gasp when I see the walls. Gruesome drawings of animals cover nearly every inch of the walls. The innards of dogs, cats, horses, birds and more are drawn with hyper-realistic detail. Pictures that would make sense in an anatomy text but on the walls of a bedroom look like the backdrop for a horror movie. These drawings weren't here before Eve died. *Nola is ape-shit crazy*, I think as I back out of the room and down the stairs.

Instead of going out the front door I decide to go through the kitchen and exit through Nola's back door in case my dad wandered into her backyard. The floor is damp with large muddy footprints. The footprints of someone who scuffed along with some difficulty. The footprints begin at the back door and end at a rug at the edge of the basement steps.

The door to the basement is standing open and a dim light glows at the bottom of the stairs. "Nola?" I call. "Nola, are you down there?" No response.

Like an invisible string is pulling me forward I move down the steps. The basement is as cluttered as ever, but I notice immediately that something is different. A table is pushed aside to reveal a pocket door, slightly open, with a wedge of light peeking through. Step by step I pick past the swollen garbage bags and overflowing boxes and bins and up to the door. "Anyone there?" I ask. I slide the door open and look inside. A heavy stainless steel table sits in the middle of the room. A small shape, covered with a sheet lies at the center of the table. It's the size and shape of an infant. Instinctively my hand goes to my hip in search of my sidearm. Of course it's not there.

I move toward the table. The only sound is my breathing and the crackle of electricity from the overhead florescent lights. With trembling fingers, I reach for the sheet. I pull it away and it flutters to the floor like a feather to reveal a metal tray lined with surgical tools. Scalpels and scissors and glinting silver tools with hooks and sharp points that I don't know the names for but look terrifying.

I step backward, at once relieved and horrified. I need to find my dad and it's clear he's not here. I turn to leave and in front of me a cat sits as if sleeping on a shelf just above my head.

Heart pounding, I slowly move forward. The cat remains still. I don't see its chest rising and falling. I reach my hand out to touch its tawny fur. Its jade eyes snap open and it swipes at my arm, taking a claw-full of my skin with it. I turn and trip, slamming into a tower of plastic bins beneath the stairs.

The bins crash to the ground, plastic cracking and the contents tumbling out. Glass Christmas ornaments shatter at my feet and cheap plastic garland wraps around my ankles. But there is something else that catches my eye, that renders me rooted to the spot. A human skull lolls back and forth on the concrete floor surrounded by what looks like human femurs and ulnas. I clap a hand over my mouth to stifle a scream.

I watch as the skull rolls to a stop at my feet. I lower myself to one knee to get a better look. Careful not to touch any of the bones I peer down at them. There's no way to know how long they've been down here. They've been cleaned well. There's no sign of blood or tissue left behind but an odd odor emanates from them.

"Nola, what have you done?" I whisper to myself. I thought by aligning myself with Nola I was protecting my baby and Shaun from what I had done decades ago but instead I've joined forces with the devil.

I have to get out of here. I retrace my steps, with one hand holding my belly and the other slapping at the lights, I head back up the stairs. I fall twice, banging my knees on the hard wooden steps. Once at the top, I pause, trying to catch my breath. I try to tell myself that there has to be a logical explanation. Nola is a doctor. It makes sense that she would have bones, right? She's a vet though. I'm not an expert, but even I could see those bones were human.

My next instinct is to call for backup, to get Francis here so we can process the scene, but then I stop. I entered Nola's house as a private citizen, not as a police officer. Technically I'm trespassing.

But I can't unsee what I've seen in this freak show of a house and as a good cop I have a duty to report what I've seen to an on-duty police officer. But I can't deal with this now. I need to find my dad and I don't want Nola to have any idea that I was in her home. Once I get my dad home safe and sound I will figure out what to do next.

Using my shirt, I wipe away the smear of blood on my arm from where the cat scratched me. I stare down into the dark basement and try to steady my breathing. I don't want to go back down there, but I have to. I hurry down the steps hoping that Nola won't come back and find me here. I do my best to sweep up the broken ornaments and replace the items, even the skull and bones, back inside their bins. I think of the makeshift surgical setup she has in her back room, the anatomical drawings that cover her bedroom walls, and shiver.

I scan the basement and when I'm confident that I've covered my tracks, I head back upstairs. I step from Nola's house and warm rain strikes my face. I need to find my dad. I don't know what to do, where to go. The street is deserted.

Suddenly I hear shouts. Moving as fast as my heavy stomach will allow, I sprint over to the Harpers' yard.

"Stay there! Don't move!" I hear someone yell. It's not the order of a police officer to a perpetrator telling them to freeze, but of a person begging someone to stay still for their own safety. I bang through the gate and race through the yard, the wet grass soaking the hem of my pants. By the time I reach the far end of the yard that opens up to the bluffs, I'm soaked, struggling for breath. I have a stitch in my side.

Cam points a flashlight and through the wobbly beam of light and from about twenty feet away I see my dad teetering at the edge of the bluff. Nola is standing just a few feet away from him.

"Dad," I cry and move toward him but Cam pulls me back. At his touch a spasm of disgust runs through me and I yank my arm away. "Dad," I say again, taking a tentative step toward him. "What are you doing out here?"

My dad turns, barefoot and dressed in his pajamas. He squints through the glare of the flashlight and seems surprised to see me. "I'm waiting for Charlotte," he says. A scruff of beard has sprouted on his face, giving him a neglected air. I want to weep. He looks frail, lost. His eyes shift from me to Nola. A crease forms between his eyebrows. "I know you," he says.

"Dad, it's the middle of the night," I say, taking another step toward him. "And Charlotte's in the hospital. She had a bad fall, remember?"

"I'm supposed to give her an update on the case. Every week I do. I'm supposed to give her an update," he insists.

"She'd like that," I say, inching toward him. "But Charlotte's not out here. You're all wet." He looks up, noticing the rain for the first time. "Come toward me." I stretch my hand out to him.

"No, I'm supposed to talk to Charlotte. But don't worry, Maggie, I found it," he says. As he takes a step backward the ground beneath him begins to crumble.

"Dad," I scream. "Don't move. Stay right there. I'll take you to Charlotte. I promise."

"No." He shakes his head. "I'm going to wait right here."

Out of the corner of my eye a shadowy streak bolts toward the bluff and rams into my dad, causing them to vanish from the flashlight's glow. Next to me, Joyce screams and for a second I think they have both fallen over the edge of the bluff. Cam whips the flashlight left and right, searching for where my dad and Nola landed, scanning the rocky ground and finally coming to rest on a knotted heap of limbs.

I dart toward them, drop to my knees, jagged points of rock biting into my skin. "Get off, get off!" I shout as I pull on Nola who is atop my dad. She peels away from him, breathing hard. My dad is lying on his back staring up at the black sky, unseeing. For one terrifying moment I am reminded of Eve's eyes the night we found her. "Are you okay? Are you hurt?" I ask, searching for any sign of injury.

Nola gets to her feet. She is sopping wet and her dyed red hair is flattened against her head and she is slick with mud. I look up at Joyce. "Call an ambulance." This order seems to bring my dad back to us and his eyes clear.

"No, I'm fine," he says, slowly trying to sit up.

"Lie back down," I tell him. "Something might be broken."

"I'm fine," he insists. I stand and hold a hand out to help him up and Nola does the same.

I knock it away. "You could have killed him," I snarl. "You could have taken him right over the bluff. Stay away from him. Stay away from all of us." Tears spring to my eyes and I'm grateful for the rain.

"He was about to go over the edge of the bluff," Nola snaps back. "I saved him."

Cam steps forward and together we lift my dad to his feet. I don't meet his eyes. I don't say thank you. I just lead my dad back through the gate and through the yard until we are on the street. Shaun, who had taken the truck to go look for my dad, pulls up and leaps from the truck.

"What happened?" he asks as he helps me guide my dad up the front porch and into the house.

"I don't know for sure," I say though a possible picture is beginning to form in my mind. My dad wanted to talk to Charlotte and wandered over to Nola's house. He was inside that house. I know it. I saw his muddy footprints. Did he see the same things that I did? Did he go down to the basement and see Nola and all the surgical equipment? Even in his confused state, he would know that what he saw wasn't right, wasn't normal. Did he run from the house or did Nola lead him away and to the bluffs?

"I don't know what happened," I say, knowing that I can't relay my fears to Shaun, that I can't tell anyone about what I saw in Nola's basement just yet. I wasn't supposed to be in there. I have to manage my own secret first. Then I'll deal with Nola.

Dripping wet, Shaun and I settle my dad into a kitchen chair. Shaun makes hot tea while I wrap my dad in a blanket.

"I really need to talk to Charlotte," he says over and over.

"I need to give her an update. But don't worry, Maggie, I found it."

This is the third time my dad mentioned something that he found and I want to ask him what it was, but I'm afraid of the answer.

"It's after midnight, Dad," I say. "It's too late for updates. It will wait until tomorrow," I soothe. "You can tell her in the morning." I'm hopeful that when he wakes up he will forget about everything that happened tonight.

Colin rushes through the front door. "Where is he?" Colin asks, looking around the room frantically. "Is he okay?"

"He's fine," I say dropping into the nearest chair, all the adrenaline seeping from my body. "He was behind the Harper house, right on the edge of the bluff. He could have fallen." I prop one elbow onto the table and drop my forehead into my hand. This isn't the time to fall apart, I tell myself. I straighten, wipe my eyes and stand. "We need to get him cleaned up and into bed."

"Jesus," Colin says, closing his eyes. "I'm so sorry. This could have gone so bad." I know Colin is waiting for me to say that it was okay, that it wasn't his fault. It's true but I can't quite bring myself to say it out loud.

"You can't beat yourself up." Shaun says what I can't. "These things happen. Now we just need to make a plan so that it doesn't happen again."

"Well, I won't forget to set the door alarms again," Colin says, rubbing a hand across his face. He looks exhausted.

Our dad needs more than alarms on the door, I think. We are going to have to have some tough conversations. But not tonight. We get my dad showered and settled into bed. Colin starts to head downstairs but I tell him that I want to stay with our dad a little bit longer.

I settle into a chair next to his bed as his eyes begin to grow heavy. I should just let him be, let him sleep, but the curiosity is too much. "Dad," I begin, "what did you mean when you said, *I found it*, earlier? What did you find?"

He looks sleepily up at me and I wonder if he's already forgotten saying it. "The scarf, Maggie." He licks his lips and speaks so softly that I have to lean in to hear him. "I found the scarf, honey. A few days after Eve died, hidden at the bluffs." A small gasp escapes my lips and he reaches for my hand, his fingers dry and papery. "I got rid of it for you. You don't have to worry anymore," my dad says. His eyes flutter shut and just like that he is asleep.

I want to jostle him awake. He knew that I killed Eve. A cold sweat breaks out on my forehead. I scan my memory for any indication that my dad suspected me, but find nothing. Did he see me that afternoon running down the bluff after Eve and when he learned that she was killed put two and two together?

How did the scarf end up hidden in the bluffs? I know I didn't take it with me. Was Eve even wearing it in the caves? Everything was so chaotic, I can't be sure. Maybe she dropped it when she came down the bluff.

It's the dementia, I tell myself. *He doesn't know anything.* My dad is the most ethical person I've ever met. Would he keep this kind of secret for twenty-five years to protect me?

I sit in the dark listening to his slow, steady breathing and think about how close he came to dying.

And I think about how close my dad and Colin live to pure evil. Once I'm confident that my dad is fast asleep and not going anywhere, I rise and make my way down the stairs. I hear Colin and Shaun talking in the kitchen and instead of joining them I go to my dad's office.

There're no remnants of my dad's earlier tantrum except for the shattered picture frame that I dropped into the wastebasket next to my dad's desk. I pull out the frame that still holds some jagged remnants of glass smeared with Nola's blood, and wrap it in an old newspaper.

I offer to stay the night at the house but Colin insists we go home.

Shaun and I say goodbye, step back out into the misty night and climb wearily into the truck. On my lap is the newspaper-wrapped picture frame. "What's that?" Shaun asks.

"My insurance policy," I murmur. Shaun gives me an odd look but doesn't press the question further. I see Nola sitting on her mother's front step. I'm so pissed at her for luring my dad to the edge of the bluff. He could have died.

With Nola's hair glowing ruby-red beneath the soft light of the porch she could be Eve. I bite at my cheeks to keep the tears at bay. How cruel Nola is. Always has been. How could she sit there, hair dyed red, in some kind of twisted Eve Halloween costume?

Nola knows exactly what she's doing. And I think I finally know what her endgame is. Our eyes lock as Shaun's truck drives past and she gives me a small, friendly wave. I don't wave back.

MAGGIE KENNEDY-O'KEEFE

Monday, June 22, 2020

All weekend I waited for Nola to approach me and accuse me of being in her basement but she never did. Maybe I cleaned up well enough that she has no idea I was there. I'm sure my dad was in her house though. He got it in his head that he needed to talk to Charlotte about Eve and wandered over there in the middle of the night. I think Nola was working in her basement and found him in her house and I think she led him out and toward the bluffs just like she did with little Riley Harper thirty years ago.

At my insistence, Shaun and I spent most of Sunday at my dad's house, keeping a close eye on things. He seemed okay. Tired but had no recollection of the night before. I kept waiting for him to bring up the scarf again, but he never did. At one point during the day, I pulled Colin aside and asked him if he could take my dad to visit his sister in Wisconsin. He balked, of course, giving all the usual excuses how it's too far, how Dad doesn't do well with change. In between my Braxton-Hicks contractions I managed to convince Colin to go after explaining that I thought the fire at our barn was intentional, that investigators were looking into whether I was targeted and by association, my family.

That finally got his attention and he agreed. They're leaving this morning. At least I know they will be safe until I figure out what to do about Nola. I'm thinking an anonymous call to the police will do the trick. I'll let my colleagues come into Nola's house, find the bones and go from there. Hopefully, Nola will have no idea that I'm involved.

I come into the station extra early this morning to finally pack up the evidence in Eve's case and personally deliver everything to the state lab in Des Moines. As I sit at my desk and review the evidence list I think of Nola and what she's asked me to do.

I think of Nola's determination to pin Eve's death on Nick Brady.

I don't have the proof that Nola is responsible for our barn fire and for posting lies on the Wrecked Nest website but I do know that she is intent on destroying my life. How stupid was I to think that she wanted to help me, to protect me? I'm just another person Nola wants to enact revenge upon. Not that I can blame her. I don't. I killed her sister.

What I am sure of is the house of horrors that Nola lives in. The makeshift surgery setup; the scalpels and knives. The bones.

I pull up the *Missing Person Information Clearinghouse* website and see that there are three hundred and fifty-six individuals that are considered officially missing in the state of Iowa. In the Operating Agency search box, I enter Grotto and get zero results. This isn't a surprise to me—if there were any open missing-person cases in town I would know.

Nola is a big animal vet and her work takes her all over the county so I expand my search to Ransom County and thirty-two names pop up. To my untrained eye, the bones did not look like they belonged to a young child so I narrow the search to individuals thirteen years old and up. That brings the number to thirty. Not much help. With a sigh I log off my computer and push my chair back from the desk. It's time I get on the road.

I sign out each piece of evidence and with the help of another officer load up my car. Before leaving I go into a storage closet and find an old box of evidence labels and envelopes. I pull out several of each and stuff them into my pocket. Back in my office I reach into my bottom desk drawer and stare down at the three items each stored in their own individual evidence bag: the needle filled with Nick Brady's DNA, the cigarette butt I got from the Harpers' backyard and the shard of glass from the broken picture frame that Nola cut herself on.

It's time to a make a decision. I grab all three bags and drop them into a larger manila envelope. All I would need to do is insert the manufactured evidence into one of the old envelopes, slap on a label and forge my dad's signature and date it as December 1995. It would be so much easier than I thought. I'll decide on the road, I tell myself. Besides, I don't dare tamper with the evidence here.

By noon I'm ready to leave. I drive for an hour and just before I hit the interstate I pull off onto a gravel road. I step from my car, pop open the trunk and remove the lid to the cardboard box holding the evidence.

I keep an ear out for any approaching cars and pull out the large sealed paper envelopes that hold the boot and jeans that Eve was wearing the day she died and I climb back into the driver's seat. In a few hours all the evidence in Eve's case will be back in the hands of the state crime lab where decades of advancements in forensic testing await it.

I stare at the three items I've spread out on the passenger's seat. A needle, a cigarette butt, a shard of glass. This is it. The last chance I have to make sure I'm never implicated in Eve's death. I have a decision to make. It might not work, but this may be the only way that I have to protect my family. Do I follow Nola's orders and inject a smidgen of Nick Brady's blood into the envelopes that hold Eve's boot and her jeans? In high school I got adept in forging my dad's handwriting. It would be easy to fill out an old label and sign my dad's name to the evidence list. Do I add the broken glass or Cam's cigarette butt into the box? All I have to do is choose one.

Here I go again, playing God. With tears streaming down my face I take a deep breath and make my choice.

THERAPY TRANSCRIPT

Client Name: Nola Knox, 13 years
Therapist Name: Linda Gonzalez, LMHC, NCC
Date of Service: April 16, 1996

LG: Good morning, Nola. How are you doing today?

NK: Today's my last session. So pretty good.

LG: I wanted to talk to you about that…

NK: It is my last day. The court order was for fifteen sessions. This is the fifteenth.

LG: Yes, that's true, but I think we are making some really good progress together. I think that if we continue to work on strategies that you can use to help handle challenging situations…

NK: But this is my last session. I've done everything you've asked. I even apologized to Nick Brady. I said I was sorry. No. This is our last session. I'm fine now. Everything is fine.

Notes:

4/16/1996

In my assessment, Nola would benefit from long term therapy in order to address anger issues and coping skills. I approached Charlotte Knox encouraging her to continue sessions and she agreed.

4/23/1996
Nola did not show up for today's session. Phone
calls to the mother went unanswered.

MAGGIE
KENNEDY-O'KEEFE

Monday, June 22, 2020

Once I deliver the evidence to the state lab I drive the three hours back to Grotto but instead of heading straight to the orchard I make a split-second decision and make a sudden turn off onto an old service road.

I've avoided coming to this spot since Eve died. I had no reason to return unless it was work related and somehow I managed to dodge any calls relating to these caves. Now, after all these years, I've come here of my own accord.

I open the car door and step out onto the pavement. It's still god-awful hot and my stomach hardens with the Braxton-Hicks contractions that have been plaguing me all weekend. I reach back into the car and take a big swig out of my water bottle, hoping that I won't have to pee anytime soon.

I grab my department-issue flashlight, step from the car and begin the trek to the caves. It's not far but I have to travel through a wooded area with no clear path and I have to fight annoying gnats and low-hanging branches and a tangled carpet of weeds and fallen logs. I move slowly, carefully so as not to trip. Daylight filters dreamily through the canopy of leaves and I'm reminded how magical this place once felt to me. Now all I feel is dread.

As children, Eve and I would pack sack lunches and play tag here, chasing one another around tree trunks until we were sweaty and out of breath. We'd look for secret paths and bear cubs, unsuccessfully of course. The only things we managed to find were Nola lurking after us and poison ivy, but we still had fun.

Above me I hear what I hope is the scuttle of a squirrel or a raccoon. Supporting my belly with two hands I pick up the pace. Eventually the trees thin and I find myself standing in front of Ransom Caves.

The three caves sit before me like a disturbing series of Halloween masks. One with an entrance in the shape of a wide, gaping smile, another with a half-closed sneer and a third with a tight-lipped, nearly impassable smirk. Eve died just inside the gaping smile known as Rattlesnake.

We were forbidden to go inside Rattlesnake because it was known to flood in heavy rains and it had a dizzying number of paths and with one wrong turn you could get hopelessly lost. We were supposed to stick to the sneer. Of course we didn't listen and we spent hours exploring Rattlesnake and it became as familiar to us as our backyards.

I don't know why I'm here, except that maybe things have come full circle. This is where the story of my last twenty-five years began and now ends. The evidence is in the custody of the state lab. It's out of my hands. The sun is beginning to set but I have no intention of staying long, just long enough to talk to Eve. To apologize, to ask for forgiveness. I move toward Rattlesnake and take a hesitant step inside. Immediately the temperature drops and the cool air feels good against my skin.

"Hello," I shout and the word bounces right back to me. We did that as kids, shout random words into the dark and listen as the sound waves spring wildly against the cave walls like a bouncy ball.

I turn in a slow circle, trying to take in as much of my surroundings as I can before the sun completely fades. Fireflies wink back and forth to one another and I have a flash of nostalgia. Me and Eve and Nola chasing after lightning bugs, holding them carefully in our cupped hands. Except for Nola, who would spread the wings out wide and then peel away the golden orb.

I duck my head to avoid striking my forehead on a rocky low-hanging dip. A dank, mildewy smell fills my nose and my heart bangs against my ribs. A shallow river trickles along a fissure in the stone and collects in a wide, deep crevice. I'm standing on the spot where Eve was found. The crime scene photos flash in my head. Eve's wide, unseeing eyes. The red-rose bloom of blood haloing her head. "I'm so sorry, Eve," I whisper and then sway and reach out for something to hold on to and find the uneven, cool rock wall.

I move more deeply into the cavern until I'm at the spot where the cave's ceiling opens up into a natural skylight. Above me the evening sky is marbled blue and pearl gray.

"Maggie?" a voice says. "Are you okay?"

I startle. "Nola?" I ask, turning toward the sound. "What are you doing here?" Her red hair is scraped back from her face in a messy ponytail and she's got a backpack on her shoulders.

"Now what are the chances of the two of us running into each other this way?" Nola asks breezily.

My stomach feels crampy and a surge of heartburn threatens to bring up my lunch. "I'm guessing zero," I say trying to keep the fear from my voice. The last place I want to be is anywhere alone with Nola. "What do you want?" I ask. "What are you doing here?"

"Obviously, I followed you," Nola says, her eyes scanning the cave walls. "I wanted to make sure you delivered the evidence to the state lab."

"You followed me to Des Moines?" I ask in disbelief. How could she have tracked me all the way to the state lab and back without me noticing? I wonder if she saw me pulling off onto the gravel road earlier in the day. Nola just stands there with a nasty grin on her face.

"I did what you told me to. Now can't you just leave me alone, Nola?" I ask. I'm so tired. My pelvis aches and I feel vaguely nauseated.

Nola rubs her arms as if she's cold. She looks around, and the smugness is replaced with sadness. Is it genuine? Maybe. Just outside the cave, the sun gives its final gasp and disappears behind a black curtain of clouds.

"It's getting late," I say, stepping past her. "I'm going home."

"No, wait," Nola says, latching on to my wrist. "I just want to talk to you for a minute."

I squirm away from her grasp. "Seriously, Nola, I'm really tired and feel like crap. I'm going home, put my feet up and count the number of minutes between contractions."

"If only I thought you were truly sorry," Nola says, sliding the backpack from her shoulders. It lands on the stone floor with a thud.

My head is pounding and my stomach is queasy. Despite the cool air, sweat trickles down the back of my neck. I glance over my shoulder toward the cave's opening. Why do I feel like I'm being ambushed? There's no way I'll ever be able to outrun her. "But I am," I say. "I am sorry. I'm so, so sorry that I hurt Eve. If I could go back and change what happened I would. I would trade places with Eve in a heartbeat."

Nola flips on her flashlight and folds her arms across her chest, a bitter smile on her face. "So you say."

My belly tightens and releases again. It doesn't exactly hurt but it's got a bite to it. I can't be in labor, can I? It's too early. The baby isn't ready to come yet. *I'm* not ready for the baby to come yet. I look around and find a ragged boulder to sit on. I take a few deep breaths and after a minute the world stops tilting.

"You okay, Maggie?" Nola asks.

I nod and look up at her. "I'm fine," I say but inside alarm bells are clanging.

Nola situates herself next to me on the rock and tucks the flashlight beneath her chin, the shadows distorting her face like a kid getting ready to tell a ghost story around the campfire. "I just want to talk to you. We need to talk about Nick."

"What do you mean?" I ask. "I told you, I did what you asked. I used the blood you gave me and I added it to the evidence. You saw me drive it to the lab…"

Nola waves away my words. "Yeah, I know but the more I think about things, the more I wonder if screwing with the old evidence is enough."

"Of course it is," I say, my voice taking on a desperate tone. "You said it yourself. DNA doesn't lie. Once the forensics come back, Nick is…"

"Are you really going to lie to me here?" Nola interrupts. "It's where you killed my sister. You can't lie to me in the spot where your best friend took her last breath."

"Lie to you?" I ask. "How have I lied to you?" I want to be more outraged, more indignant but a wave of nausea overtakes me.

"Pay attention," Nola says tapping me on the head with her flashlight. "I've been watching you and I'm beginning to think that maybe you don't have the stomach for this." She points the light toward the gullet of the cave. But even the strong beam can't penetrate the absolute darkness.

"Nola, you're wrong…" I argue but Nola taps my head again. This time harder.

"You talk a big game, Maggie, but I think I'm going to need a little more assurance. Why did you send your dad and brother away this morning?"

Another contraction hits me, this one intense enough to make me groan. Nola waits patiently until it passes. "I didn't," I begin but she gives me a look that shuts me up.

"You were in my basement," Nola said with disappointment. "You probably saw some things that you shouldn't have. You aren't planning to tell your coworkers about what you found, are you?"

"I don't care about your things, Nola," I say, struggling to get to my feet. "You must know that. I'm not going to say anything about what's in your basement. As far as I know they are just fake. Your Halloween decorations. You hold all the cards. I'm not going to say a word. We've got a plan in place. I don't intend to change anything so you don't have anything to worry about." A burning pain spreads across my pelvis and I bend at the waist.

"Okay, then," Nola says, plucking my phone from my back pocket. "I can text Shaun for you." She scrolls through my contacts and quickly types out a message. "I told him I was going to drive you to the hospital and for him to meet us there. You, my dear, are in labor."

"I think I am," I breathe. "But the baby won't be here for a long time, right?" I ask, my voice taking on a tinge of desperation. "Especially since it's my first?"

"Depends," Nola says, shining the light on my face. I wince at the brightness. "You could squeeze that baby out in a matter of minutes or it could take hours."

"We should probably go then," I say moving toward the exit. It's going to be okay. Nola realizes that I'm no threat to her. I'll get to the hospital, have my baby, put all this ugliness behind me.

"Wait, wait," Nola says playfully moving the flashlight like a maestro, causing the light to dance across the ceiling of the cave. I catch glimpses of a rocky shelf. It's a ledge about ten or fifteen feet above the ground and runs deep into the cave much like a catwalk high above the stage of a theater. It must have been a bitch to get up to, slippery and narrow.

"That's where you hid," I say, realization spreading through me, "the night that Eve died. That's where you were when you heard our argument." I clench my teeth against another contraction. I turn my face and throw up onto the ground beside me. A cold sweat breaks out across my skin and I begin to tremble. The sour smell of vomit is overpowering.

"We better go, Nola," I say, wiping my mouth with the back of my hand. "We can talk about this later. Shaun will be waiting for us." I imagine him at the hospital, the bag filled with a set of clothes for me to wear after the delivery and an outfit for the baby.

"Don't worry, Maggie," Nola says, "I was just kidding. Shaun isn't waiting for you at the hospital. He thinks you're still in Des Moines. Flat tires are a bitch."

"Flat tire?" I repeat dumbly. "What do you mean?"

Instead of answering, Nola sets the flashlight on the ground and spreads out a large plastic tarp like a beach towel.

"What are you doing?" I ask fearfully.

Nola reaches into a black leather bag situated on a rock ledge next to her and pulls out two syringes. One small, like the one she gave me that held Nick's DNA and one much larger. Instinctively, I cover my belly with my hands and begin to edge backward. "Surprise," Nola whispers, her eyes feverish and a small smile playing on her lips as if we share some kind of secret.

NOLA KNOX

Monday, June 22, 2020

Maggie's eyes flicked back and forth between the syringes and just past Nola's shoulder in search of an escape route.

"Sorry, Maggie," Nola said, fingering the syringes in her hand. "We need to finish our chat," she said as if they were sitting down for tea, "and I'm afraid we might not be done before the baby comes. But first of all I need your gun." Nola slipped one of the needles into her pocket.

"I'm not giving you my gun, Nola," Maggie said through clenched teeth as another contraction overtook her. In that second, Nola was on Maggie, the point of the larger needle pressing against her neck.

As Nola unsnapped the gun from its holster Maggie reached for it at the same time. They wrestled for it, their fingers clawing at the cold metal. It fell to the ground with a clatter along with the syringe. Maggie knew she was no match for Nola's speed and strength and kicked out at the revolver, sending it skittering across the cave floor and down into a deep crevice filled with water.

A shiny layer of sweat gleamed across Maggie's face and her breath came in desperate hitches. "I don't understand what's happening." Maggie planted one hand against the cave wall. "I did what you asked me to. Why would I double-cross you?

You hold all the cards, Nola. You can trust me," Maggie said through gritted teeth.

"I don't think so," Nola said regretfully. "You know all my secrets now."

"And you know all mine," Maggie gasped. "I need to get to a hospital," she whimpered. "I can't have my baby here."

"Well, you really aren't in a position to make any demands now, are you?" Nola snapped as she slipped on a pair of latex gloves over her fingers.

A contraction overtook Maggie and she pressed her palms against the coarse wall of the cave with a low guttural moan.

"Five minutes apart now," Nola said looking at her watch. When the spasm passed, Maggie lowered herself to her knees as if in prayer and pressed her forehead against the limestone.

"Do you want me to turn myself in for killing Eve? I will. I'll do it. I'll do it right now. But please, you have to get me to the hospital."

Nola sighed as if dealing with an annoying petulant child. "I still want Nick to take the blame for this. I will take great joy watching him being taken into custody. Now if only I could count on you to keep your mouth shut." Nola shook her head.

"I won't tell," Maggie cried. "I promise. Please," she begged. "Please, call for help." Maggie felt a rush of liquid and then blood bloomed between her legs. "Oh, God! Please, Nola, something's wrong. Call 911."

"Lie down, Maggie," Nola ordered. "The baby is coming."

"No, no," Maggie shouted, shaking her head from side to side. "Someone help! Please, help me!" Tears streamed down her face and she struggled to catch her breath.

Nola was a little bit afraid of this. Maggie going into full panic mode. Nola wasn't worried that someone was going to hear her.

"Shhh, now," Nola said pulling a scalpel from her backpack. "Lie down and I'll take care of you." she cooed.

"Please don't let my baby die," Maggie beseeched. "Please, Nola, please." She reached up and grabbed a fistful of Nola's shirt. Her eyes were wide and haunted. "Eve wouldn't want this. She wouldn't want you to do this."

Using her free hand, the one not holding the scalpel, Nola smoothed Maggie's hair, slick with sweat, away from her face. "You have no idea what Eve would have wanted. You killed my sister and I'm afraid you're going to have to pay for what you've done."

EVE KNOX

Friday, December 22, 1995
3:20 p.m.

Eve stared down at the red piece of paper. The *C* had to mean Cam Harper, Eve thought as she folded the paper back into its bird shape. She had heard Cam call Maggie a little bird. More than once. Eve debated whether to confront Maggie with it. Not to use against Maggie. But to help her, in case Maggie needed proof. They could show it to Maggie's dad or maybe to Miss Cress. Miss Cress would know what to do. Eve couldn't wait until this awful year was over. 1996 had to be better, right?

The house phone rang and Eve picked up the receiver absentmindedly. "Eve, what's wrong?" Nick asked. "Why won't you talk to me?"

Eve's mind swirled with thoughts of Maggie and Cam Harper. "I can't talk right now, Nick," she said and hung up the phone and seconds later it rang again. She lifted the receiver and pressed it to her ear.

"I mean it, Eve," Nick said. "I'm coming over there. You have to talk to me."

"I don't have to talk to you," Eve snapped back. "Do not come over here, Nick. I don't want to see you. It's over."

"It's not over. I'm coming over right now and you are going to talk to me. You can't do this," Nick was shouting.

Eve slammed down the phone and when it started ringing again she pressed her hands to her ears. Nick was acting insane and she knew that he would be here in a matter of minutes and when he arrived Eve didn't want to be around.

She grabbed her coat and rushed from the house and over to the Harper house where she knew that Maggie was babysitting. They needed to talk about the note. How could Maggie have kept this from her? They were best friends. It was so wrong. Eve wasn't angry at Maggie but enraged *for* her. Cam Harper was an adult. A married man with two kids and Maggie was only fifteen. It was gross. People went to jail for things like this.

Eve hurried down the steps and out the front door. Without looking around, she crossed over to the Harpers' yard and heard laughter coming from the side of the house. She followed the giggles and found the twins bundled up in their parkas and stocking hats, kicking a soccer ball back and forth. They were engrossed in their play and Eve decided not to interrupt them. She knocked on the front door but got no answer. Tentatively, Eve opened the door and stepped inside, careful to wipe her feet on the rug. "Maggie," she called out and wandered toward the kitchen and the scent of brown sugar and vanilla. The sink was filled with measuring cups and mixing bowls. Maggie must have made cookies.

With Riley and Rebecca outside, Eve and Maggie could talk uninterrupted and maybe Maggie could explain to her what was going on. Eve searched the main floor but Maggie was nowhere to be found. Eve made her way up the stairs. She paused to look out the window and could see the twins still playing on the side lawn, their shouts floating up toward her.

The twins' bedrooms were empty as were the two guest rooms. The bathroom door was ajar and it was dark inside. Eve turned to go back downstairs when a noise startled her. The door to the master bedroom was shut but she could hear a man's voice on the other side. It was low and honey-warm and made Eve's stomach roil. It was Cam Harper's voice.

Eve heard creaks and soft moans and the unmistakable sound of two people having sex. Not sex, Eve thought. Rape. Maggie was only fifteen. Eve wanted to throw up, wanted to run from the house but the thought of Maggie in there with that man stopped her.

Before she could stop herself, Eve was pounding on the door. "Maggie, Maggie," she called. "Are you in there? Are you okay?"

She was met with silence, then heard the rustle of clothing. "I'm okay," Maggie finally called through the door, her voice unnaturally high. "Go home, Eve. I'll call you later."

Tears burned Eve's eyes as she rushed down the steps and hesitated about what to do next. She had hoped that it had all been a mistake, that she had misunderstood what was written in the note, but it was all true. There was no way she was leaving. She slipped into the hall closet. She would wait for Cam to leave and she and Maggie would talk.

Above her she heard one low, angry voice in tandem with a desperate one. The rat-a-tat of footsteps coming down the steps echoed through the house.

"Jesus," Cam growled. "Your friends just walk into my house like it's their own?" Eve held her breath. She had never heard Cam so angry.

"I'm sorry," Maggie cried. "Eve won't say anything. I promise."

"Dammit," Cam said. "You need to tell her she made a mistake. That it wasn't me. That you brought some high school kid in here. I mean it, Maggie. You have to fix this. I wasn't here this afternoon. Got it? I don't care what you have to do, but you make sure that she keeps her mouth shut."

Their voices faded as they moved through the house. Then it was quiet again and Eve's face burned at the thought of what Cam and Maggie had been doing upstairs. He was an old man. It was gross. Sick. Finally, she heard the click of the back door closing.

A cacophony of footsteps filled the front entryway and a rush of cold air crept in. "I'm hungry," came Riley's voice.

"Me too," came Rebecca's. Then came the sound of zippers and the shedding of coats and boots.

"Come on," Maggie said, her voice shaking. "Grab a cookie and you can watch TV until dinnertime," Maggie said, her voice shaking with emotion. "One each," she called after them.

Eve stayed hidden as she listened to Maggie and the kids pound down the stairs to the television room. The frenetic music from a cartoon drifted upward. A few minutes later Eve heard Maggie's heavy footfalls as she came up the steps.

Eve emerged from her hiding spot and found Maggie in the kitchen leaning against the sink, crying. "Maggie," she said softly, "what have you done?"

Maggie looked up, her face awash with fear. "Eve, it's not what you think."

Eve shook her head. "I heard you with Mr. Harper. Maggie, why? He's *old*. And married."

"You heard wrong," Maggie said flatly and crossed her arms across her chest as if daring Eve to argue with her.

"Maggie, don't lie to me," Eve said. "I heard you. I came upstairs to find you and I *heard* you."

"So?" Maggie said. "So what? It's none of your business. Worry about your own boyfriend, not mine."

"Boyfriend?" Eve's voice rose. "Mr. Harper isn't your boyfriend. He's a pervert. You're only fifteen! It's against the law."

Maggie flinched as if she had been slapped. "You aren't going to say anything, are you?"

"I have to," Eve said, her voice filled with sorrow. "I have to say something. It's not right. We'll go to Miss Cress. She'll help you."

"You can't do that. Please, Eve," Maggie begged.

Eve opened the front door, desperate to get out of there, and saw Nick Brady pounding on her own front door. She couldn't go that way. She turned and made her way through to the back of the house with Maggie right behind her. "Please, Eve, if you tell I swear to God I'll never forgive you. I swear our friendship is over." Eve hurried through the kitchen.

"Stop for a minute." Maggie pulled at her elbow but Eve brushed her off, opened the back door and stepped out into the cold.

Eve had to tell someone. Her mother? No, her mom was useless in times of crisis. Mrs. Harper. God, no. She couldn't see herself calling Maggie's dad. How could she tell him that his daughter was having sex with a grown man?

Eve ran toward the pine trees that edged the bluffs. From there the only place to go was down the trail that led to the caves.

Part of her wanted to stay with Maggie and try to talk some sense into her but Eve knew Maggie too well. If Maggie wasn't ready to talk, she wouldn't. She would fold her arms across her chest and refuse to speak. But they were best friends; they would get through this. Eve would stick by Maggie no matter what; that's what friends did.

NOLA KNOX

Friday, December 22, 1995
3:55 p.m.

The snow was just beginning to fall when Nola rounded the corner. Nick Brady's car was sitting in front of their house. *Great*, she thought. He was pounding on the front door but no one answered. Nola paused. She didn't especially want to run into Eve's stupid boyfriend. Though Nola was only thirteen years old she knew better than her older sister what bad news Nick was. Nola scoffed at their relationship, told Eve she was stupid for being with such a jerk, but she was truly worried about her sister. Nick slammed his fist on the door one more time and then turned, rushed to his car and sped away.

Nola jogged the rest of the way to the house and pushed open the door. It was quiet. No music or television blaring. "Eve," she called out. She slipped off her coat and hung it on the hook by the door. She had decided to come home to try to talk to her sister again, to get her to understand that what happened with the dog was no big deal. "Eve," she shouted again. No answer.

Eve had it all wrong. The dog was already dead. Nola had happened on it by accident. Pissed off at Eve and the assholes at the bus stop, Nola needed to be by herself and decided the caves were as good a place as any. No one would look for her there except for Eve of course.

Nola hadn't seen any obvious signs of traumatic injury on the dog's body. She'd taken off her glove and buried her hand into its thick fur. The skin beneath was still warm. She searched for a pulse and found none. Maybe the dog was hit by a car on the highway and then dragged itself to the caves to die. Maybe it had died of old age. It would be hard to tell without checking more closely.

Nola had pulled out her pocketknife, not ideal but it would work. She sliced only once. An even measured cut, her hand steady. She felt something that she had never encountered before, something that she couldn't put a name to. But then Eve came upon her and ran away horrified.

It wasn't fair, Nola thought. People just didn't understand.

Nola went upstairs in search of Eve. She pushed open her bedroom door and found it empty. Eve's bed was rumpled, the book she was reading sitting on the pillow. Nola picked it up and returned it to the bookshelf. She wandered to the window. From this high vantage point Nola could see the entire neighborhood. It was quiet now. Most of the adults off at work. Mrs. Olhauser was probably in her kitchen baking spritz cookies.

A flash of color streaked across the Harpers' long backyard. Eve, hurrying toward the bluffs, then disappearing as she stutter-stepped down the side of the bluff. *Interesting*, Nola thought. Then a few moments later came Maggie running after Eve. Even more interesting.

Something was happening. Nola rushed down the stairs, grabbed her coat. Felt for the heaviness of the knife in her pocket. It was getting colder and the snow was coming down in lazy loops. The cold, Nola thought, would help with preserving the dog but the moisture from the snow could cause a problem. Quietly, Nola fell into step behind Maggie Kennedy.

NOLA KNOX

Monday, June 22, 2020

Nola, scalpel in hand, looked down on Maggie whose eyes were glazed over with pain. This was taking too long, Nola thought. An hour had already passed since they arrived at the caves and the chance of someone coming across Maggie's car was growing. Nola needed to speed things up. She had to admit, though, that this was more fun than she thought it would be.

"Focus," Nola said sharply and gave a quick slap to Maggie's cheek. Maggie's eyes snapped open with fear. "I need you to listen to me, Maggie. Did you really think I would let you get away with killing my sister?"

"I'm sorry," Maggie said bracing herself for another contraction. "I swear I didn't mean for it to go that far!"

"Are you sure?" Nola asked, unconvinced. "You killed her, Maggie. It sure seems like you were more than willing to let it go that far."

Maggie moaned in pain. "I don't understand why you are doing this," Maggie cried. "Just tell me what you want."

"It's pretty simple, really," Nola said curtly. "I want Nick Brady to go down for what he did to me. And I want you to pay for what you did to my sister. See if you can keep up." Nola stood upright and tapped her chin thoughtfully. "Nick beats up Eve and gets away with it. You kill Eve and get away with it. Nick sexually assaults me and gets away with it. See a pattern here?"

"I was hurt too," Maggie tried to explain. "Cam Harper hurt me. Please, we can stop all this right now. We can end it."

"Damn right, we can," Nola said triumphantly. "So this is what's going to happen. Or at least what people are going to think happened. Nick killed Eve. With the new investigation you began to suspect Nick. The DNA will eventually back that up. In the meantime, Nick kills you. Nick gets arrested for two murders." Nola smiled as she held up another small syringe, this one filled with what looked like blood. "What do you think, Maggie? Does that cover things?"

EVE KNOX

Friday, December 22, 1995
4:00 p.m.

Eve carefully picked her way down the bluff. The rocky terrain was slick and she held on to spindly tree branches to help steady herself. She was afraid for her friend. Mr. Harper knew that Eve was in the house, that she was aware of what was going on between the two of them. Eve needed a few minutes to catch her breath, to clear her head so she could figure out what to do next. And she needed to make sure that Nick wasn't staked out in front of the house.

If Cam Harper was horrible enough to have sex with a teenage girl, what would he do to try to keep it quiet? She shivered at the rage she heard in his voice when Cam told Maggie to take care of things.

Behind her, Eve could hear Maggie calling her name. She hoped that Maggie would give up and go back to the Harpers'. Eve didn't want to be talked out of this. Loose stones shifted beneath her feet and she reached for a branch, the pine needles leaving behind a sticky sap on her palms. She stopped, regained her footing and cautiously continued downward.

When she finally reached the bottom of the bluff she was breathing heavily and her legs ached. The caves loomed in front of her. She would stay here for a little while, then go back home. Nick couldn't sit outside her house forever.

Eve peered into the scowling mouth of the cave. It was dark and still. Daylight was fading fast and Eve was hesitant to step over the threshold but she was curious. She had never been here in the dead of winter and had never come alone. When she and Maggie came during the warmer months, they were used to the sound of dripping water, a constant plunk, plunk that Eve found comforting.

But now it was quiet. Too quiet. And too dark. When they did come, they always made sure to come armed with flashlights. Without a beam of light to guide her way, Eve felt naked, exposed to whatever might be lying in wait behind each limestone corner. Thoughts of coyotes and bats crossed Eve's mind.

"Eve," came another shout and her name bounced back to her in soft whispers. Eve whirled around and Maggie was standing there.

"What are you doing here?" Eve asked. "Did you leave the kids all alone?" She looked behind Maggie, almost expecting to see Rebecca and Riley. "Did Mr. Harper come back home?"

"No, and if you tell on us he will never talk to me again," Maggie said, her voice heavy with tears. "Why did you have to come over? Why can't you just stay out of it?"

"Because it's wrong. I want to help you," Eve said. "It's going to be okay. Maggie, we can work this out together," she pleaded.

"It's not okay and I don't want to work it out," Maggie lashed out at her. "Eve, I'm pregnant. If you tell, it will scare him away. I need time to figure out how to tell him."

Eve stood there, stunned. Maggie pregnant? This was bad. "Maggie, he's not going to want a baby. He has two at home already. With his *wife*. He should have left you alone. It's against the law. Come home with me," Eve begged.

"No," Maggie said defiantly. "We aren't going anywhere until you promise you won't say anything."

Eve shook her head in frustration. "Well, I'm leaving."

As she turned to leave, Maggie tugged on her shirt. "You ruined it. You ruined everything. I hate you for this, Eve, I hate you!"

Eve shook her off. "Come on, Maggie, knock it off. Let's just go. It's dark and you left the kids all by themselves."

"Not until you promise me you won't say anything." Maggie roughly grabbed at Eve's arm.

"Let go of me." Eve pulled her arm back but Maggie held tight.

"No," Maggie said defiantly. "You can't tell anyone. I won't let you."

"How do you think you're going to stop me?" Eve scoffed. "The man's a rapist."

Maggie's hand shot out and connected with Eve's cheek. The sharp slap reverberated throughout the cave. They both stopped, not believing what just happened. In all the years that Eve and Maggie had been friends, they had rarely argued and it certainly never came to blows.

At first Eve thought that Maggie would apologize, say she was sorry. But Maggie's shocked expression turned stony and she squared her body so that Eve couldn't move past her.

"Get out of my way, Maggie," Eve said, angry tears filling her eyes. Maggie refused to budge. Eve shook her head with disgust and tried to step past, her shoulder connecting with Maggie's sending them both off balance.

Eve was the first to right herself and kept moving, eager to get out of the caves and back home. "I'm sorry, but he's just using you," Eve said apologetically, "and the sooner you figure that out the better."

With a cry of rage, Maggie grabbed onto the back of Eve's coat and the two fell to the ground in a knotted heap. "You can't tell," Maggie said through clenched teeth. "You can't. I love him."

"Get off!" Eve tried to squirm out from beneath, but Maggie wouldn't let go. Eve kicked out, striking Maggie in the belly with her heavy boot. Maggie inhaled painfully and then bent over, cradling her stomach. Eve scrambled to her feet. She hadn't meant to kick Maggie so hard but she was being so unreasonable, so crazy. Eve was done. She was going home.

Behind her, Maggie's moans of pain turned to a roar. Stunned silence. Eve staggered to her feet and eyed the narrow patch of light that lay before her. Nightfall came early in the winter and they had moved too far into the cave and Eve knew she had only a few minutes before they were plunged into complete darkness.

Eve began to move forward when in the distance a shadowy silhouette dropped from above and landed with a soft thud. Nola. The two gazed at one another for a brief moment and then Nola was gone so quickly that Eve wondered if she imagined that her sister was there at all.

NOLA KNOX

Friday, December 22, 1995
4:20 p.m.

Nola had decided she couldn't watch one more second of her sister's fight with Maggie. She was disgusted by what she had just witnessed. Eve was getting the crap knocked out of her by the person who was supposed to be her best friend. *Serves her right*, Nola thought.

Just that morning, Eve had ditched Nola when the group of kids were messing with her. *See how Eve likes it*, Nola thought. What had Eve said? *Do whatever you want to her. I don't care.*

Well, I don't care either, Nola thought and she turned away leaving Eve alone with Maggie. *She's got to learn to stand on her own two feet. May as well be right now.*

EVE KNOX

Friday, December 22, 1995
4:22 p.m.

Eve began to call out to Nola when she felt a shove from behind. Eve skidded forward and tried to break her fall by thrusting her hands out in front of her. A sickening thud filled her ears as her temple struck the stone floor. Maggie was on top of her again, her face twisted with fury, the ends of Eve's scarf gathered in her fists. Eve couldn't breathe. Panicked, she kicked and kicked until she heard a cry that wasn't her own.

Maggie gasped, releasing the scarf and falling backward. "Oh my God," she groaned.

Stunned, Eve lay there trying to assess her injuries. Her head throbbed and her right wrist blazed with pain. Eve ran her fingers across her scalp and felt a warm, sticky river of blood flowing from the wound.

Eve was tired. So tired. All she wanted to do was to go home, to forget this terrible day. Next to her, she felt movement, heard the soft hitches of Maggie crying. Eve closed her eyes and heard the whispery shuffle of retreating footsteps.

Why hadn't Nola stayed to help her? "Nola?" Eve called out once Maggie was gone. There was no answer and Eve unsteadily got to her feet. Blood trickled down her face and tickled her neck. Her head ached and her wrist throbbed. "Are you there?" Eve's voice bounced back to her in soft whispers.

Eve limped away from the comfort of the slowly fading light that fell through the opening in the cave's ceiling knowing that it would be dark soon. She tried to remember which twists and turns led to precarious drop-offs and which ones opened up to almost magical spaces with stalagmites rising from the ground and stalactites hanging from the ceilings. She tentatively put one foot in front of the other, her hands stretched out for protection from walking face-first into a rocky ledge. Eve needed to be careful. One wrong turn and she could be stuck in the caves for hours.

"Nola," she called out again. "Are you in here? Please, I need your help."

Eve rounded a corner and though the sun hadn't completely disappeared, a gray veil had been lowered in front of the cave's mouth. Because of her injured wrist she wouldn't be able to hold on and crawl back up the bluff but she could take the long way along Ransom Road. How she would explain her injuries, she didn't quite know. She had used the *I tripped* and the *I walked into a door* excuses one too many times to explain the bruises that Nick had given her. How long were people going to buy these lame explanations?

She'd figure out the details later. All she wanted to do right now was get home. Ahead of her, just beyond the cave's opening, a figure stepped into view. Eve heard the echo of footsteps. Maybe it was Nola or Maggie coming back to help her. She couldn't believe their fight had gone this far. It made Eve sick to her stomach to think that they'd actually laid hands on each other. She'd kicked Maggie in the stomach over and over and Maggie had tried to choke her. The world had officially gone crazy.

Eve rushed forward and as the figure came toward her, she quickly realized that the person in front of her was much too big to be Maggie or Nola. When Eve stopped, the shadow stopped too. "Hello?" she called out. There was no response.

A spasm of terror coursed through her. The man from the library, the man in the red sweatshirt? Had he followed Eve here to the caves? "My boyfriend is right behind me," Eve said, forcing confidence into her voice. She glanced behind her shoulder, almost wishing that Nick would appear.

"No, he isn't, Eve," the man answered. Eve strained to see who was speaking but in the fading light his features were blurred in the velvety darkness. "There's no one here now but you and me." It was then that Eve recognized the voice. Cam Harper. "I'm afraid we have a little problem here."

Fear made Eve's skin buzz, numbing the pain in her head and her wrist.

Eve considered her options. She could try to talk her way out of here, tell Mr. Harper that there was no problem. That what was between him and Maggie wasn't her business. She could turn around and try to navigate to the opposite end of the cave and to the other exit. Or she could try to get past Cam Harper, out of the cave and to safety.

He didn't give her a chance to decide. Before she could speak Mr. Harper was at her side, his fingers digging into her arm, trying to drag her more deeply into the cave. Eve managed to wriggle free but lost her balance and stumbled to the ground. Eve's fingers swept the floor in search of some kind of weapon and her hand landed on a jagged piece of limestone. She clutched onto the rock and with a cry of frustration she swung her arm hoping to strike him but only cut through the damp air. She tried again and this time managed to graze his scalp.

"Goddammit." Cam released her and his hands flew to the back of his head.

Good, thought Eve, *I've drawn blood.* Eve tried to get to her feet but Cam latched onto her boot and yanked, his fingers snagging like talons into her shoelaces and bringing her back down.

"No," Eve cried, tearing away from his grasp, and ran toward the cave's opening, hopscotching over jagged stone. *Almost there*, Eve thought as her right foot plunged into a narrow crevice and she tumbled forward.

The sickening snap of her ankle filled her ears and Eve howled in pain. Using her good hand, she tried to push herself up to her knees but her right foot was still entangled. Only twenty yards more and she would be free of the claustrophobic confines of the cave; she would be away from Mr. Harper. Behind Eve, the sound of gasping, ragged breath came closer, pushing her into action. With one desperate yank, Eve pulled her leg free of the rocky snare, tearing skin and losing her boot in the process.

She army-crawled across the rough stone toward the mouth of the cave, the ends of her scarf cascading down her back as she moved. Almost there. Suddenly, Cam was there, one leg on each side of her. He bent down and grabbed the ends of her scarf, pulling it tight against her throat. Eve froze but still the pressure built. She scrabbled at the fabric, trying to desperately slide her fingers between the wool and her skin, but failed. Eve's legs felt weak and her lungs screamed for oxygen.

Night had fallen and the only light came from the houses far up atop the bluffs, twinkling, tiny beacons. *Only a little bit farther*, Eve thought. *I'm so close.*

With one frantic effort, she managed to flip onto her back but the scarf didn't loosen. It tightened, cutting more deeply into her throat. Her screams became lodged in her chest. Her vision blurred and her arms fell uselessly to her side. Above her, Eve found Cam's eyes. They were filled with rage. There was no fear, no regret, no sorrow.

How did things go so wrong? Eve wondered. *Why?* Just beyond the cave night had fully arrived and snow came down in dizzying swirls. Dark places made it so much easier to be cruel, to enact revenge. Eve just wanted to be a good friend, a good sister. Nothing more.

Air couldn't pass through to her lungs. The cold crept through her skin, settling deep into Eve's bones until she became one with the icy limestone.

MAGGIE KENNEDY-O'KEEFE

Monday, June 22, 2020

I try to comprehend what Nola has just told me. She's going to kill me and pin it on Nick? I search Nola's face for any clue that this is all a joke but I know that she is crazy enough to do it. "It will never work," I say. I pull myself to my feet. I have to get out of here. I need to get home.

"Oh, I think it will," Nola shoots back. "I've got plenty of Nick's blood left to leave right here at the scene. DNA doesn't lie, remember?"

I ready myself for another contraction but to my surprise one doesn't come. Maybe they are slowing down. Maybe I do have time to talk my way out of this. "Be reasonable," I tell her. "If you kill me you have to make sure that none of your DNA is left behind. You have to make sure that Nick doesn't have an alibi."

Nola rolls her eyes. "He doesn't have an alibi, Maggie. Nick does the same thing every single night. He closes up the shop, stops at the café to pick up dinner and then goes home alone to sit in front of the television." Nola looks at her watch. "He's probably watching *SVU* reruns right now. I guarantee he has no alibi. Now lie down, Maggie," Nola orders. "The baby is coming."

"No! No, she's not!" I cry. "It's not time." I may be a first-time mother but I know that this baby isn't going to come until I have the urge to push. I've been having full-blown contractions but not that primal need to bear down. I pray that the baby doesn't come for hours. I have to find a way to overpower Nola and to get to safety.

"Lie down, Maggie," Nola says, dragging her scalpel across my arm. I scream in pain and terror as a thin line of blood oozes from my skin. "Now shut up before I cut this baby from you."

There is no way I'm going to lie down. If I do that, I'm as good as dead. My mind whirls trying to think of a way to reason with Nola but how do you reason with crazy?

"Please, Nola. Please whatever you do, don't hurt my baby. She's innocent in all of this. Can you promise me you'll make sure she's safe?"

"Like you did with Eve?" Nola asks. "Why would I do that for you?" Another contraction rolls through me, this one bringing me to my knees. "Now let's get those pants off you. Your baby will be here soon."

I know she's right. There is no stopping this now. I can't escape and now I'm at the mercy of a crazy woman who is going to kill me and my baby and make it look like Nick Brady did it. I lower myself onto the tarp and Nola helps me remove my shoes and pants. It's mortifying but my embarrassment doesn't last long. I'm in too much pain. My lower back seizes up and I grit my teeth and moan. I'm beginning to realize that I've probably been in labor all day. My water has broken and the contractions are minutes apart. I'm having this baby and soon.

The contractions come one after another and though I'm terrified, I look helplessly to Nola for reassurance. She's the only one who can help me deliver and I'm completely reliant on her. I struggle to keep my eyes open and sweat pours down my face. I'm so thirsty, the roof of my mouth feels like sandpaper. At the peak of each contraction my fingers scrape against the rocky ground until all my fingernails are ragged and my fingertips are bruised and scraped raw.

Time is marked by the brief, blissful pauses in contractions but the reprieves are few and far between. Minutes or hours could have passed; I have no way of knowing for sure. All I know is that I feel like I'm going to die. Suddenly, the pain shifts and the need to push overwhelms. I bear down and push. The pain is unimaginable, then fades and returns with a fury. I push, try to catch my breath and push again. Over and over, like being buffeted by violent waves.

"I see her," Nola says excitedly, a look of pure rapture on her face. I barely feel the burning, tearing sensation as the baby rips through me. I grit my teeth and a howl explodes from me.

"Here she comes," Nola says and I look between my legs to see the baby's head emerge and then slide into Nola's waiting arms. I hate that the first person who touches my daughter is so evil.

"Why isn't she crying?" I whimper, struggling to sit up on my elbows to get a better look. My baby is so small, her tiny mouth opening and closing, fighting for air.

Still no sound comes. No welcome cries. "Please, Nola," I beg. "Please help her." Nola turns away from me so I can't see what she's doing. Seconds past. I count them. Five. Then ten. Thirty seconds. A full minute. She's dead, I think. My baby never had a chance.

Finally, a robust wail fills the air.

"Congratulations," Nola says over the cries. "You have a beautiful baby girl."

"Oh, thank God," I weep. "Please don't hurt her. Please, I'll do anything."

Holding the infant in the crook of her arm, once again she reaches for the scalpel. "Of course you will," she says.

Nola kneels above me, my baby in one arm, a scalpel in the other. She is crazy. She's going to kill my baby, make me watch and then kill me too. How could I have been so stupid? I had let my guard down and ended up in this godforsaken spot that I swore I would never return to.

"Please let me have her," I beg. "Please give her to me."

"Not just yet," Nola says and reaches behind my head and retrieves her jacket, spreads it out on the ground right next to me. She carefully lays down my wailing daughter.

"What are you going to do?" I ask. My legs are shaking and I can't stop shivering.

"Stay still," Nola says as she pulls the elastic tie from her hair and bends over the baby. I can't see what she's doing and I try to slide myself a little closer to them. "Whoa, now," Nola says, grabbing for the scalpel. I freeze and watch as she saws through the umbilical cord with the sharp blade. Now the only thing left connecting me to my baby is gone. She lifts the baby, wrapped in her jacket and lays her on the ground several feet away from me. I haven't even got to touch her yet.

Horror washes over me. "Please give her to me. Please don't hurt her, she's just a baby. Please, Nola!" I beg. Salty tears blur my vision.

"Don't worry, Maggie," she says, her red hair brushing against my cheek. "I'm not going to hurt your baby. I'm not a monster." With the scalpel still in one hand she reaches into her backpack and pulls out a scarf. For a second I think it's the scarf that Eve was wearing the day she died, but it isn't. The colors are different. Nola holds it in her hands like a garrote.

I don't think—I just act. In one fluid movement I rear back then surge forward, butting my head into Nola's knees. I hear the snap of ligaments like elastic being stretched too far too fast. Nola falls backward, the scalpel flying from her hand and tumbling across the limestone and out of sight.

Nola lands on her back, her head hitting the ground. I

scramble to my knees. My first instinct is to go for my baby but I know there is power in light so I dive for the flashlight.

I keep the light trained on Nola as she sits up, stunned. Disoriented, she blinks into the blinding light. The beam of the flashlight glints off the bloody scalpel lying on the ground. We both dive for it at the same time and by some miracle I get there first. I clutch it in my fingers and once again focus the light on Nola.

I have the weapon but now Nola is sitting between me and my baby. With a sly smile Nola reaches for my baby and I lunge toward her, burying the blade in her shoulder. Nola screams and writhes on the floor as she tries to extract the scalpel, but her hands are covered in blood and the exposed end keeps slipping from her grasp. I scramble past her and sweep the baby up in my arms. Her shrill cries wrap themselves around me like a warm blanket.

Frantically, I grab the flashlight with one hand, my baby in the other and scan the cave floor for my cell phone. It's not there. I am naked from the waist down but I barely feel the sting of cold. I snag my pants from their spot next to the tarp and step into them. Feeling the weight of my car keys in the front pocket, I begin limping toward the cave's opening.

I hear the rasp of Nola pulling herself across the cave floor. "Come back, Maggie," she calls out. "Don't go, don't leave me here."

I try to move faster but I'm weak and still losing blood. And I know that I'm not done yet. I still need to deliver the placenta and need to get help as soon as possible.

When I step from the cave the sky explodes above me in a navy blue canopy and a thousand stars wink down on us. I want to drop the flashlight now that I can see what's in front of me, but I don't dare. It's the only weapon I have left. I'm hoping that I injured Nola enough that she can't come after us. In my stocking feet I move slowly but methodically through the trees, careful not to squeeze the baby too tightly. Her cries have turned to soft mewls and I worry that she might not be strong enough to survive the walk.

Finally, my car comes into view, right where I left it on the service road, hidden behind a thicket of scrub trees. The contractions are starting again. The placenta is coming. "No, no," I whimper, sure that Nola is right behind us. I lurch to the car and wrestle the keys from the pocket of my pants. I climb into the car and relock the doors. Holding the baby to my chest, I reach for my belt radio that I had taken off before I went to the caves.

"This is Detective Maggie O'Keefe," I say, my voice thick with exhaustion. "Please send help."

I'm holding my baby, intently watching the rise and fall of her little chest when Nola staggers from the trees and toward my car. Panic squeezes at my chest and I lay the baby on the seat next to me and reach under my seat for my second gun. There is no way that I will let Nola get the upper hand again.

I unlock the door and step from the car and the bull-like bellow of bullfrogs thrums in my ears, masking the rapid pounding of my heart. Nola is weaving unsteadily toward me. She managed to extract the scalpel from her shoulder but must have dropped it along the way. Her shoulder and arm are drenched in blood.

"Stay where you are," I order. "Don't come any closer." Nola briefly leans against a birch tree for support but then lurches forward, leaving a bloody handprint behind on the papery, white bark.

"Goddammit, Nola! Don't make me shoot you." I almost wish she would keep coming so I could put a bullet between her eyes but she stops.

"What would you have done?" Nola asks as the wail of approaching emergency vehicles fills the air. "You killed my sister. Eve was the only person who really ever cared about me."

"Get down on your knees," I command. To my surprise she complies. "Keep your hands up," I say.

Nola stares at me with flat, dead eyes. "What would you have done, Maggie?" she asks again. "I miss her. I miss my sister."

The dark erupts in an explosion of sirens and pulsating lights as half a dozen police cars and an ambulance appear. Behind me is the sound of car doors opening and slamming. There is shouting and the slap of approaching footfalls. "I miss her too," I whisper as Officers Francis and Weaver rush toward Nola, pull her arms behind her back and shove her head to the ground.

SIX MONTHS LATER
MAGGIE KENNEDY-O'KEEFE

Tuesday, January 5, 2021

"Maggie, you'll want to see this." I look up from my desk to see Chief Digby standing there holding a manila envelope in his hand. Digby doesn't need to tell me what the envelope holds. I know what's inside: the forensic testing results on the evidence from Eve's case. I've been waiting six months for this to show up on my doorstep.

As he hands me the envelope, I examine Digby's face for any clue as to what the results show but his expression gives nothing away.

This afternoon Shaun and I are supposed to take Eleanora Eve, Ellie for short, for her six-month checkup over in Willow Creek. She's doing great despite her eventful entry into the world. After the appointment we're going to go to my dad's house for a dinner to celebrate another big art sale for Colin. I hope I get there.

I open the envelope and pull out the packet of papers and flip to the final page. One name jumps out at me. I look up at Digby who is grinning widely. "The boot was a gold mine. The DNA from the boot didn't match anyone in the system but then the lab compared it to profiles on a genealogy site where his son had submitted DNA. Once we had that partial profile match we were able to get a sample of his DNA from a coffee cup he threw away. It's a perfect match. They found his blood on the laces and inside of the boot. The lab even found more of his DNA from the initial evidence submitted. We got him."

I stare down at the name, my mind racing. *Cam Harper.* "Maggie, you okay?" Digby asks. "We did it. We solved Eve's case. Do you want to do the honors and call Charlotte Knox and let her know we caught her daughter's killer?"

"No," I say. "I think you should."

Digby nods with understanding and hands me the signed warrant for Cam's arrest. "Take Francis with you," he says. "Congratulations."

"Thanks," I say numbly as he leaves. I set the document aside and open my bottom desk drawer. I reach inside and pull out another envelope, this one holding a syringe, a piece of glass and a cigarette butt. I toss them into my purse to throw away. I never used them. When I sat on that gravel road last summer trying to decide whether or not I would doctor the evidence, trying to decide who I would frame—Nick, Cam or Nola—I knew that the lies had to end.

I was fully prepared to take the blame I deserved for killing Eve. I even considered turning myself in but then Nola ambushed me in the caves and I realized that I wanted whatever time I could get with my baby. I decided to let the forensic testing speak for itself. And now it had. Cam Harper had murdered Eve. He must have followed us to the caves and attacked her after both Nola and I had left.

Eve was still alive when I left her there. I didn't kill my best friend. Relief floods my body but is quickly replaced with a heavy sadness. What would have happened if Cam had caught both of us there? Would we both be dead? Or would we both still be alive?

I think of Nola and the hatred she has harbored for me all these years. How it ate away at her from the inside out, how it made her crazy from grief. In the days after our encounter at the caves, the Grotto PD did a thorough search of Nola's house and the bones I believed to be human were just that, except she bought them legally off some site called The Bone Garden. As for the hatbox and the tackle box in Nola's house, they also held bones and teeth but from a variety of different animals. Absolutely twisted and creepy but Nola wasn't the mass murderer I believed her to be. No connection could be made between Nola and the arsons. The fires just stopped. As for the posting on Wrecked Nest, I never found out who did that either.

Believe it or not, I went to bat for Nola. She did save Ellie—got her breathing after a full minute without drawing a breath. I owe her Ellie's life. I got her charges reduced to simple assault and instead of sitting in jail she was sent to a mental health institute in Cherokee for a month. Once she was stabilized, I went to go see Nola. We talked for the better part of two hours.

I apologized for what I did to Eve and told her that I forgave her for what she did to me. I thanked her for saving Ellie. I also told Nola that I would do everything possible to make Nick Brady pay for what he did to her. Though the statute of limitations has expired on her complaint, I've kept my promise. Guys like Nick don't change their ways and with a little digging I found out that he had been knocking his new girlfriend around and I had the pleasure of arresting him. The publicity around Nick's bad behavior was not good for Grotto Gifts and it closed down about a month ago.

Nola still hates me but not in a homicidal way. Part of Nola's sentence is a restraining order that says she must stay away from me and my family. Nola and her mother ended up selling the house and moving to the far end of the county. I keep close tabs on Nola and always will.

"Ready to go?" Francis is at my door, enthusiasm for a big arrest radiating from him.

I push back from my desk and grab my coat. "You drive," I say.

"Park in front of my dad's house," I tell Francis as he pulls onto the street. I called Cam Harper's law firm and was told by his administrative assistant that he wasn't in for the day. Arresting him in the house where he victimized me will be quite satisfying.

"Wait here for a sec," I tell Francis as I step from the car.

The January sky is forlorn and gray. The day is cold and blustery, not unlike the day Eve was murdered but I don't feel the chill. I trot up my dad's front steps and push open the front door.

"Hey, Dad," I say. He's sitting in his favorite chair watching a morning talk show.

"Maggie," he says with surprise. "Do we have plans today?" He's always surprised to see me. I'm just grateful he remembers my name today. Some days he doesn't.

Leanne steps out from the kitchen to say hello and then goes back to whatever she was doing.

I sit on the ottoman in front of my dad's chair and reach for his hands. They are warm and completely envelope mine. "Dad," I say, my voice already shaking with emotion. "I know what you did for me." His eyes are clear, alert. He knows exactly what I'm talking about. "I know you thought I was the one who killed Eve. I thought so too. I know you found Eve's scarf and took care of it."

"Maggie," he says with alarm, looking around in case someone can hear.

"No, it's okay, Dad." I squeeze his fingers. "I wanted you to know that I didn't do it. I didn't kill Eve. I promise you. It was Cam Harper. We are going over to arrest him now."

"Cam Harper?" he says in disbelief and gets to his feet. "Why? How?"

I stand too and wrap my arms around his neck and lay my head on his shoulder just like I did during our dad-daughter dance at my wedding. "I promise I'll tell you, but right now, I just need you to know that I didn't do it. I didn't kill Eve." I know that in a matter of minutes what I've told him will drift away like dandelion fluff. I say it again over and over again, *I didn't kill Eve*, hoping that my words will imprint themselves on his soul so that somehow he'll know. That he'll never doubt me again.

We stand like this for a long time until my dad pulls away and looks down at me. "Do we have plans today?" he asks.

I kiss him on the forehead and tell him that I'll see him later tonight for dinner and go back outside to where Francis is still waiting in the squad car.

I rap on the window and say, "Let's do this." Together, we walk up to the Harpers' front door. I pull the arrest warrant from my coat pocket while Francis rings the doorbell.

Joyce Harper opens the door and looks from me to Francis, dressed in his uniform, in confusion. "Maggie? Is something going on? Did something happen?"

"Is Mr. Harper here?" I ask ignoring her questions.

"Yes, he's upstairs. Did something happen?" Joyce asks fearfully.

"Can you please go get him for us," I say evenly though my pulse is racing.

"Of course," Joyce says, stepping aside to let us in.

"Nice house," Francis murmurs as Joyce disappears up the steps. *Nice house, with dark secrets*, I want to say but don't. I know my relationship with Cam Harper will eventually come to light but I'm okay with it. I'll finally be able to speak the words that I haven't been able to. I'll be able to say, *This is how I lied, and now this is my truth.*

"Maggie?" Cam Harper asks cautiously as he comes down the steps. "What's going on?"

"Cameron Harper," I say, steel in my voice, "you are under arrest for the murder of Eve Knox."

"What?" Joyce Harper says in disbelief.

"You have the right to remain silent," I say, watching Cam's face, which has been leached of all color. "Anything you say can and will be used against you in a court of law."

"What are you doing, Maggie?" Joyce cries. She turns to Cam. "This is a mistake. Cam, tell them it's a mistake!"

"It's a mistake, Joyce," Cam says. "Don't worry. Go call Jerry, tell him to meet me at the station."

I lock eyes with Joyce and in that brief moment there is a fissure in her devotion to her husband. I've seen it before. It won't be today or even tomorrow, but eventually Joyce Harper will turn on her husband and she'll cooperate with us.

"Joyce, go call Jerry," Cam snaps and Joyce scurries away.

"You have the right to an attorney," I continue. "If you cannot afford an attorney, one will be provided for you. Do you understand the rights I have just read to you?"

"This is bullshit," Cam says arrogantly. "No one will believe it."

"Do you understand the rights I have just read to you?" I repeat.

"Yes," Cam says bitterly as Francis pulls Cam's hands behind his back and snaps a pair of handcuffs around his wrists.

Francis leads Cam outside to the squad car. The cold air burns my eyes and I watch as Francis places Cam into the back seat. After he's situated, I lean in and whisper into his ear. "You are finally going to get what you deserve. You're

331

going to pay for killing Eve and for what you did to me and to any other little girl you raped."

For the first time I see alarm in Cam's eyes but he recovers quickly. "You don't have any proof," he says dismissively. "I'll be back home in a few hours."

"We have the proof," I tell Cam and the fear returns. I can smell it on him. "DNA doesn't lie."

Hours later I'm sitting in Ellie's bedroom. She's asleep in my arms, her wispy hair still damp from her bath. I breathe in her powdery scent and watch her pink lips form a perfect O. I stroke her soft, plump cheek and a smile blooms. Her eyes flutter open and then close.

After arresting Cam and after Ellie's doctor appointment I finally sat down with Shaun and told him everything. I told him about my argument with Eve at the caves and about Cam Harper and the baby. I was expecting him to grab Ellie and run. He was shocked and then enraged but not at me. At Cam.

Shaun held me tight as I cried and told me that it was going to be okay, that he wished I had told him about everything sooner. I wish I had too.

I slowly rise and carry Ellie over to her crib, kiss her cheek and gently lay her down. Her little fists wave until, with a contented sigh, her thumb finds her mouth. For the first time in a very long time, I know I will sleep through the night. Though I know there are murderers and thieves and monsters out there, tonight I will go to bed knowing that I'm not a killer and that a killer and a predator is behind bars. Cam Harper won't be able to hurt anyone else.

I feel Shaun come up behind me and together we look down at Ellie and I think of Eve. "Sleep well," I whisper. "Sleep well."

★ ★ ★ ★ ★

ACKNOWLEDGMENTS

The long road from initial idea to publication is a long one and I couldn't do it without the help of many.

Thank you Mark Dalsing, Amy Gilligan, Jennifer Hosch, Christine Fortin, and Emily Gudenkauf for your time and expertise.

Special thanks to early readers Jane Augspurger, Amy Feld, and Emily Alexander —your input and assistance was priceless.

Thank you to my editor, Erika Imranyi, for believing in me during the times when I doubted myself. Her perspective and suggestions are always right on and help me be a better storyteller. Thank you, Partner.

My agent, Marianne Merola, not only supports me as a writer, but as a friend. I'm so thankful for her encouragement and guidance on this journey.

Kate Studer's keen eye and suggestions were invaluable as we brought the book into the final stretch. Thank you!

Much gratitude goes to my publicist, Emer Flounders, for championing my work behind the scenes, and to all the folks at HarperCollins, Harlequin and Park Row who get my books into the hands of readers.

A special shout-out to my childhood friends: Lenora Vinckier, Sara Anderson, Laureen Retzer, and Carrie Pederson. Our laughter-filled weekend together reinvigorated me and reminded me of the importance of keeping in touch with those who helped me become who I am. Thank you.

Finally, thank you to my dear family. My mom and dad, Milton and Patricia Schmida, have been my greatest supporters as have my brothers and sisters. And love always to Scott, Alex, Annie and Grace—I couldn't do it without you.